The dream was always the same. Myrmeen looked up and saw she was an adult dressed in silver armor with a phoenix head-dress. The sword that had been forged for her by her second husband was in her hand.

"I'm dripping," her father repeated. "I hate that."

This time she saw what he meant. His flesh was leaking from his bones, his eyeballs drooping to his jaw.

"Honey," he said insistently, though his tongue was now curling up in the back of his skull, "can't we do something about this?"

THE HARPERS

A semi-secret organization for Good, the Harpers fight for freedom and justice in a world populated by tyrants, evil mages, and dread creatures beyond imagination.

Each novel in the Harpers Series is a complete story in itself, detailing some of the most unusual and compelling tales in the magical world known as the Forgotten Realms.

THE HARPERS

THE PARCHED SEA
Troy Denning

ELFSHADOW
Elaine Cunningham

RED MAGIC
Jean Rabe

FORGOTTEN REALMS

FANTASY ADVENTURE

THE
NIGHT PARADE

Scott Ciencin

THE NIGHT PARADE

First Printing: June 1992
Printed in the United States of America.
Library of Congress Catalog Card Number: 91-66504

9 8 7 6 5 4 3 2 1

ISBN: 1-56076-323-X

TSR, Inc.
P.O. Box 756
Lake Geneva,
WI 53147 U.S.A.

TSR Ltd.
120 Church End, Cherry Hinton
Cambridge CB1 3LB
United Kingdom

To Michele Nicholas, with fondness and appreciation for being my friend and confidant on this and many other projects. To Laura Ciencin-Guild, with every hope for a glorious future. And especially to Eric Severson, Mary Kirchoff, and Jim Lowder, TSR's finest.

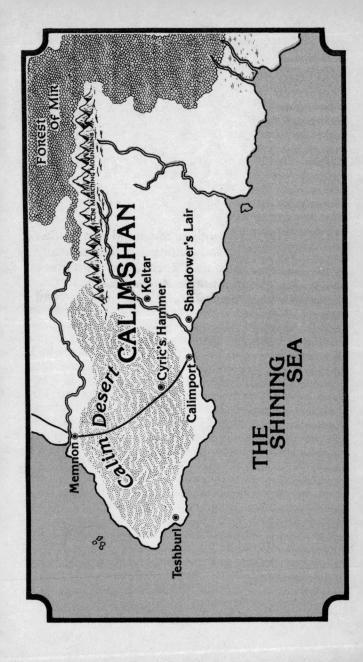

One

She hated the storms.

Staring out at the walled city of Arabel through the grand window of her private chambers, Myrmeen Lhal closed her eyes and listened as the rain beat a staccato rhythm against the thick glass. The sound should have been comforting; it reminded her of a nervous habit her father had possessed, drumming his fingers on the side of the lute he had played for passersby on the streets of Calimport. She could still picture him as he sat on the pavement, entertaining the rich from sunrise to sunset, their gold dropping into the plumed hat at his feet. Turning her thoughts from that image, Myrmeen forced herself to smile. Tonight she did not want to think about her early life. At thirty-four she was the ruler of the second largest city in Cormyr and there was no reason for her to give in to the sadness that awaited her in the past.

It had been the storm, of course. The haunting sounds of the rain had brought back moments that were better left forgotten. Better to concentrate on more pleasant memories,

1

such as the young sculptor's touch as he had expertly worked her tender flesh for the past ten evenings, as if he were attempting to make her into one of his highly regarded works of art. Across the room lay a present that he had left for her: a bust of the ruler wearing her most wicked expression and little else. Behind her was the huge, round bed they had shared, topped with teal and black silk sheets that had been wrestled into unnatural formations by their efforts. On the floor lay a pile of black and gold pillows that had been tossed from the bed in a frenzy that continued to delight Myrmeen when she thought of it. The chamber was lined with several sculptures and paintings; many were abstract works of expression and all were joyous celebrations of life and love.

She clutched at the thin black sheath she wore as she hugged herself and sighed. Her life had turned out better than she had ever believed it would. She would not allow herself the ridiculous indulgence of self-pity. For as long as she was able, she would push away the growing realization that for all her wealth, for all the dreams she had made real, her life was hollow and empty.

"Myrmeen?"

The tall, beautiful, dark-haired woman turned from the window in surprise. A decade ago, when she had been a ranger operating under the Harpers' direct supervision, Myrmeen instantly would have been aware of the lean, pale-skinned man who stood next to her. The storm had distracted her, she told herself.

"Is something wrong?" he asked.

"Foolish thoughts," she said in a failed effort to banish them. "It's late, Evon. What do you need?"

Evon Stralana, Arabel's minister of defense, shifted uncomfortably. Myrmeen suddenly realized her state of near-undress. Out of respect for his more delicate and refined sensibilities, Myrmeen turned from the man as she retrieved a robe from beside her heated, ivory bath and slipped it on, tying the sash tightly around her small waist. Her generous figure was accentuated even more by the clinging silk robe. Stralana glanced at her long, beautiful legs, exposed by the slit at the side of the robe, then trained his gaze on her eyes and did not allow it to wander, though he would not have offended her if he had. Myrmeen restrained a smile.

"We have a prisoner who claims he must speak to you on an urgent matter. He murdered a man at the Black Mask Tavern. My guess is that he wants to plead for his life."

"That's not unusual, Evon. But you generally don't come to me with such requests. Why is this man so special?"

Stralana's head tilted slightly to the side. "He's something of a sight. A filthy man dressed in rags, with wild eyes and hair everywhere you look." The immaculately groomed minister of defense wrinkled his nose in disgust. "From the stench I rather doubt that he's bathed in months. But he had a message that I thought you should hear."

"What did the vagrant say?"

"He said to tell you that the Night Parade is real."

Myrmeen recoiled as if she had been struck.

"He said his name is—"

"Dak," she interrupted.

"Yes. He said that you know him."

"I knew him," she said, correcting the thin man. "Once. From the way you've described him, he doesn't sound much like the man I remember."

Behind her, she could hear the whisper of the storm.

Crossing her arms over her breasts, Myrmeen set her face in a grim expression and narrowed her eyes. "Have him cleaned up and brought to me."

Why had it suddenly become so cold? she wondered.

"Here?" Stralana said, aghast. The pale, dark-haired man surveyed her opulent bedchambers.

"Hardly," she said, her voice as cold and hard as her eyes had become. Bright yellow slivers floated in her deep blue eyes, ships of gold adrift on a sea with no stars. "I want him brought to my private court. I'll meet you there in an hour."

"Of course, Myrmeen," he said sheepishly. "My apologies."

Stralana exited her chambers without another word. Myr-

meen looked back to the window and gazed at the rooftops of
Arabel as the rain streaked downward, then studied her own
reflection in the glass. With the exception of the barest hint of
lines around her eyes and mouth, her flesh had lost little of its
soft, youthful appearance. Her strongly defined cheekbones,
piercing eyes, full, blood-red lips, and flowing brunette hair
served to better define her beauty. Her figure was generously
proportioned, and she trained daily to stay in peak condition.

Myrmeen spun away from the window and sat down hard
upon her bed. "It's been ten years, Dak," she whispered
hoarsely. "Why didn't you stay away?"

From somewhere far off, as if in reply, she heard a rumble.
But it was only the storm.

Or so it seemed.

An hour later, Myrmeen waited in her private court,
dressed in her ceremonial armor. A jewel-encrusted sword
hung at her side. Her hair was tucked neatly within a shining
silver headdress modeled after the legendary phoenix, and a
host of red gems were embedded in the steel mesh that encased her trim body. The only flesh that was exposed was that
of her face.

Stralana brought Dak into the room. The prisoner's ankles
and wrists were secured by chains, and he moved in a halting
fashion. Even hunched over, the man was imposing, standing
close to six and a half feet. He was gaunt, his eyes bloodshot.
His damp hair had been cut as if someone had placed a bowl
over his head, then shaved. A series of nicks lined his face,
causing Myrmeen to wonder if he fought whoever had been
assigned the task of making him presentable. Still, the man
was handsome, with jade green eyes, soft black hair, and
strong, chiseled features, dressed in a simple white frock.

Dak laughed when he saw Myrmeen sitting upon her
throne. Grinning, he raised his hand slightly, indicating her full
battle regalia. "A little extreme, don't you think, Flower?"

Myrmeen's expression revealed nothing as she ordered
Stralana to leave them alone. In moments he was gone.

"Dak," she said stiffly. "It has been a long time."

"The years have been kinder to you, Myrmeen."

She advanced on him. "You knew that Arabel was mine. You must have."

"I knew. I've been here before. I've seen you at the ceremonies. You did not see me."

"You bastard," she said finally. "How dare you mention the Night Parade?"

"I had to get your attention," he said in a deep, gravelly voice. "Besides, it's true. The monsters *are* real."

Memories exploded unbidden in her mind. She thought of the first time she had heard the name of the Night Parade. She had only been six years old and her mother had tried to comfort her by explaining where the soul of Myrmeen's stillborn sister had gone. Myrmeen had been told that the Night Parade had come that evening with singers, dancers, clowns, acrobats—and they called out to her sister with voices that were too tempting and too sweet to resist. Her mother's voice returned to her:

"Now your sister is a part of that wonderful procession, happy for all time with others like her who were not meant to be a part of our world."

The story was meant to comfort Myrmeen. Instead it had terrified her. She saw the Night Parade as a demon horde come to steal the souls of the innocent. Dak was trying to unnerve her by bringing up her childhood nightmares, which she had shared with him in better times, and she could not allow him to succeed.

"They tell me you killed a man," Myrmeen said.

"Yes. I was drunk. I admit it. It was a mistake."

"You struck him down from behind after he humiliated you. I always told you that your temper was going to get you in trouble one day."

"You'll never stop judging me, will you, Flower?"

"Don't call me that again," Myrmeen said, unsheathing her sword, aiming the point at his exposed throat. The cold steel pricked his flesh and he did not back away.

Dak grinned. "I've never stopped loving you, you know."

"I stopped loving you," she said, her voice trembling, the sword's fatal edge lowering almost an inch, her hand wavering. She could tell he was lying. He had never been able to deceive her. Myrmeen wondered if he could tell she had lied, too. As much as she hated herself for it, she still loved him.

"Myrmeen," he said, his tone suddenly somber, his eyes revealing his true desperation. "I made a mistake. I need your help."

"There's nothing I can do for you, Dak. You broke the law. You must be treated like anyone else. The man you killed had a family and friends."

"I have information that's worth—my life," he said haltingly.

"What information?"

"Not so quickly, Myrmeen. I want your guarantee that I'll be taken out of this city. I wish to be secreted away tonight. They plan to kill me tomorrow."

"What could you possibly tell me, Dak? Do you mean to frighten me with stories that the nightmares of my childhood have flesh and form?"

"They do," he said gravely. "Myrmeen, think back, fourteen years ago, the night of the great storm, in Calimport."

I don't want to be reminded of that, she thought, but she refused to give in to his manipulations. From outside, the sounds of the storm increased. The window flashed searing white as lightning struck a tree in the courtyard.

"Do you remember?" he asked.

"*Yes.*" Her knees almost buckled as she spoke that single, damning word. Thunder rolled, causing the windows to shake in their housings.

"You were pregnant with our child. The child was delivered that night during the great storm."

I don't want to hear this, she thought, but I will not give in to him. I will never give in to him again.

The rain beat at the window like a thousand tiny hands begging for her to let them in, for her to stop denying the truth. Lightning flashed again, from farther off.

"The baby died," he said.

Stop it, she thought. Stop it, damn you.

"Or that's what you were led to believe."

Suddenly the sounds of the storm fell away and became distant once more. "What are you—what are you saying?"

"Myrmeen, our daughter did not die that night. She was not stillborn. She was healthy and strong. I sold her."

"No."

"I sold her to the Night Parade. To a man named Kracauer. He is still in Calimport."

"You're lying. You bastard, you are lying." Deep down, however, she knew that he was telling the truth. A baby's scream returned to her, a cry that had been dismissed as part of her fever dream. The delivery had been difficult and she had been delirious with pain. That night, he had never said that the baby had died. All he had said was, "She's gone, Myrmeen. Our daughter is gone," and that was true.

They had rarely spoken of their child from that night on. She could no longer stand to be touched by him, to speak to him, to be reminded of what they had lost. Within a year their marriage had been dissolved.

"What did you do with the money?" she asked. She could not yet focus on the unbelievable truth.

"There was no money. I was in debt. Kracauer took our child as payment." Dak lowered his head in practiced shame. "Myrmeen, I'm sorry. I thought that we would be able to have more children. I didn't know that the doctor would turn out to be a butcher, I didn't know what he would do to you—"

"No more!" she screamed. Dak fell silent. Myrmeen fought back the tears that welled up in her eyes and the racking sobs that threatened to erupt from within her soul. "Is she alive?"

"I don't know," he said, "but you could find out. With your skills and your resources, you could go back to Calimport and follow the trail. You could do what I have never had the courage to do. You could find her."

There was silence in the court. Only the persistent drumming of the rain intruded. The storm was moving on, heading south, Myrmeen guessed, south to Calimport.

Dak raised his head and gazed at Myrmeen with an expression of humility and sadness that she was certain he had carefully rehearsed. "Now, tell me how you plan to smuggle me out of the city."

"In the undertaker's wagon," she said as she turned her back to him, her head hung low.

"A smelly and unpleasant journey, Flower," he said with a laugh, "but I'll take it."

"Yes, you will," she said, and suddenly whirled on her heels, her sword flashing as lightning struck once again. The bright burst of light reflected off the razor-sharp edge of her sword as it swept through the air and separated Dak's head from his shoulders. Blood spurted from the headless corpse, spraying the walls and Myrmeen's shining armor. His body collapsed a few seconds after his head struck the floor and rolled to the corner, an expression of surprise permanently etched upon his features.

"You asked if the information was worth your life, you smug bastard," she said as she watched the pool of blood from his corpse slowly ease toward her. "I'd say that it was."

She went to the door and summoned Evon Stralana. When the thin, pale man arrived, she said, "Have this removed. I want it secreted from the city tonight. Burn the remains in Beggar's Field."

The bloody sword was still in her gloved hand. Stralana did not look down at the weapon. "Is there anything else?"

"Yes," she said softly. "I want you to arrange a meeting for me. I'll give you a list of names. Some of them might be difficult to find, but do your best."

"Of course," he said. She was about to leave when he stopped her and gestured toward her gore-drenched sword. "Would you like me to have that cleaned for you?"

"No," she said stiffly. "His blood is the one thing I would prefer to keep, as a reminder."

With that she left him alone in the bloody court.

*   *   *   *   *

Three nights later, Myrmeen sat by herself in a private booth at the rear of the Hungry Man Inn. Myrmeen often appeared in public without benefit of her royal bodyguards; the people knew they were far better off with her in command of the trading city, and thoughts of assassination were a minor concern.

"You're not touching your food," Zehla said.

Myrmeen looked up from her plate and stared at the old woman's heavily lined face. She had questioned Zehla extensively about her connection to Kelemvor Lyonsbane in the days when the gods walked the Realms, and the two women had surprisingly become friends.

"I'm meeting someone," she said, embarrassed. "A few people, actually."

"I know. That's why you need your strength."

Myrmeen shook her head and pushed the plate away. "I can't. I haven't seen these people in a long time. My stomach is in knots as it is."

"Then you better untie it quickly. I've already seated the Harpers at my best table. They're wondering when you're going to join them."

Glancing over in shock, Myrmeen saw the party of five for whom she had been waiting seated at a table near the door. A bearded man with pale blue eyes and a red cape lifted a tankard to her.

"Burke," she said in a whisper. Suddenly her nervous feelings vanished, replaced with a girlish enthusiasm she had almost forgotten that she once had possessed.

Zehla smiled and collected the untouched plate as Myrmeen rose and crossed the inn, stopping before the table where her old friends were seated. Her heart sank as she realized that she only recognized four members of the party. Sitting close to Burke was his wife, Varina, a lithe, blond-haired woman who wore black armor with red trim, the same as her husband. Across from the couple was a man in his early forties. He had tightly curled salt-and-pepper hair, dark eyes, and skin that was deeply scarred by a childhood disease he had survived.

Despite his shortcomings, he was an attractive man, though not as dazzlingly handsome or thoroughly at ease with himself as Burke. His name was Reisz Roudabush, and he once had been in love with Myrmeen. Although she had cared for him deeply, she had not returned his affections. Reisz nodded and looked away, as if the mere sight of her was painful to him, even after a decade of separation. Sitting next to a chair that had been left open for Myrmeen was a tall, attractive woman who could have passed for her sister. Of all those who had come in answer to her summons, it was this woman, Elyn, who mattered the most to Myrmeen's plans. In the corner was a thin, young brown-haired man whom Myrmeen had never seen before.

"There were ten of us," Myrmeen said as she sat in the vacant chair.

"We are all that remains," Elyn said. "I'm sure you know everyone but young Ord, here."

The dark-haired man nodded. He did not seem pleased to be at the inn.

"What happened to the others?" Myrmeen asked.

"Everyone but Morlan is alive and well, retired from the life, and prosperous," Burke said in his jovial voice.

Morlan had been a magic-user, a mage who had possessed a trove of available spells that had saved the group on many occasions. He also had possessed a collection of filthy jokes that Myrmeen continued to draw upon to this day.

"How did he die?"

"Fighting another wizard," Varina said. "His death has been avenged."

"You should have contacted me," Myrmeen said. "I should have been a part of it."

"We shouldn't have *needed* to contact you," Reisz said bitterly. "You should have been with us. If you had been—"

"It would have made no difference," Burke said strongly.

Reisz returned his gaze to the drink he had yet to touch. "Probably not," he agreed. "Of course, we'll never know."

"Ignore him," Elyn said, placing her hand on Myrmeen's

wrist. "I wouldn't be surprised if he left the womb with his dour attitude."

Myrmeen became cold at the reference.

"What's wrong?" Elyn asked, instantly alarmed at the change in her friend.

Myrmeen told them everything. In moments she was surrounded by a din of sympathy and outrage, oaths of vengeance and curses at fate itself. Reisz slammed his tankard on the table and the discussion abruptly ceased.

"She didn't come to us for our pity," Reisz said. "She needs something from us. Hear her out."

Nodding slowly, Myrmeen said, "He's right. I'll need your help if I'm going to find my daughter after all these years."

"Tell us what you want us to do," Elyn said softly.

"I'm going to have to leave Arabel for a time, and that's not as simple a task as it sounds. This place was ruled by anarchy before I took control. If I were to leave tomorrow, it wouldn't be long before it returned to that state. I don't know how long I'll be gone, but I do know that I don't intend to allow what I've accomplished over the last eight years to be lost to me. I need someone to safeguard the city while I'm gone." Myrmeen turned to the dark-haired woman beside her. "Elyn, I need you to pretend to be me for a time."

Elyn shuddered. "Myrmeen, I'm a warrior. I'm not meant to sit on a throne and pass judgments. Besides, no one would believe that I was you without—"

"Magic," Myrmeen said as she withdrew an amulet from her pouch and laid it on the table. "An old acquaintance of mine forged this trinket and cast a spell upon it that still works. Whoever wears this amulet will assume my image. We had needed some time alone and so one of my serving maids assisted me in the deception."

"Let me see that," the young Harper said as he reached across the table, snatched the amulet, and pulled it tight around his neck. There was a tiny snap as he fixed the clasp behind his neck and suddenly there were two Myrmeen Lhals sitting at the table. Only their style of dress distinguished them from one another. The boy looked down at his hands, then clawed at the amulet until he was able to release the clasp, the illusion suddenly dispelled. Hands shaking, he dropped the amulet in front of Myrmeen as the others laughed.

"Myrmeen, why me?" Elyn said.

"Because I need someone who would rule as I would; someone who would appreciate the responsibility and maintain Arabel in the manner in which I will instruct them."

"What about the rest of us?" Burke said.

"I need only Elyn. I don't need anyone else."

"Of course you do," Varina countered. "Why else would you have summoned all of us?"

Myrmeen hesitated. She did not have an answer.

"I'll do it," Elyn said, "on one condition: that the others go with you to Calimport. If the Night Parade is real, then it is the Harpers' duty, as lord protectors of the Realms, to destroy it."

"I don't know," Myrmeen said.

"You'd better decide soon," Elyn said, smiling. "The offer is only good for a short time."

"She's right," Reisz said. "You are too valuable to Cormyr to risk in the foul pit of Calimport. You must let us accompany you."

Ord sat back, crossing his arms. "She doesn't want our help. That much is clear. Why should we risk our lives—"

"Because she's one of us," Elyn said sharply. "When you join the Harpers, you become one for life."

"But I never officially joined you," Myrmeen said.

"A technicality," Burke said as he offered his hand to Myrmeen. She took it and nodded in agreement.

"An error that perhaps we will see righted before this business is done," Reisz said as he finally raised his tankard and drained the contents.

From somewhere close, Myrmeen thought she heard the low rumble of thunder. She dismissed the thought and settled back to spend the evening with her only true friends.

Two

The group arrived in Calimport a few weeks later, before sunrise. At Myrmeen's insistence they spent their time stashing caches of gold, false papers, and weapons throughout the city. They made a full circle of the port city and saw opulent mansions sitting side-by-side with shantytowns. Traveling down a street at random sometimes led them to fantastic outdoor markets where the finest jewelry and clothing could be found, along with the most succulent of foods. That same journey just as often led them to scenes of abject horror, such as children with bellies bloated from starvation fighting their parents for the disease-ridden rats they had captured in the gutters, or street people openly relieving themselves before the disguised Harpers.

The group's youngest member, Ord, was especially disgusted when a young man tried to sell himself, his sister, his mother, or anyone the warrior might desire, for the night's comfort. The boy preferred life in the wilderness to the casual degradations he and his companions frequently encountered in the city.

Close to nightfall, they returned to the inn that first had caught their attention when they had passed through the city's gates. They were in one of three rooms they had rented for the first leg of their stay, and the cook sent one of his apprentices with a pair of baskets containing their dinner. The Harpers devoured the meats, wines, and sweetbreads with barbaric speed, or so it appeared to Myrmeen. She had been used to taking her time with a meal and preferred to conduct business that strongly affected her city or her romantic life while sipping from crystal goblets filled with the most expensive wines in the land. Those days would have to be put aside, she realized, if she wanted the acceptance of not only the Harpers with whom she rode, but also the commoners whose assistance she would need if she was to find her daughter. Snatching the wine bottle from Reisz's hand, Myrmeen threw her head back and took a slug. The wine was of a crude vintage and burned going down her throat. She did not betray her discomfort as she handed the bottle back to the older man.

"It's very good," she managed to say.

Reisz's smile was tight as he watched the sudden flush brought to her face by the liquor. As he continued to stare at her, his smile deepened and the battlefield of scars on his face joined with the deeply driven age lines surrounding his eyes and mouth; together they bunched up as if they were an army of warriors raising clenched fists to the sky. He could not look away from her.

"You've had almost a day to think about it," Reisz said as he moved to Myrmeen's side in the darkened chamber. "Have you come up with a suitable identity yet?"

Myrmeen looked away and sighed. She was almost too exhausted to think about it any further after the busy day she had endured. Burke and Varina sat on the floor, cuddling like children who believed they had invented the concept of love. The bearded man with pale blue eyes gave his wife a quick kiss, then said, "Reisz is right. You're the one who insists on using another name. Let's hear it."

Myrmeen tried to appear brave as she said, "Magistra, the mage, teller of men's fortunes, diviner of their souls."

She gestured with a weak flourish and tried to convince herself that it was the poor wine that had inspired this lame attempt at creativity. Silently cursing herself for mentioning this one out loud, especially in light of the blank stares she received from her friends and allies, Myrmeen thought of the half dozen scribes and poets whom she could boast as lovers. She wished she had possessed the foresight to have assigned one of them to this task before she had left Arabel. Merely rolling around in passionate embraces with them had not, apparently, led to any of their inventiveness rubbing off—not with words, anyway.

"And you're the one who's supposed to be leading us?" Ord said with a bitter laugh. "Your name's not that uncommon. Just use it."

Burke placed his head in his wife's lap. "I'm afraid the boy's right. That was perfectly dreadful. Better than most you've come up with today, but still dreadful."

"Tact, husband," Varina countered as she lightly slapped his forehead. "Tact."

"He *was* being tactful," Reisz said. "I mean, the phrase 'cow dung' didn't enter into his evaluation, now did it?"

Ord raised an eyebrow. "From the way you smell, old man, I'm not surprised that's one of your preoccupations."

Reisz sniffed himself under the arm and sadly agreed. Myrmeen joined the others in a healthy round of laughter. Soon the moment passed and Myrmeen took advantage of the conversation's lull to bring up their purpose for coming to the city in the first place: "If everyone's rested enough, I feel we should think about making some inquiries about this baby merchant that my ex-husband mentioned."

"Yes, I certainly hope that all divorces aren't conducted as such in Arabel," Ord said, the wine beginning to affect him. Burke said the boy's name in a tone of warning, and Ord looked away with a casual shrug.

"There's no better time to start gathering information than

at night, when the city's foulest scum come out," Myrmeen said, trying to ignore the boy's words.

"That's a profound observation," Ord added as he rolled his eyes. "Tell me again, how long has it been since you've performed this line of work?"

"Child, I'm warning you," Burke said gravely, "you could be back on your parents' farm, working in the fields, if you would prefer."

"My parents are dead," Ord said coldly. "Or don't you remember how I came to you?"

"They might be gone, but their fields are still waiting," Burke said. "Now keep your impolite thoughts in your head. If I want to hear your wit and wisdom, I'll come over there and shake them out of you. Am I making myself understood?"

Ord lowered his head. "Indeed, sir." Without raising his gaze, Ord said, "My apologies, mistress Lhal."

"No harm done," she said softly. "You have a right to your opinion."

"No, actually he doesn't," Burke said. "Just trust me on this, will you?"

Myrmeen shook her head, surprised at the unexpected turn in the relationship between the Harpers. Burke obviously had assumed the role of Ord's surrogate father, and from the subdued manner of the formerly nasty and boastful young man, it was a responsibility he took quite seriously.

"Besides," Burke said, "we can't go yet. We have to wait for Cardoc to make contact with us."

"Yes," Myrmeen said, anxious to move away from the tense exchanges between Burke and Ord. "You mentioned him briefly. He's to be our mage for this mission." Frowning, she said, "Do you really think it's wise to bring in another body? There are enough of us already that we're going to draw some attention."

"This city is filthy with magic," Reisz said darkly. "Doing business in Calimport is one of the rare times when I welcome any help we can get, even if it comes from a damned spook like him."

"What are you talking about?" Myrmeen asked. "What's wrong with Cardoc?"

"Oh, there's nothing wrong with him," Varina said as she stroked her husband's lustrous hair. "He's just a very private person. And the last thing you have to worry about with him is his getting in the way or drawing attention to himself. He's very good at what he does."

"And what is that exactly?" Myrmeen asked, suspicious.

Burke sighed heavily. "Some things about Cardoc have to be seen to be understood."

"That is true," a voice said from the darkened corner of the room. Myrmeen whirled in surprise as a tall, dark man wearing a shining black vest, a white shirt, and black leggings and boots appeared, several cloaks in his arms. With alarm she noticed that the coat rack had vanished the instant he had made himself visible.

"That can't be done," Myrmeen said in astonishment, though what she really meant was that Cardoc's spell could not have been achieved easily. During her reign, she had been showered with magical items as gifts from admirers, and before that she had been witness to mystical sights that would have driven a lesser woman insane. She simply could not accept that Cardoc had so easily deceived a room full of the Realms' finest defenders.

Myrmeen rose from the bed and introduced herself. She quickly learned that such niceties were totally wasted on the man, whose stoic expression made him appear part of the furniture even when he was visible. Cardoc was a tall, dark man in his forties, with rich brown eyes, sharp features, and full brown hair. He took her hand and bowed slightly.

"I vow that I will do all I can to help reunite you with your daughter," he said in a deep, sensuous voice. Despite her initial disquiet, Myrmeen was thoroughly charmed.

"Is Cardoc your only name?" she asked.

"No," he said softly. "I am called Lucius."

"Humph," Burke muttered. "I didn't know that."

Cardoc looked over to the man. "You never asked."

Ord stared at his plate and mumbled, "So that's where that damned piece of sweetbread with honeyed jam went."

Burke hugged his wife and rose from the floor. The blond woman took his hand for support and sprang to her feet, too. "We should split off into teams if we want to make the most of our time here. We need to learn all we can about this Kracauer gentleman. Varina will come with me. Ord, you go with Reisz. Cardoc—Lucius—if you would accompany Myrmeen, I would appreciate it."

"Perhaps you should still call me Cardoc," the mage said to Burke, then he turned to Myrmeen. "You may call me whatever you like, gentle lady."

Varina whispered, "I have never heard that many words come out of that man's mouth at one time, ever."

"Maybe he's in love," Burke said jokingly.

His wife observed the manner in which the usually solemn mage regarded Myrmeen and said, "Perhaps you're right at that."

Reisz, who was close enough to hear their hushed conversation, hissed, "Come on, boy. Let's go!"

Ord glanced at Burke, then nodded and dutifully followed the swarthy-skinned man from the room.

An hour later, Myrmeen had learned little more about Lucius Cardoc than she had known before they had left her chamber. His silence did not bother her and she found his presence strangely appealing. She had never felt comforted, particularly, by the proximity of a man. The men she had been with normally had a single agenda that they were pursuing when they were in her company. Their attempts at bravery or merely jovial entertainment led back to their painfully obvious desire to land her in bed. Cardoc had not seemed the least bit interested in achieving any goal but the one he had promised to aid her with, and she found his old-fashioned gallantry enormously appealing.

They had set off to find what he had described as the "rat traps," the establishments favored by the city's criminals. Soon they discovered what they had been looking for in the darkened gambling rooms of a pub known as the Two-Headed Mare. Myrmeen had asked Cardoc about the tavern's unusual name, and he had told her that it related to the time of Arrival, when magic and nature had produced many such oddities. The bar's owner had been a simple man with very little to his credit but his mare, which had been transformed into a freak by the strange magic unleashed during the arrival of the gods. A rich man in Calimport learned of the creature and paid an exorbitant amount for the horse. The man who had sold it used his newfound fortune to open the tavern. His daughter had been quite fond of the mare, and to appease her, he named the tavern after the horse.

"What a wonderful story," Myrmeen said, though she was taken more with Cardoc's graceful delivery than with the story's content. Myrmeen sighed. She liked Cardoc, but she had a more important agenda to keep her thoughts trained on. The time had come to start asking questions of the lowlifes who populated the establishment. "Lucius, I'm going to—"

She stopped suddenly. The mage had vanished, leaving her alone. Covering her mouth as if she were yawning, she said, "You *are* still here, aren't you?"

There was no reply.

Myrmeen was taken back by his abrupt disappearance and decided that he was a powerful man who could certainly take care of himself. For that matter, she was capable of the same. Sauntering up to a group of men in the midst of an intense game of chance, Myrmeen set her hand on the back of a chair occupied by an enormous, red-haired man dressed in a single boot and a strapped-on codpiece. His body was perfectly sculpted, without a trace of fat. The pile of clothing that rested at the next table obviously belonged to him and to three others seated at the table. The man who was still dressed in full mails and leathers was the evening's winner. Myrmeen had no interest in him.

"Dragon's teeth!" the nearly naked man howled as he threw down the strangely marked cards in his hand. He shoved his chair back with little regard for Myrmeen, who darted out of the way. Unlacing his last boot, he threw it on the pile, then looked down at his final remaining item of clothing.

"I'm out," he said sullenly.

Myrmeen cleared her throat. The attention of all six men was suddenly directed to the luminous, dark-haired woman who stood before them. The man who had been winning, a younger man with straggly blond hair and hazel eyes—which burned with sudden desire—reached to the next table and dragged a chair over.

"Would you like to join us?" he asked lasciviously. "The game is not difficult. The stakes, well," he said as he examined her from top to bottom with an eager gaze, "I'd say you have much that interests us."

Myrmeen smiled and patted the shoulder of the red-haired, nearly nude man whose chair she stood beside. She leaned down and said, "I'll buy back all you've lost if you're willing to answer a few questions."

The red-haired man raised an eyebrow. He was intrigued. "Depends on what kind of questions you have, now doesn't it?"

"I'm trying to find a man," she said.

An instant too late, she realized that her phrasing had been a bit too general. The other players rolled with laughter. Nearly every man at the table volunteered his services. Their comments became increasingly vulgar and surprisingly creative. The red-haired man was the only one who had simply laughed and not bragged about his qualifications for the job. Myrmeen reached down and placed her hand on his breast.

"A bit cold in here, wouldn't you say?" she asked.

The man's companions shifted the aim of their taunts and focused fully on his unfortunate condition.

"Come with me," he growled and dragged her by the wrist to a table at the back room's far end, where they could speak without being disturbed. "All right. Show me your gold. Prove to me that you can buy back my clothes."

Myrmeen removed a single token. With it he would be able to purchase new leathers and boots at the marketplace and still have enough to cover his lodgings for a week.

"So tell me why I shouldn't just take it from you, along with whatever else I want," he said in a growling voice.

"To begin with, I'm not alone," she said, wishing that Cardoc, if he were present, would do something to help her make her case. Nothing happened. "I'm here with friends. Besides that, I'm very good with a knife. If you tried to take any more than I was willing to offer, I'd hack off that piece of equipment you seemed so proud of just a few minutes ago. I hope my position is clear."

"Indeed," he said with a broad smile as he rubbed at his clean-shaven face. "You know, I even lost my beard in that game. They made me shave it off right there at the table!"

"I don't have all night," Myrmeen said as she slipped the token back into her pocket. "Will you help me?"

"All business, are you? Well, ask your questions," he said, his smile fading.

"I'm looking for a man named Kracauer. He's a—"

"I know him. I know where to find him. What else do you want to know?"

Myrmeen thought of the first words that she had heard from Dak after ten years of separation: The Night Parade is real. Every night after she had slain Dak, she had been unable to force away the nightmares from her childhood. When she closed her eyes she dreamt of monsters coming to take her soul. She knew it was unwise, but she also knew that if she did not ask about the nightmare people, she would regret it.

"What can you tell me about the Night Parade?" she asked. In response, the red-haired man slapped his hands on the table and rose so quickly that his chair skittered back across the floor.

"The Night Parade?" he shouted. "I thought you wanted to talk about serious business. The Night Parade is for children and the insane. What kind of fool do you think I am? Who put you up to this?"

The red-haired man's booming voice had captured the attention of everyone in the back room. "Come with me!" he shouted as he grabbed her arm and yanked her back to the table where his friends were in the middle of another round. Before she could move to defend herself, the brawny, sweat-drenched, nearly naked man heaved her against the table. She fell on her back, the impact startling her but not causing any real pain.

"Here's my new stake for the game!" he cried. "Whoever wins gets to have her first!" The edges of his mouth curled up in a vile expression. "After me, that is," he said as he reached down for the release of his brass codpiece. He was surprised to see Myrmeen's steel-tipped boot racing up to greet his hands, and he screamed like an infant as her foot connected with the metal. The warrior cried out in pain, turned, and sank to the floor. Four of the gamblers rose to their feet, while the man who was winning crossed his arms and sat back to watch the show. He grinned at the man beside him, who stood ready to defend him and was obviously his bodyguard. Two of the gamblers reached for Myrmeen's arms. Myrmeen twisted out of their way, then bounded from the table, spun on her heels, and stood ready for their attack. The man she had kicked was on the floor five feet to her right. He was no threat.

The closest of the three who came for her was the wiry man. He foolishly hurled himself in her direction and received a punch in the throat for his efforts. She moved aside so that he would trip over her out-thrust leg. The wiry man fell clattering into a chair at the next table, which he broke on the way down.

The last two came at her as a team, circling around the table, one approaching from her left, the other, her right. The closer man, a gray-bearded fighter with blackened teeth, was to her left. She angled in his direction as he rushed in low, trying to gather up her legs, as his companion, a black-haired man with a paunch and a scar running the length of his face, tried to pin her arms from behind.

Myrmeen's only surprise was that their effort nearly succeeded. She knew the proper way to block them, but her body was not in the same condition it had been ten years earlier, when she would have disposed of louts such as these without any perceivable effort. She allowed the black-haired man to her right to grab her arms from behind. Using the leverage he unwittingly afforded her, she kicked off from the floor and brought her boots to either side of the left man's head, kicking him with satisfying force. He fell to his knees. Then she spread her legs wide, hooked her heels behind and beneath his arms, and drove him toward the man who was holding her from behind. There was an ugly crush of bone as the full weight of the gray-bearded fighter collided with the other man's knees. The man behind her yelped in pain and released Myrmeen's arms. With the grace of an acrobat, she planted both feet on the back of the man who had fallen beneath her and leap-frogged onto the top of a second table.

"Damn it, Cardoc, if you're here, do something," she said as she saw the red-haired fighter rise before her. He had recovered more quickly than she had expected. The others were still down, and the pair of gamblers across the table did not move. The redhead's face was a bright pink, his eyes dark and smoldering with anger. The fighter grabbed her by the waist and lifted her from her feet. She toppled forward, reaching down to grab at his hair, then yanked brutally as she allowed her weight to carry her back to the top of the first table, where she again landed on her back. The gambler who had been winning merely sat and watched with amusement. A group of men stood behind him, watching the fight. Several nudged each other and pointed at her with smiles.

The red-haired fighter howled as he saw the great gobs of hair in Myrmeen's hands. Enraged, he launched herself at her in an awkward, brutish lunge, seeking to pin her to the table with his weight. With blinding speed she rolled to one side of the table, snatched a large flagon that had been overturned in their fight, then brought it down on his head as he crashed onto the table, belly first. The flagon shattered on impact, stunning the brutish fighter but not rendering him unconscious. Myrmeen surveyed the back room to ensure that there were no other enemies approaching and that the men she had put down were not preparing to rise again. Then she spun on the table and straddled the man's back, grabbing him by the hair a second time as she unsheathed her blade and laid it against his throat.

"I asked you a simple question," she said. "All you had to do was answer me. But, no, you had to be a complete ass about this. Now, all I want to know is whether or not the Night Parade is—"

Totally unmindful of the knife at his throat, the fighter reared up and stumbled back until he was able to slam Myrmeen into the wall. The impact caused her to drop her blade and lose her hold on the man. She fell to a crouch, and the few seconds it took for the red-haired fighter to turn and face her was all the time she needed to rise up on a single leg and raise her free foot into the air. Before he even guessed what she was about to do, Myrmeen brought her boot down upon the man's instep, crushing several bones in the process. The man squealed in pain and dropped to his knees before her. With an open fisted blow to his exposed ear, Myrmeen struck the man a second time. He jerked to the side as his head collided with the table's edge. Then he sank to the ground.

This time he did not get up again.

Myrmeen was breathing hard as she fell back against the wall and tried to catch her breath. She was covered in sweat and her tangled hair was matted to one side of her face. Suddenly, she was greeted with a shattering round of applause. Most of the men gathered behind the blond gambler howled with laughter and cheered her victory. The gambler shrugged philosophically and parted with nearly all the gold he had accumulated.

"You were taking bets on me?" she asked, stunned.

"Actually, I was betting against you," the man said as he paid the last who had wagered and won. Myrmeen approached him and sat down hard in one of the few remaining chairs that had not been overturned in the fight. "That did not turn out to be prudent."

Myrmeen grinned and removed the coin she had offered the

red-haired fighter. "Would you like to make some easy money?"

He nodded and Myrmeen asked him about Kracauer. He was about to respond when a cold hand appeared and closed over hers, covering the coin. She looked up sharply to see the dark-haired mage standing beside her.

"That will not be necessary," Cardoc said.

Angrily rising from the table, Myrmeen stared into the tall man's dark eyes. "Where were you?"

"Here," he said.

Her mind reeled. "You were right here the entire time and you did nothing? I thought you were supposed to help me if I was in danger!"

The mage cocked his head slightly. "But you were never in any real danger. You acquitted yourself very well."

Myrmeen fumed.

"I could tell that you were doubting yourself at first," he said, "and I would have stepped in if I thought you were going to be hurt. Time has not dulled your edge, Myrmeen. If anything, it has made it sharper."

"How would you know what I was like ten years ago?" She was not about to forgive him this easily.

"I saw you fight once, in the battle for Evermeet. You were magnificent. I would not have thought to insult you then by offering assistance when you clearly did not need it. I would not do so now."

She exhaled deeply. No matter how hard she tried, she could not remain angry with him. "Next time, Lucius, just jump right in, all right? I won't feel insulted."

"Excuse me," the gambler said. "I wanted to give you this address and get paid. You remember that, don't you?"

"Like he said, that won't be needed," a man called as he broke from the crowd gathered at the door to the tap room.

"Burke," Myrmeen said. He wasn't alone. Varina, Ord, and Reisz were with him. "How much of this did you see?"

"Enough to know that you can still handle yourself in a fight," Burke said brightly, "and enough to know that you still have a rare talent for causing a brawl when a few friendly words with the barkeep can get you all the answers you need." He looked down at the bodies scattered on the floor. Several of the men were still moaning.

"At least no one appears to be dead," Reisz said as he moved forward and examined the red-haired fighter, "this time."

"Wait a minute, we had a deal," the gambler said.

Burke clamped his heavy hand on the man's shoulder and leaned in close. "Shut up if you want to keep breathing."

The man fell silent.

Varina bent down and retrieved Myrmeen's knife. "You really must try the bar across the street. They gave us a tankard of ale and Kracauer's address for a gold piece."

Myrmeen smiled in defeat. "Well, perhaps we should—"

The mage looked around in distress.

"What is it? What's wrong?" Burke asked.

Cardoc's brow furrowed and he shook his head. "It was nothing. For a moment I thought I sensed something that could not be. I'm sorry. Perhaps we should leave."

"It's about bloody time one of you thought of that," Ord said. "We've attracted a crowd."

*   *   *   *   *

At the other end of the tavern, beside a table in the room's darkest corner, a young serving maid named Hilya approached one of her husband's indentured servants. The boy was no more than eleven, and he was standing alone, staring at an empty table.

"What's the matter with you?" she said, anxiously watching the crowd that had bottlenecked near the gambling room. She would have to keep a close watch to make sure no one tried to get away without paying his bill.

"He went," the boy said.

"What are talking about? Who went?"

"It was a man," the lean, blond child said. "I *think* it was a man. He was very dark. I could never see his face. It's like he was always in shadow, even when he was standing by the fire."

"Well, what about him? There's work to be done."

"He got up from the table and went to watch the fight with everyone else. Then he came back to his table, drank his mead, and went."

"You mean he didn't pay?" she said, her anger swelling. "Why did you let him go? Why didn't you call someone?"

"There wasn't no time," he said. "One second he was there, then he just went."

"Went where?"

"I don't know," the boy said. "It was like he just stepped into the shadows and disappeared. Like he walked right into the wall."

The woman pressed her lips together and slapped the boy on the top of the head. He hollered and she grabbed his arm. "That was for lying." She reached back and slammed his bottom. "That was for letting a customer go without paying his bill, if that's what happened. Now come with me."

"What?" he cried. "I didn't do anything."

"I'm going to take you back and let Andros give you the once over. You probably took the man's money and pocketed it for yourself."

"I didn't, I didn't," the boy said frantically. Andros was the serving maid's husband and the Two-Headed Mare's owner. He also possessed a temper that was easily ignited and a strap the boy had seen one time too often. "Wait, Hilya, look there!"

She glanced back at the table, where the boy was pointing, and squinted. Then she released his arm, picked up a candle from a nearby table and walked close to the wall. There, against the hard oak, was a shadow that was deeper than all the others, a night-black silhouette in the form of a man. As she brought the candle closer, the shadow did not disappear. It seemed to absorb the flame's light.

With a trembling hand, Hilya reached out and touched the

shadow on the wall, then yelped in surprise and drew back her fingers, which were burned and bleeding. She gasped as she saw a tiny red trace of her blood vanish into the deepening shadow. Without warning, the entire silhouette disappeared as if it had never been there at all.

Hilya felt faint. She looked at her hand once again and saw that the darkness that had been on the wall was spreading from the tips of her fingers to engulf her entire hand. For an instant she felt as if a river of ice had traveled through the blood in her veins and had taken hold of her heart. Her mouth cracked open and she felt a staggering pain. The boy watched as a tiny cloud of black smoke escaped with her breath, then he leapt back as she fell to the floor, her eyes already glazed over in death.

Tears welled up in his eyes as he saw the smokelike shadow trail across her flesh one last time before it vanished.

Finally, he began to scream.

Three

The death of the proprietor's wife drew the attention of the onlookers who had gathered to view Myrmeen's brawl and the aftermath. When the crowd parted, Cardoc received a brief glimpse of the body and froze. Something clearly troubled him, but even when the Harpers were back on the street, several blocks from the Two-Headed Mare, he refused to say what that was.

Burke, Varina, Reisz, and Ord agreed to return separately to the inn, as a large group would have drawn too much attention at this late hour. Lucius and Myrmeen traveled down the dark, silent street on foot. In many sections of the city, mounts were only allowed for the city's guardsmen and commercial carriages. The streets often were so congested with people that horses panicked and bolted in the street, causing injuries among the wealthy tourist trade. Anything that was bad for business in Calimport was strictly prohibited.

Lucius and Myrmeen walked down a ruined street, passing houses and other buildings that often were the survivors of fires or simply the victims of age and neglect. Myrmeen turned to Cardoc and said, "I grew up here. This place hasn't changed. The government does nothing to help the poor."

Myrmeen knew that the city's underdeveloped, less afflu- ent sections actually lent to Calimport's allure. Wealthy citi- zens often paid guides to take them through the worst parts of the city so that they could shower the destitute with the occasional coin or scrap of food. They would return to their mansions and tell their peers of their morally correct, chari- table endeavors. In truth, the suffering they witnessed gave them grist for their dinner party conversations.

"In Arabel, you encountered a similar situation when you became ruler," Lucius remarked.

"Even before," Myrmeen said as she saw a pair of children playing at the end of the street. "My second husband, Haver- strom Lhal, was a good man. But, like many politicians, he catered to the needs of those with money who could most ben- efit his career."

"You brought about changes, government reforms to aid those who could not find work and could not afford to house and feed their families."

"How do you know so much about me?" Myrmeen asked.

Cardoc tilted his head slightly, like a wolf. "I am a Harper. We are the lord protectors of the Realms. It is my business to know who will most benefit these lands and who will bring to them the greatest threat. Your husband died?"

"Yes," she said softly. "There was a plot, a conspiracy in- volving the leaders of several races, to find an object that might have ended human dominance on this world. My hus- band went off with several others to investigate these rumors and left the city in my care. I had already been given an equal hand in the running of Arabel, and the programs you men- tioned had gone far in bringing the people of my city together. They accepted me immediately."

"And your husband?"

"He never returned. He was killed in an ambush, his head placed on a pike. I never would have believed his death, had I not seen his remains myself." She became quiet. "Lucius, I'd rather not speak of this."

"Of course."

Soon they reached a hostel, a gathering place for children who were homeless or had been made wards of the state, and decided that the direct approach would be best. Walking through the front door, they roused the interest of a man in his early fifties who had a wisp of white hair on his head. Hard, square features dominated his face. The hostel itself once had been a beautiful house of lodgings, subsequently sacrificed to the same decay that had eaten many Calimport neighborhoods. The two Harpers were close to a grand, winding staircase that led to a spacious second-floor landing. Myrmeen had the feeling that the children's actual quarters were closer to the size of closets than the luxury suites the place once had afforded.

"If you're here to see one of the children—" he began.

"In a manner of speaking," Myrmeen said quickly so that the balding, older man would not have a chance to voice an objection. "You see, my husband and I are unable to have children of our own, and we were told that a certain Master Kracauer might be able to help us."

The man pursed his lips. "Lord Kracauer is not here at the moment. Perhaps if you tell me your names and where you're staying, I can have him get back to you."

Myrmeen understood. Kracauer would have to be certain that she and her "husband" were not agents of the local authorities, or bereaved parents trying to find a child of their own who had been taken by slavers. The hostel was an ideal place for a flesh merchant; so many of the children already had been shuffled from one place to another. If a few turned up missing, no one would notice, or care.

Cardoc surged forward, his towering form and wild, intense eyes causing the smaller man to back away in alarm. "You are Kracauer," Cardoc said as he drove the man backward into a tiny room that Myrmeen had not even noticed. She followed and gently closed the door behind them, locking it so that they would not be disturbed.

The room was a simple office with cases for strange curios from several parts of the world, old, square bound texts, and tightly wrapped scrolls. Cardoc backed the man up to the open window, where soft bluish white moonlight filtered in. The mage wanted Kracauer to see his face as clearly as possible to know that he was not in a mood to be sociable.

"You are Kracauer," he said again. "I recognize you from the description we were given."

"All right," Kracauer said, "what do you want?"

"Your head on a stick if you won't cooperate," Cardoc said with a nasty smile. Myrmeen was surprised to note that his accent had changed from the flat monotone with which he usually spoke to a hard-edged gutter dialect that most of her friends had employed when she had been a child in the poor sections of the city. Burke had warned her that Cardoc was a chameleon at times, changing his appearance, wardrobe, and dialects to suit the needs of the moment.

"Just tell me what you want," Kracauer said.

"We want you to think back," Myrmeen said, "to fourteen years ago, the night of the great storm. Do you remember?"

He nodded swiftly. "How could I forget? Everyone remembers the storm. In a city like this, they are rare."

"You were selling children then, just as you are now. You sold a child during the great storm. A baby girl—"

"Who are you people?" Kracauer asked, his panic causing him to inch away from Cardoc. The mage grabbed him by the collar of his waistcoat and slammed him against the window frame.

"Answer her question."

"There were so many children," he mewled. "How can I possibly remember that one?"

"He's lying. Should I kill him?" Cardoc asked, then pulled his hand back and whispered a phrase. Suddenly a ball of flame appeared in his hand, the fire generating enough heat to cause Kracauer to break into an immediate sweat.

"You're one of them!" he cried. "Please, I've told no one. Lord Zeal, please!"

Myrmeen felt her heart thunder in her chest at the name.

"One of who?" Cardoc asked, bringing the flame closer. His hand, amazingly, did not appear to be damaged by the flames. "And who is Lord Zeal?"

"This is a test," he said, shaking his head quickly. "I don't know. I don't know anyone named Zeal, I don't know anything about you people."

"What people?" Cardoc said, bringing the fire close enough to singe the man's eyebrows.

"The Night Parade!" he shouted. "There! Satisfied?"

"Tell us about the girl," Myrmeen said excitedly. "A man named Dak gave you the child to cover his gambling debts. You sold her—"

"There were two others," Kracauer said, his fear overtaking him. "It wasn't just me, you know."

"What are their names?" she asked.

"Johannas and Nehlridge. They're both still in the city. They might remember. They might know. I only remember bits and pieces of what happened that night. I know there were children, many, many children, and the nightmare people came. They wanted the children, and they paid handsomely for them, all the children born that night—"

With a short, choking cry, Kracauer fell silent, his eyes rolling back into his head, the tip of a blood-drenched knife jutting from his larynx. Cardoc grabbed Myrmeen and threw her to the hardwood floor, the flame in his hand vanishing. She heard the sound of a blade slicing though the air above their heads like the hiss of a snake breathing out in warning. It struck the wooden door she had locked when they had entered the room. The mage was already crouched beside the open window, reciting several spells, always leaving out the last few words so that he could trigger them at any time. He leaned against the wall as he eyed the window suspiciously and motioned for Myrmeen to crawl as close to the wall as possible. There was only one window in the room, one possible entrance point for other weapons.

Kracauer had fallen facedown onto his desk. The handle of

the blade that had killed him was buried deep in his neck. The force that had been used to throw the weapon must have been considerable, Myrmeen wagered, as only the hilt could be seen. She glanced at the door, where the second dagger had struck. Its blade, too, had passed entirely through the hard wood, leaving only the glittering black hilt exposed.

Suddenly Cardoc jumped to his feet and turned to face the window, his hands curled in an arcane gesture, ready to propel the force of some powerful spell against the assassin who had been standing in the alley. His hands relaxed as he snatched a small mirror from the desk and thrust it outside the window. He checked the area on either side of the window, then above and below the frame.

"The killer is gone," Cardoc said.

Myrmeen nodded and used the wall for leverage as she stood up and went to Kracauer's body. She was about to touch the dagger's hilt when Cardoc screamed for her to stop. She froze where she was, her fingers inches from the cold, sparkling metal. Something about the weapon's design seemed familiar.

Suddenly, she saw a wreath of darkness separate from the weapon and hang just above the dead man like a deadly, nebulous cloud. It quickly descended into the dead man's body, sinking deep into his flesh. Across the room, where the second blade had struck, a large, round band of darkness was eating into the wooden door. In moments, it vanished as well. The hilts of both weapons now shone gray, as if they had been covered in black tar that was now completely washed away. Their bizarre design reminded her of lightning bolts. They caught the light and reflected it back as if to reinforce that notion.

Cardoc nodded toward the window. "We must leave."

Myrmeen followed him through the open window, into the alley beyond. She took a final glance inside the office and suddenly knew why the knives had seemed so disturbingly familiar: She had seen them in a dream.

No, she corrected herself, not a dream. A nightmare.

Four

Lucius Cardoc escorted Myrmeen back to the inn, then told her that he would spend the night trying to discover the location of the two men Kracauer had mentioned.

"You need sleep, too," she had protested. "And it may not be safe for you on your own."

"I do my best work when I am alone," he said, giving her no choice in the matter as he became invisible. She reached out to where he had been standing, but he already had moved away. With a sigh of defeat, she turned and went upstairs to join the others.

Ord had fallen into a deep sleep with Burke silently watching over the boy. Myrmeen told the group all that had occurred and relayed Lucius's promise to return with information by morningsun.

"The best thing for us to do is wait," Varina said.

Myrmeen agreed. Reisz went back to the room he had planned to share with Ord. Myrmeen retired to her private chamber. She slept fitfully, waking every thirty minutes to an hour. The last time she wrested herself from her sleep, she awoke frightened and felt as if she were being pulled away on a tide that had overpowered her senses.

Slivers of her last nightmare remained as she got up and paced. She did not feel like going back to sleep and so she performed an exhausting series of exercises and practiced with her heavy sword, hoping to tire herself. Finally, when she had given up on a decent night's sleep, Myrmeen sat before the small window, looking out at the city of her birth. A single image from her dream refused to fade:

She had seen a man standing on the muddy earth in the middle of a terrible storm, a dark man who raised his arms to the sky. Two ragged bolts of lightning shattered the night with their blinding intensity, their jagged paths cutting across the horizon from opposite directions. Suddenly they met where the man stood, each of his out-thrust hands receiving a single blast of lightning. He became transparent for a moment as the searing white light coursed through him, and Myrmeen could see that his anatomy was not that of a man, but of something considerably older and more threatening.

Was this Talos, god of the storms? She was not a worshiper of any particular god, but if she had been, Talos would have been her last choice. Storms terrified her.

Myrmeen felt an odd scratching sensation on her left arm and held the arm out to the soft blue-white illumination from the window. She was shocked to see three sets of black eyes open on her forearm.

Suddenly she was aware of a knocking at her door. Myrmeen yawned and felt a strange warmth on her arms. She looked up and saw sunlight pouring through the open window. The raw heat of the day caressed her. Examining her left arm several times, she found no trace of the curious eyes that had materialized within her flesh. She did not remember falling asleep after she shook herself from her nightmares and sat before the window, but the eyes must have been part of them. Worried that the line between her dreams and her waking reality was beginning to blur, Myrmeen became anxious to fill her mind with other thoughts. She checked her dress to ensure that her gown would not offend her visitor's sensibilities and said, "Come!"

The door opened and Lucius Cardoc stepped inside. She was not surprised. From the tentative nature of the knock, she had guessed that it would be him.

"Myrmeen," he said as he entered and lowered his gaze in a form of respectful greeting. The mage looked exactly as he had the night before. If he had missed out on a night's sleep, the effects had not manifested.

She stepped away from the chair that she had been straddling and turned to face him. Her neck and back ached. She had fallen asleep in an awkward position, her head resting in the crook of her arms. Unconsciously, she raised her arms over her head and reached back to link her fingers behind her neck, stretching like a cat. Then she suddenly became aware of the sensuous image she was providing for the mage. Her thin shift had hardly been shocking, but it was not modest either. She was aware that the light from outside was serving to reveal her body's perfect lines.

Cardoc did not seem embarrassed in the least, and she found that she liked his reaction. He came to her from behind, raised the back of her shift, and said, "Sit on the side of the bed."

With a tentative smile, she did as he commanded. He delivered a powerful and soothing massage to the tense, knotted muscles in her back. His hands were stronger than she had anticipated. She resisted the urge to let him know exactly how pleasurable his touch was becoming as she bunched her hair in her hands and lifted it to give him clear access to her neck. He somehow knew exactly where to touch her and with how much pressure.

She appreciated that he said nothing of the scars lining her bare back.

"I have the information," he said, a trace of amusement in his tone as he gently lowered her shift and backed away. "Would you like a few moments to dress? I could wait downstairs with the others."

She almost asked him to stay, then thought better of it. Her heart was racing as she turned to see him exit the room.

An hour later, the Harpers were on the street. They had retrieved their mounts from the stable master, who had charged them an inflated fee, a common occurrence in Calimport, and rode through one of the designated routes set aside for intracity travel. They brought their supplies.

Reisz chose to ride beside Myrmeen, with Lucius taking point. A thought had weighed heavily on him for the last few weeks, since he had responded with the others to Myrmeen's summons and listened to her story. During the long ride to Calimport and through the trials that followed, there had been no appropriate moment to bring up his observation. Now, he felt, was as good a time as any.

"Myrmeen, you said that your mother first told you of the Night Parade to explain what happened to your stillborn sister. Isn't it possible that the monsters took her, too?"

She drew a deep breath, as if she had been stung by his words. "Anything is possible," she said evenly, betraying the fact that the thought had occurred to her, too.

Lucius called for the company to halt, and he pointed at the sight that had arrested his attention. They were close to the shipping lanes, traveling between endless rows of buildings that had been converted into warehouses. Ahead they could see the bay's sparkling, clear waters, along with nearly one hundred ships in the docks. Above one of the ships, like an angry black fist, rose a cloud of smoke. A small boat had been set on fire and was sinking into the waters.

The mage dismounted and led his sleek black horse to the others. Reisz took the animal's reins as Lucius offered to go ahead and learn what had happened. Myrmeen and Burke agreed. As they waited for him to return, she thought of Kracauer, the baby merchant who had been slain by the strange weapon charged by a form of magic that had unnerved Cardoc. She considered the possibility that the assassin had been close enough to hear the names Kracauer had given them. Having mentally traced the trajectory of the second blade, the one, presumably, meant for her throat, Myrmeen knew that, without Lucius's interference, the knife narrowly would have missed her.

The killing had been a warning.

Lucius came back and announced what Myrmeen had already guessed: The boat that had been sunk belonged to Ivan Nehlridge, the smuggler who frequently shuttled Kracauer's stolen freight from the city. Witnesses had seen him engulfed in flames, screaming for his life, as the boat had gone down.

"Martyn Johannas is the only one left," Lucius said. "What I learned about him was a bit more vague. That could work in our favor."

"Perhaps," Burke said as he ordered the company to follow the mage. They left the docks and cut across the dark heart of the city, the meaning of Cardoc's words apparent: Their only possible advantage depended on the quality of the information received by the killers, who were attempting to seal off Myrmeen's avenues of inquiry. If they had been given the same odd phrases as Cardoc to explain the whereabouts of Martyn Johannas, then the Harpers had a fair chance of getting to the man first.

The morning was a bitter memory by the time they arrived at the outskirts of the city's financial district. Guardsmen ordered them away from the busy streets. The Harpers put up their mounts at the first stable they spotted, which had been filled nearly to capacity. Myrmeen was doleful at the idea of leaving the mounts in the oppressively hot stables. Fortunately, the stalls they rented were the responsibility of a young stable boy who seemed to genuinely love and respect the magnificent animals left to his care. She gave him an extra coin for his troubles.

Before they left, the boy took her to a private room, where she changed into an elegant gold-and-white dress from her travel bag. When she emerged from the room, her hair was piled up in a regal style and held in a beautiful headdress. She wore white gloves that covered her forearms and ended above her elbows. Her shoulderless gown plunged in the front, revealing the creamy tops of her breasts, which had been thrust upward by a wire corset that chafed against her skin. Her bearing and style of walk had changed, too.

The Harpers had decided that they would draw far less attention if they posed as servants and bodyguards to a finely dressed lady. For Myrmeen, her companions' expressions at her emergence as a woman of wealth and privilege made it worth slipping out of her battle-worn leathers, mails, and thigh-high boots. Her only mistake in choosing this outfit had been her sandals, which revealed her calloused feet. Cardoc nodded at her approvingly, his gaze lingering perhaps a moment too long.

The group left the stable and walked for several blocks. They were surprised as they turned a corner and were suddenly swallowed up by a torrent of citizens. The people rushed blindly forward, heads down, their gazes carefully set to take in any obstacles at a glance without making eye contact with anyone. As Myrmeen had imagined, the passersby were dressed in the finest, most brightly colored gowns and business wear that the city's markets had to offer. Many people had entourages similar to Myrmeen's, and her group drew little attention, except for the occasional stare inspired by Myrmeen's hypnotic beauty. They had not traveled far before Myrmeen realized that Lucius had vanished into the crowd.

The buildings lining the financial district's long, central street had been designed with the care and expense usually devoted to fine palaces or halls of study. Myrmeen had seen it all before. The merchants were so touched by petty rivalry that each had attempted to make his or her establishment more spectacular to gaze upon than all the others. Their childish infighting, something that would not have been allowed in Arabel, had led to impressive spurts of towering architecture; several buildings had bridges suspended twenty feet above the ground, linking them with covered walkways. Others had statues of fierce lions or creatures of myth built into their walls. A few of the designers had opted for simple but elegant spires and ornately decorated, concave walls.

Cardoc had been told to look for "the house of the griffon" and to "regard kindly the temple of the sun." Myrmeen found the trading house situated between a building guarded by a pair of stone griffons and a church made of glass. She and her party went inside the establishment and proceeded to the currency exchange bureau, where they found a tall man with slicked-back hair tied in a ponytail. He busily marked entries on a scroll and did not look up until Myrmeen set her gloved hands on either side of his parchment and leaned forward to whisper, "Martyn Johannas?"

He looked up, stunned. "Yes," he said.

Myrmeen smiled. She had seen the expression before. At that moment, she was certain that he would have agreed to anything she proposed. Her entourage kept its distance, allowing her to delicately take a seat before the man, her gown parting slightly to reveal her firm, lightly tanned legs, which she crossed to add to the effect.

"You don't even know what I'm going to ask," she said in a haughty, teasing voice.

"I don't think that will change the answer," he said as he scratched his neck, "but ask away."

Myrmeen looked around, making a show of it. "Is there somewhere we can go that's more private?"

Johannas angled his gaze toward her companions. "That depends on whether or not they come along."

A throaty laugh escaped Myrmeen. She had softened him up enough, she decided. "I wish to trade some currency," she said. "I seem to have a surplus of pearls from Amn."

The man shook his head, his expression slowly becoming serious. "And how many Roldons do you have to exchange?"

"More than a thousand," she said. "This trip, anyway. You see now why my personal assistants follow my every move."

He breathed out heavily. "Yes. That is a healthy sum." Glancing at some papers on his desk, he rattled off the rate of exchange as of that morning. "Naturally there will be a short period of waiting while the coins are authenticated—merely a formality, you understand."

She shrugged. There was a slight rustle of cloth as she shifted in her chair. She had to get him away from the exchange in a manner that would make the accompaniment of her guards seem reasonable. Her only reason for playing the seductress was to unnerve him, and hopefully shake his otherwise stolid sense of judgment.

"Is there nothing that can be done to speed up the process?" she asked. "Perhaps we could go where you could authenticate the coins personally and hurry the exchange."

The lines at the corners of his eyes crinkled as he smiled. "Am I to assume that these coins are fresh from the vats and have not yet cooled?"

"That would a reasonable assumption," she said, and gave the name of Lucius's contact who had said that Johannas was experienced in such transactions. Stolen coinage from Amn would have engraved numbers that could be traced.

"You understand that I can only pay half the going rate? The coins will have to be melted and recast—"

"Of course," she whispered, absently wetting her lips. "Now it's my turn to say yes to whatever you desire."

He rose from behind the desk. "Wait a few moments, then follow me into the alley at the rear of this building."

She nodded and watched him leave. The man had been a thorough professional the moment he realized that he was about to make a personal profit. She turned to her fellows, who had been unobtrusively following his movements. Burke nodded, and she casually walked through the crowded establishment, the Harpers directly behind her.

Within moments they were in the alley. Johannas was already waiting. Two men stood beside him, each carrying a large black bag. Before Myrmeen could give her companions the command to take all three men, Burke, Reisz, and Varina had sprung at them, shoving them against the next building's wall as they placed their blades at the men's throats. The pair of bags dropped in unison. Notably absent was the clink of shifting coinage as the bags struck the ground.

"Are you sure you want to do this?" Johannas said without emotion. "I have a reputation in this city. Steal from me and you will be hunted down for what you have taken. Kill me and prepare to die in return."

"All I want is information," Myrmeen said. "You can keep your money."

"I see," Johannas said as he glanced toward the blade held tightly at his throat. He shifted his gaze to Myrmeen as he raised a single eyebrow. "This is not necessary."

"Let him breathe, but stand ready to cut him if he tries to run or call for help," Myrmeen commanded.

Burke eased off with his knife but kept his grip on the man's velvet topcoat. Ord stood to the back of the group, beside the door, ready to deal with anyone who made the mistake of entering the alley from the trading house. He suddenly became acutely aware of the deepening shadows in the alley, though the sky above had not changed to a discernable extent. The alley ran the length of the trading house, which had been deeper than the glass temple or the house of the griffon. Buildings blocked the alley at either end, but there was a narrow passage that appeared to lead back to the street they had traveled or forward to the next street. The alley formed an **H** and they stood at its vulnerable apex. Burke wondered if Cardoc was with them as he watched the shadows lengthen and again looked up to see a bright, perfect sky.

A rustling from the shadows made Ord start. "Burke," he called, "there's something you should look at!"

Burke shook his head. He was not about to give Johannas the opportunity to escape. "Quiet, Ord."

Myrmeen licked her lips, which had suddenly become quite dry, and said, "You handle the financial end of a lucrative business run by a man named Kracauer. He sold children for a living. You handled the money. Ivan Nehlridge took care of the freight, the human cargo. Now Kracauer and Nehlridge are dead. You're going to tell me everything you know about the children that were sold to the Night Parade fourteen years ago, during the great storm. My daughter was one of those children. I want to find her. You will help me contact the Night Parade and together we will find my child. If you do not cooperate, there won't be enough left of you to fit into those sacks your men brought with them."

Johannas smiled. "Those sacks are already occupied. You should take a look."

Myrmeen glanced down at the sacks and saw her own shadow lengthen. "Let me see that," she said to Varina. The warrior gave the bag a quick kick, and the bag's mouth came open, its contents spilling out. Myrmeen gasped as she saw a human head roll in her direction. Then she recognized the face as that of Martyn Johannas.

Burke looked away from the face of Johannas's perfect double when he heard Myrmeen's small cry of surprise. The doppleganger took advantage of the man's distraction by shoving his own shoulders back and drawing a breath. His frilly shirt burst apart and a black, gore-drenched arm shot forward, snatching Burke's hand. It twisted the hand savagely, causing the warrior to drop his blade. Another hand erupted from the man's stomach and caught the falling weapon, then drove it at the warrior's chest.

Varina had seen the incredible display. She shoved the man she guarded to one side as she lashed out with a kick that knocked the weapon from the gnarled second hand of the creature that held her husband.

Johannas, or whatever the monster's true name was, threw Burke to the opposite wall without effort. It then began scratching at its neck once again. Myrmeen finally understood that it was not a human gesture at all. As it clawed at its skin, great gobs of pink flesh tore off, revealing a charred, blackened surface beneath.

"You should have taken our warning," the thing said. "To appear during the day is abhorrent to our kind. But we were forced into it by your foolish tenacity, which you are now going to pay dearly for." The doppleganger tore away the rest of its fleshlike covering and revealed a black, misshapen head. Only the perfect white teeth and glaring red eyes broke the monotony of its night-black flesh.

The shadows grew and deepened at either end of the alley, sealing it off. Myrmeen heard the chattering laughter of creatures that had plagued her dreams since she had been a child. She had come to Calimport in search of members of the Night Parade. Now, it appeared, she had found them.

Ord reached for the door, but it was covered in shadows and would not budge. The black-skinned creature looked at Myrmeen and laughed. It gestured with the additional two black arms that jutted from its stomach and chest, the palms open in a gesture of regret. "If they had told me you were so beautiful, I would have arranged to have you to myself for a time before I killed you."

No one had to give the order to attack. Reisz was about to slice the throat of the man he held when another creature emerged from the shadows, a man whose body seemed to exude darkness. The shadow man hauled Reisz from its companion, throwing the fighter at Varina. The humans fell to the ground.

Myrmeen backed away as the black-fleshed monstrosity rushed toward her. She snatched Burke's knife from the ground and cut away the flowing skirt of her dress. Hurling the fabric at the creature's face, she sidestepped it easily and spun to kick it face first into the opposite wall.

All I want is my daughter! We don't have to fight! she wanted to scream, but she knew her words would not gain the warriors the respite they needed if they were to escape from this trap. Her own weapons were bundled in the parcels the warriors had left at the stables. She knew that each Harper wore a sword and carried at least one dagger. Reisz had kept a scimitar strapped to his back. Ord carried a pair of steel truncheons. Reisz, Ord, and Varina were on their feet, drawing their weapons. Burke was still down.

Varina had come best prepared for a deadly encounter. The leather gloves covering her hands flared at the forearms, covering the weapons she had carefully wired into place. By raising her fists and turning them in a quick motion, so that her

palms faced her chest, she caused a set of blades to rip from
her gloves and spring forward, clearing her hand by half a foot.
The identical blades, which now appeared to be extensions of
her arms, looked like straight pikes with curled blades attached beside them that reached ever farther, and a short dagger that extended away from her body. She had more
surprises hidden in her boots and on the pads covering her
thighs and upper arms.

Myrmeen, on the other hand, had her bare legs, worthless
sandals, and cleavage. She had clearly not taken the inherent
dangers of this quest seriously enough. Under her breath she
swore that if she could just make it out of this alley alive, she
would never make the same mistake again.

Varina and Reisz stood back-to-back, prepared to face the
onslaught. Ord helped Burke to his feet and stood beside the
man. Myrmeen moved close to them. The four-armed, black-
skinned man-thing, its two companions, and the form whose
body seemed to drink in light and reflect only shadows, closed
around the Harpers. The creatures grinned to one another,
forcing the humans back into a circle. Myrmeen did not understand why they hesitated to attack. Moments ago they had the
humans separated and could have taken them one at a time.
This way, they had allowed the party to merge into a position
where they could use their strengths and support each other.

A moment later, she had her explanation.

"Zeal," the creature who had posed as Johannas said, "we
have them for you. Burn them!"

Myrmeen drew in a deep breath and looked up. At the edge
of the opposing roof she saw one, perhaps two figures looking
down at them. She thought of Kracauer's distress when he
saw the illusionary fireball in Cardoc's hand and recalled the
name he had used to address the mage. The man who had
been called was going to rain fire upon them from above. She
gritted her teeth and waited for the flames.

Nothing happened.

The doppleganger looked up in surprise. "Zeal?"

Myrmeen wasted no time and hurled the knife she had been

carrying. It struck the black-skinned creature in the throat. The monster gurgled in surprise and clutched at the weapon with all four of its arms, which now got in the way of one another. Twitching, it fell back to the pavement, oillike blood dripping from its wound.

As the first one fell, the Harpers launched themselves at the other three creatures. Each still possessed the appearance of humanity. Even the shadow lord looked like a man, though a very dark and featureless one. The man closest to Varina was thick-chested, with a full black beard and impossibly blue eyes. Varina plunged her blades into his throat and realized that his handsome appearance was nothing more than a disguise. The man's head had tilted as the blades approached, and the bones of his neck slid impossibly out of the way of the sharp edges, sliding to the opposite side of his neck, where they caused the flesh to ripple and change shape. The skin that had been pierced by the center staff stretched outward with the weapon's tip, then sprang back into shape as it forced the blade out of his throat, leaving a wound the size of a gold piece that immediately sealed itself. The creature grinned and snarled. "My turn!" it shrieked.

Varina leapt back as the man advanced on her, his upper and lower jaws expanding to three times their normal size. The bones in his hand ripped from their fragile coverings of flesh and reformed into identical copies of the weapons that Varina had produced. His ribs burst from his chest, clean, with no blood, and stood straight and razor-sharp as he tried to gather her in a lethal embrace. Reisz crossed in front of her, swinging his scimitar at the creature's malleable arm. The weapon sank deep into the monster's flesh, then stopped dead as it struck bone that was as strong as tempered steel.

Beside Reisz, the second member of the Night Parade who had not yet abandoned his human skin, a tall man with a wild mane of yellow hair, grabbed hold of the warrior's arm. Reisz screamed as the man's flesh bubbled and cut through the heavy leather padding on his arms as if it were concentrated acid. He released the scimitar, which was quickly expelled by the first creature's rubbery flesh, then tried to pull away from the second man's burning grip.

Varina grabbed hold of Reisz's body and yanked hard. The swarthy-skinned Harper clenched his jaws as he saw a long pink-and-red glob stretch away from his arm as it adhered to the blond-haired man's hand. He could not feel the skin and muscle that tore away from his arm; the wound had been cauterized instantly by the man's touch. Finally the bond between them snapped and Reisz looked down in shock at the smoldering black mass on his upper arm. Varina turned as she heard the shadow-man's singsong voice from the other side of the group, where Myrmeen, weaponless, stood between Burke and Ord, whose swords were drawn and crossed before the woman they had sworn to protect.

Nevertheless, Burke's anxious face was turned in his wife's direction as she dragged Reisz away from the grotesque, bony monstrosity that chattered and giggled as it slowly advanced with its companion. The handsome man with the touch of death winked at her, then raised his fingers and wiggled them in her direction. She realized suddenly that her attack on the nightmare people and their retaliation had only taken a few seconds. Soon her back was inches from Myrmeen's and there was nowhere left to go.

"Humans are such easy prey," the lord of the shadows said as he bent low and picked up a large rock. The stone was instantly coated with an impenetrable layer of darkness, and he tossed the rock to Ord in a friendly, underhanded motion. "Catch!"

Myrmeen saw Ord's hand go up instinctively, and she recalled the murder of Kracauer with the ebon-coated, lightning-shaped blades. Seconds before the stone would have fallen gently into Ord's unprotected hand, Myrmeen grabbed the teenager and twisted him out of the way. The rock struck the wall behind them and sizzled as it made contact, a deep black cloud rising from where it hit.

The two creatures before Varina and Reisz backed up. The man with the corrosive touch said, "Take them, Roderik."

The shadow lord smiled and sank into a crouch, his hand reaching toward the pavement. Myrmeen understood what would happen. He would touch the ground and his lethal shadows would snake across the distance separating him from the Harpers, engulfing them from their boots to their vulnerable flesh. The shadows would kill the humans upon contact. She had to stop him. Snatching one of the truncheons from the belt at Ord's waist, Myrmeen ducked below the crossed swords that were meant to protect her and hurled the weapon at the man's head. It struck him in the forehead with a sharp crack, causing him to bound to his feet, his arms pinwheeling in the air as he tried to regain his balance. Myrmeen gasped. The second he fell, his hand would touch the ground.

From the end of the alley came the sound of thunder. A blinding bluish red bolt of lightning snaked through the air and struck the shadow lord. The arcane fires hit him between his shoulder blades and emerged from where his heart had been an instant before. Then they crackled and dissipated. Through the hole that had been created in the shadow-creature's chest, Myrmeen saw Lucius Cardoc's sweaty, worried face. Buckling at the knees, the lord of shadows fell back. His hand struck the ground, but his power had vanished with his life.

Cardoc raised his hands again, his lips forming words that she could not hear at such a distance.

"Get down," Myrmeen shouted, and the Harpers dropped to the hard pavement as a second stream of mystical energy snapped across the alley and struck the chattering creature with the skeleton made of shape-changing steel. The monster was lifted from its feet by the powerful energies. Its torso was ripped apart by the initial blast, its twisting bones fused in a spiderweb of intricate designs that quickly melted and cooled into a shapeless mass.

The blond man with the deadly touch backed away in fear, then broke into a dead run toward the opposite end of the alley, where the shadows quickly swallowed him whole.

* * * * *

Inside the swirling black cloud of shadows and smoke, the handsome, almost human creature ran a few more paces, then stopped suddenly as he heard the familiar sound of inhuman legs scampering down a wall and saw a fiery-haired man leap down to stand before him.

"Imperator Zeal," the man said, his heart leaping into his throat.

"Callistraon, is it not?" the red-haired man said. His hair was tightly curled and his skin was hot, his body drenched in sweat. He wore a loose-fitting white frock with the sleeves rolled up, a simple yellow sash tied around his waist. His feet were bare, and the patch of tight, curly red hair that grew on his perfectly honed chest glistened with beads of moisture. He frowned in confusion. "You have a mission, do you not?"

"Imperator, they have a mage that killed two of the other Inextinguishables. They—"

Zeal pointed at the heavy curtain of shadows at the man's back. "You are supposed to be back there, killing them, disposing of the humans. Am I wrong in this, or are you not one of those I assigned to the task?"

From the wall where Zeal had descended came a rough sound, like leather brushing leather, followed by a piercing shriek that was not unlike the sound of two heavy blades scraping together. Zeal angled his head toward the sounds. "It's the wife. She wants to get on with it."

"Get on with what?" Callistraon asked in a small voice.

"Punishing you for your cowardice," Zeal said as he raised his hand to reveal a fiery, yearning abyss within his palm that seemed to reach into the depths of some hellish dimension.

* * * * *

Moments before, at the middle of the alley, the Harpers had tried to regain their bearing. Cardoc stumbled forward. Myrmeen realized for the first time that he had been hurt. His flesh was crisscrossed with burns that appeared to have been lashed into his flesh with a whip. The channeling of the tremendous forces that he had called upon also had served to drain him.

Ord had crossed to where the black-skinned corpse had lain and had knelt beside the creature, curious about its inhuman nature. The monster's blackened arms had retreated into its chest and a new covering of soft pink flesh was sewing itself over the creature's leathery black skin. The dark man suddenly came to life, snatching Myrmeen's blade from its throat with one hand while it grasped Ord's wrist in the other. He dragged the boy into the ink-black shadows near the wall. They were smothered by the gathering darkness.

"Ord!" Burke screamed.

At that moment, a massive tongue of flames reached out from the mouth of the alley where the blond-haired man had vanished. A fireball rolled in their direction, instantly consuming the blond man, who stood in its path. The great sphere of flame unraveled long before it reached the Harpers, exploding against both walls of the alley, leaving a blackened, charred carpet on the pavement to mark its path.

The flames had burned away the darkness, and Myrmeen was able to see the red-haired man whose right hand sweltered with flames. She had seen him before, in a dream when she was only six years old, a dream that she had only been able to recall in flashes until now. Suddenly the dream was before her, its image burned into her mind. She would not forget it this time. To do so would be deadly, she realized. Twice already she had made the mistake of underestimating her enemy. She would not do so again.

Standing behind the man was a tall, lithe woman with creamy skin and long, shiny black hair. Wrapping her arms around him from behind, one arm around his ribs, the other over his right shoulder, she nuzzled at his neck. Then her hands reached into his shirt and caressed the rock-hard landscape of his chest. The woman whispered something in his ear. Whatever she was saying had caused the fire lord to hesitate and not simply turn his power against the humans.

Suddenly, from the shadows where Ord and the black-skinned man had vanished, the tall, lanky teenager appeared. He seemed dazed as he cried, "My face! He was trying to take my face!"

Another figure burst from the darkness, a young man who might have been Ord's twin. This boy's face was contorted in a mask of rage, and he launched himself at the wobbly-kneed teenager with undisguised hatred. The first Ord turned and drew his sword at the sight of the advancing doppleganger.

The entire party's attention was drawn to Ord and his duplicate. Varina was the first to respond. Without hesitation she released a set of blades hidden on her right arm, then she drew her hand back and propelled the center spike toward the back of the teenager who had first emerged from the smoky mist. The sharp blade burst through the soft leathers of his back, piercing his heart from behind. An inhuman scream filled the alley as the true Ord snatched his sword away from the duplicate, who had fallen to his knees in agony. Ord cleaved the creature's head in two, his sword sinking down to the monster's collarbones. Blood as dark as ink sprayed from the creature as it fell in a heap, twitching and convulsing.

Ord backed away, trembling. "How did you know?"

"His face," Varina said. "It was fresh and new. Your old scars had not appeared."

Cardoc glanced down at the corpse, which had not stopped moving. The two sections of its head were merging, healing. "This one is still alive. We may get some answers from it."

"By the gods," Ord muttered, "what does it take to kill these things so they stay dead?"

The mage felt a sudden chill in the air, the same sensation he had experienced an instant before the red-haired man's fires had erupted seconds earlier. He gestured quickly, casting a sphere of protection around the adventurers.

The red-haired man stood at the end of the alley, a separate spear of fire bursting from each of his hands and mouth. Each of the three ragged tongues of flame struck the walls and were deflected perfectly to incinerate the bodies of the monsters downed by the Harpers. The flames never approached the obsidian sphere hiding the adventurers.

Seconds later, it was over. The corpses were nothing but ash that was quickly dispersed by the heavy winds that followed the arcane fires. At the end of the alley, the deep shadows once again congealed around the spot where the red-haired man and dark-haired woman had stood. They were nowhere to be seen.

Cardoc released the sphere of protection and surveyed the area for further threats. Burke finally spoke. "Where in the fiery hells of Cyric were you?"

"Ord closed the door in my face. I cannot walk though walls. I had to go around the long way. Those shadows" the mage shuddered—"were alive and tried to stop me."

Myrmeen moved past the others, then ran toward the end of the alley. Cardoc and the Harpers followed. The man and woman were gone, and the shadows were quickly dissipating. All evidence of the Night Parade's presence was vanishing before her, along with all hope of ever finding her daughter.

Ord pointed upward. "Look!"

The Harpers trained their gazes at the rooftops. "I see nothing," Burke said. "What was it?"

Ord shook his head. "The leg of a spider, I'm certain. It scampered over the edge of that rooftop."

"The spider would have to be the size of a man for you to be able to see it at this distance," Reisz said.

"Yes," Ord said as he took a few tentative steps forward, "I know."

* * * * *

On the rooftop, Imperator Zeal glanced down at the humans, the fires within his breast continuing to rage.

"Tamara," he said, his voice distant, the call of the fire surging within him like a drug. The beautiful, lean, muscled woman approached him, a dangerous smile upon her exotic features. She appeared in her mid-twenties, and her hair was a very dark brunette, almost black. Zeal turned and ran his hand through her gorgeous, shining hair, which was long and given to curls, then he stared into her fine, dark eyes flecked with crimson. Only the most delicate traces of lines could be seen beneath her eyes and around her mouth. Her complexion was soft and light. She had a small bust, generous hips, and long legs. There was an elegant flow to the lines of her body. She wore a black-and-red shift that would fall away quickly when she made the change. Sandals protected her feet and a waist sash carried her valuables.

"My love," she whispered as she leaned close and kissed him, her tongue snaking into his mouth to taste the intense heat within him. She pulled away and caressed his face.

"You know why I didn't help the others."

"Of course," she said with a knowing laugh. "No man may command Imperator Zeal, save for Lord Sixx."

"And yet a woman can bend me to her will," he snapped.

"He humiliates you and you take it. He treats you like a buffoon, a servant, and yet you give him nothing but love and loyalty. Perhaps he is justified in his treatment of you.

"He's jealous of you," Tamara said for perhaps the hundredth time. "He fears you. He does not understand that every time his words lash you in public, he merely strengthens the love of the people for you."

"Even if that is true, his fears are not warranted," Zeal responded. "I am not an ambitious man. What would I do with the power of the Night Parade at my command, if that is what you are urging me to take?"

Tamara gave no answer. Imperator Zeal suspected she had another motive for wanting him to depose Lord Sixx, as wealth and power had never especially interested her. In his heart he prayed that his beloved and trusted friend would not force him to choose between them.

She touched his lips with her finger. "I love you, husband. If you wish me to keep my opinions to myself, I will do so."

Zeal shook his head. He knew that was a lie, and even if it were true, he valued her counsel and the audacious fire that burned within her. Glancing at the alley once more, he saw that the humans were leaving. The assassins that Zeal had sent against the humans had been his Inextinguishables, the elite of his enforcers. Many of his kind could be killed with a simple knife thrust; they were as vulnerable as any human. How would it look if he allowed the killers of the Night Parade's finest to go free?

"We should kill them," he said. "It would be a simple matter for us. Even the mage—"

"Let them live," she urged. "The edicts of our kind tell us that we are to avoid direct confrontation whenever possible. This scene will draw attention."

"They will not stop," he said.

"They must. There is nowhere left for them to turn."

Zeal's hands bunched into fists. "They know we exist."

"Who would believe them?" she said as she kissed his throat and licked a single bead of sweat that descended along the hard, glistening muscles of his neck. Below, the humans on the street were quickly out of view.

"You are certain they will stop?" he asked.

"Of course," Tamara said as she turned the red-haired man to face her. "What choice do they have?"

With a passionate cry, she threw her arms around her husband, kissing him full on the mouth. He returned the kiss greedily, roughly caressing her hard, trim flesh. The call of the flames rose up within his body.

As they kissed, small piles of trash burst into flame on the rooftop.

Five

 Temples with healers who were not above taking a healthy contribution to the church in return for treating heathens were not difficult to find in the financial district. Reisz's wound appeared worse than it actually had been and when the healer was finished with him, a new layer of bright pink skin had appeared on his arm and he had regained the limb's full use. Several of Ord's minor cuts and bruises were removed by the healer before they left the temple and walked back toward the stables.

Burke admonished Cardoc for his independent ways, ordering him to stay visible at all times and keep close to the party. The Night Parade would be most worried about him, and his visible presence might cause them to stay away rather than move in for a second attack. Reisz eyed everyone on the street with suspicion. The Night Parade's members had expertise in disguising themselves as human and he stood ready to attack anyone who made the slightest move in his direction.

Varina had stayed close to her husband, who was overcome

with shame. He had done nothing in the fight, and his wife had almost been killed. The incident had weighed more heavily on the strongly built warrior than on his lover, who was grateful that they had made it out of the ambush alive.

At the stables, Myrmeen found the stable boy once more. He gazed at her with distress, but respected her privacy and did not ask what had happened. He led her to the small office, where she changed back into her warrior's attire. She emerged to hand the boy the remains of her dress with a straightforward command: "Burn this."

Myrmeen returned to the others, who were gathered near Cardoc's sleek black mount. Burke had been severely shaken. He looked at Myrmeen with a tired, haunted expression. "Last night I dreamt that if we didn't leave this city by nightfall tonight, we would all die here. My dream nearly came true this day."

"When I was little, the other children said that the Night Parade could make you have strange dreams," Myrmeen said. "Some would come true. Others would not."

Burke shook his head. "We've taken a vote. The consensus is that we should take what we've learned to the local authorities then flee this nightmare-infested city."

"There are five of you," Myrmeen said quietly. "Did anyone vote to remain?"

"My wife and the mage."

"You didn't ask me," she said, angered at the thought of being forced to give up on the child she had never seen.

"We're asking now."

"I can't go back," Myrmeen said. "I picture the girl in my mind. I wonder what her first words were. I need to know what they did to her, Burke."

Reisz cleared his throat. "I have something to say to Myrmeen in private, if that's all right."

The others nodded and Myrmeen allowed the curly-haired fighter to lead her to another part of the stables. Once they were alone, he ran his hand through his salt-and-pepper hair and stared at her with hard, dark eyes that had witnessed more death and brutality than Myrmeen would ever believe possible. "I must speak plainly," he said.

"Yes."

"You know that I have feelings for you. I always have. You are the only woman I have ever loved."

"Reisz, please," she said, her tension drifting away as she caressed the side of his face with a compassion she had worried was lost after the day's horrors. He tensed and gently forced her hand away. Her touch was more than he could bear.

"I was married for a time after you left us," Reisz said. "The woman loved me. I found that I could say, 'I love you,' easily enough, but the words were meaningless. After a time, she understood this and turned elsewhere to find the love I could not give her."

Myrmeen's compassion suddenly flared into anger. "Reisz, I don't know why you feel it necessary to bring all this up now, but I'm not going to accept the role of the woman who ruined your life. I never led you on and I never lied to you. You can forget it right now if you—"

"Shut up," he said painfully. "That's not it at all."

She stood before him, chest heaving in anger, waiting for him to continue.

"I'm telling you this so you understand that what is in the past is not always buried as deep as we would like to think," Reisz said. "You left us behind because we were reminders of what you had lost. Then you found yourself in the arms of a man who could give you what no man had offered you before: peace of mind, a chance to stop running, an opportunity to reinvent yourself. But none of that was what you really needed, was it?"

"I don't know what you mean."

"Did you love Haverstrom Lhal?" he asked.

"He was my husband."

"That does not answer my question."

She hung her head low, then looked away. "In my way, yes, I felt love for him. But after what Dak had put me through, I knew that I could never give myself completely to another. My body, my loyalty, and affection—these I could give. But my ability to love died with my child. It died that night, during the storm."

"Lost, perhaps, but not dead. If that were the case, you wouldn't be here. But there is a danger to what you are doing, a danger beyond the threat to our lives. Myrmeen, you have always been more interested in the quest, in the hunt for the prize, than in dealing with the rewards and the consequences of what you bring about. What will you do if we find your daughter? She will be a stranger to you, and you to her. You will have to try to love her, Myrmeen. It will change your life forever. Do you think you can do that?"

"I don't know," she said, a single tear threatening to fall from her eye. "But I need to . . . I need to find out, Reisz. I need to know if I'm really dead inside, or if I have something left to give."

Reisz nodded and tried to draw her into a comforting embrace. Myrmeen placed her hand on his chest to stop him.

"No," she said. "If you want to help me, you know what you have to do."

He touched her face gently, then turned away. They returned to the group. Burke and Ord were talking with the stable boy, getting the best directions back to the city's main gates.

"You won't be needing them," Reisz said. "I've changed my vote. We are Harpers, sworn to protect the Realms. I see no greater threat now than the villains we faced today. I say we stay and try to find them. After we've forced them to tell us what they know of Myrmeen's child, we will bring their organization to the end it deserves."

Burke looked at his wife and understood that he would receive no support there. Ord shook his head, anger and fear coursing through him. "Where do you suggest we start looking?" the boy spat. "Our dreams or the shadows that gather when the sun falls from the sky?"

Myrmeen glanced at the stable boy and held out another coin. "Tell us the name of the most disreputable house of criminals in this vile city."

"Keep your money," he said with a laugh. "That one's too easy. All you need do is go to the Gentleman's Hall. Ask for Pieraccinni. He's the one in charge. If you like, I can draw you a map. . . ."

* * * * *

By nightfall the Harpers once again were near the docks. They had found lodgings nearby and had dined and rested. The directions that the stable boy had produced were perfectly accurate. The Gentleman's Hall was an abandoned temple that had been converted into a surprisingly stylish and restrained meeting place for thieves, hired killers, and others with similarly low aspirations. The Harpers were stopped at the door and politely requested to check their weapons by a young, golden-haired man named Alden, who possessed soft green eyes and a rakish smile. He raised an eyebrow when Cardoc approached.

"You reek with the stench of magic," he said brightly. "I've been requested to inform all mages that there are wards throughout this establishment whose sole duty is to capture any magic that is discharged and turn it back upon its sender twofold. Now that you have been warned, please try to enjoy yourselves without causing any trouble. There are gambling rooms, musicians, poets, and women and men of severely loose morals if anyone is feeling in need of company."

Myrmeen said, "We would like to speak to a man named Pieraccinni."

The name caught the young man's attention. "Who should I say is calling?"

"The mistress of pearls," she said, holding out a handful of platinum coins.

"Remember our restrictions," Alden said as he waved a finger before her, then turned and motioned for her to follow. The Harpers were led past several rooms where men and women who would normally be found hiding in shadows, nervously waiting for fresh prey to arrive, were openly laughing and trading stories over drinks. Others played good-hearted games where the stakes were kept low for the enjoyment of all. A dark-eyed serving maid winked at Ord, who strained to look over his shoulder at her passing form until Burke grabbed his shoulder and reminded him to stay alert.

Soon they stood before a great set of double doors that had been painted blood red. Figures had been chiseled from the marble door, representations of many gods, including the hawk-nosed lord of the dead, who once had been a man in Myrmeen's employ. Alden used both hands to manipulate the heavy knocker. Only when he had heard an invitation lost to the hearing of all the others did he move to the side of the door and throw a lever. The doors swung inward, revealing a spacious office that contained a gigantic four-poster bed, a wealth of statues, a small kitchen, and a desk, behind which sat a hulking, bald man who rose to greet his visitors with a disarming smile. The Harpers moved to enter the room and Alden's hand shot up.

"Only her," the young man said. "She will be safe, I assure you."

Myrmeen entered the chamber and heard the door swing shut behind her. Pieraccinni was not handsome, but his features were bold and strong. He wore a sleeveless teal frock, with an ornate belt made of gold and covered in rubies. Similarly designed bands graced his thick upper arms and wrists. The man was strongly built, but the muscles of his bare arms and partially revealed chest were not meticulously defined. He walked barefoot upon the floor, which was carpeted in a fine, eastern-style weave, and paused before the red silk curtains of his black marble four-poster bed. He wriggled his fingers at the curtains, and a slight, feminine giggle sounded. Myrmeen suddenly became aware of movement behind the silk and the hushed whisper of conversation.

"Twins," Pieraccinni said proudly, "from the desert of Anauroch. Incredibly talented lovers and highly efficient assassins. Would you like me to bring them out for you?"

"No," Myrmeen said. "I have other needs."

Pieraccinni linked his hands behind his back and nodded with a forced compassion, his smile still in evidence. "I see," he said. "And what might they be?"

"Information. On the Night Parade."

The bald man's stride did not falter, nor did he seem surprised as he stopped before Myrmeen and crossed his arms over his chest. "I could give that to you, I suppose. Charge you some outrageous fee, so that you feel you've gotten your money's worth. They'll kill you, of course. I'll feel regret for at least a second or two, then go on to my next bit of business. Yes, I suppose I could do that, Mistress Lhal."

Myrmeen tensed, worried that she had walked into another trap. Sensing her distress, Pieraccinni allowed his hands to fall to his sides, palms forward, in a gesture of acquiescence.

"There is no harm to be found here," Pieraccinni said. "These hands and my heart contain no malice for you."

"You must be mistaken—"

He raised his hand, his features twisted in distaste. "Please. Don't insult my intelligence. You've been making inquiries in violent and extremely public ways. That gets people talking. I always listen when people talk. Not two months ago, your former husband, Dak, lay on that bed with an acquaintance of mine, a delightful young lady. Some wine, the pleasure of her rather athletic abilities, and he was ready to tell me everything of his plans to extort funds from you for the information concerning your lost child. He was a thoroughly unlikable man. I hope you don't mind me saying as much."

"That's fine," Myrmeen said. "Are you aware that Dak was killed in Arabel?"

"Oh, yes," Pieraccinni said as he looked at her strong arms. "It takes great strength and terrible desire to sever a man's head with a single blow. You seem to possess both, in great abundance."

"Will you help me find the Night Parade?"

"There's no need," Pieraccinni said as he retreated to his desk, drawing Myrmeen deeper into the room as she moved to follow him. She glanced back at the bed and rested one leg on the edge of his desk so that she would not have her back turned to the women behind the curtains.

"What do you mean?" she asked, suspicious.

"I have something more valuable. Once I had learned that poor, foolish Dak had been married to you, I urged him to think about anything he knew about the fabled ruler of Arabel that could be used to blackmail her. Not that I would have, you understand, but I enjoy this type of thing. The entertainment value. You understand."

"Go on."

"I have found your daughter," he said as he scratched a set of numbers on a sheet of parchment, then slid the paper toward her. "That is my price for what I know."

Myrmeen let out a deep, ragged breath as she thought about the figure. "You must know that I would not carry this kind of money with me."

Pieraccinni shrugged. "After you have the girl, come back here and pay me what you can as a show of intent. I will be happy to take payment on the rest after you go home."

Myrmeen thought about his offer. "How do I know you aren't lying?"

"Well, you don't, of course. But I think you can see that I am a businessman. I see a need, I fulfill that need—for a price. Your needs are considerably more apparent than you seem to realize. That is why I ask for nothing up front and trust you to follow the terms of our agreement, provided this information proves to be of value."

She cupped her face in her hands, thinking it over, then she locked her gaze with his. He did not flinch or look away. She would have to wager that he was telling the truth.

"All right," she said. "Tell me how to find my daughter."

Six

Cyric's Hammer was one of the few significant landmarks in the vast Calim Desert. Djimon, the leader of the highly successful band of desert raiders known as the Black Scourge, knew them all. The towering spire of rock was a particular favorite of the short, powerfully built man. His unusual brown hair and soft blue eyes had marked him as a pariah in his own culture, a bastard child who had been abandoned because of impurity in his blood. He did not know his parents and so he did not know if the stigma he had suffered under had been warranted or not. What he did know, however, was that once he had reached adulthood, no man or god had been safe from his wrath.

During the time of Arrival, Djimon had slain a man who claimed to be the human avatar of Malar, the Beastlord, the god of bloodlust. The man's random attacks along the trade route that Djimon had clearly staked as his private territory had made a challenge inevitable and the man's continued existence extremely bad for business. In truth, Djimon's nemesis was an insane, murderous wizard with delusions of grandeur. Nevertheless, Djimon had earned the name "Godslayer" among his people. His band of killers and thieves had gained a taste of even greater notoriety, for which they were grateful. Keeping his underlings happy had been the single most important aspect of his continued success in an enterprise where death was often the ultimate reward.

Djimon turned at the sound of the familiar, piercing shriek that he had been forced to put up with for the past week, ever since his last excursion into the city. It was midafternoon, and he was sitting atop Cyric's Hammer, a dangerous perch that boasted only one safe path from its base to its wide, flat head. Rumors had it that a hundred men had died trying to find a nontreacherous route to the top. When they mere inches from achieving their desire, the stones would shift to dislodge all who were foolish enough to challenge the rock, sending them screaming to the sharp rocks at the base. The pillar had earned its name when a wandering sage pronounced the rock accursed by the god of misery and death.

Djimon had shrugged off all rumors and had scaled the five-hundred-foot pillar without trouble, further adding to his near-mythical standing. He now looked to the horizon and saw the portents of what would be a terrible storm when it finally arrived. A tiny flicker that might have been lightning flashed in the heart of the deep gray clouds, a rare sight in the Calim Desert. He decided that he would give the buyers another half hour to appear, then he would give his men the order to abandon the Hammer. The storm troubled him. Last night he had dreamt of a storm that carried with it a collection of piercing, merciless eyes; there were eyes everywhere in his dream, and they were always in sets of three, groups of six eyes. What did they signify?

The scream came again. "What?" he shouted impatiently.

A voice that he instantly identified as belonging to Jurgon Rutsche, his tall, swarthy-skinned second-in-command, called, "She tried to leap off again. The child seems to think she can fly!"

Djimon sighed. A part of him wished she had succeeded, though her death would have been difficult to explain to the buyers. There was no sense in trying to avoid his duties. The girl had lived, and so it was time for his daily speech. He screwed his most nefarious expression into place, spat twice, then gestured for his second-in-command to bring the girl to him.

The child was young, just past the age where she would have experienced her first bleeding. She wore the traditional wrappings expected of a woman in their nomadic society, though she refused to keep her face covered. He stared into her devastating blue eyes, studying the unusual slivers of gold he found there. The child was a brunette with a trim, athletic build. Her cheekbones were high and strong, and her lips were full, a rich scarlet without augmentation. Jurgon Rutsche had pinned her arms behind her back and was shoving her in front of him with considerable effort. She had lost one sandal by trying to dig her heels into the unyielding stone and was now struggling like a creature possessed to free herself from Jurgon's hold. There were chains around her wrists and ankles, but they barely restrained her.

The first thing out of her mouth that was not a high-pitched, eardrum-rattling scream, was a curse she had learned in Djimon's language, linking his parentage to goats, demons, and whores.

He struck her with a backhanded blow that caused her head to whip around with a sharp crack. She looked back at him with a wicked, triumphant expression as she licked the blood from the corner of her mouth. "Now I'm damaged goods."

Djimon forced himself to gain control of his emotions. A large, ugly bruise was already starting to form on the child's face where she had been struck. He moved in close so that she could smell his rancid breath.

"Know this, child. If we had not found a buyer for you so quickly, I would have allowed my men to take you. They would not have stopped until they had drunk their heart's content of the pleasures your young body has to offer. Then I would have fed you to the vultures for the trouble you have caused."

"Charmer." She spat and tried to kick him in the crotch. Only his sharp reflexes allowed him to move out of the way in time. He restrained himself and did not strike her again. His buyers had been promised a fourteen-year-old blue-eyed virgin in perfect condition, and, by Cyric's fiery hell, he was going to make good on that pledge. On the other hand, the degradation and shock of being brutally raped by a dozen or so of his men might serve to break her spirit and make her a more docile—and therefore more valuable—commodity.

He was contemplating this issue when the girl began to scream, "Kill me! Kill me!" at the top of her lungs. The raider marveled at the girl's talent for widening his options.

He leaned close and said, "Child, I warn you—"

With a howl of delight she brought her knee up to the space between his legs. This time the short desert raider was not able to move out of the blow's path. He squealed as her knee connected, then he doubled over, his face inches from hers. She leaned in and bit at his exposed ear even as Jurgon yanked her away from his master. Djimon screamed even louder as the lower half of his ear was torn away. In alarm, Jurgon relaxed his grip on the child's arm, giving her the opportunity to slip from his hands and launch herself forward, toward the lip of the pillar's flat top. Her chains caught her legs and she tripped, spitting out the bloody chunk of flesh that she had bitten from Djimon's head. She did not allow the bonds to defeat her; the freedom of death was within her grasp, a mere ten feet away. Rolling with her fall, the girl used her momentum and twisted her body until she had covered the ten feet and was about to make one final turn, which would send her plunging to her death.

She stopped and laughed at the men who were now running toward her. "My name is not 'child,' you ignorant spawn of whores. My name is Krystin!"

With that, she rolled off the edge and somehow suppressed a scream as she plummeted through the air, the ground rapidly reaching up to meet her.

At the lip of the flat, Djimon and Jurgon came to a halt, their chests heaving with exertion. Djimon held his savaged ear and issued a stream of curses.

He stopped only when he heard the sound of laughter from the pillar's base. Kneeling, he looked over the thin, crumbling ledge to see Krystin suspended in midair, her flight impossibly arrested. For once, the child was speechless. She floated gently downward, toward a group of six people that included a tall, gaunt man who was pointing his hands at the girl and gesturing: Magic.

Djimon ignored the pain long enough to issue yet another curse. His operations had proceeded without the opposition of mages for close to a year. The formerly stringent measures he had taken to protect himself against practitioners of the art had become lax, a seemingly unnecessary burden on himself and his people. He considered himself fortunate to realize his error in this manner. The party below had been shielded by a spell of invisibility, or some type of cloaking incantation that had allowed them to blend with the endless vista of sand as they approached. From Cyric's Hammer, he could see the main route between Calimport and Memnon in the distance. Even now his buyers appeared on the well-traveled road. He thought of the humiliation he would face for the rest of his life when the story got out of how a fourteen-year-old child had taken the legendary Godslayer's ear, and the thought was almost too horrible to accept.

From the ground below, Djimon heard the group's youngest member, a man close to twenty years in age, howl, "Well, that solves the problem of how to get her down without having to engage all of these louts." The young man rested his hands on his thighs and shook his head in amazement.

"They actually think this is over," Djimon said as he rose to his feet and barked a string of commands to his people. He could not control the future, but in that moment he swore that he would have his vengeance on the child and her rescuers.

At the base of the pillar, Lucius Cardoc levitated the girl to the ground, then fell back, exhausted.

"You've done well, mage," Burke said as he caught the man and helped to steady him. All the Harpers' faces were red and blistered despite the hoods they wore to protect their skin. Varina and Reisz still sat on their mounts, holding the reins of two other horses.

"Would that all of our quests were completed with such ease," Reisz said darkly.

"What's that supposed to mean?" Burke asked.

"Nothing. I hope."

Several feet away from the party, the girl they had rescued held up her chained hands. Myrmeen broke from the group and approached her tentatively. The sun was in Myrmeen's eyes and she was not able to get a decent look at the child until she was practically on top of her. For an instant she felt as if she were staring at a much younger reflection of herself: The child had her eyes.

"If you're done gawking, could you break these chains?" Krystin asked impatiently. "We have to get out of here."

Myrmeen smiled. The strange, deep-blue eyes with slivers of gold were not all the girl had inherited.

"I'm serious. Djimon keeps guards down here," Krystin said urgently.

"No more," Myrmeen replied, indicating with a slight nod the trio of bodies lying in the shadows near the pillar's base, where Djimon's route to the top began. She could not keep herself from staring at the girl in adulation, though she knew she must have appeared to be a dull-witted fool from her vacant expression and hesitancy. This was her daughter; it was actually her. Dak had told her the truth.

"Damn," Krystin said as she slid one of the blades from Myrmeen's waist, then scurried to a rock, where she rested the chains and began to pound at the links with the weapon's hilt. They snapped quickly and she immediately went to work on the chains binding her feet.

A warm, frothy euphoria filled Myrmeen's heart as she watched her daughter. The logical part of her mind told her that her actions were not those of an intelligent, calculating woman. She was giving Djimon a chance to react, and the operation was supposed to have been a quick, clean slash and grab: take out the opposition, steal the prize, get out as quickly as possible. But for some reason she was completely enchanted and unable to think of giving orders.

Then she remembered her overconfident bearing at the bar in Calimport and the ambush she had blundered into behind the trading house. The memories were sobering.

The group had stayed close to the pillar's base, underneath the overhanging lip, where the raiders would not be able to fire upon them with arrows or any other weapons they possessed. When they departed, Lucius would have to cast a deflecting wall at their backs until they were out of range of Djimon's archers. Fighting in an environment where any form of exertion could bring about heat sickness, vertigo, and exhaustion was not a desirable option.

"Don't worry about your captors," Myrmeen said. "We severed their lines with arrows. Young Ord turned out to be an expert marksman. They're trapped up there, with no means of getting to the ground. I'm sure they have archers, but—"

"It speaks," the girl said as she sprang to her haunches.

"I'm Myrmeen. My name is Myrmeen—"

"Fine, I'm Krystin. And, yes, Djimon has archers and a damn shade more than that. Let's get out of here!"

"What do you mean, more than that? What—"

"They have magical weapons, too!" she said as they both heard several cries of terror and rage from above. Suddenly a group of four men leapt from the edge of the flat, each holding one corner of a sleek black sheet that might have been a cloak. They fell quickly, but not with the speed that would have killed them. The Harpers were drawn from their mounts by the sight of the falling men.

"A cloak of levitation," Lucius said as he watched the raiders drift slightly faster to the ground. Ord broke out his bow, nocked an arrow, and loosed a shaft at one of the four men, who squealed as the arrow narrowly missed his face. His surprise caused him to let go of the cloak's edge, and he fell another hundred feet to his death.

Ord nocked a second arrow and fired again. The raiders' descent had been slowed by the loss of the fourth man's weight. This time the teenager was able to strike one of the men dead center in the chest. One of the two remaining fighters reached and grabbed the dead man's hand, catching him before he plummeted and caused their descent to slow even further. Ord was preparing a third arrow when he saw that the raiders, who were now only twenty feet from the ground, had decided to take their chances with a free-fall. They released the cloak and fell to the ground in heaps, rolling and groaning at the impact. Myrmeen was certain she had heard the snap of bones. Neither survivor attempted to get up.

"They have more than one cloak like that!" Krystin warned. "I bet Djimon and the others went down the other side—"

"Very astute," a voice sounded. Djimon stepped around the curved base of the pillar, his crossbow aimed at Krystin's head, and fired without hesitation.

The bolt whistled past Myrmeen's ear as she shoved the girl from the iron rod's path and hurled herself at the swarthy-skinned, brown-haired man. She knew that she could not afford to give Djimon a chance to reload his crossbow.

Myrmeen collided with the short, powerful man and drove him to the ground. She straddled his chest and prepared to deliver an open fisted blow that would drive the cartridge from his nose deep into his brain, killing him instantly. Suddenly she heard the slight crush of boots and looked up to see three archers, arrows nocked and ready to fire. The middle archer stepped away from the others and aimed his shaft at her face. She realized that Djimon probably had sent another contingent around the other side of the base with the intent of catching the Harpers in crossfire, slaughtering them quickly and efficiently with their arrows. She heard the sounds of conflict from where she had left the Harpers and knew that she could expect no help from them.

"Get down!"

Myrmeen did not question the voice. She threw herself

upon Djimon and heard two sounds: A blade slicing through
the air above her head and the familiar gurgle of a dying man
with a dagger lodged in his throat. Then she heard the slump
of a body and the snapping of a bow caught beneath a falling
man. The archer was dead.

Beneath her, Djimon had regained his breath. The man
shoved her from him, then scrambled to his feet, unwittingly
saving the life of the child he had wished to kill as he found
himself standing between his two remaining archers and Krystin, who had thrown the blade that had saved Myrmeen's life.
The archers pointed their shafts upward when they saw their
master.

Krystin took a running start and leapt into the air, planting
both feet on Djimon's back. She kicked him with all her
weight, then expertly rolled to the sand as she fell. The kick
drove Djimon forward, past Myrmeen, who also rolled out of
the way and into the arms of his warriors, where all three collapsed in a tangle.

Suddenly, Burke and Varina were on either side of Myrmeen, running for the fallen men. Varina snatched Djimon's
hair, slid her drawn sword beneath his throat, and executed
him without a word. His blood splattered on the closest of the
downed archers, who screamed in his own language for
mercy. Burke had already driven his sword into the other
archer's chest and was about to finish off the pleading man
when a sound made him hesitate. He heard the scrape of a
sword leaving its scabbard and registered that Krystin was removing the sword from the scabbard at the side of the still-
twitching body of Djimon and was preparing to haul it over her
head and decapitate the last man.

Myrmeen grabbed her arms, restraining her, and Varina
slashed the last archer's throat.

"You should have let me do it," Krystin said, her chest heaving, her mouth caked with dried blood.

Myrmeen considered her daughter's murderous rage a
frightening sight and not one that she had been prepared to
witness. She turned to Burke. "The others?"

"Lucius, Reisz, and Ord are dealing with them. We should see if they are—"

"We're fine," came a reply from behind the Harpers. Burke turned to see Ord standing before the older men, his tunic splattered with blood. "They're all dead, except the two who hurt themselves on the way down, the ones who were supposed to distract us."

"See to them," Burke said.

Krystin sat back, staring at the bloody remains of her former captors, then glanced to the west and said, "The scum these bastards were going to sell me to are on their way. I can see their caravan."

Cardoc wiped the sweat from his brow. "I can shield us again. We can ride past them and they will never know it."

Burke listened to the screams of the last two raiders, whom Ord and Reisz were busy putting to death, then said, "I feel as if I can barely breathe in this heat. Mage, are you certain your strength is enough—"

"We will find out," Cardoc said in a cold, efficient manner. Burke nodded and gave the order for the Harpers to retrieve their mounts and prepare to ride. In moments, Myrmeen and Krystin were alone, regarding each other warily.

"We've got the same eyes," Krystin said slowly, only now registering the similarities between herself and the woman twenty years her senior.

"Yes," Myrmeen said guardedly. "I noticed that, too."

It had not been the reunion Myrmeen had anticipated.

Seven

 The caravan had come and gone, its occupants pausing only long enough to verify Djimon's corpse. The buyer who had been promised the blue-eyed fourteen-year-old had been livid and had kicked Djimon's body several times before returning with his escorts to the caravan. They rode off with haste to avoid the gathering storm.

The first drops of heavy rain struck the corpses, which had been left in the open to rot. Only two of the bodies had not begun to show signs of death. The rain pelted their still faces. Suddenly, the eyes of the first man flashed open. "Are they gone?"

"I no longer care. My back is starting to ache."

Both men rose from the sand. The first was a tall man with dark skin. Crow's feet bunched around his eyes and a heavy beard covered much of his face. His companion was short and lean, clean-shaven, and possessed a dour expression. They both had been run through with swords, the bearded man's heart cleaved in two, the shorter man gutted, a second blow having fractured his skull. Each man opened his tunic and placed his open palm over his wounds, waiting patiently as the flesh stitched together. The internal injuries would heal with time. The men allowed the falling rain to wash away the blood.

Closing their tunics, the two members of the Night Parade surveyed the human corpses strewn about the pillar's base. "Mortals are so fragile," the short man said. "The smallest injury, and they surrender to death."

"We can die, too, you know."

"Yes, but not so easily. The Draw favored us."

The bearded man looked away from the Hammer, toward the distant road. "Did you see which way they went?"

"The mage cloaked them. I couldn't tell. Back to Calimport, I would wager. The woman still has to pay Pieraccinni."

"Of course." The bearded man was silent for a time as he threw his head back and allowed the rain to caress his face. Five hundred feet above, lightning struck the flat of the hammer and thunder shook loose a hail of small rocks from the pillar's surface. The short man jumped out of the way of the falling stones. His companion stood, arms stretched wide, unmindful of the danger. The rocks seemed to avoid him.

"Is the girl really her daughter?" the short man asked.

"I don't know. Does it matter? She will believe it, and because of that, she will leave and trouble us no more."

"Just curious."

The bearded man grinned. "I have curiosities, too." With that, he leapt to the side of the pillar and began to climb, his hands digging into the solid rock as if it were soft clay.

"Come down here," his companion shouted when the bearded man was already one hundred feet up the side of the pillar. His commands were ignored. "We're supposed to follow them!"

"We will," the bearded man called. "They'll make camp. They won't travel in this. We'll catch up easily." Within a minute, the bearded man had scaled the pillar and disappeared over the rim.

"You're such a child, Zandler," the short man said as he sat down hard on a rock and placed his head in his hands, waiting for his partner to finish indulging his infantile impulses. It was true that Zandler had the more spectacular ability, but he had powers of his own. Gesturing at the sand, the short man with smoldering gray eyes watched as several sand creatures burrowed out of their holes, a host of scorpions rushing to the lead. Within seconds a small army of arachnids had gathered at his feet. He remembered the last man he had tormented then killed, an older man with a paranoid fear of cockroaches. The gray-eyed man had played with his victim's dreams for weeks before making his nightmares come true.

He heard a shuffling in the sand behind him. "Zandler?"

"No," an unfamiliar voice said with a malice that could not be mistaken for anything but murderous intent. Before the gray-eyed man had a chance to order the sand creatures to attack his unseen enemy, he convulsed in searing agony. Looking down, he saw a hand erupt from his chest. The gloved hand burned with a bluish white energy laced with crackling strands of green fire. He had seen those cold flames once before.

"The apparatus!" he shouted as he fell forward and died. His corpse struck the sand, scattering the arachnids he had summoned.

The dark man with the weapon turned it a few times, examining it for damage. The dead man was wrong. It was not the apparatus, but it had been charged from the energies of that object. The design was extraordinarily simple; in truth, it was little more than a steel glove. When it was activated, however, claws made of mystical fires stolen from the apparatus would leap from the moldings above each knuckle. The blue-white talons mimicked the actions of his true fingers and allowed him to take the lives of those creatures who laughed at human conceits such as mortality. As always, the weapon had performed admirably.

"You're going to miss everything," a voice called from above. The dark man looked up in the direction of the voice and smiled.

On the flat, the bearded man stood, hands held out to the

sky, the worsening storm raging directly above his head.

"Come to me," he shouted, "Come on, come on, come—"

Suddenly two streaks of lightning burst from the clouds, tearing jagged paths across the darkened sky, streaking down toward the bearded man. He screamed with delight as lightning struck each of his hands and his entire body quaked with the impact.

"Yes!" he shouted as his body absorbed the lightning. His entire form became a brilliant white mass with slight indications of what may have been human anatomy within. He held the lightning within his body for as long as he could stand, then pointed both hands at the horizon. Twin bolts of white energy sailed from his fingers and struck the ground below. Then he was human again, but his clothing had been burned away.

"Crolus, you moron, you missed the whole thing," he shouted.

"I didn't," a voice said.

Zandler turned and saw a man materialize before him. His heart seized up as he saw the shimmering hand of the dark man. He did not even have time to scream as the assassin attacked.

Seconds later, the dark man stood over the smoldering remains of the second monster. He concentrated and caused the arcane talon to vanish.

"So they're going to Pieraccinni's," he said. "I'll pick up their trail there."

With a rustle of cloth, the dark man removed two gold pieces and dropped them beside the dead man's hand. "The first one is for the information," he said. "The second is to pay your passage into hell, you miserable excuse for a nightmare."

The man stepped back and vanished into the storm's fury.

*   *   *   *   *

The Harpers had avoided the main road and pitched their tent when the storm made it too dangerous to continue. Inside the tent, as the heavy rains of late afternoon fell, Lucius elected to keep watch near the partially opened flap. He declined the meal the others devoured with their usual lack of decorum. Myrmeen was too exhausted and famished to do anything but join them. Stones were laid in the middle of their enclosure, and a small fire blazed there. Burke had unwrapped and skillfully prepared several slabs of meat, most of which had been snapped up by the dark-haired, fourteen-year-old girl whom they had rescued.

"So," Burke said, determined to slap Krystin's hand away if she grabbed at another serving before he could distribute the meat to the others, "is anyone *else* hungry?"

"You mean she actually left something for the rest of us?" Reisz said as he spat out the seeds from a mouthful of grapes. Ord had consumed an entire loaf of bread and was eyeing the blackened slabs of meat with lustful intent. Myrmeen had gnawed three apples to their core.

"Come now, the girl has been through an ordeal," Varina gently coaxed, her stomach rumbling almost loud enough to be confused with the rolling thunder outside.

Reisz growled, "How are you, girl?"

"Fine," Krystin said, the word delivered hard and fast, like a blow.

"You feel well?"

"Fine," she repeated sharply. Her tone became demanding as she said, "Who are you people?"

"We told you, we're Harpers," Varina said gently.

"That's right," Reisz hissed. "No matter what you may think, we are not rival slavers. We are the lord protectors of the Realms."

Krystin nodded. "So you just run around doing good deeds. You help people and don't expect anyone to pay you."

"Well," Varina said, "essentially. But we have lives away from our duties as Harpers."

Krystin bit off another chunk of meat. As she chewed, she said, "You people are either the worst liars I've ever met or the biggest fools."

Ord raised his hands and smiled. "Well, at least she's grateful we saved her life," he quipped.

"You saved it," she admitted, "but for what?"

Reisz unconsciously glanced at Myrmeen. She had been staring at the child and was alarmed to discover that she had absolutely nothing to say to her. They had decided on the long ride into the desert that, at least for a time, they would not disclose Myrmeen's last name or her position as ruler of Arabel. To Krystin, Myrmeen would be simply another of the Harpers who had rescued her.

"What?" Krystin said nastily. "The dullard has something to tell me?"

"Stop calling me that," Myrmeen said, her anger simmering within her heart.

"I'm just surprised you understand the meaning of the word," Krystin said with a shrug. "You do, don't you?"

Myrmeen fought back the urge to strike the child. She had been resisting that impulse for hours. "Where were you educated? It wasn't just on the streets."

"What makes you think I'm educated?" Krystin said. "I know I must seem that way to you, slow-wits—"

Reisz suddenly reached over and grabbed the girl's wrist as he roared, "That's enough!"

Krystin fell silent, a catlike grin on her face. She looked down at his meaty hand on her pale, thin wrist and shamed him into releasing her without saying a word.

"There are limits to our patience," Burke said. "It's best not to test them."

"I'll consider myself warned," Krystin said, her smile deepening. She had learned when she was very young that those who ultimately revealed themselves to be the most threatening often approached wearing benevolent faces. By provoking these people, she had hoped to force them to reveal their true agenda.

Nevertheless, she was troubled. Normally she assumed the worst and did not bother to wait around to be proven incorrect. For some reason, she actually wanted to trust these people, and trust was an almost impossible commodity for the streetwise teenager after the brutalities of her early life. She decided that when she had a chance, she would steal one of their horses and escape.

"Why are you like this?" Myrmeen asked. "We're just trying to help you."

Krystin shrugged and tore another chunk of meat from the bone she had been nursing as Burke distributed the remaining meat among the Harpers. She said nothing as she slowly lowered the picked-clean bone to her lap and stared at the slab of meat that Varina was about to bite into. The child's eyes widened and her shoulders slumped. She pressed her lips together and allowed the tip of her tongue to flicker out of the corner of her mouth, just for an instant. Varina slowly lowered the meat and held it out to the child.

"Don't give her that!" Burke snarled.

Krystin sat back and laughed. "I'm not hungry anyway. But thank you for the offer. You're a dear."

Varina screwed up her features in disapproval, then took a healthy bite of the meat.

"You people are so easy," Krystin said. "It takes almost no effort to get to any of you. You're all a bunch of raw nerves waiting to be irritated. You're so full of yourselves I could almost believe you are—what name did you use? Harpies? Helpies? Heifers?"

"Harpers," Myrmeen said coolly.

"That's right," Krystin said. "Thank you."

Ord had been staring at her as if he she belonged to a different species, one that he was unable to identify, at least until now. Suddenly it came to him: "I think you just want attention."

The girl's smile dropped and her eyes became hard as she returned his stare.

"You're not subtle, you know. I played that game when I was your age. But I was better at it. You're sitting there fishing with a meat hook, thinking nobody's going to notice."

"*Fenghis-sla!*" she said, backing up her foreign curse with a hand motion in case he did not understand the words.

"You're the one who is so easy," he said wryly.

Krystin froze. The others glanced at one another and smiled. Burke slapped Ord on the back and led his comrades in a tension-breaking round of laughter. The girl drew her knees up and stared at the crackling fire's orange glow.

"Dullards," she said, but her heart clearly was not to the insult. Her gaze drifted to the open flap at the tent's entrance, where Lucius Cardoc sat, looking out at the storm. The heavy droplets of rain pelted the hard leathers with the force of meteors that had slashed across the blackened afternoon sky and exploded against the enclosure. The relentless pounding made her wonder if it had become a hailstorm. The sound reminded her of the constant drumming of insistent, curious fingers. Water cascaded down the sides of the tent, dripping to the large puddles where the companions had cut ditches. The sound of running water was making her insane. All she wanted to know was how long the storm would keep up.

She nearly dropped her tin cup filled with fresh water as she saw a flash of lightning in the distance. The heavy clap of thunder made her jump. Varina instinctively reached out to put her hand on the girl's arm in a comforting gesture, then stopped herself, remembering the way Krystin had swatted her hand away the last time.

Myrmeen moved closer and sat down beside Krystin. "I hate the storms, too. I have a lot of terrible memories tied to storms like this one."

"I suppose you're going to tell me all about it," Krystin said nastily, resisting Myrmeen's attempts to distract her from the storm.

"No," Myrmeen said. "I'd rather talk about you. I'd like to know why you're afraid of storms."

Thunder rolled, somewhere close. Myrmeen tensed. So did Krystin. "Why should you care? You're not my mother."

Myrmeen flinched. She closed her eyes and let out a deep breath. "Who are your parents, then?"

Krystin appeared to shrink into herself. She set the cup down and hugged herself. Myrmeen tried to get the child to look in her direction, but Krystin shook her head. Despite the way it frightened her, she would not take her gaze from the storm. "I don't know," she said in a small voice.

"Who raised you, then?" Myrmeen asked.

She swallowed hard, shuddered. "Monsters." Suddenly, Krystin came to life. Expectantly, she asked, "Are you people with them?"

"Who?" Burke said. "The monsters?"

"No," Krystin replied, shaking her head as if she were being ridiculed and no longer cared. She bit her lip and said, "The demon killers. The hunters who are killing off the Night Parade's monsters."

Ord grinned. "We killed four of them last week."

Krystin sank to her knees and planted her hands on her thighs in awe. "Four? That many. At one time?"

"Yes," Burke said, getting some idea of Ord's destination. The younger man was trying to find a way to make Krystin show them some respect. With a smug laugh, Burke placed his hand on his wife's back and said, "I expect we'll be up for a few more before we leave Calimport."

A shudder passed through Krystin. Her expression changed to one of sheer panic. Without warning, she scrambled to her feet and bolted to the partially open tent flap. Lucius turned and grabbed her, wrapping his arms around her from behind, pinning her arms at her sides. She began to scream and wail incoherently, shouting phrases in a language that no one understood.

Myrmeen went to her. "Krystin, what's wrong? We're not going to hurt you."

Krystin kicked at the mage's legs, then leaned down and bit the fleshy part of his arm. He winced at the pain but did not let her go.

"Stop that," Myrmeen said. "Lucius is your friend. We all are."

"Let me go!" she screamed. "You didn't say we were going back there! That's where they live. That's where they hide. That where they do things to you!"

"Krystin, we have to go back to Calimport. There is a man who has to be paid for his services. Once that's done," she said, looking back at the Harpers, "then we'll leave."

Reisz nodded, closing his eyes then opening them slowly.

"I'm sorry." Krystin started weeping. "You're not stupid. I'm sorry I said that. Just don't take me back there."

Ord laughed. "It's just an act. Look at her, she's—"

"She's terrified, Ord," Myrmeen said, the yellow slivers in her rich blue eyes appearing to burn with the flames of her anger. Ord looked away.

Krystin's body relaxed as she watched Myrmeen. She turned her face in Cardoc's direction. "I won't try to run. You can let me go."

Sensing the truth in her tone, Lucius released her.

She turned to him and said, "I'm sorry about your arm."

"It will heal," he said, "unlike some wounds you cannot see that sometimes take a lifetime to heal."

Myrmeen nodded. He had been looking at her as he spoke. She placed her hand on Krystin's shoulder. The girl did not try to force it away. "What did they do to you? What did those monsters make you do?"

"I'd find people for them," she said, lowering her head in shame. Myrmeen guided Krystin back to the circle, and they sat with the others. She kept her arm around the girl, and the shivering fourteen-year-old did not protest.

"Those creatures don't need humans to do their work for them," Reisz said. "We've seen them. They can pass for human at any time."

"Some of them can," Krystin said darkly. "Not all."

"So you found people for them," Myrmeen said. "Then what happened?"

"Don't you know?"

Myrmeen shook her head.

"You don't know what the Night Parade monsters do to their prey? How they survive? What they live on?"

The Harpers were silent.

"Really?" she asked in stunned disbelief. "But you wish to

make war on them. You slaughter them without understanding the reasons for what they do."

"It sounds as if you're defending them," Ord said as he saw their dinner fire slowly die.

"No," she said. "No, kill them. Kill them all, if you can. I just don't think you know what you're dealing with."

"So tell us," Myrmeen said.

"You're not the hunters," she said. "You're not the ones that have been seeking them out and killing them for the past two years."

Ord raised an eyebrow. "Why do you say—"

"Enough," Burke said. "No. We are not the ones. We only arrived in Calimport a short time ago."

Krystin buried her face in her hands and drew a sharp breath. She laughed a hollow laugh and shook her head in amazement. "How many of you are there? What's the size of your army?"

"Why would you ask us that?" Myrmeen said.

"Because I only see six of you in this tent," Krystin said slowly. "And I can guarantee there are over six thousand of the monsters in Calimport alone. . . ."

Outside, the rain began to level off. The storm rolled on, moving deeper into the desert. A sharp crack of lightning sounded in the distance.

Within the tent, Burke stoked the fire. He felt comforted by the warmth and watched the reddish orange glow of the flames as he quietly said, "Tell us everything."

Krystin nodded and began to speak. Myrmeen listened to her daughter's words with mounting fear. She gained an education into the nature of an evil that astonished even her jaded sensibilities, and the thunder that eventually followed sounded like a promise that the storm soon would return.

Eight

"That is all I can give you," Myrmeen said.

Pieraccinni sat behind his desk, regarding the pile of coins and jewels before him with an amused expression. "I know I said a small token of faith would suffice, but I didn't expect it to be this small."

"You'll get all that's coming to you," Myrmeen said stiffly as she stood before the merchant. "Or do you not trust the word of Myrmeen Lhal, ruler of Arabel?"

Pieraccinni's gaze slowly rose from the riches on his desk to the piercing stare of the magnificent brunette. Her unusual blue-and-gold eyes were hard and unyielding.

"Why do I get the feeling you told Dak something very similar before you lopped his head off?" he asked.

Myrmeen leaned forward. "Perhaps because he tried my patience, too."

The bald merchant of arms and men leaned back, rocked in his chair, and laughed. "If you ever get tired of your post in Arabel, I hope you will consider giving me a chance to employ you."

"In what position? On my back or bent over your desk?" Myrmeen asked bitterly, tired of thinly veiled propositions.

Pieraccinni shook his head and opened his hands. "As a *negotiator*. You are far too suspicious."

Myrmeen glanced around the room. There was movement from behind the red satin curtains of his four-poster bed. "Somehow I find it difficult to accept a serious job offer from a man who keeps a bed in his office."

Pieraccinni pursed his lips. "No one told you? No, from your expression I see that they did not. I never leave this room. I have a rare malady that keeps me here."

The statuesque adventurer stepped back from his desk.

"Don't worry. What I have is not contagious and what I've told you is public knowledge." He tapped his shining, bald pate. "What I suffer from has been diagnosed as a disease of the mind, but that does not make its effects any less real. If you were able to drag me beyond those doors I would collapse with fits and seizures within a minute's time. Of course, you would first have to get me out there."

Myrmeen heard the scrape of weapons sliding from scabbards. She glanced back at the shadowy figures behind the blood-red curtains. "The twins are highly protective?"

"They are, along with all my employees. Not one of them has ever had it this good before. They don't want their comfortable lifestyle to be ruined, and they are aware that my skills are all that ensure their continued employment."

"I understand," Myrmeen said.

"All I want from you is the promise that the next time you have business in Calimport, you will come to me first."

Myrmeen reached out and shook Pieraccinni's hand. "You have my word."

"And you have your daughter. May your life with her be as rewarding as it will be interesting."

Walking to the door, Myrmeen stopped midway. "That sounds like a warning. Do you know something I don't?"

"I have five sons and two daughters," Pieraccinni said. "Believe me when I say you are embarking on your most challenging and perilous adventure yet."

Myrmeen knocked twice and the doors swung outward. She left Pieraccinni's chamber without another word. The doors slammed shut behind her. The boy, Alden, appeared from a secret doorway at the other end of Pieraccinni's room. He hurried inside, rushing to the bald man's desk.

"I have need of your special skills," Pieraccinni said. "Assign Marishan your duties, then follow Lhal and her group. I want confirmation that they have left the city."

"You will have it," Alden said agreeably.

* * * * *

Outside the Gentleman's Hall, Myrmeen joined the Harpers. Krystin nervously glanced at every shadow, though it was midday and the sunlight was glaring. The child had made her rescuers promise that they would enter the city and leave once more while the sun was there to protect them. The nightmare people despised movement during the day.

Myrmeen had not given Pieraccinni all of the riches she had secreted in the city. She left many of the caches in place as a contingency in the event that she one day returned to Calimport, but she said nothing of this to the others.

The group stopped at a nondescript eatery for one last decent meal before the long ride to Arabel. They were greeted by a fiery-haired serving maid whose pleasant smile faded as she caught sight of the Harpers. They had been in the desert for several days without bathing or changing clothes and they had the look of ruffians.

"A private table might be best," she said as she took the small group to a pair of tables near the kitchen and promised to return shortly with tankards of ale. As she left, the girl was stopped by an older woman, who whispered in her ear, eyeing Myrmeen and her crowd suspiciously. The red-haired girl shook her head and raised her voice as she said, "You're right, of course. I would have thought their kind would keep to the

Hall."

Krystin was about to hurl a heavy wooden container of
ground pepper at the back of the girl's head when Lucius
grabbed her arm.

"That is not civilized," he said in deep, rich tones.

"And you think I am?" she asked. "The cow has it coming."

Myrmeen glanced at her daughter. She was beginning to no-
tice that they used many of the same phrases and wondered if
Krystin was trying to emulate her. The thought appealed to
Myrmeen and she smiled broadly.

An hour later, they were riding toward the city's gates,
passing through another run-down neighborhood. Myrmeen
drew up her mount's reins, and Krystin held on tightly as the
horse neighed and brought them to a halt. Cardoc had been
riding beside her, taking point.

"What is it?" Lucius asked as he raised his hand to signal
the others to stop. The gaunt mage had followed Burke's orders perfectly, maintaining his visibility at all times. "What
have you seen?"

"This place," Myrmeen whispered as she nodded toward a
large, **U**-shaped building across the street. "I didn't even recognize the neighborhood, but that building is where my nightmares started. That's where I was born and raised."

"Your family had that entire estate?" Krystin said with
amazement.

"No," Myrmeen said. "The family that had the building con-
structed left when the area was taken over by the working
class and the poor undesirables, like my family. When the estate was given to the city, it was turned into cheap housing."

"But you're wealthy, cultured—"

"That came later, much later."

"It looks abandoned," Krystin said.

Myrmeen nodded. The building where she had played as a
child, where she had later experienced her first kiss, now appeared to be deserted. Vines covered the walls of the two-
story dwelling and overran the courtyard. The fountains had
dried up. Most of the windows were shattered and covered

with boards. The balcony that ran the length of the second floor was stained with mildew and its railing was shattered in several places. Strangely, while the building had not been maintained, neither had it been vandalized. There were no signs that it had been overrun with families of squatters.

"Why are we stopped?" Burke called. "What's happening?" When no response came, Burke and Varina rode to either side of those riding point. Burke was surprised by Myrmeen's softening features. The lines around her eyes and mouth, which had seemed to deepen over the past several weeks, appeared to vanish as she surrendered herself to the embrace of warm remembrances.

"Did you want to go inside?" Varina asked.

Myrmeen thought it over. Suddenly she heard her father's warm, booming laughter as he went off to work on that last, fateful morning, riding off to a private audience from which he would never return. She had clung to that image for years, then forgotten it until just now, as she saw the window of the bedroom that once had been hers, in the building's east wing.

"Yes," Myrmeen said, "for a moment. Then we'll leave."

"I have no objection," Burke said benevolently.

Krystin turned her gaze to the sun. There were many hours of daylight left, so she did not allow her fear to overcome her. Reisz and Ord followed behind the four horsemen who led the party beyond a crumbling marble fountain, upon a stone walkway and deep into the central courtyard. In moments they were flanked by the two long arms of the building, and they dismounted before the easternmost of two sets of stairs, the only way up to the second floor.

The curly-haired fighter tapped Ord's shoulder. "I don't like this," he said candidly.

"That's the joy of riding with you, Roudabush. You don't like anything."

Reisz nodded. Ord never used Reisz's family name except to signal that he, too, was very worried.

Myrmeen was already climbing the stairs, her boots trampling the vines underfoot. Krystin remained at her side, feeling a disquieting compulsion to stay close to the woman whose hair and eyes were identical to her own. Burke told Myrmeen to go ahead, that he and his wife would follow at a comfortable distance. Reisz and Ord were ordered to remain behind and watch for horse thieves. Cardoc went off to explore another section of the building but promised to remain within earshot.

"It's so much smaller than I remember," Myrmeen said as they reached the second-floor landing.

Krystin walked a few steps to the right and peered through the slats into one of the rooms. Frowning, she said, "I don't think you're going to find much. Look here."

Myrmeen went to her side and squinted as she bent slightly and stared at the ruins of what had been the main living chamber of a single-family dwelling. Staring at the demolished furnishings and piles of rotted wood strewn about, Myrmeen felt the urge to abandon the search. After all, she did not want to see her childhood home in such condition.

An urge that she could not resist propelled her forward. She led Krystin back along the gallery to a hallway at the top of the stairs, which had been scorched by flames. There were no rats or roaches, though she did find the occasional wisp of a spider's web.

"Can't we walk around this ledge?" Krystin asked.

"We can't get in that way. The front doors were all walled up after a few children died after running through the doors and not looking where they were going. The guardrail was a joke."

Myrmeen swallowed hard. She had known one of those children, an unfortunate little boy, and had been schooled with his sister. They both had lost siblings, and the experience had bonded them together.

"Myrmeen?" Krystin asked.

Shuddering, Myrmeen took Krystin into the hallway and turned to face a darkened central corridor that subdivided the second floor. "I don't know how safe this is. Let me go first."

"All right," Krystin said.

Myrmeen entered the black corridor, her hand against the wall as she found the spot where the passage angled to the left. She gestured for Krystin to follow. The girl entered the corridor, barely able to see Myrmeen's hand, which she clung to as she was led down the night-black avenue to a door that Myrmeen did not need to see to recognize. They heard the footsteps of Burke and Varina following behind.

"It's not locked," Myrmeen said as she pressed her weight against the door and shoved. The door came open easily and Myrmeen was shocked by what she found on the other side.

"Someone's still living here," Krystin said.

"Yes," Myrmeen said in a tiny, stunned voice. "I am."

The chamber they faced was decorated exactly the way Myrmeen remembered it from her childhood. A heavily worn sky-blue rug was thrown across the floor. Wooden shelves and cabinets lined the walls. Oversized pillows, which her mother had woven and stuffed with feathers that she and Myrmeen had spent weeks gathering, lay on the floor beside a lute identical to the one that had disappeared with her father. There were paintings on the wall, and one in particular arrested Myrmeen's attention: It was a portrait of herself as a child, sandwiched in a happy, loving embrace between her mother and father.

"No," Myrmeen whispered as she fought back the tears that welled up in her eyes. Her trembling fingers grazed the painting's surface, lightly touching her dead father's hard, proud face.

Krystin wandered past the main chamber and called to Myrmeen from one of the two adjoining bedrooms. Myrmeen glanced at the rocking chair near the partially boarded up window, then at the chests shoved against the wall, the dining table, and the small kitchen. Food had been prepared here recently; she could smell the succulent aroma of chicken basted with imported spices from her father's village in far off Velen, near Asavir's Channel and the Pirate Isles.

"Myrmeen!" Krystin yelled.

Glancing at the doorway, where she expected to see Burke and Varina appear at any moment, Myrmeen wondered what was keeping them. She turned away and followed the sound of her daughter's bright, expectant voice. She felt as if she were no longer moving of her own volition, as if she were being dragged along by forces that she could not hope to control. Looking down, she became aware of the changing perspective and the steady motion of her legs, one before the other. A part of her was terrified to go any farther, but she had no choice. She reached the doorway to her old room and felt as if twenty years had vanished. Myrmeen stared at a living portrait of her early life, with Krystin playing her role.

The room was perfectly preserved. Krystin rolled on the bed, clutching the scented blankets to her chest. Myrmeen was stunned by the wealth of small items that she had forgotten about, such as a drawer in her nightstand that still contained the wretched love poems of her first suitor. On the dresser sat an empty vial of perfume that she had drained in an eight-year-old's attempt to emulate her mother's daily ritual of bathing and scenting her soft, beautiful skin.

Above the bed was a painting that caused her tears to finally burst free. The image captured on the canvas had remained in her dreams and fantasies for her entire adult life, though she somehow had blocked its origin. The portrait revealed a sky at twilight, where a soft, bluish white mist rose from a valley that was hidden by a rise in the foreground. A handful of pine trees stood as lone sentinels to watch a comet whip across the sky. Its trail entered the frame at the top, arced first to the right, then suddenly sped in a downward curve to the left, gaining momentum and intensity, to flare at the deep blue, starry sky where the veil of night slowly fell.

Myrmeen had dreamt of that rise many times. In some of her dreams, she made love with magnificent strangers on that fantastic landscape as the comet streaked by. In others, she lay there alone while a haunting melody played on a lute.

"What's wrong?" Krystin asked.

Myrmeen turned and wiped away the tears. "Nothing. This was a foolish idea."

"Tell me."

Pressing her lips together, hugging herself tightly, Myrmeen looked at the painting a second time. "My father gave me that painting. I still remember the morning he woke me up to look at it. Somehow he had put it up while I was still sleeping. It was a month after my sister had died. Stillborn. My father looked at me and said, 'You are that light for me. You rescue me from the darkness.'"

"What happened to him?"

Myrmeen shivered. The room was growing colder. "My father was put to death because his music displeased a rich man who had heard him play on the street and had requested a private audience. Father spent the entire previous night worrying over what selections to play for the man, and he had chosen a classical ballad for his lead. He had no way of knowing that the song had been a favorite of the wealthy man's wife, who had betrayed him and then 'took her own life' in shame for the transgression. The rich man had been certain that Father had been paid by one of his enemies to play that piece of music. He went into a blood rage, beating and kicking Father until he died. Father was a gentle man who had never learned to fight. Then the servants left the body in the streets and claimed that thieves had killed him before he ever arrived at the palace."

"But you got even."

"Yes."

Krystin nodded slowly. "Good."

Myrmeen was touched again by the deep feeling of loss that had plagued her for the last decade. She missed her family and looked to Krystin with hope.

A scream sounded from one of the other quarters.

"Varina," Myrmeen said in alarm, racing from her old bedroom, through the main quarters, to the corridor beyond.

Three doors along the formerly darkened corridor had been opened. The closest door, six feet ahead and to her right, led to the rooms on the other side of the wall from Myrmeen's old dwelling. A dull orange glow radiated from the doorway, partially illuminating the corridor. The next two doors that were open lay fifty feet away at either side of the corridor's end, before the bend the mother and daughter had taken earlier. Shafts of murky sunlight burst from these rooms, intersecting like crossed swords. A long patch of darkness stretched between the light at the end of the corridor and the dull luminescence from the nearby doorway.

Myrmeen suddenly became aware that she was not alone in the corridor. Something rose from the darkness and flew at her. Her view of the light at the end of the corridor was obscured by whatever had just taken flight, though she could not make out anything more than a vague, large shape in silhouette and could not tell how far away it had been when it began its flight. She could hear the beating of leathery wings and a steady, high-pitched squeal that grew louder with each passing second.

From the rooms next to Myrmeen's childhood home came Varina's scream a second time. Myrmeen looked back into her old quarters as an explosion shook the corridor. Suddenly the wall separating her old home from the next apartment was no longer there. Myrmeen saw the wall disintegrate, the portrait of herself with her family suddenly destroyed. A glistening, pulsating tentacle twice the size of a man hurled Burke's limp body through the opening that had been created. The bearded warrior smashed against the far wall, his heavy, armored body shattering the reproduction of her father's cherished lute.

Myrmeen heard the squeal before her grow more intense, and she redirected her gaze to the corridor. The flying creature was almost upon her. By the dull, caressing glow from the next apartment, she caught a glimpse of the monster in the light. But before her mind could assimilate what she had seen, the creature was upon her and she was overcome by its hot, sweet breath, which smelled of honey.

She reached for her sword, but by then it was too late. Tiny hands clawed at the exposed flesh of her face as Myrmeen felt a strong hand dig into the meat of her upper arm. There was a sharp tug, and she was dragged out of the monster's path. Myrmeen fell into her childhood home as the creature flitted past and disappeared from sight.

Looking up, Myrmeen saw Krystin, then noticed that there was more light in the dwelling. Apparently, at the first sign of trouble, Krystin had run to the window and had been trying to pry loose the boards that covered it in a haphazard fashion. Gaps had been left between the wooden planks, allowing streaks of light to show through and illuminate the dwelling without revealing its secrets to the world. Krystin had been successful in removing one wooden board and a second seemed ready to give.

"This is one of their lairs!" Krystin screamed. "You idiot, you led us right to them!"

From the corridor Myrmeen heard the fluttering wings of the creature outside. Before she could react, it appeared in the doorway and hovered for a moment. In that instant, Myrmeen was able to see it fully.

She was surprised by the strange beauty of the monstrosity. It had four clear, colorless wings with the intricate designs one might find on a butterfly's wings. The creature's body was black and gold, shaped in segments, with dozens of tiny arms branching off, each with distinctly human hands. She looked up at the creature's face and saw that it was not the face of a monster at all, but that of a magnificent and beauteous child with red eyes containing black, catlike slits. Its pouting Cupid lips suddenly drew back to reveal sharp, glimmering, carnivorous teeth.

Myrmeen heard a low groan behind her and knew what had captivated the monster's attention. Although she was unwilling to look away from the creature as she drew her sword and rose to face her adversary, she had caught a glimpse of Burke's unnaturally twisted body when she had been yanked into the room. He had been facing away from her, his head turned to the wall. His legs were bent at unnatural angles, obviously broken upon impact.

Burke had been one of her first teachers after her actions had gained her the attention, then the assistance, of the Harpers who had helped her to bring her father's murderer to justice. The cardinal rule that Burke had taught her about proper conduct during a battle was to never allow yourself the luxury of emotion. Step out of yourself, he had told her time and again. If a person close to you falls at your side, you can do nothing for them if you allow feelings to get in the way. Take care of the job at hand.

Myrmeen looked at Krystin's cold expression and realized that the child, at fourteen, already knew this lesson.

She also heard a soft, wet, flopping sound and knew it was the tentacle. She had seen that it could not reach more than five feet into the main body of the room, and so Burke was safe from it. In morbid fascination, she wondered what the tentacle was attached to and what had spawned the dragonfly-child, as she now thought of the creature.

"Stop dreaming!" Krystin said as she rushed forward and slammed the door shut on the creature's face. From the corridor, they heard the telltale squeal of the dragonfly-child as it prepared to launch another attack. The door buckled with the impact as the monster slammed into the hard wood then fell to the floor. Its wings beat furiously and its tiny hands reached under the door, trying to gain access. Krystin smashed one of them under the heel of her boot. With a yelp of pain, the creature retreated from the door. Krystin threw the latch and locked the door tight.

"I told you they're not human," Krystin said. "Not all of them. Why didn't you believe me?"

Myrmeen had other matters to think about. "Varina!" she screamed. "Where are you?"

"Trapped," a muffled voice responded from the next room, through the shattered wall. "Boxed into a corner. It can't get me and I can't get out. My husband! Myrmeen, is he alive?"

Krystin ran to the other side of the room and returned to the task of prying loose the boards before the heavy glass window. She knew that their only avenue of escape was to break the glass, leap to the gallery, and lower themselves to the ground, where their mounts waited.

Myrmeen had gone to Burke's side and had placed her hand on the man's neck. She felt a cool torrent of relief splash upon her as she registered a weak but steady pulse.

"He's alive!" she screamed. "But he's going to need help. I don't know if we can move him."

"We have to get out of here," Varina screamed. "Where are the others?"

"I don't know," Myrmeen said as she left Burke's side and gradually angled herself so that she could see into the room where Varina was trapped.

"Myrmeen, come on!" Krystin shouted impatiently. The girl was struggling with the boards and desperately needed help. She did not turn when she heard the sound of absolute disgust that rose from Myrmeen; Krystin had already looked into the next room and learned its secrets.

"What are you?" Myrmeen whispered, entranced by the sight of the grotesquerie in the next room. Then she corrected herself, as 'what aren't you,' would have been a more appropriate question.

The creature's body resembled a gluttonous, red-and purple-veined flower. Its quivering layers of flesh pulsated with clear sacs containing shiny black pearls the size of a man's fist. A half dozen tentacles rose from its base like the limbs of a starfish. At the core of the monster, surrounded by the obscenely pulsating pedals of flesh, was a wormlike, gelatinous trunk from which long, thin stalks protruded. At the end of each tiny stalk sat a human head. Some appeared to be alive, their eyes darting back and forth with madness and fear, their mouths working in silent screams. There were close to a dozen heads in all. Not all were alive. The necks of those who were dead seemed to be shrinking, as if the lifeless heads would be ground into the sickening mass of the creature, where the bones of humans were clearly visible. A shattered vertebrae poked out of its mass.

Myrmeen felt as she were going to be sick and forced down the mounting bile in her throat.

"Save my husband," Varina called from her unseen niche in the room. "I'll get away from this thing."

Myrmeen turned from the hole in the wall and looked to her

daughter.

"I've seen worse," Krystin said as she finally managed to pry the board loose. The next one did not appear to be as firmly mounted. Myrmeen ran to her side and slid her sword under two of the boards, using her leverage to yank them loose. They pulled the boards free and exposed a section of window large enough for Krystin to fit through, once the glass was shattered. Suddenly, the squeal of the dragonfly-child rose in the distance. It was not alone.

Myrmeen heard Varina scream again, the sound coupled with the flapping of wings. She turned to see four identical dragonfly-children sail into the room, the wingspan of each close to four feet.

From the other side of the glass window before Krystin, two figures suddenly appeared. The girl slammed at the glass as she shouted, "Myrmeen, Reisz and Ord are right outside!"

As if the creatures had understood Krystin's words, or were instead drawn by the sound of her screams, the group of dragonfly-children heightened their own squeals and dived straight at the tall brunette and her thin, hard-muscled daughter. Without hesitation, Krystin dove out of the way, rolling on the floor until she was within reach of the tentacle from the other room. Realizing the danger, Krystin rolled again as the heavy limb slapped the floor where she had been. Myrmeen raised her sword to fight, then realized how quickly her flesh could be ripped from her bones by the creatures' talons, which were less similar to human hands than she first had believed. She followed her daughter's lead and dove to the ground, rolling until she was halfway across the room. Then she bounded to her feet, her sword raised before her.

Krystin was at the door, her trembling fingers about to turn the lock when an inhuman hand punched through the door from the other side, causing her to cry out and stumble back. The hand had a large, flat thumb and two fingers each the size of a pair of human fingers fused together. The muscle covering the hand looked as if it had been stripped of flesh. Krystin fell to the floor, scrambling away from the hand, and shouted when her back touched Myrmeen's sturdy legs. She grabbed Myrmeen's waist and pulled herself to her feet.

Myrmeen was immobile, standing with her sword held out from her body to one side, in a traditional stance of readiness taught to her by Burke. The dragonfly-children congregated by the window, holding their position. They had cut off Myrmeen and Krystin from their only avenue of escape and waited to prey upon their rescuers. The Harpers beat at the heavy glass from the outside, shattering parts of it with the hilts of their swords. Ord tried to reach inside to punch away a sliver of glass, and one of the dragonfly-children darted at his hand, its teeth fastening on his palm. The young man screamed, and Reisz's sword was thrust through the window, into the gold-and-black body of the creature, which writhed on the sword blade, then reached down and shattered the steel with its many hands. The broken shaft of metal was still in its bloated body as the creature flitted into Myrmeen's room. It proceeded to wail and throw itself against every wall in agony before it fell silent in death.

Suddenly Krystin heard noise at the door. She turned to see the red arm of their new assailant as it reached through the hole it had made and tried to unlock the door. Krystin had been allowed to keep one of Myrmeen's knives. She drew the weapon and threw it at the arm. The blade sank deep into its flesh. The creature that owned the arm did not flinch; at least, the arm did not. With a sharp click, the door was unlocked. Krystin gasped as the arm retreated through the hole it had made. The door swung open, and she saw the creature, who had the lower body of a slug and the torso of a man. Its head was graced with wildly protruding jaws, which chattered as a thin, long tongue darted around in its mouth.

"Krystin," Myrmeen said, her voice laced with fear, "there's something you have to know about me—"

A sharp hiss came from beside Myrmeen. She leapt back in surprise as she saw Lucius Cardoc fade into existence at her side. "May I assume that this is one of those times that interference will not insult you?" Lucius asked.

"You know it," Myrmeen said.

"I thought as much." Lucius turned, whispered a phrase, and aimed his hands at the torso of the red-skinned creature. The monster slid across the floor with considerable speed. A thunderclap that was deafening in the confines of the small room accompanied the release of the mage's spell. Myrmeen barely heard the sizzle and the crack as a burst of reddish blue light erupted from the mage's hands and struck the wormlike man. The creature did not have time to scream as the arcane fires ripped it to pieces. Sections of its body left dents and cracks in the wall as they hit. The eruption of gore and blood splattered the Harpers.

"That's really disgusting," Krystin said.

"I will keep your criticism in mind," Lucius said as he turned to the window, where the dragonfly-children squealed and hurled themselves in the mage's direction.

"Reisz, Ord, jump clear, now!" Myrmeen screamed. The Harpers leapt, and Lucius released a second burst of energy that incinerated two of the dragonfly-children immediately and went on to collapse most of the far wall, sending debris spurting into the courtyard beyond.

"Run!" Cardoc said. "I'll free Varina and levitate Burke to the ground. Ready our mounts. There are bound to be more of these creatures!"

Myrmeen chose not to argue with him. She grabbed Krystin's hand and started for the collapsed section of wall. Teetering, Lucius placed his hand on his head, the drain of the spells he had used finally catching up with him. The final dragonfly-child circled the room and headed directly for him. Myrmeen released her daughter's hand, raised her sword, and took three steps in the direction of the mage when the roof suddenly collapsed upon them. Heavy wooden beams smashed to the floor, one of them striking Lucius on the back, knocking him to the ground. Myrmeen raised her hand to her face and looked away as a rain of dust and splinters fell upon her, along with chunks of wooden struts. She was vaguely aware that something else had fallen with the ceiling. A sound had come, separate from the others, the sound of heavy boots striking the carpeted floor.

The sounds had come from either side of her. Myrmeen's vision cleared and she saw a man who was not human standing several feet before her. The creature winked and smiled. She could only see the other man from the periphery of her vision, but she felt him touch her shoulder. His hand glowed and a vibrating current ran through her arm.

"Krystin, run!" she screamed as she spun and described an arc with her blade that caught the closest of the two men off guard, grazing the side of his head and sending him back, staggering, with his hand to his bloody scalp. She had no idea what had happened to her daughter. With a prayer that the girl was not buried beneath the rubble from the ceiling, Myrmeen looked at the face of the remaining member of the Night Parade. Its face was incredibly pale, with skin as withered as ancient parchment. It had a long, hooked nose and soft blue eyes. Ducking beneath her blade, the creature touched the floor, which instantly transmuted into liquid.

Myrmeen shouted as the floor gave out and she found herself falling into the darkened chamber below, along with everything else that had been in her childhood home. The impact when she struck bottom knocked the wind from her and she fell on something that bruised her ribs. Her free arm twisted behind her back and she felt a tearing in her shoulder, along with a sudden stab of red-hot liquid. Debris crashed around her, but somehow she had managed to hold onto her sword. She used the weapon as a crutch, digging into the settling wreckage, using its strength to help her climb to a kneeling position. Everything surrounding her was soggy. A sheet of harsh white light came in from the collapsed second story wall. The roof itself was still intact; it was the floor of the attic that had been destroyed.

"Hello, hello!" a figure said as it sprang up before her. Myrmeen found herself looking into the delighted face of the wrinkled, white-skinned member of the Night Parade who had changed the floor into water. His features ran like candle wax.

The creature reached toward her with dripping hands. "Tell me how you want to be immortalized. Glass? Steel? Porcelain? I'm an artist, but I like to be accommodating." The waxman giggled insanely.

Myrmeen knew that by the time she drew her sword, the creature would be upon her. She wondered if Lucius or Burke had survived the fall, and if her daughter had made it out alive.

Suddenly there was a groan from above and the pale man looked up in surprise. "No," he said, "it's spreading. It wasn't supposed to spread!"

His power was causing the wall beside them to disintegrate, along with the floor upon which Varina was trapped by the tentacled creature. As the wall beside them turned to liquid, Myrmeen saw that heavy support beams had been placed in the next room to help manage the tremendous weight of the monstrosity above. She could not help but wonder why they did not simply allow the creature to stay on the first floor. Then there was no more time for thought. The floor beneath the creature transmuted, sending Varina plunging into the darkness as her massive enemy sank like a weighty sponge. It made no sound as it was impaled on the many support beams, its body and tentacles writhing madly as it lashed out in pain, then surrendered to death.

Myrmeen had not stood by as a spectator. While the waxlike man had watched the scene in horror, Myrmeen had withdrawn her sword, scrambled back over the debris to put some distance between herself and the creature, and thrown her sword at the pale man's head. He threw his hands up in alarm, his body twitching as the sword pierced his skull, the weight dragging him down to lie on his side in convulsions.

She heard a moaning sound, then the pounding of sword hilts on glass from the first floor. Myrmeen looked around and saw something moving within the wreckage. A man.

"Lucius?" she called as she walked closer.

The figure rose unsteadily and turned to her. It was the second man who had leapt down from the collapsed floor of the attic. The man had long black hair, azure eyes, and a tremendously well-developed body. He was tall and handsome. His expensive clothing was cut to reveal his washboard stomach, thick arms, and powerful legs. Bright, bluish white energy crackling with green flames engulfed his hand.

She was unprepared for his speed as he grabbed her arm and yanked her toward him, pulling his hand behind him for an instant, then shoving it forward. The pain she had anticipated never arrived. She heard a scream behind her.

Looking over her shoulder, Myrmeen saw that the man's hand was buried deep in the chest of the man with the waxen face. There was no indication that her sword had ever touched him, though she had seen it buried in his skull. The creature writhed for a moment, then fell back in a heap and did not rise again.

"I am Erin Shandower," the man who'd grabbed her said. "I am human, like you." He held out his glowing hand, the talons of energy quickly fading. "This gauntlet is my weapon against them. With it, I can kill almost any—"

"My daughter," Myrmeen said. "Help me find her. She was up there when the floor gave out."

Shandower nodded, and together they began the search. Across the room, Myrmeen registered that the pounding at the window had stopped. She had assumed that it was Reisz and Ord, trying to get in and free them. Something had made them stop, and that frightened Myrmeen.

"I've found someone. A man," Shandower said.

Myrmeen went to his side and helped him to drag Lucius from the waterlogged wreckage. The mage was dazed, barely conscious. She heard the sloshing of footsteps and turned, worried that she would find another enemy. Varina walked past her, desperately plunging her gloved hands into the debris, trying to find her husband's body. The lithe blonde was frantic. She ignored the gaping cuts lining her legs and back.

The desperate search went on until Varina gave a single, grief-filled cry. She had found her husband. Miraculously, he was still alive. His eyes flickered open at her touch and he reached up to caress the side of her face. "So beautiful," he whispered hoarsely.

Varina lowered her face to his, kissing him gently.

Myrmeen raised another chunk of debris and realized with disgust that it was a severed wing from one of the dragonfly-children. She dropped it immediately. Krystin had not been trapped below the heavy wings. The tall, beautiful brunette tried to fight off her growing hysteria. She could not have come all this way to find her daughter, only to lose the girl so quickly.

"I have only one question," a voice called from the darkened corner of the room. " 'My daughter'?"

Myrmeen spun around in surprise. Straining her eyes, she was able to see Krystin sitting on a pile of wreckage a dozen feet away. She heard footsteps above. The sections of the floor that once had held the dining and kitchen area of Myrmeen's former dwelling were still intact. Something fell from the crumbling ledge above. Two lengths of rope.

Reisz and Ord leaned down over the edge. The older man gestured wildly. "Everyone out of there, quickly. There may be more of those things!"

"Why didn't you just break through the window on this floor?" Myrmeen asked as her daughter left her perch and joined the others.

"We couldn't. The walls, the glass, they've all been changed to steel. Something didn't want us getting in."

Myrmeen thought of the creature with the power of transmutation. It had nearly succeeded in trapping them.

Shandower grasped one of the ropes and tugged. The rope was secure. "I can take the tall one over my shoulder. Then I'll come back for the one who was hurt."

"Good plan," Reisz said. "Who was hurt and who in Cyric's hell are you?"

Ord suddenly noticed Burke's twisted body and screamed the man's name. The teenager grabbed one of the ropes and was about to slide down when Reisz threw his arms around the boy and held him back.

"Ord!" Burke shouted, somehow raising his hand in a fist.

"Listen."

The boy stopped fighting the older man long enough to shift his gaze back to the pit of wreckage below.

"I want you to prepare the horses for our escape," Burke said. "Now."

"I'll come down, I'll help you—"

"No. Go outside. I'll be along."

Desperation flashed in the boy's eyes. His true father had been horrible to him. Burke was the only man who had showed him kindness and discipline.

"Go on," Burke said. "I'll not have my only son disobeying my orders in front of all my friends."

For a brief instant, Myrmeen was certain that she saw a face looking in on them through the first floor window, which may have had the consistency of steel but was still translucent. Then the face was gone.

Above, Reisz clamped his hand on Ord's shoulder. "He'll be fine."

"Go, Ord," Varina said, wiping away the tears that were suddenly streaming down her face. "We'll be with you soon."

Ord nodded sharply, then turned and vanished. They heard his footsteps recede and Varina said, "We'll be with you always."

Burke stared into her eyes. "You know, don't you?"

"I do," she said, her chest heaving with grief. Burke took her hand. He was not going to last much longer. His injuries were too severe.

Suddenly a chorus of high-pitched squeals erupted from where the dead tentacled creature rested. Myrmeen looked on in horror as hundreds of fist-sized black pearls cracked open and a swarm of yellow-and-black dragonflies rose in the air. One of the creature's many layers of skin had fallen away in death, freeing the black eggs.

"We have to get out, now!" Shandower screamed as he hauled Lucius over his shoulder and began to climb.

Myrmeen watched Varina, who stared at the swarm as if its arrival had been inevitable.

"We have to go," Myrmeen said.

"I'm not leaving him," she said. "I won't leave him to them."

Burke touched her hand. "You know what to do."

"You be quiet," she said, her hands trembling.

"Please," he said, though he would not beg. "I love you, my wife."

"Don't make me," she cried.

Krystin ran for the ropes. Both were free. Reisz already had helped Shandower and Lucius over the side. Without a look back, she started climbing. The swarm buzzed angrily and had started to drift in their direction.

"Myrmeen, go. This is private," Varina said solemnly. "I'll be right behind you."

Nodding, Myrmeen crossed to the ropes and took hold of the one that Krystin was not using. Then she hauled herself upward.

Below, Varina took her husband's head in her hands and said, "I love you."

"Forever," Burke replied.

Behind her, Myrmeen heard the sharp crack of bones snapping. She hurried up the rope and felt hands upon her, helping her over the edge, and suddenly she was facing a blinding white curtain of midday sunlight.

"Varina, come on!" Myrmeen shouted as she heard the swarm's flapping wings and high-pitched squeals. She pictured their razor-sharp mouths and talonlike claws; they would be like piranhas.

In the near darkness below, Varina rose from the body of her husband and quickly disrobed. She took her knife and opened several cuts in her flesh, then began walking in the direction of the swarm, diverting its attention from the Harpers who waited above.

On the second floor, Myrmeen saw this and had to be dragged from the edge of the ruined floor. Her last sight of her friend had been as the swarm descended upon her, covering her instantly. Varina never screamed.

Reisz shoved Myrmeen outside, to the gallery. "Don't make her sacrifice count for nothing. Come on!"

Something in the kitchen caught her attention. She broke from him, tipped over a large oil lantern, and struck a piece of flint. In seconds the fire she had started began to bloom. Reisz dragged her outside and together they swung over the side and slid down the ropes that had been anchored by the fountain below. The others were already waiting.

"Where—where are they?" Ord stammered, looking back to the building, which already belched clouds of black smoke.

"They loved you very much," Myrmeen said. Then she struck him in the solar plexus, just beneath the rib cage, with the stiffened fingers of her right hand. He collapsed in a heap, and Reisz loaded him onto his mount, securing him quickly as he eyed the burning building, expecting a new host of monstrosities to erupt at any time. Shandower took the first of two mounts that had been left behind by the deaths of Myrmeen's friends, and said, "I know a place."

"Show us," Myrmeen said.

The Harpers rode out, Myrmeen taking one last look at the remains of her childhood quarters before she quietly followed the others to safety.

Nine

Alden McGregor had not anticipated a journey of discovery when he first began to shadow the Lhal woman and her companions. Their detour to the Knight's Kitchen for a last meal in the city before their long journey had not seemed out of line. Even the stopover at the Tower Arms had appeared innocuous enough at the outset; after all, they were pointed in the correct direction, riding toward the city gates. Then he heard the sounds of battle. From the vantages he secretly had taken, including a position outside the steellike glass of the east wing's first floor window, Alden had received his first taste of a world completely alien to his own, a world that apparently had existed side by side with his for a frighteningly long time. When the building was left a flaming ruin, Alden was relieved.

There were monsters in Calimport, entire lairs of nightmarish creatures unlike anything he had seen except in his dreams. The past week he had dreamt that eyes were watching him, hard, flat eyes that stared at him as if he were nothing more than carrion. The eyes had grown from the walls in his dreams, burst from his flesh, and hung before him in the mists and shadows that pervaded his nightmares. They always appeared in sets of three pairs, a total of six eyes each time. A voice had accompanied his most recent dreams, a finely cultured voice that reverberated with power.

"You know," the voice said enigmatically, "don't you?"

Alden never thought much about his dreams, but after witnessing the battle at the Tower Arms, he had begun to wonder if demons could escape the dream world.

The blond teenager had followed Lhal and her people from the burning building. They had ridden for close to an hour, snaking through forgotten paths in the city, until they came to a one-story stone edifice. The building once had been a sewing shop, where dozens of women had sweated out the day to weave cheap imitations of fine clothing. One day the authorities had learned of the shop and closed it down. The place also had been a warehouse for a time, until fire had destroyed the contents several times over. Currently it sat vacant, the locals claiming that it was accursed. Alden smiled. A little bad luck and any location would be proclaimed as such. His mentor, Pieraccinni, had taught him that, and also that men make their own luck.

The long-haired man with the strange, arcane gauntlet had led Myrmeen and her companions through a side entrance to the building. Alden had sat in the darkening alley for a time, waiting for them to come out. When they did not, he decided it was time to return to the Gentleman's Hall and give a full report.

Before nightfall he was back on the docks, indulging himself at the expense of the many guards Pieraccinni employed as he circumvented their best efforts to keep out intruders. Distracting the forty-year-old mercenary at the kitchen entrance by preying upon his sole weakness, a fondness for cats, Alden watched the tabby he had lifted from a gutter several blocks away mewl piteously as the man bent down and fed it some kitchen scraps. He had slipped past the man and was inside the building so easily that the game was losing its allure.

Alden weaved through the service hallways and tunnels until he reached the private door that only he and Pieraccinni's ladies of the moment were allowed to use. He heard voices from inside Pieraccinni's rooms and was about to turn around when he recognized one of the voices. "You know," it said, "don't you?"

Alden froze. The voice was the one from his nightmares. A part of him wished to turn and run from the Gentleman's Hall, but another more curious and insistent voice within him urged the young man to carefully open the marble door a crack and peak inside.

He saw Pieraccinni kneeling before a tall man with a black widow's peak, angular features, and a trim, athletic body. The man was cloaked in black leather and gray steel. There were three sets of eyes in his head, one set above and below the natural pair, allowing him to look to the front and each side at all times. Clusters of six eyes appeared throughout his body. He had three sets of eyes on each arm and leg, three on each breast, and six on his back. His clothing had been designed to protect his many eyes, with holes cut out to allow the eyes vision and hard crystal of many colors protecting the vulnerable orbs.

Alden wondered if the man had been born with so many eyes or if he had acquired them from his victims. His curiosity made him ponder what function each of the various sets of eyes performed.

He watched as the tall man reached for one of the strange, edged weapons at his waist and drew the blade slowly, the metal scraping its scabbard. Pieraccinni looked up, sweat exploding on his bald head as he stared at the jagged, curved knife. His master touched one of the three gems on the hilt, causing the two flat metal surfaces that made up the knife to separate. A thin strand of wire sprang upward from between the deadly blades.

Alden tried to imagine the damage such a weapon could perform if it were already inside a victim.

"You know, don't you?" the man repeated as he gestured

with the knife. "What dreams may come? Dreams of darkness and death from which you may never wake, or prosperous dreams of wealth, power, and women of such great beauty and talent that you would never wish to wake. The latter is what I have given you. I could take it away in an instant."

"Please, Lord Sixx. I meant no disrespect."

"Pieraccinni," the one called Sixx said with a knowing smile. "How long do you think this life of yours would last if everyone were able to look through my eyes? If they could see past your illusions and know you for what you truly are?"

Lord Sixx waved the knife. From his hiding place Alden winced and felt a sudden wave of nausea as the scene before him suddenly changed. Pieraccinni was no longer a man. His skin was dark blue, with red and green veins visible beneath the surface. The merchant's head was oblong, with tiny, heavily hooded eyes, a small mouth, and pulsating openings along his neck to allow for the intake of air. The man's body had a roughly human shape, but his flesh quivered like a jellyfish under tremendous pressure beneath the ocean. Alden clamped his hand over his mouth as Lord Sixx waved his knife a second time and Pieraccinni changed back to a man.

"I will tell you anything," Pieraccinni blubbered.

"Of course you will. That is your duty and your compulsion to he who commands the Night Parade," Sixx said as he looked down and sighed. "Get off your knees. I'm tired of looking at your bald head."

The merchant of arms and men did as he was commanded.

"Tell me about the Lhal woman," Lord Sixx said.

"She has been dealt with. She will trouble us no further," Pieraccinni mewled.

"That's what you said the last time. Now four of our number have died and two more have disappeared."

"Zandler and Crolus have always been unreliable. I will ask Imperator Zeal to discipline them when they return."

"I doubt that they will. I believe he got to them."

"Who, milord?"

Sixx grabbed Pieraccinni by the front of his shirt and hauled him into the air with inhuman strength, the blade pressed against the man's throat. "Who do you think, idiot?"

The shirt ripped and Pieraccinni flopped to the ground. Lord Sixx retracted the wire and sheathed the knife. "Him. The Slayer. The human who stole the apparatus and uses it to kill more and more of our kind. The presence of the Lhal woman has been a minor disruption compared to the affront this man committed against us. Years have passed and we are no closer to finding him. We need to hold a festival, but we cannot until we recover the apparatus and punish this man who denies us our blood rite."

"Lord Sixx, I assure you that our best agents have been assigned to the task. The Inextinguishables will—"

"I want results, not reassurances," Lord Sixx roared as he raised both hands into the air. The walls suddenly buckled inward. From his vantage point, Alden felt a strange, arcane wind that prickled his skin and nearly sucked him into the room. He dug his heels into the door frame and held on to the door so that it would not fly open and alert the two men to his presence. Alden saw strange energies swirl and coalesce around Pieraccinni's body, shredding his clothing as he writhed in agony. Lord Sixx casually leaned against the desk and crossed his arms over his chest, as if he were not affected by the supernatural gales.

"Enough," Sixx said. The winds died away instantly. The tall man scratched the side of his nose. "Without the dampers I installed in this lair for you, exactly how long do you think it would be before you started to draw not only the ambient magic so prevalent in this city, but also a chunk or two of the weave that surrounds this world? You know what happens if you get too much magic, don't you?"

"Yes," Pieraccinni said, once again on his knees.

"Then we understand each other. Find the thief or I will lower the gates and let you drown," Lord Sixx said as he glanced at the closest of several large oil-burning lamps and gestured. The room was engulfed in pitch darkness for an instant, as if the eye of their ancient god had closed for a moment. Then the light returned and Lord Sixx was gone.

Alden watched Pieraccinni lie on the floor, sobbing and quivering until his fear and shame had passed. As the man rose and walked to the large clothes closet, stripping off his ruined tunic, Alden closed the door quietly and considered his options. After waiting in the hallway for several minutes, Alden knocked at the door.

"Come," Pieraccinni called.

Alden entered the room, his face cold and without emotion as he said, "Milord, I have something to report. . . ."

* * * * *

Across the city, in the deserted building that had been a clothing mill and warehouse, Erin Shandower placed a new dressing on the cut above his left eye.

"So, you're the one," Krystin said excitedly. "You're the Slayer. That's what they call you, you know."

"Flattering," Shandower said, laughing bitterly as he regarded his rapidly aging face in the mirror.

"What? You're not going to tell me your life's story?"

"Not unless I have to," Shandower said as he regarded the other members of the group he had brought to his safe house. There were few comforts here. A cot, blankets, salves to treat wounds, stores of food, lanterns, and empty wooden crates were all that could be seen except for a few broken looms left against the far wall and a mound of debris that he had swept into the corner. The woman and her companions had barely spoken in the last few hours.

Krystin had railed against Myrmeen to explain why she had called the girl her daughter, but the beautiful brunette's dark eyes revealed only weariness and grief. Krystin gave up and lay down on the cot, pretending to sleep in the hope that the adults would talk about her. After a time she abandoned her ruse and went to Shandower, fascinated by his gauntlet and the power she sensed within him. Power, perhaps, to banish all of her nightmares.

"Erin Shandower," she said. "Why do I know that name?"

"This is not the time for discussion," Shandower said. "Perhaps in the morning we will talk."

Lucius rose. "I'll tell you why his name is familiar: He was a wealthy man. He secured the financing for much of the city's rebuilding fourteen years ago, after the great storm devastated Calimport. He was known for his public works and his talent for increasing the city's wealth."

Myrmeen looked up. "What are you talking about? The two of you know each other?"

"I know of him," Lucius said. "I told you, I take my responsibilities seriously."

"We all do," Reisz said as he placed his hand on Ord's shoulder. The young man sat beside him, quietly managing his pain over the deaths of his surrogate parents. He knew why Myrmeen had struck him: there was a good chance that more of the nightmare creatures were in the building and the fire would have driven them out of hiding. Although he had known the moment he had seen the flames that Burke and Varina were beyond saving, he would have tried to rescue them and probably would have lost his life in the effort. His adopted parents had wanted more for him than that and he had silently vowed to honor their lives and their wishes—after he saw the Night Parade destroyed. Ord looked up and listened intently to the conversation.

"According to all public record, Erin Shandower passed on about four years ago," Lucius said.

Myrmeen nodded and shifted her gaze to the long-haired man who walked across the room and joined them, Krystin close behind. "Do you want to explain that?" she asked.

Shandower pulled up a crate and sat across from Myrmeen. "You understand what I do?"

"Yes," Ord said, breaking his self-imposed silence, "you kill monsters."

"I'm waging a war," Shandower amended.

"The odds are six thousand to one," Reisz said stiffly.

"It doesn't matter. Four years ago, when I decided to undertake this mission, my name was too well known. Erin Shandower had a position and responsibilities. The idea of a public entity like myself fighting a secret war against the people of nightmare sounded absurd to me and so I arranged for my own death. A fire. The body they found was one of the Night Parade's, one that appeared human. I haven't used my real name in years. I don't know why I did today."

"You've been following us," Myrmeen said.

"Of course," Shandower said. "I wanted to see if you were true allies in my cause."

"I don't believe any of this," Reisz said. "Why would you give up all you had? Why throw your life away?"

Shandower's face darkened. "I was not born wealthy. When I was young I fell in love with a beautiful, exciting woman who was as poor as I was, or so I had believed. Shortly after we married, I learned that she was heir to a fortune. A year after our union, she inherited. I found that the breezy life of a rich man did not suit me. I had been a warrior. Restless, I fell in with practitioners of the art and went on a journey of discovery with them that lasted half a year. All I learned was that I had been a fool to go away.

"When I returned to Calimport, my wife was dead. She had gone mad and taken her own life, or so the story went. I didn't believe it, and my investigation led me to forbidden knowledge. I found her killers."

"The Night Parade," Lucius said.

Shandower nodded. "I learned a great deal about them, including the fact that the great storm of fourteen years ago was not a storm at all. A festival of evil occurred here."

"But I remember the storm," Myrmeen said.

"Of course," Shandower said. "The monsters mask their festivals by creating false memories in the survivors, such as storms, plagues, attacks by raiders, whatever they like. During the festival, they take every child that is born that night. The time was approaching for them to hold a new festival. I decided to try and stop them."

"How did you find them?" Reisz asked, suspicious.

Shandower shook his head. "I had secreted away a sizable fortune, then arranged for my own 'death.' Months after my estate had been picked apart by the government and my business associates, I once again became a public figure, albeit one of a very different kind. I knew that there were agents of the Night Parade everywhere. As the city I called my home had been the site of their last festival, I guessed correctly that several of the monstrosities would still be present in Calimport.

"Disguised as a mad prophet, I walked the streets dragging signs that proclaimed, 'The Night Parade is coming. Protect the souls of your children!' I was jailed several times as a public nuisance, but eventually my efforts paid off. I was attacked by a member of the Night Parade who wished to silence me. I was able to overcome the creature, and I tortured the being until it revealed all the secrets of its kind.

"With the knowledge I had gathered, I was able to steal the apparatus the Night Parade needed to begin its next festival. The Night Parade has been trying to retrieve the object and punish the thief, but it doesn't know who I am.

"No matter the cost, we must stop the Night Parade creatures from gathering again and slaying thousands; they can only do this if they regain the apparatus, which I've kept safely hidden."

Krystin was silent. For a moment she felt faint as bizarre images sliced across the theater of her consciousness without warning or invitation. For a moment she thought she was being chased, though she did not know by whom, or for what reason. The images vanished as quickly as they had arrived.

I was their dog, she thought. They sent me to sniff out their prey.

Self-loathing surged through the girl. Hugging herself, she noticed the odd manner in which Myrmeen was staring at her. "If you have something to say, say it," Krystin spat.

Myrmeen exhaled a ragged breath. "My name is Myrmeen Lhal. I am the ruler of Arabel. Fourteen years ago I had a child that my husband told me was stillborn, like my younger sister. He lied to me and sold the child to the Night Parade."

Krystin stared at her without blinking. "Me."

"Yes," Myrmeen said warmly, a trace of the wonderment she first had experienced when she saw Krystin in the desert returning. "You are my daughter."

"Perhaps, perhaps not," Shandower said. Myrmeen looked up at him sharply. "I have another story that I believe you will find interesting."

"Tell me," Myrmeen said cautiously.

Shandower related what he had learned in the desert from the Night Parade members who were among Djimon's men.

"You're saying that they arranged for us to find Krystin? Why would they go to such measures?" Myrmeen asked.

"Because they wanted a peaceful way to get you out of the city," Shandower replied.

Reisz gave a bitter half smile as he glanced at Cardoc and said, "The spook must have frightened them."

"Perhaps," Shandower said without looking away from Myrmeen. "I believe they thought that if you had your daughter, you would leave. By this time they knew who you were and exactly how much attention your death would have attracted. They prefer to keep to their own, to keep to the shadows. You were forcing them to expose themselves to the light, to risk discovery. This way would be easier. Now we must address the issue of the girl."

"I have a name," Krystin said.

"Yes, you have much to lay claim to," Shandower said.

"I don't have to listen to this," Krystin said. "I didn't ask to be rescued by you people." The child shot an angry glance at Myrmeen. "And I didn't ask for your name."

"Nevertheless, you would have it," Shandower said. "It might be desirable to them to place one of their own in succession for your throne, Myrmeen. They often need money and favors. In time, you could pass on and she—"

"But you can see our resemblance," Myrmeen said, fighting to preserve what she now perceived as a fragile illusion. "Look at our faces, our eyes."

Shandower laughed bitterly. "And how many of the Night

Parade have you encountered who possess the gift to change their appearance?"

A river of ice suddenly leapt from Myrmeen's heart. She felt an unexpected vertigo and tried to calm herself.

"That's it!" Krystin said. "I've had about as much of this as I'm going to take. You think I'm one of them?"

Shandower said nothing. Myrmeen looked at Krystin with an expression of fear intermingled with hope. Prove him wrong, she seemed to plead with her eyes. Krystin suddenly felt Myrmeen's overwhelming need, and the sensation made her uncomfortable. She crossed her arms over her breasts and stared at Shandower with her best, most penetrating gambler's stare. The man did not flinch, but he eased back a few inches. Restraining a grin, Krystin said, "All right. That glove of yours. When it's charged, the magic will kill any of them at a touch, right?"

"Yes," Shandower replied.

She held her hand out, palm down. "Then do it."

"Krystin—" Myrmeen began desperately.

"Shut up," Krystin said. "If you are the woman who gave birth to me, you waited a damn long time to come get me. I don't much care if you think it was worth the effort. But no one says I'm one of those things. How do I know the whole lot of you aren't with the Night Parade? This whole thing could be a punishment for me. They like to play games. That might be why you dragged me back to this filthy city."

Shandower regarded Myrmeen with the detachment of a professional assassin. "Do you wish this?"

"Forget her," Krystin said. "This is what I want." She placed her hand over his gauntlet, suddenly realizing that the flesh around his wrist was fused to the metal. "Do it."

He nodded and called upon the energies residing within him. The glove exploded in brilliant bluish white light. Snakes of green fire slithered up Krystin's arm. She remained perfectly still, only the sudden sweat that had broken out on her forehead revealing her fear. Then she smiled, the beautiful soft lights flickering in her eyes.

"What about the rest of you?" she asked.

One by one the Harpers rose and took the gloved hand. When it was over, Shandower allowed the mystical fires to retreat. Myrmeen placed her hand on Krystin's arm, attempting a weak smile. The girl shook her head impatiently and pulled away. The tall brunette felt her last embers of hope smolder and die within her heart.

Several minutes later, Lucius said, "As long as there is a chance that Krystin is not your daughter, as long as there is doubt, I will remain at your side. Both of you deserve to know the truth."

"But who can tell us?" Myrmeen asked.

"They can," Krystin said. "The monsters. They're probably the only ones."

"Do you want to go to Arabel?" Myrmeen asked. "It will be safe for you there."

"No." Krystin rose slowly and walked past Myrmeen and the Harpers. Without looking back, she said, "I've spent fourteen years not knowing who my parents are. I didn't think it mattered." She looked over her shoulder, at Myrmeen. "But it matters. I'm not saying that you can ever be my mother or that I could ever be your daughter, but it matters anyway."

Ord nodded. "Yes. More than you know."

"I can't ask the rest of you to continue," Myrmeen said.

"You don't have to ask," Reisz said. "Remember Morlan? We avenge our own. I'm with you."

"As am I," Ord said.

Myrmeen stood and addressed the group. "If we're to do this thing, it should be for the right reasons, not for vengeance, and not for personal gain." She looked down and shrugged, her hands open at her sides. She never knew what to do with her hands when she was making a speech. "I sound so pompous." She laughed. "It's just that I think of my friends, those we lost today. Burke and Varina were family to all of us. If they had a vote, they would vote to do this only to fulfill the sacred duty and obligation of the Harpers. That is what they died for, as much as anything else. More importantly, that's what they lived for. I think we should honor their memories as best we can."

The Harpers conferred alone and decided that they would stay with Shandower, gain his trust, and learn his secrets. They were particularly interested in this apparatus that the Night Parade wanted so desperately to reacquire. They wanted to send at least one of their number to the Twilight Hall to alert the other Harpers. However, they knew that Shandower's suspicion would have been aroused if one of them suddenly departed. This was not information that they could trust to a messenger. For now, they were on their own.

"If you will have us," Myrmeen said as she returned to Shandower, "we will join you."

"Allies are hard to come by in this war," Shandower said. "I'm honored."

Suddenly there was a rustling from the pile of debris at the warehouse's far side. The Harpers were stunned to see a blond youth standing beside the mound of trash. He made the rustling sound on purpose, to draw their attention.

"The boy from the Gentleman's Hall," Myrmeen said.

"Alden McGregor," he said brightly. "And considering my wealth of experience, dear Madame Lhal, I would hardly describe myself as a boy. Young, maybe, but certainly a man. So, how would you like one more ally?"

The boy's wet hair was matted to his scalp, and he walked toward the Harpers, brushing at his fine clothes in a vain attempt to remove the ingrained filth from his black shirt, boots, and leggings. He had left his fine red jacket outside.

"Excuse the stench," he said sheepishly. "I had to crawl up through the sewage tunnels to get in here. You really have a very secure location—"

Shandower grabbed the teenager and forced him down over one of the grates. Alden yelped in surprise. "I've come to help you!"

"We'll see," Shandower said.

Reisz tapped Ord on the shoulder. "Take a lamp and check the grating. Make sure there are no more."

"I will," Ord said, hurrying to the task.

His back upon the crate, Alden stared up at Shandower and said, "You seemed so even-tempered."

"You work for Pieraccinni," Shandower said. "He's—"

"One of them, the monsters, yes, I know," Alden said as he quickly explained the task he had been set to and his discovery at the Gentleman's Hall. He described Pieraccinni's transformation in great detail, and Lucius deduced Pieraccinni's nature, that of a living siphon of magical energy.

Ord returned. "We're clear. Reisz and I are going to check the perimeter."

"Good," Myrmeen said, drawing close to Shandower. Krystin joined her.

"Listen," Alden said, "if I wanted to betray you, I could have led those things back here to you. I didn't. I told Pieraccinni I saw your party leave the city gates. They'll think you're gone. They won't be expecting anything from you."

"Let him up," Myrmeen said. "I believe him."

Reisz and Ord returned. The building was secure.

"Why betray your employer?" Shandower asked.

"I might not always be on the side of law and morality, but I insist on sticking with my own kind," Alden said. "You have something those monsters want, some kind of apparatus, and I have the feeling that if they get their hands on it, there's going to be a lot of human blood spilled."

"You're right," Shandower said. "But trust does not come easily. It has to be earned."

"Don't be so stiff," Alden said. "Whatever it is you want me to do, I'll do it. That's why I'm here."

He winked at Krystin. Her eyebrows went up in surprise.

Shandower suddenly noticed the gaunt mage's dark, burning stare. "Cardoc, did you have something to add?"

"Only that I think we should find a way to hurt these monsters, and I have an idea about where to begin. . . ."

Ten

The cloud of flame reached into the night sky like an angry fist. The building seemed to shudder, its foundations rocked by the assault. Myrmeen stood a comfortable distance away, on a low rooftop, with Reisz and Ord flanking her and Krystin standing off to the side with a sullen expression. Both the Harpers and Myrmeen were armed with bows.

"There's one," Myrmeen said.

"I've got it," Ord said quickly, a flickering light playing in his eyes. The source of the light was not the fire across the street; instead, the shimmering luminescence came from the bluish white arcane fires in which the shafts had been immersed, courtesy of Shandower and his sorceries.

Below, a creature with long, twisted horns growing from its head raced out of the building. It fell suddenly as Ord's shaft pierced its chest. Soon there were more of the monstrosities flooding into the street, driven there by the dual attacks of Lucius and Shandower, who had sealed off all other means of escape from the burning building. As the monsters ran outside, they were quickly dispatched by the sure arm of the archers across the street.

For the past week, the Harpers had been mounting similar assaults against the clandestine homes of the Night Parade. With the information Shandower had gathered on his own and the invaluable help of Alden, who had been their eyes and ears at the Gentleman's Hall, the Harpers had been able to rout the creatures from a half dozen lairs in the low towns. Tonight marked the first attack on one of their nests in the garment district. The Harpers were dangerously close to their hiding place, which lay only blocks away.

Myrmeen saw a shambling creature break from the doorway below. Without hesitation, she placed a mystically charged arrow in its chest. Although some of the monsters fell to cold steel, magic was required for the rest.

Krystin moved to Ord's side. "Erin and Lucius should have been out of there by now," she said with concern.

"They know what they're doing," Myrmeen said sharply. "We've all been at this a lot longer than you have."

Flinching as if she had been struck, Krystin hissed, "I'm sorry I said anything."

Ord glanced at her. "Your mom's got a case of nerves."

"She's an idiot," she whispered harshly.

"There is that, too."

Krystin stared at the young man as if she were seeing him for the first time and smiled. Below, two figures raced from the burning building. Reisz drew back from the edge of the roof. "Cardoc and Shandower are out. Time to go."

As a group, Myrmeen, Krystin, and the Harpers retreated to the back of the building, where they were met by Lucius, who levitated them to the ground. Shandower waited at the end of the alley, waving his hand for them to follow.

Within ten minutes they were back at Shandower's safe house. While the others celebrated the victory, Myrmeen remained alone, examining the looms stacked in the corner.

During the last several days, Myrmeen had immersed herself in the work of helping to plan their attacks against the

Night Parade. In her spare moments, she trained with Shan-dower and Reisz, learning new and more deadly techniques of hand-to-hand combat. Her only contact with Krystin had been when she shared her lessons with the girl, and that had been at Reisz's urging. Reisz had taken a keen interest in the girl, and had been saddened by the steady disintegration of her relationship with Myrmeen.

Krystin went to Myrmeen. "You couldn't be less subtle."

Myrmeen turned suddenly. "I don't understand."

"On the roof you wouldn't give me a weapon. When we're in the field, you don't want to hear anything I have to say. I'm amazed you're willing to turn your back on me."

"I told you, when you're as accomplished as the rest of us, we'll arm you."

Krystin hugged herself. "Why are you lying to me? If you don't want me around, just say so and I'll leave."

Cocking her head slightly, Myrmeen raised an eyebrow and said, "You mean you want to go to Arabel?" She hated herself for the excitement that had crept into her voice.

"No," Krystin said firmly. "I can survive on the street. I have the feeling that I'd be more welcome there."

Myrmeen's mask of indifference fell away at once. "What are you talking about?"

"You don't want me here," Krystin said. "If you can't be honest with me, then at least be honest with yourself. I can pack up and leave at any time if you want me to go."

The tall brunette seemed to shrink. Her shoulders fell and she leaned against the filthy wall. "That's not what I want. It's just that I don't know how to be a parent. I've never been responsible for anyone except myself."

"You think you're *responsible* for me?" Krystin said, aghast. "What makes you think I want that?"

Myrmeen was silent. She bit her lip and looked away. Krystin had a point. Myrmeen had been on her own at a young age, and she would have resented a complete stranger walking into her life, trying to dictate her actions. Frustrated, she cried, "What is it I'm supposed to do? If I pay too much attention,

I'm crowding you. Too little, and I'm being cold!"

Krystin shuddered. "You hate me, don't you?"

"No," Myrmeen said, though it was true that she felt tight around the girl, unable to be herself. Staring into Krystin's eyes, so like her own, the uncomfortable feeling deepened. "I just don't want to make any mistakes with you."

"You've already made the first. You just lied to me."

"Krystin—" Myrmeen began as she reached for the child.

"Leave me alone!" the girl cried as she turned and stormed off. Walking away, Krystin firmly resolved not to bring up the true reason why she had approached Myrmeen. For the past week she had been witnessing brief flashes of scenes playing before her eyes. The images felt like memories, but they were of events that she had never experienced. Over the past two days, the visions had come with increasing frequency. Although they only lasted a second, no more, the faces she saw were clear and distinct. One, in particular, an old man with a kind, gentle look, had returned more often than any other. She wanted to know if the others were experiencing such waking dreams, as the visions had disturbed her. But when she saw the distrust in Myrmeen's eyes, the naked suspicion with which Krystin was still regarded, she chose not to bring up the subject.

"You're going to walk into a wall if you don't look up," a voice said.

Krystin glanced upward and saw Ord approaching. She realized that she had crossed the length of the warehouse and looked around to see Shandower gathering Myrmeen and the Harpers to an old table they had appropriated from a nearby alley. Scrolls and scraps of paper were strewn about.

"Shouldn't you be attending the planning session with the others?" Krystin asked.

"I will when my opinion means something around here."

"I can appreciate that," Krystin murmured. Gazing into Ord's relaxed face, she was certain that she was watching a carefully maintained performance. He was still grieving for Burke and Varina. "How are you, Ord? How are you, really?"

"Quite good, I've been told."

Krystin felt suddenly flushed. "Will you stop," she said, embarrassed by how easily he had made her blush.

"Only if I have to."

"Well, you have to," she said, shaking her head.

"What?" Ord said with a laugh.

Krystin shrugged. "Don't let it go to your head, but the only time I feel good anymore is when we're together."

Ord stood close to her, his hand lightly brushing hers. "I feel the same way."

"It's not that I feel that I can't get away with anything when I'm with you."

"Of course not. You can get away with anything you like," he said. She took his hand, gave his fingers a slight squeeze, then sighed heavily as she heard Myrmeen and Reisz call out for the youngest members of the group to join them. Krystin shot an anxious glance in the direction of the others. She was worried that they had seen the slight touch and the look that had passed between Ord and herself. The young man was smiling and he seemed thoroughly unrepentant.

"You're dangerous," Krystin said, "very dangerous."

"I know," Ord replied as he led her to the table, where they listened to the plan for their next attack.

Later that night, Lucius left the safe house and took to the streets. His departure went undetected by the other Harpers, just as it had for the past three nights. Soon he was deep in the residential district adjacent to the financial quarter, waiting across the street from the entrance to a lavish inn known informally as the most fashionable spot in Calimport for illicit rendezvous.

Alden McGregor emerged from the front, traded pleasantries with the elegantly dressed doorman, then entered the street, moving quickly as he blended with the shadows. Above, in one of the many windows, a candle was blown out and a young woman stood near the glass, watching him depart. Lucius followed Alden at a comfortable distance. The boy soon left the main streets and became one with a maze of alleys and side streets. Lucius lost sight of the young man several times, and he was surprised when he rounded a final bend and felt something hard and flat dig into his side.

"Snick!" Alden whispered. "You're dead."

Lucius turned as Alden removed the hilt of the spring-loaded blade from his ribs. The mage's stoic expression served to disguise his unease. No one had been able to surprise him like this before, and Alden had managed to do it two nights in a row.

"I hope you don't mind," Alden said as he replaced the weapon. "No one else offers much of a challenge."

"I understand," Lucius said, wondering if his age was beginning to show, if he was beginning to slow down. "We all must take our sport where we can find it." He paused. "What do you have for me this evening?"

"This," Alden replied as he withdrew a scroll from his jacket and handed it to the mage, who opened it up and examined the parchment. "I traced this from a map that one of Pieraccinni's men left with his clothing while he was being entertained by the twins. You can see the piers, the shipping lanes, the checkpoints. Use your imagination if you must, but trust me, the Night Parade is in our hands."

"Alden, they are going to know that someone in their organization helped us get this information," Lucius said gravely. "Before they may have suspected that we were getting help from the inside, but now they'll know."

"That doesn't bother me. I'm above suspicion."

"What makes you think that?" Lucius said.

Alden shrugged. "Pieraccinni treats me like a son. I have his trust and the respect of all who serve him."

"This isn't your war," Lucius said. "Have you thought of that, Alden?"

"But it is. This is humanity's war. Besides, where's the fun if there's no risk of being caught?"

The mage had no answers for the boy. Alden's words filled him, not with comfort, but with an all-consuming fear for the safety of them all.

Eleven

 Night had arrived. Myrmeen and Lu-
cius were stationed in a derelict vessel
that had been left less than a mile from
shore on the far side of the city, practically beyond the border. The area had
proved to be a popular dumping ground
for ship owners who did not wish to in-
vest in repairing their unsafe vessels. If
the information that Alden had gathered was correct, the darkness would bring a black ship that was owned by the Night
Parade. According to the course Alden had laid out, the vessel
would pass directly between the ship bearing Lucius and Myrmeen and another that sat a thousand yards across from them,
where the remaining Harpers waited with Shandower.

Alden had supplied them with the names of the guards working the port where the ship would arrive. The guards had spot-
less records, primarily due to their absolute loyalty to one
another. Before arriving at Calimport they were mercenaries
who had never lost a single man in their twelve years together.
No one suspected that they had become corrupted along the
way.

The black ship was bearing a cargo of contraband weapons, firesticks that could kill at a distance. Despite, or perhaps because of, Calimport's strict ordinances against these weapons, Pieraccinni would be able to sell these weapons for an exorbitant profit. But the Night Parade's true gain would be in the terror these weapons would inspire.

The Harpers' plan had been simple enough: Capture the Night Parade's ship and pilot the vessel into less corrupt waters, with as many living, inhuman prisoners on board as possible. By the time the guardsmen from the shore could arrive, Myrmeen, Shandower and the Harpers would be safely away. They had taken rooms at a small inn nearby and would return to the safe house in the morning, when the sunlight would burn away any advantage the Night Parade would have tracking them.

In the derelict vessel, Myrmeen looked out to the choppy waters mournfully.

"Your daughter was not happy with your decision," Lucius whispered in the darkness.

"My daughter's not happy about anything I do," Myrmeen said. "We had to leave her behind. It wasn't safe."

"I know that, but I doubt she is convinced."

Myrmeen was silent.

Lucius suddenly whispered, "I have a daughter."

A shudder passed through Myrmeen. "What did you say?"

"She is not as old as Krystin, but she is approaching that age. I have a son also. He is much younger."

Myrmeen stared into his perfectly set face. She wanted to ask him if he was having a joke at her expense, but she knew what an insult that would be if he were telling the truth. His modest reserve with her from the beginning suddenly made sense. "Do any of the others know about this?"

"No. They have never asked," he said.

Myrmeen looked out at the dark waters. The moon was resting far above the horizon; the evening was the brightest she had seen since she had arrived in Calimport. She was worried about the operation and did not want to become distracted. However, she knew that the others were in place, and that they could be trusted. Myrmeen turned back to Lucius. "You understand, this is somewhat surprising. I mean, no offense, but you seem very solitary, not the type to raise a family."

"I suppose. Is something wrong?"

"It's nothing," she said as she turned away. She did not want to deal with this now.

"Look at me," he commanded in his rich, dulcet voice.

She did as he said. "You have the most perfect brown eyes I've ever seen," she said hoarsely.

Lucius blinked. Twice. The lines around his eyes crinkled and his brow furrowed slightly.

"I don't know where that came from," Myrmeen said. She looked away, licked her dry lips, and wondered how she had suddenly become one long, raw nerve. "I'm sorry."

"Do not be."

"Lucius," she said slowly, angry with herself for the words that were tumbling out of her mouth, "I had the feeling you were somewhat, um, interested in me."

"Of course I am. I am interested in the welfare of all people."

"That's not what I meant."

"I know."

She laughed. "You're good. You're very good."

"So I've been told."

Her eyes flashed open in amazement. "Was that an off-color remark? You can tell me. We're friends."

Lucius rested his hand on her wrist. "Myrmeen, I would like to think that we *are* friends."

The warmth of his hand surprised her.

"We are," she said, taking his hand in hers, holding it tightly. "This is a frightening place."

"It is."

"In Arabel I'm in control. Here, in so many ways, I'm lost." She stared directly into his brown eyes. "When we're away from all this, can I ask you some questions about having a daughter?"

For the first time since they had met, Lucius smiled. "We have a few minutes. Tell me what you're thinking."

"It's hard to put into words. It's just that I had all these ideas about what it would be like to have a child. I thought it would solve all my problems, but I was wrong. Everything's more complicated. My time with Krystin seems unreal. I feel detached. There's a wall between us and I can't take it down, even though I put it there."

Lucius squeezed her hand. "It is hard to trust anyone."

"You don't understand. There's this part of me that was relieved when Shandower said she might not be my daughter. Inside, I almost want that to be the case."

"Perhaps you should try to see her not as your daughter, but simply as herself."

"I suppose you're right, I—"

Lucius looked up sharply. "They are here."

Averting her gaze from his rich brown eyes, Myrmeen saw the black ship stealing close from the horizon. "How long have they been on the approach?"

"For as long as you have been talking. I saw no need to raise the alarm prematurely."

"Damn," she whispered. "We have to signal the others."

"No. They can see the ship. Let us prepare ourselves. I am certain they are doing the same."

Scowling at the mage, Myrmeen walked across the deck of the abandoned vessel and crouched near the guardrail. At her feet she found a child's toy, a doll. Angrily she kicked it from the deck and winced at the slight splash it made.

The group had been outfitted in dark clothing that would not weigh them down as they swam. Their weapons were sealed in bags that Lucius had made buoyant with his spells. Soon the black ship came within a thousand yards. Myrmeen nodded to Lucius, who lowered her into the waters, then joined her.

They swam toward the ship, Myrmeen afraid that her legs would suddenly cramp up, that she would drown alone and helpless in the dark waters. Then she heard the steady, comforting breath of the mage beside her and her fear slowly dissipated, replaced with a resolve to complete this mission as quickly as possible and try to make amends with her daughter.

They approached the vessel's side, Lucius ahead of Myrmeen. He gripped the rung that jutted from the side of the ship and climbed upward, unencumbered by weapons of any kind. Myrmeen was bothered by the dead weight of the heavy bag slung on her back, the strap pulling on her throat as she climbed. They made it over the top and walked directly into a pair of sailors. Darting out of the way, they were not surprised to go unnoticed; Lucius had cloaked them in a spell of invisibility. They could see each other, but no one else would mark their presence.

Myrmeen and Lucius did not speak as they walked quickly to the bridge. The fighter clutched the molded grip of a blade as they approached the ship's navigator. Beneath Myrmeen's boot, a floorboard groaned loudly. The man at the helm turned suddenly and stared directly at the tall, gaunt mage and his beautiful companion. Then he frowned and turned back to the large wooden wheel that he gripped tightly.

Human, Myrmeen thought with dismay, or so he seems. Lucius glanced down at her foot, then turned his gaze to her face and motioned for her to step on the creaking floorboard again. She leaned on the wooden plank a second time, causing the sailor to spin around in genuine alarm. The man was on edge and Lucius capitalized on this fact as he held out his open palm and blew a handful of dust into the man's face. Myrmeen quickly sheathed her blade as the man fell forward. She caught his limp body with both hands. Dragging the man a half dozen feet, she carefully laid him beside several coils of rope, then she speedily disrobed. Removing his jacket, Myrmeen slipping it over her shivering, waterlogged body, then donned his leggings, boots, and the dark cap he had worn.

Lucius held the wheel for her. She took it as the mage hurried to the unconscious man's side and covered his pale, pink body with a blanket from the adjoining deck. Lucius then released the spell of invisibility that cloaked them. Myrmeen wondered if the others were on board, then committed the ship to its new course. The sailing vessel veered abruptly, engaging on a route that would take it parallel to the shoreline.

"What in Cyric's hell are you up to?" someone shouted.

Looking over her shoulder, Myrmeen saw that several members of the crew were racing in her direction. Lucius stepped before her, his lips moving, his fingers gesturing. The advancing crewman were suddenly lifted into the air, their legs yanked upward as if they had been plucked by gigantic, invisible hands. The men levitated into the rigging, where they grabbed hold, screaming in anger and fear. Two of the seven men Myrmeen counted nearly floated beyond the reach of the sails, into the sky, but they managed to grab hold of the flapping canvas sails and save themselves. Three men approached from the rear of the ship and Myrmeen relaxed as she recognized Shandower and the two Harpers, who were all soaking wet.

"There were five more, but we subdued them," Ord said, watching the floating men above his head in amusement. The sailors cast creative variations of all-too-familiar curses at their vessel's usurpers.

"They were all human," Shandower said as he spat on the deck with disgust. "I should have guessed that the Night Parade wouldn't leave itself exposed like this."

"Perhaps we'd be better off sinking this ship after we check the hold," Ord said. "It would be a short journey from the city lockup to ready buyers in the streets for those weapons if we allow them to be confiscated—only the suppliers would change."

Myrmeen nodded. Their goal had been not only to interfere with the smuggling operation that would give the night people more gold for their dark purposes, but also to bring them from the shadows of myth and children's whispered tales to the light of scrutiny from the authorities. That plan depended on encountering at least a few of the monsters on board and securing their capture.

"Ord, you take the helm from Myrmeen," Reisz said. "The

rest of us will go below."

The young man started to protest, then fell silent when he registered the look in Reisz's eyes. "Of course," Ord whispered, "Roudabush."

Reisz nodded and followed the others below decks.

Lanterns lighted the first deck to which they had come and a full search netted the adventurers only two frightened deck hands who had run at the first sign of trouble. Shandower agreed to test these boys, firing his weapon into brilliant, blue-white life as he touched each of their hands. The first boy fainted, his fear causing him more harm than the gauntlet's touch. The second was slightly more at ease after realizing that the Harpers did not plan to kill him. He touched the glove voluntarily and was relieved when all he felt was a slight racing of his heart as the green lightning coursed through him. The unconscious boy was bound and left behind, the second taken with them as they found the door to the cargo hold.

The teenager, a rail-thin boy with thick, dark hair, angular features, and a scar above his left eye, shouted for them to stop before they pulled back the heavy, square door that secured their cargo. Reisz, who had been holding the rope that would pull open the wooden door, shuddered as if his worst fears had been confirmed.

"What's down there?" Myrmeen asked as she heard a groan that had not come from the wood-frame ship's shifting.

"It's not the crew," Reisz said as the rope fell from his hand. "It was never the crew."

Beneath them, the floor undulated and they heard a heavy thud. Something incredibly large and strong had struck from below. The sound came again and Myrmeen decided that whatever was making the noise wished either to gain their attention or escape from the hold. Lucius took Myrmeen's arm. "We must leave. We can sink the ship from a distance."

Myrmeen thought of the ambush they had walked into at her childhood home, the nest of nightmares they had uncovered and to which they had lost two of their oldest and dearest friends. She quickly scanned the faces of those who had boarded the ship with her and wondered who would die next if they did not follow the mage's urging.

"No!" Shandower shouted. "This is what we came here for, proof that the nightmares are real. There were never any forbidden weapons on this ship, only more of their kind, beings who could not pass for human and needed special care."

Myrmeen stared at the madness she saw in Shandower's eyes and was grateful that she had decided to spare Krystin this sight. A part of the assassin had hoped for this—a part of him had wanted to fight the monstrosities even if it meant sacrificing all the others to satisfy his needs.

I want to make the monsters go away.

The words were branded into her memory, but she could not recall if it had been her father, Dak, or her second husband who had spoken them.

You can't, she suddenly understood. No one can make the monsters go away but me.

"Myrmeen," Reisz urged, "we made a mistake. Let's leave while we still can. If he's right and those things escape—"

"Retreat," she hissed, still watching Shandower's eyes, worried that the fervor she saw within him might one day stare out at her when she looked at her own reflection.

"I'm not going without seeing what's down there," Shandower said as he shoved Reisz out of the way, took the heavy rope in his hand, and yanked the door upward.

Looking over the assassin's shoulder, drawn in perverse fascination, Myrmeen was certain that she was staring into the pit of ultimate damnation. Dozens of monstrosities lay below, their bodies intertwined as they writhed frantically. Many were climbing the walls and two were on the stairway leading up to them. At the center of the gathering lay an obese, grotesque creature that appeared to have the power to manipulate its own body as if it were clay, stretching its muscles and tendons into shapes that seemed strangely familiar to Myrmeen. The monster's stomach was immense, lined with a set of jaws large enough to swallow a man whole. Its face was marked with huge, egg shaped eyes, and a wide, gentle smile.

Myrmeen suddenly recognized the shapes it was forcing its body to create: Musical instruments.

Blood-soaked tendons stretched to the consistency of strings for a large pink harp, while hard muscle coalesced to form a lute near the base of the monster's incredible bulk. A long, thin appendage shot from beneath its layers of fat that had been its jaw, with holes suddenly appearing to mark it as a wind instrument. The host of smaller, equally inhuman creatures stopped and turned, their mad, chattering sounds dropping away in anticipation.

"Lucius!" Myrmeen shouted.

The mage was already gesturing, his hands stretched before him. The sound of thunder roared in the confined space and a flash of lightning burst from Lucius's hands. The light was so intense that it nearly blinded those gathered above the hold. The fleshy harp and lute were destroyed by a deadly bolt of bluish red light, and the monster wailed in agony, odd music accompanying its screams.

Myrmeen suddenly felt drowsy and saw her companions exhibiting signs that the effect was not limited to her. "Lucius," she screamed, "again! Kill it before—"

A geyser of water burst through the hull beneath the monster, revealing a horrible rip in the craft's shell. The music stopped suddenly as the creature was blasted upward by the force of the water. The ship tilted, and two of the smaller monstrosities vaulted out of the hold. Then the door crashed downward, shaken by the motions that had knocked all but Shandower from their feet. The deckhand who had been with the group turned and ran.

The first creature looked as if it had been sewn together from the bloody remains of corpses on a battlefield. It squatted on four arms, each poised in a different direction, and had a thick, ball-like torso. Its head drooped and peeked out from between the cage of arms. The monstrosity beside it was female, with overly large arms that hung to the floor and tiny hands growing from every part of her body, including the hollows where her eyes should have been. The first creature spoke:

"The crew, the guards at the shore, they were meant to be our feast, our payment for enduring this awful journey. We hunger. Vizier Bellophat promised us sustenance."

"Feast on this," Shandower said as he ran his glowing hand through the monster's fatty torso, its body collapsing. The woman with too many hands drew back, her hands suddenly detaching from her body, falling to the floor, and racing toward the assassin. The probing fingers closed over the startled killer, their razor-sharp nails biting into his flesh. Reisz drew his sword and buried it in the skull of the woman who had spawned the hands.

"Idiot," she said, gore running down her scalp as the flaps of her head sealed around the weapon. She drew Reisz close and kissed him full on the mouth as a new set of hands began to manifest on her body.

Suddenly, Shandower pushed himself forward and plunged his glowing blue gauntlet between her shoulder blades. The multitude of hands fell away as the woman collapsed. Reisz did not try to retrieve his weapon.

"We have to get out of here," Shandower said in alarm, awakened from his bloodlust to embrace the reality of their imminent deaths. The group raced through the corridors leading to the stairway, then climbed to the main deck as the ship pitched to one side. Myrmeen prayed that the monsters in the hold would be trapped there, drowning before they could escape.

Ord greeted them at the top of the stairs. "The men who had been floating, they fell!"

Lucius nodded. "I had to release that spell."

"They mostly jumped overboard. Before that, one of them lost his grip, then floated out into the sky."

"It doesn't matter," Myrmeen said impatiently. "We have to get back to our boat."

The craft they had rented to take them to the derelicts was anchored near the ships that had helped them stage their ambush, its rotting appearance making it look like another corpse in the graveyard of boats. All but Lucius leapt over the edge into the icy waters. The mage remained, gathering his will, and sent another blast of energy straight down, into the hold. The ship buckled and he was thrown free into the waters. Myrmeen swam to his side, rescuing him from drowning, as he had been left weak and trembling after using his power. Behind them, the black ship was in flames, Lucius's second bolt of energy sparking the conflagration.

They made it back to their boat, disturbed by the sight of a small craft embarking from the harbor. As they sailed into the night, Myrmeen prayed that they would avoid the members of the corrupt merchant company. Averting her gaze from the smaller vessel, she watched as the black ship containing its cargo of monsters went under, one end pointing out of the waters until it was sucked down by its own weight, disappearing beneath the surface without a hint that it had been there at all.

* * * * *

Krystin had been ordered to wait at the inn. Naturally, she was now more than a mile from that location, on her way to visit a shopkeeper named Caleb Sharr. Sharr had always been generous in supplying a scrap of food when she had needed it the most, or a bit of sage advice when she desired it the least. Nevertheless, she loved the grizzled, middle-aged man and had missed talking to him. She knew that soon she would leave Calimport forever, and she wanted him to know that she was well. He often had called himself an old fool where she was concerned and she would not have had him any other way.

The Lhal woman, on the other hand, had been particularly cold and distant tonight, her thoughts even farther away than the storm she had heard engulfing some part of the desert. The rains gathered on the outskirts of the city like a skulking thief waiting for the right moment to enter Calimport and strike.

Krystin turned her thoughts from the storm and recalled her conversation with Myrmeen in detail. The woman had explained the dangerous nature of the operation they were undertaking tonight and said that, despite Krystin's training, the girl was not yet ready for a mission with such a high degree of danger.

"In other words, I still can't be trusted," Krystin had said, to which Myrmeen had no reply. The woman had left her side, an icy breeze marking where she had stood. Seconds later, Ord had joined Krystin.

"In other words," he had whispered in his sly voice, "that woman has no idea who you are."

Krystin had turned to him, her anger dissolving the moment she saw the perfect blue of his eyes. "Who am I?"

"Someone very special," he had said softly, caressing her arm. "And someone who had best be here when we return."

"Now you're giving me orders?"

"No. But I can see that you'll be out wandering tonight, and if you didn't return, I would miss you."

Her lips had opened slightly and she had felt her hands tremble at his touch. She waited for him to kiss her, but instead he had backed away, his own sadness gathering over him like the clouds she had seen on the horizon.

"Nothing I do gets past you," she had said. "I like that, Ord. I like that very much."

He had smiled and left to join the others, but his smile had been cloaked in sadness, his words, even at their most seductive, laced with a texture that was bittersweet. He was not dealing with the loss of his parents, she knew, and the forces inside him one day would tear loose and destroy him if he did not accept the grief and allow himself to heal. She wondered if there were any way she could help him, or if she even should try.

One thing was certain, he had been correct in his assumption that she would not stay locked up in the inn, waiting for Myrmeen's return. She now was within a city block of Caleb Sharr's market house and her heart was filled with excitement at the thought of seeing him.

Krystin turned the final corner and stopped dead. The shop

was gone. For a moment she gazed about, familiarizing herself with the streets and various landmarks. She needed to make absolutely certain that she had not taken a wrong turn and ended up someplace other than where she wished to be. There had been no mistake. She was on Heridon Way, but the shop where she had found shelter was gone. There was no evidence that it ever had been there to start with. In a daze, Krystin wandered the street, occasionally stopping to ask other shopkeepers if they knew Caleb Sharr. When she asked if they had ever tasted the succulent meats that he prepared for his special clients, basted in spices from faraway lands that no one but he could procure, they treated her as if she were insane.

Krystin felt a sudden shortness of breath. For a moment the world seemed to spin, and she grabbed hold of a stranger's arm. The man shrugged her off with a casual curse. He shoved her to the ground, where she was ignored by the dozens of men and women who briskly walked past her. Their downcast eyes carefully avoided the skinny fourteen-year-old with dark hair and beautiful, practically unique eyes. Suddenly, Krystin realized that she was shrinking back, heading for the shadows of an alleyway. She bolted to her feet and thrust herself into the crowd, avoiding the places where the Night Parade moved freely. A chill passed through her as she felt a drop of rain strike her shoulder, then she realized that it was a tear that she had shed.

There was no storm; there had been no storm.

Thunder rolled in the distance.

There was one person who would remember Caleb Sharr: Melaine, a fellow hunter for the Night Parade, a girl who was a year younger than Krystin. Melaine had been Krystin's responsibility on several occasions when she had made mistakes. Krystin had put herself at risk to prevent their keepers' wrath from falling upon the girl. She wondered why she had not thought of Melaine earlier; they could have rescued her, taken her away from the life of horror that she had known practically from birth.

Of course, there was a danger that Krystin would fail, that the keepers would capture her again. The creature that had served as her master had been named Byrne. For a moment she was curious to learn if he had been the old man whose face had come to her in flashes of memory.

Why do you even have to ask these questions? she wondered. You remember Byrne. He had scorpions for arms and snakes for teeth. His tail had been wrapped around your tender throat a thousand times and his eyes held the secrets of twilight, the end of humanity, the beginning of something new and repulsive.

That was not entirely true, she reminded herself. Sometimes he was human. He even appeared handsome and kind. Did he change, or did he create illusions? It did not matter. He was one of the nightmare people; that was all that was important. He would die with the rest of them.

An hour later, she arrived at the estate where she had been housed for the better part of her childhood. The building was deserted, overrun by weeds that clung to the sides of the two-story building. She stared at the estate in shock.

Not possible, she thought. This is not the way I remember it. The iron gate surrounding the estate had been rusted shut, and she was forced to climb over it. The dogs that had prowled the grounds were silent. Deep down, a part of her knew that she had heard the barking of Byrne's hounds for the last time. The estate had changed to an impossible degree. She had been here less than a month earlier, just before the desert raiders had taken her from the streets that had been her home after she had left the estate.

She heard a rustling behind her. Krystin spun and drew one of the daggers Myrmeen had begrudgingly allowed her to keep. When she saw the figure standing before her, she lowered the knife immediately.

"Malach Byrne is dead," the child said in a singsong voice, her head tilted to one side, her body as thin and drained as a wilting flower. "Malach Byrne is my Daddy, and Malach Byrne is dead."

"Melaine," Krystin whispered in shock.

"Daddy's dead, Daddy's dead," Melaine sang. She stopped suddenly when she saw Krystin, a gasp of terror choking off her words as if hands had closed about her throat and were strangling her into eternal silence. The child was dressed in rags. She carried something in her hands that appeared to be the scalp of a man. Long, stringy hair was woven between her pale fingers.

"Melaine, what's happened?" Krystin said.

"Who are you?" Melaine spat, clutching the black, hairy object to her breast as if it were a toy she had played with in her childhood. Her eyes were the pale gray Krystin had remembered, her features plain, her small nose upturned.

"Don't you recognize me?"

Melaine backed away, her small, bare foot catching on the root of a large tree. She fell back, the impact knocking the wind from her. Krystin rushed to her side and placed her hands on Melaine's arms. The young girl tried desperately to wriggle out of Krystin's embrace, but she was weak and malnourished, her flesh mottled with bruises and sores.

"Melaine, it's Krystin. I'm your friend."

"Daddy's men will find you. They'll hurt you. They won't let you touch me, they won't!"

Krystin tried to hold back her tears, but she could not restrain the racking sobs that escaped her. "Melaine, we've been friends all our lives, please!"

"Daddy's men will find you. Daddy's dead, but his men will find you. They can't find me. I'm too smart for them. They want to take me away in a cart, like they did him. They want to bury me in the ground, or burn me. I know, I've seen. I followed them. I watched them. I know what they are. I know what they want to do with me!"

"Melaine, please, don't you know me?"

The straw-haired girl stopped wailing long enough to look into Krystin's face. Sanity briefly flickered in her eyes, then the light of reason faded and her head came up suddenly, her teeth snapping like those of a ravenous animal. Krystin let her go and flung herself back to avoid the attack. Melaine sprang to her feet with unexpected grace and ran off, singing, "I don't know you, I never did, I never will. I only know Daddy, and Daddy's dead, but before they burned him, I took his hair, and soon, and soon . . ."

Her voice trailed off, and Melaine quickly vanished into the night. Krystin sat for a long time and allowed herself to cry for the friend she had lost. Finally she could cry no longer. Her strength drained from her, Krystin returned to the gates, managed to drag herself over the top, and began the long walk back to the inn.

Along the way, she felt drawn to a certain house at the end of a deserted street. Candles burned within the house. A party was in progress. Krystin heard people laughing. She stole close to the window, then looked inside. The man she had been looking for was dancing with his wife while several of his friends laughed and applauded.

"Impossible," she whispered. He should have been dead.

She remembered finding this man for the Night Parade. He had been insanely jealous and suffered from an all-consuming fear of losing his wife to another man. A handful of human-looking creatures had attached themselves to him like leeches wearing the faces and forms of newfound friends. In this capacity, they had manufactured lies about his wife's infidelities and told him that they could not turn away while his wife made a fool of him. He had murdered his wife, then himself, and the Night Parade had feasted upon his anguish.

Krystin returned to the inn without allowing herself any further detours. She arrived ten minutes before the Harpers returned, quiet and shaken after their escape from the harbor authorities. Only Ord sensed her distress, and when he tried to find out why she was upset, she pushed him away.

*   *   *   *   *

The next day, Myrmeen woke Krystin and insisted that the child share morningfeast with the others. Krystin moaned and complained that she was not hungry and only wanted to be left to herself, to sleep.

"There's nothing planned for today," Myrmeen told her. "Why don't we spend it together?"

"Yes," Krystin said dully. "I suppose."

She had spent the night in a deep, dreamless sleep. The visions that had been troubling her waking hours did not intrude. All she wanted was to return to that blissful state of oblivion, but she knew from Myrmeen's tone that the woman would not be put off. Myrmeen was making another one of her concentrated efforts to play mother to Krystin. The girl knew that Myrmeen's pleasant smile was forced, her words carefully rehearsed. Nevertheless, she did as Myrmeen requested. They spent the morning touring the markets, with Lucius maintaining his invisibility and watching them at a comfortable distance.

They stopped before a merchant selling clothing from the eastern nations and Myrmeen said, "I had a scarf like this once." She ran her hand across a brilliantly colored length of cloth that displayed a beautiful golden dragon. A sigh of disappointment sounded from her. "Unfortunately, our gold is running low, not something I'm used to dealing with."

"Like abstinence?" Krystin said. The words had surprised Krystin. She had no idea why she had said them.

Myrmeen's pleasant mood faded. "You have quite a mouth on you, you know that?"

Krystin shrugged. She had wished that Myrmeen would simply talk to her rather than at her. Their conversation consisted of sporadic bursts of speech followed by lengthy, unbearable stretches of silence. In the marketplace, with so many people noisily haggling over prices, Krystin could not evaluate the quality of the silence between Myrmeen's words. She needed something to think about, something to take her mind from the startling revelations of the previous night. Arguments with Myrmeen had become a normal, almost comfortable way to spend her day.

"What is your problem?" Myrmeen spat.

"You are," Krystin said without thinking.

Myrmeen grabbed her arm and fought down her impulse to slap the girl with the back of her hand. "By the gods, you're lucky we're in public, the way you speak to me."

"You want to hit me? Go ahead. I don't care. I've been beaten by the best of them. There's nothing you can threaten me with that's going to make me care. You don't know anything about me. You haven't even asked. I had a life before we met—a terrible one, but a life. My life."

"So did I!" Myrmeen howled.

They both stared at one another. Krystin did not need to gauge the quality of the silence this time. She could see the confusion and anger in Myrmeen's eyes, along with the guilt that had motivated her in the first place. The chasm between them was widening with every quiet moment.

"What did you, um," Myrmeen said haltingly, "what did you want to tell me?"

"Nothing," Krystin said with a tired laugh. "Nothing, Myrmeen. It doesn't matter." Say that it does, she thought. Say that you want to know. Let me tell you who I am. Stop thinking about who you want me to be.

Myrmeen was silent.

"What about the scarf? You were about to tell me something," Krystin said.

"No. Like you said, it's not important." Myrmeen sounded tired and defeated.

They continued through the marketplace in silence and soon allowed themselves to be separated by the crowd. Krystin did not object; even with Myrmeen beside her, she felt more alone than ever.

Krystin found a merchant selling tiny brass figurines. The statuettes were of elven folk. They were taken from a collection of stories that had been read to her by Madame Childress, the woman who had tended to the daily needs of Byrne's hunters at the estate. Krystin never knew if Childress was a Night Parade member or not. The woman had shown the children compassion and light, even as Byrne had embodied the

shadows that always appeared to be watching them. Her
memories of that place were vivid and overpowering.

*The estate was overrun. Melaine didn't know you. And the
storm is coming closer, Krystin. You can feel it.*

"May I be of assistance?" a voice asked.

Krystin looked up to see a muscular, sun-baked blond man
with a dark-haired child in his arms. The little girl he carried
buried her face in his chest and took only a quick peek at Krystin. From the glimpse that Krystin had of the child, she could
tell that the three-year-old would be a devastating beauty
when she grew up.

"I was admiring your handiwork," Krystin said.

The man laughed and hefted the girl into the air. He kissed
her forehead. "You see, my dear? I'm not the only one who
thinks you're pretty." The man looked back to Krystin. "Or
were you talking about my other handiwork, the ones on sale
before you?"

Krystin smiled. "Your daughter's very beautiful."

The girl peeked out, chanced a slightly longer look at Krystin, then turned away and held on to her father for all she was
worth. The man grinned.

"She's very shy," he said. "She's adopted."

Krystin asked the man if he had ever heard of Malach Byrne
or his daughter, Melaine.

"Yes, it is very sad," he said. "Malach secured his fortune in
the wake of the great storm—he was a builder. The city
needed builders at any cost. He was a good man, though a
trifle vain. He lost his hair and insisted on wearing a wig to
make himself look younger."

The hair Melaine clutched to her breast, Krystin thought.
The fact that she had not sliced it away from his cold flesh was
comforting to Krystin.

"When did he die?" she asked.

"A year ago."

Krystin flinched.

"His daughter was never found. They say she hides somewhere in his old house. New tenants do not stay long. They

are certain the place is haunted. I saw poor Melaine once at the outskirts of town, picking through refuse for her evening meal. A poor, sad child, no longer sane."

"A year," Krystin repeated dully. In her memories, Byrne had been alive three weeks ago.

"Dear miss, forgive me for inflicting sadness upon you. There are happier subjects. My figurines, for example. Each comes with its own personal story, which I will tell you—"

"I have no gold, I'm sorry."

The man smiled gently. "If I did not need to feed my princess and keep the roof above our heads, I would gladly part with one of them for you."

"No, you've given me all I need. I thank you."

Krystin turned and left the merchant, waving good-bye to his retiring young daughter. She envied the girl the life of love and happiness that would stretch before her in the coming years, then realized that there were no guarantees in life. A totally unselfish thought, something that even she would admit was quite unusual for her, came in that instant:

May she always know happiness. Don't worry about me. Protect the girl.

She stopped in the marketplace and wondered if that had been a prayer to some god or another; if so, it had been her first. Perhaps exposure to Myrmeen and the Harpers was changing her after all.

Suddenly a glint of green fire caught her attention. She stopped and found herself captivated by a beautiful emerald pendant. The item hung from the fat arm of a dark-haired woman who had her own booth in the marketplace. Several other necklaces were displayed on the woman's pale, meaty forearm, but it was the emerald pendant that arrested the girl's attention. Upon closer examination she realized that it was a locket. As she stared at its polished surface, Krystin began to see images form. Suddenly the world fell away. She was no longer aware of the crowd surrounding her, of the suffocating shroud of voices that had hung upon her. For a single, precious moment, all that existed in the world was the locket.

Within its emerald depths, she suddenly knew, lay the answers that she so desperately sought. A face began to form as she stared at the locket, the face of the old man from her waking dreams.

"There you are," a voice called.

The sounds of the crowd fell upon her like a wall of distress. She turned from the locket and saw Myrmeen standing before her with an expression of impatience.

"I thought I told you not to wander far," Myrmeen said.

"Did you?" Krystin said absently, her gaze returning to the locket, which now held only a glimmering promise of the magic she had felt within it only seconds before. Hope seized up within her as she took Myrmeen's arm. "Buy it for me."

"What?"

"Please, Myrmeen." She swallowed hard. "Mother, if you like. The green locket. Buy it for me. You can afford it."

"Let's get out of here," Myrmeen said darkly.

"No," Krystin wailed. "You have more money than can be found in any temple in this city. Buy me the locket!"

Before them, the fat woman stared at the mother and her child with amusement. She shook her arm, making the chains rattle slightly. "I like a customer who knows what she wants. Go on, buy her the locket. It's cheap."

Myrmeen grabbed Krystin's arm and yanked her away from the booth, where the fat woman urged them to come back, offering to cut the price in half.

"Didn't you really look at it? It was dented and cracked," Myrmeen said. "If it's baubles you want, I'll give you a cartload when we get to Arabel. But for now we're low on gold and we can't squander it on cheap costume jewelry."

Krystin looked over her shoulder. She was able to glimpse the locket for another moment, then the crowd intervened and the fat woman disappeared.

For the rest of the afternoon, Krystin lapsed into a sullen mood. Late that evening, when Myrmeen brought the evening's meal, Krystin refused to acknowledge her presence. Myrmeen set the tray down carelessly, the loud crash of steel plates and utensils causing Krystin to tense momentarily, then relax once again.

"Fine," Myrmeen said. "If you want to act like a child, then I might as well treat you like one. You can sleep in this room alone tonight. I'll make other provisions." Myrmeen waited for a nasty retort. When none came, she frowned and left the room.

Several hours passed. When the hunger in the pit of her stomach became too overwhelming to be ignored, Krystin went to the tray and bit into the corns and meats that had been left for her, though they now were cold. In the gleaming metal of the picked-clean dish, Krystin saw the reflection of the room behind her. She thought of the terror that once sought her out in the darkness, the nightmares that until recently had come for her every night. They had gone away only when she had begun to sleep in Myrmeen's presence. Bringing a metal cup to her lips, Krystin drank deeply and was surprised by the pleasant surprise of peppermint bubbling in her mouth, a treat that she had told Myrmeen she treasured when she was a little girl.

Suddenly, out of fear and loneliness, Krystin began to sob. When her tears had run their course, she left her room and tried to find Myrmeen. She decided that she would tell the woman about the strange images that she had seen. Her memories seemed to be unraveling like a tapestry with a single thread that was slowly being pulled loose.

The door to Reisz's quarters was ajar and Krystin heard voices within.

"That's all that's left," Reisz said.

"We're all right," Myrmeen replied. "I chose this place for a reason. There's a depository less than a mile from here. In the morning, I want you to take this claim ticket and retrieve the cache I left there for emergencies. The gold you'll find should be enough to get us through another week or two, if we're careful."

"They're open all night. Why not go now?"

"Because the Night Parade revels in the darkness. We don't

want to be seen by the burning man who nearly had us before, now do we?"

"Good point."

A sudden change came over Krystin. She thought once more of the locket, of the strange images that had come to her as she stared into its jade depths, and she knew that she had to own that locket, had to possess it no matter the cost.

Krystin crept back to her room and waited for midnight, her fear of the darkness all but forgotten in her excitement. When she was certain that the hour had come, Krystin returned to the room shared by Reisz and Ord. She found the door unlocked and quietly entered, using every technique of stealth that Myrmeen had taught her. She froze when she saw Myrmeen lying on the floor, her face turned to the wall, then relaxed and moved to the small nightstand beside the bed where Reisz lay. The claim note rested in plain view. She took it without incident, then retreated from the room without disturbing the others' sleep.

As she walked down the hall, Krystin heard Myrmeen sob quietly in her sleep. She stopped for a moment, thought about going back, then hung her head low and proceeded down the stairs.

Twelve

Krystin was painfully unaware that dawn had arrived. She had lost most of the night staring into the emerald depths of the prize she had betrayed her benefactor to acquire. Procuring Myrmeen's cache of valuables had been a simple task. The locket had been waiting for her in the marketplace. She had divided the gold that she had not spent, burying most of it in the soft, well-packed earth of a deserted, fire ravaged barn. The money would serve as insurance that, in the event the others did not survive the war on the Night Parade, Krystin would have a stake to begin a new life elsewhere—in Arabel, perhaps.

Returning to her room at the inn, she had sewed the remaining gold into the lining of her sash and the inside of her boots. Then she had curled up on her bed and held the emerald locket before her. Thin white beams of moonlight had sliced into her room and fallen upon the locket, reflecting the light with brilliant, prismlike shards.

It was not the beauty of the object that accounted for its

fascination to the young woman. Krystin knew that if she had been pressed to explain the locket's significance, she would fail in the attempt. All she knew was that she had seen this locket, or another trinket that looked identical to it, once before. She sensed that if she could remember exactly when and where she had glimpsed it the first time, she would be on the way to solving the mystery of what had happened to Melaine, Byrne, and Caleb Shar. She had to know if she could trust her memories.

As the night went on, her world had become a sparkling green field, a beautifully woven tapestry of hazy, indistinct images. She shuddered in anticipation as the fog encompassing her vision stepped up to the threshold of clearing then hesitated. Figures danced back and forth in the emerald world. They gestured broadly, inviting her into their land with words that she could not hear and actions that she could not quite discern.

Suddenly she was aware that it was morning. She glanced out the window and watched the final stages of the sun rising above the city. Her fingers closed over the locket in frustration. Krystin could not tell if the visions she had glimpsed had been inspired by the locket, or if she had imagined them all. She felt exhausted. Realizing that further examination of the locket would have to wait, she hid the item by carefully sewing it into the fabric of her sash.

For the first time she understood that she should have felt guilty for stealing from Myrmeen, but there was no emotion attached to the knowledge. The woman should have purchased the locket for Krystin in the first place. She had more gold in other caches in the city. The Harpers would not have starved.

Krystin no sooner had looked up after hiding her stolen sewing kit than the door swung open wide and Myrmeen entered the room. The older woman came to a sudden halt, obviously surprised to find Krystin awake and fully dressed.

"I didn't bother getting undressed last night," Krystin explained truthfully.

"Get your things. We're leaving here," Myrmeen said. "There are not only rats and spiders in these rooms, but vermin that walks on two legs, too."

Krystin shrugged as Myrmeen left the room, closing the door behind her. She had seen no trace of either spiders or rats during the night. Myrmeen's terrible dreams were returning, and, in Calimport, the line separating dreams from reality was as thin and sharp as the cutting edge of a sword. The claim note's theft obviously had been discovered, and the thief was closer than the woman ever would have expected. Krystin gathered her few belongings and left the room, pausing only to touch her sash and feel the locket's comforting weight.

The others were waiting for Krystin downstairs. They wasted little time after paying for their lodgings, and within the hour Krystin once again was standing before the Blood-Stained Sword. Myrmeen emerged from the building, shaking her head.

"What are we going to do?" Krystin asked.

"What else can we do?" Reisz said in annoyance. "We'll have to go to the next cache, that's what."

Myrmeen held the claim note. "They have it in their logs that I came here last night and retrieved my property with this. Gonzmart, the gentleman who was on duty last night, was fired this morning. They say he was drunk."

Krystin ran her hand over her face. "Maybe he took your things," she said, careful not to mention that she knew that it was gold they had come to retrieve.

"I doubt that a drunkard could have slipped into our rooms last night," Myrmeen said.

"Unless he had an accomplice," Reisz said. "Go back in and tell the day manager, Myrmeen. We may never see your gold again, but the Harper in me wishes to see justice done."

"Does it matter?" Krystin said nervously. She had decided that intimating the guilt of the night guard would avert attention from herself, but she had not stopped to think of the consequences. If the man were caught, he would be able to identify her.

"He took what was mine," Myrmeen said. "If this were Arabel, he would see damned quick exactly how much that matters."

"I understand," Krystin said, "but wouldn't he have left Calimport by now? Or at least found a hideout that he knew was secure? We could spend days trying to find him—"

"She has a point," Erin Shandower said, breaking the long silence that had suffused the others.

"I agree," Ord said as he turned to look at Krystin. "Our mission is not to capture and punish common thieves. My mother and father did not give their lives so that we could waste the time they purchased for us with their blood."

For a time, no one spoke. Ord's words had struck deep within the hearts of Myrmeen, Shandower, and the Harpers. Krystin felt an elation that was difficult to hide when Myrmeen finally hung her head and whispered, "We shouldn't have made it so easy for the thief in the first place."

Reisz frowned and looked away. "Let's move on. We'll be more careful next time."

The group remained together in a tight formation as they made the journey back to the inn, where their mounts were tethered. The streets already were filled with people, and Krystin wondered if there ever was a time when Calimport truly slept. The people of the city seemed to maintain shifts to keep the busy trade streets bustling at all times. The Harpers merged with the crowds whenever possible. On a barren street they would have attracted attention, but here they were invisible.

They passed street performers who sang of sad, mournful times, then collected the guilt and sympathy of the crowds in the form of their loose change. A contortionist executed a bone-snapping arrangement of his limbs that had the two dozen men and women gathered about him clapping and shouting in approval. Krystin watched a dark-skinned young man place a series of towering obstacles in his way. He approached them with a running start and vaulted over them, one after another, without touching them with any part of his body. The display was impressive, and Krystin felt a slight flush in her cheeks as she watched the young man's sweaty body as he spiraled in midair and surmounted each obstacle with matchless grace. Moments later the boy walked past her and the musky scent of him made her weak for an instant.

She did not know why the sight of him had affected her so strongly. She had never felt much of an interest in boys; most of those she had met were not worth her time. Nevertheless, since Ord had been paying her such close attention, Krystin had found herself thinking about them with increasing regularity.

Krystin suddenly felt a sharp tug at her waist. She looked down in time to see a curved blade slicing at the golden threads of her waist sash with practiced ease.

"No!" she shouted, realizing that she was about to fall victim to one of the city's many thieves. Twisting away from the blade, not caring if she was cut by its razor-sharp edge, Krystin unwittingly helped the thief slice open her waist sash. There was a slight ripping noise that was absorbed by the sounds of the crowd in the marketplace, and the fistful of gold that she had sewn into the lining rained down to the paved street. With a cry of agony, Krystin dropped to her knees, searching desperately for the emerald locket, which might have fallen as well.

"Krystin!" Myrmeen shouted in genuine distress. All she had seen was Krystin doubling over, as if she had been stabbed. From the periphery of her vision Myrmeen thought she had seen the pale gray arc of a steel blade slicing through the air like a hawk closing in for the kill.

Then she saw the gold at Krystin's feet. A frenzy had already begun. Strangers coalesced on the spot, dropping to their hands and knees to snatch at the gold pieces that were scattered on the ground. Hanging from the girl's sash was the emerald locket that Myrmeen had refused to purchase the day before. Myrmeen snatched the locket from her daughter's waist. Krystin looked up and parted with a wail of sheer agony that brought the crowd to an abrupt, eerie silence.

"Come with me," Myrmeen said. Grabbing Krystin's limp body by the arm, she lifted the girl into the air and set her on her feet as if she were a child just learning to walk. The Harpers tried to hurry away from the pocket of rapidly swelling attention that they had caused. Only the intervention of the swarthy-skinned acrobat had kept the people from following them as if they were the newest attraction.

"Another show," he announced, his gaze following Krystin. She was too grief-stricken to respond with anything more than a tear-filled nod of gratitude. Within minutes the Harper group was far from the crowd, but Myrmeen had no interest in talking to the girl until she had her alone. They arrived at the stables and Myrmeen ordered the others to remain behind while she dragged Krystin inside and found a recently vacated stall. The stench of dung rose to Krystin's nose and made her cough.

Myrmeen held up the locket as if it were a totem of her power over the young woman. "Explain this."

"Give it back," Krystin said, her gaze riveted to the emerald surface. All of her strength was suddenly devoted to restraining the urge to leap at the woman. The palms of her hands became clammy.

"This means so much to you," Myrmeen said in a tired, distant voice. It was the same voice that had pronounced death, life imprisonment, or worse in her tribunal of justice.

Krystin recognized the tone in her voice. Myrmeen had become detached. "I'll tell you where the rest of your gold is buried if you give me back the locket."

"Why don't you try taking it from me? You took what was mine without a second thought last night. Why should this be any different?"

"I had to have it," Krystin said. "You don't understand."

"You're right, I don't."

"What is it you want?" Krystin said, amazed by the tears that were leaking from the corners of her eyes. "If you want me to leave, I'll go. Just give me the locket."

"This bauble is more important to you than learning the

truth?"

Krystin was suddenly struck with a new vision, one of a scarred, black-haired man with rotten teeth. He raised the shattered leg of a table over his head and was about to bring it down on her face. Instinctively, she backed away and cowered, her hands rising up to ward off the blow in the manner of a frightened child, not a trained warrior.

"I'm not going to hit you," Myrmeen said.

Suddenly Krystin remembered where she was. The disquieting vision had faded. Myrmeen handed the locket to Krystin. "Take it. If it means so much more to you than the trust I've placed in you, then go ahead."

The young woman did not hesitate. She snatched the locket from Myrmeen's hand. The metal was surprisingly cold and offered little comfort as she watched Myrmeen walk away. The sight infused her with a sudden panic. She did not wish to be left alone.

"I'll retrieve the rest of the gold," Krystin said.

Myrmeen did not stop.

"Just give me a chance. I'll go to the owner of the Blood-Stained Sword and confess," Krystin pleaded.

"As you will," Myrmeen said, her voice hollow. She had not slowed.

Clutching the locket, Krystin hurried after her. "I won't lie to you ever again!"

Myrmeen stopped dead, her body tensing. "Two out of three, child. I'll believe two out of three."

They walked on in silence, the fragile bond between them strained almost to breaking.

Thirteen

 Lord Sixx and his guest were seated at a table in the Gentleman's Hall. The oddities of his flesh were hidden from the casual observer by one of his many sets of eyes, which he used to influence the manner in which he was perceived.

"Is that the one? The boy?" Sixx asked.

The fat man with gnarled hands and blackened teeth shook like a dying mare with palsy. His fear was all-encompassing; he did not seem capable of lying. Nevertheless, Lord Sixx would have felt more comfortable if he could have entered the man's mind and learned his secrets directly. The best time to have attempted this would have been when the man was asleep and fully relaxed. Once inside his mind, Sixx could have manipulated the man's dreams and forced him to reveal any truth he desired to witness. The man would have awakened and thought nothing of the fact that he could not recall his dreams; such occurrences were common. He would not have known that his dreams had been stolen, that they now belonged to Lord Sixx. Sixx was a generous man, however, and he would have left nightmares for the man to feast upon in the years to come.

There was, in truth, an element of danger to this enterprise, which explained why he chose instead to accept the fat man's words. Once he would not have hesitated to overpower a man's will and invade his conscious mind; he would have looked upon the exercise as an adventure into the unknown, a grand hunt wherein he was the predator stalking his prey through the landscape of their very thoughts. Ten years ago, he would have laughed at the risks involved, for if the prey turned on him and Sixx was killed on the psychic landscape, he would die in reality, too. Today, Lord Sixx, ruler of the night people, consummate master of nightmares and terror, had trouble sleeping.

He needed the belief of his people, the unvarying surrender of their wills to his own. Without belief he would survive, but he would not grow and prosper. Inevitably, a day would come when rivals would try to slay him, just as he had slain his predecessor.

Lately, a significant portion of his time had been spent listening to oily little men like this one, then spending valuable time ascertaining whether or not their claims of dissent within the ranks of the Night Parade were valid. If he found a potential rival, he eliminated the threat. His role as leader of the Night Parade had never been in question. Under his unyielding command, the Night Parade had prospered and become a unified force that existed to best serve the needs of all its people. Their profits were measured not only in human wealth, but also in the contentment of their burgeoning numbers, who were flocking to this place called Faerun at a growing rate.

There is one threat you seem content to ignore, a voice within his mind called out. Imperator Zeal. He has the love and the will of the people within his fiery grasp.

Zeal is not an ambitious man, Sixx countered.

That doesn't matter. His wife, the widow Tamara, hates you. You know why. When you fall—when you are pushed—Zeal will have no choice but to fill the vacancy you will leave.

Do not delude yourself. No one can be trusted. Even your own blood will one day turn on you.

Lord Sixx knew who owned that voice within his skull. The voice had belonged to his father, the man from whom Sixx stole the many eyes that covered his body.

"May I go now?" the man asked.

Lord Sixx was shocked back to reality. He sat at a table with the greasy little man, who seemed to want payment of some kind for his services. Distracted, Lord Sixx slipped a gold piece into the man's sweaty hand, then ordered him to leave at once. If he had been feeling more himself, he would have smiled terribly and told the man that his payment was his life, which Sixx was graciously allowing him to keep. He looked up and realized that the fat man had already gone. Of late, his entire existence seemed to be made up of missed opportunities. That would change, now that he had the information he so desperately required.

Sixx rose from the table, snaked through the crowded hall, and entered Pieraccinni's quarters without being announced. The bald man was busy entertaining a new, young assassin from Sembia. He had already liberated her from most of her clothing and was preparing to show her exactly what was expected of her in her new position when Sixx appeared. The woman stared at him brazenly, her lack of clothing no great concern. Suddenly her expression softened and changed, fear overtaking her bravado. She lowered her gaze, gathered her silk dress, and ran from the room, leaving through the private exit. Lord Sixx allowed the illusion of humanity cloaking him to fall away.

"Lord Sixx," Pieraccinni said, nearly falling as he slipped back into his leathers. "I was not expecting you—"

"Summon the boy," Sixx commanded.

Pieraccinni froze. "Pardon me, sir?"

"The boy. Your servant. The one you call Alden McGregor. Summon him. I hunger for truth."

"Milord, you know what the boy is to me. You can't—"

"Summon him or I will cause you unimaginable pain." Sixx

snarled.

Pieraccinni dropped to one knee before his master and swallowed hard. "I will."

* * * * *

Alden had been at the bar, trying to win the heart, or at least the body, or a fresh young serving maid. When he responded to Pieraccinni's summons and entered the room, his cheeks were still flushed. He was surprised when the doors leading to the hall and the servant's entrance slammed shut, seemingly of their own accord.

Turning, Alden saw the tall man with many eyes. He felt as if he had been trapped in a sudden, unexpected downpour, with no place to go that would offer shelter from the storm. He could tell from the man's expression that Lord Sixx knew the truth. There was nothing he could say in his defense. With a speed that neither member of the Night Parade had anticipated, Alden leapt at Pieraccinni, snatched the dagger from his scabbard, and threw the weapon at where he had seen Lord Sixx instants before.

The blade cut through the red curtains of Pieraccinni's fourposter bed, then struck the soft mattress, its flight arrested and cushioned by the comfortable bed. Before Alden could turn, he felt an incredibly strong hand grip his shoulder from behind. His flesh was squeezed so tightly that he was not surprised to feel the sharp tips of Sixx's fingers bite through his clothing and enter his flesh. Alden howled in pain as he was forced to his knees. His scream was cut short as Lord Sixx slammed the boy's head into the edge of Pieraccinni's desk with enough force to knock him out, but not enough to kill him. Alden fell in a heap at Lord Sixx's feet.

"What do you plan to do with him?" Pieraccinni asked. The bald merchant knew that he could not defend the boy, as much as he would have liked to, despite Alden's crimes.

"I wish to make him dream," Lord Sixx said as he unlaced the leathers at his neck and exposed the twin sets of jade green eyes, the Eyes of Domination. Lord Sixx touched Alden's face and closed all but one of his many sets of eyes; that pair trained its wary gaze on the bald man.

Several minutes passed as Pieraccinni anxiously watched Lord Sixx's face. The black-haired man frowned occasionally, smiled, and laughed more than once. Finally his eyes came half open and he whispered, "Glorious."

"Then you have learned all you need to know," Pieraccinni said, still trying to absorb the awful shock of learning that Alden, the one he had trusted the most, had been the one who had betrayed him.

"I have," Lord Sixx said, running his hand along his mouth unconsciously, as if he had just partaken of a feast. The answers were so simple that he felt ashamed he had not guessed them sooner.

"What are you going to do with him now?"

Lord Sixx smiled enigmatically. "What I should have done a long time ago," he said as he once again reached down and touched Alden's face. Alden began to twist uncomfortably, mumbling words of denial and a final scream of agony before his body went limp and his breathing became shallow. "Have him cleaned and tended. I want him alive and healthy. If we are to recover the apparatus and punish the Slayer, this must be done."

"Yes, milord. So it shall be."

"When Alden wakes, he'll know what he has to do. Give him anything he asks for. His words are mine."

As Lord Sixx merged with the shadows and disappeared, Pieraccinni looked down at the pale, blond youth and fell to his knees. He took Alden's head in his lap and caressed it gently as he began to weep.

* * * * *

The journey to Heaven's Lathe, the largest outdoor eatery in Calimport, had taken two hours. Myrmeen and her companions had put up their mounts at a nearby stable and walked the rest of the way as the sun began to sink in the sky, casting a reddish hue on the travelers. Krystin walked beside Ord, the only member of the party who would speak to her. She brazenly wore the emerald locket around her neck.

Reisz had taken Krystin's place at Myrmeen's side. The swarthy-skinned warrior was severely distressed by the growing rift between mother and daughter; the two women now regarded each other as strangers, their familial pretenses no longer worth the effort for either of them. Erin Shandower had taken the point and Lucius had used his magic to become invisible.

The Lathe was nothing more than a series of tents that would be blown down if struck by a severe storm. Under the flaps of canvas lay, as the owners were fond of saying, "a little piece of heaven for the weary traveler." The eatery specialized in exotic dishes, and the clientele was always a vast mixture. Those who ate at the Lathe ranged from the poor, who found the prices for simple dishes within their means, to the rich, who expected and always found some new and delectable meal with an irresistibly exorbitant price. The Lathe also catered to traders from other cities, even other nations, whose faces lit up in delight when they found even the most obscure dishes from their homelands served routinely. On the rare occasion when a dish could not be found at the Lathe, the cooks would listen patiently to the requests of their patrons and create the meal to the customer's satisfaction.

Alden supped here regularly and so it had been chosen as the evening rendezvous four times a week. As they were afraid he would attract too much attention if he came there every night, alternate locations were in place for the other evenings. Lucius had the task of making contact with the lad, who regularly flirted with a particular serving maid. Alden had not, by his own admission, had any luck in persuading her that he was different from the hordes of randy men who propositioned her every night, though she had admitted that he was younger and a bit more handsome than most.

Myrmeen and her companions split into separate groups,

with Shandower dining alone, Reisz joining Myrmeen, and Ord staying close to Krystin. Myrmeen was the first to spot Alden. Once again he was speaking to the serving maid with honey-blond hair and soft gray eyes. This time, though, his manner seemed a bit less gentlemanly. The slap he received confirmed that he apparently had grown tired of waiting and had asked directly for what he desired. He laughed as she stalked off.

At a nearby table, several mercenaries from the eastern nations, many of whom could not even speak Common, had understood the boy's plight and had raised their tankards in a friendly salute. Smiling, he approached their table and suddenly stopped, his head snapping back as if someone had taken a handful of his shirt from behind and given his entire body a firm yank. Turning he stumbled away from the table and soon was deposited in a chair a dozen yards away.

Myrmeen lost interest in the sight. She had seen it too many times. Lucius would find out if Alden had learned anything of value, then join her when the conference was at an end. The serving maid who had slapped Alden arrived at her table, and Reisz gestured for Myrmeen to order first.

Within shouting distance of Myrmeen and Reisz, Shandower sat at his solitary table and watched the Lhal woman's light, easy manner. Despite the horrors she had witnessed in recent days, including the deaths of two of her oldest and closest friends, she was able to laugh and smile as if she were back in Arabel, with servants tending to her needs. He did not understand how she could feel so at ease in a city that was infested with nightmares given flesh and form. Shandower wondered if her demeanor was nothing more than a carefully created sham put in place to hide the terror she continued to battle when she tried to sleep.

They all had heard her moans and pleas in the night. By tacit agreement, no one had mentioned this to Myrmeen. She would have been embarrassed and may have lost several nights' sleep worrying about what she might whisper when the nightmares came. He glanced at her again, and for the first time realized what a beautiful woman she was. Gazing at Myrmeen, he suddenly became uncomfortably aware of the great void in his life.

With that thought, he drained the sweet ambrosia that had been delivered to his table in one swift gulp and immediately regretted his rashness. The alcohol shot to his brain and he felt as if he were being lifted out of his chair, his toes and tongue tingling with the touch of a thousand needles. His skin turned cold suddenly, and his heart raced in his chest.

Shandower caught sight of the serving maid that had brought his ale and realized that he had never seen her before. The girl grinned at him, parted her lips slightly, and allowed a forked, leathery tongue similar to that of a lizard to emerge from her mouth. It wriggled slightly, then she sucked it back between her lips. He tried to scream, but his throat seized up and he found that he could not swallow, and could barely breathe. He had been poisoned. Shandower focused his will, and his gauntlet began to glow.

At the table where Krystin and Ord sat, a covered dish was delivered to the table. The fourteen-year-old had been despondent, losing track of their conversation on several occasions as she stared at the emerald locket's hard surface.

"Krystin," Ord said, "am I boring you?"

She glanced up from the locket, her eyes only half open, as she heard a noise from the table. For a moment she thought the serving dish had moved of its own accord, then she dismissed the thought as ludicrous.

"No, of course you're not boring me," she said. "I'm sorry. I must be terrible company. Do you want to sup with the others?"

"You're not getting rid of me that easily," he warned. "I intend to recite the tale of how I was first indoctrinated into the Harpers at our secret base in Berdusk, the Twilight Hall, as many times as it takes to get a smile from you, even if it's one that's totally manufactured."

Without warning, he reached over and gently touched the corner of her mouth, causing her to smile broadly and look down in embarrassment. She heard the lid of the covered dish slide a few inches, then convinced herself that she was hearing sounds from another table.

"I got it the first time," she said. "Storm Silverhand did not realize that the floors had been mopped, and as she approached to pin the symbol of the Harpers upon your breast— the silver harp sitting within the crescent of a silver moon—she slipped and impaled you with it. Thus you earned your first scar in the service of the Harpers."

"It was an auspicious beginning, I was told by Burke."

"I fully agree," she said, reaching for the covered dish. Her mind did not register that the dish shuddered ever so slightly before her hand closed upon the lid's knob. She drew the curved metal covering from the plate and revealed a pair of intertwined, pulsating abominations. The creatures turned their lazy heads in Krystin's direction as she screamed.

Less than a hundred feet away, at the table that appeared to be occupied solely by a young man who spoke discreetly to himself, a second man suddenly appeared. The shock of Krystin's scream had destroyed the concentration Lucius needed to maintain his spell of invisibility. The mage cursed himself for committing such an amateurish mistake and immediately restored the magic that kept him unseen. The momentary lapse was all that Alden had needed. His blade was drawn and already slicing through the air before Lucius had completed his spell. A second after Cardoc disappeared, Alden plunged the blade deep into the man's chest and a spray of blood spattered the clean white tablecloth. Lucius reappeared, his fingers moving, his lips shaking as he tried to complete another spell in a hushed whisper. The blade had missed the mage's heart and was lodged just below that vital organ. Alden reached up and twisted the blade, causing Lucius to bellow in agony as he fell forward, the weight of his body driving the blade deeper into his chest. His hands clawed the tablecloth, which now contained an ever-widening blossom of rose-red blood, and he fell to the ground, the cloth falling upon him like a shroud.

"Assassins!" Alden shouted as he stumbled back, the word drawing the undivided attention of the visiting mercenaries, traders and wanderers who had gathered for eveningfeast. Although the word had been spoken in Common and had counterparts in almost every language, the sight of Lucius Cardoc's still form, covered by the white sheet that was now soaked red, conveyed the meaning all too well. Hundreds of people bolted from their chairs and a panic erupted. Soldiers from the east spied emissaries from rival countries and attacked them without warning, deciding that they were the assassins in question. Once new blood was drawn, a frenzy began. Drawn swords, oaths to gods, and promises of agonizing death filled the outdoor eatery. Minor scuffles and disagreements sprang up as the walkways became congested with people trying to escape the random knife or arrow that certainly would be loosed by the assassins.

Only a handful of people within the crowd understood that there were no assassins; not the sort that had been imagined, anyway. These individuals were capable of the same emotions as the humans that flooded past, but, in truth, they were not human. They were emissaries of the Night Parade, and their moment of retribution had come.

Two members, a red-haired man whose flesh was covered in sweat and a lissome, dark-haired woman with eyes that housed terrible secrets, stood together in the shadows provided by the tents housing the chefs and their delicacies. The couple held hands and watched as their hand-picked warriors needled their way through the crowd and found Erin Shandower lying on the ground. The Slayer had been kicked and stepped on by the crowd that was hurrying to leave the killing ground.

Shandower had retained consciousness despite the toxins in his system. The gauntlet that was fused to his flesh burned with a blinding, blue-white luminescence. Cords of green energy erupted from his clenched fist and wove themselves about his body. He looked as if he were being attacked by an army of snakes composed of emerald fire. The crackling green strands of energy disappeared within his flesh, and his body was racked with convulsions. After a few seconds, the shuddering stopped and Shandower rose, his face pale, his legs uncertain. The magic of the apparatus had burned the poison from his body. He was jostled by several members of the panicked crowd, then he raised his glowing fist into the air and shouted, "Come for me now, you bastards!"

He was only vaguely aware of the figure that suddenly appeared at his back and the whistling of a sword through the air. Shandower heard something fall, a heavy object that dropped into a sack. Then he looked at his left arm and saw that his hand and half of his forearm were no longer there. The stump that remained spurted blood. Fighting off a tide of nausea, Shandower shoved his right hand over the wound, applying as much pressure as he could. The blood continued to flow, but not as quickly.

He turned to find the pair of monsters who had taken his weapon, wondering why they had not taken his head rather than his hand. A giddy excitement overcame him as he found himself sliding down into shock. Shandower congratulated himself on the calm manner in which he was taking the loss of his hand, the butchering of his body. In another moment, he was certain, he would start laughing, then the screaming would begin.

Suddenly another figure was beside him, a man.

"Shandower!" Reisz cried, his initial shock quickly fading as he grabbed a tablecloth, tore off several strips, and wrapped them around the man's bloody stump. Reisz hastily created a tourniquet by tying the edges around the wound and pulling them tight. He quickly explained that Myrmeen had left him to check on Krystin.

"Our guard was relaxed," Shandower said as he fought off the rising delirium that threatened to overcome him. "We didn't think they would attack in public, when it was light."

"They're still here," Reisz hissed. "There's no time."

Despite his pain, Shandower understood. They had to retreat as quickly and efficiently as possible.

"Join the crowd," Shandower said. "We must retrieve my weapon. Without it—"

"Stop talking. I'll get it," Reisz said as he threw his arm around Shandower's back and helped the man. They merged with the flow of people still trying to escape the pockets of violence that bloomed throughout the court.

At a more remote table, Myrmeen had arrived to find Krystin and Ord fighting for their lives against a pair of skinless monstrosities. Startled, Myrmeen saw that the creatures appeared to grow and diminish as they fought to rake open the throats of her daughter and the thin, brown-haired young man who tried to act as her defender. The inhuman creations that attacked the young pair looked like men whose flesh had been stripped from their bones then replaced with rotted chunks of spoiled meat. Their eyes burned with a dull, blood-red glow. Ord swung his sword in wide arcs, keeping the monsters at bay, while Krystin stood ready with a pair of daggers. A man lay at their feet, apparently an innocent who had wandered into the creatures' path in his attempt to flee.

Myrmeen noticed that Krystin's arm was bleeding from a very deep gash. The artery had not been severed, but the wound was a serious one. The girl looked as if she might faint at any moment.

Shouting her daughter's name, Myrmeen launched herself at the closest of the abominations, drawing her sword in midstride. She dropped to her knees and swung her sword at the monster's knees as the creature lashed out with its talons.

A sharp crack filled the air as Myrmeen's sword hit home, biting through the bone and cartilage of her victim's right knee and the hard, leathery muscle of its left thigh. Neither limb was severed outright, but the creature toppled backward as Myrmeen yanked her bloody sword from the monster. Before she could cross to the second creature, who had not allowed its partner's distress to deter it from its mission, Ord rushed forward, stepping between the creature still standing and Myrmeen, raised his own sword, and brought it down on the fallen abomination's neck.

"Krystin!" Myrmeen shouted helplessly. Because of Ord, the creature would be upon the girl before Myrmeen could reach her. For an instant her gaze locked with that of her daughter. The absolute dread that Myrmeen felt at the thought of losing the girl whom she had gone through so much to find—the child who eventually might fill the empty hollow that passed for her heart—translated into an expression of undistilled love and primal fear. The expression startled Krystin, but she quickly recovered and moved forward to deal with the threat from which her mother could not save her.

In those critical seconds, as the monster raced at her, Krystin reacted as she had been trained to by Myrmeen. She bent her legs slightly at the knee and planted them with exactly the right amount of space between her feet. Then she flipped both of her blades so that she held them by the sharp, cold metal of their flats. Staring at the creature's eyes, she launched the daggers. Her wound made her flinch as she released them and only the first blade struck true, piercing the soft red orb of the creature's left eye. The second blade opened a bloody rivulet across the right side of its face, then clattered to the ground. The skinless creature threw its head back and howled in pain.

Myrmeen finally made her way past Ord and the member of the Night Parade that he had dispatched. Krystin was weaponless. Before the half-blind creature could retaliate for Krystin's attack, Myrmeen drove her sword through its torso. The dying thing grabbed the blade's hilt, and Myrmeen sawed it back and forth until the creature released its grip and fell back to lie beside its dead partner.

She wondered why it had been so easy to kill this pair. Compared to the monsters they had faced in the alley behind the counting house, these two seemed like little more than a distraction, though a potentially lethal one.

Ord stood, pleased with himself. "That's one less of those murdering bags of filth that we have to—"

"Shut up," Myrmeen said, her chest heaving. Ord fell silent in surprise, a hurt expression clouding his features. He had stopped Myrmeen from getting to Krystin and she had nearly been killed because of him. Krystin, however, had not died. She had performed like a warrior. Myrmeen turned to her daughter. "I'm very proud of you."

Krystin was speechless. Myrmeen shook her head and added, "Come on. We have to see to the others."

Suddenly a high-pitched scream erupted from the opposite side of the court. Myrmeen looked up and noticed that, except for the men who had started fights with other humans, the number of people at the Lathe had thinned out considerably. She was able to see two nondescript men standing near a heavy bag glowing blue-white. The first man looked down at his hands as if they had betrayed him. Collapsing to his knees before the bag, the man slumped forward and landed to the parcel's side. His partner, a heavier man who carried a recently blooded broadsword, looked down at the bag in alarm. When a tongue of green fire cut through the heavy sack and licked at the air before the second man's face, he turned and ran.

"The gauntlet," Myrmeen whispered as she futilely scanned the area for signs of Shandower, Reisz, or Lucius. She assumed that if the Night Parade somehow had gained possession of Shandower's weapon, they had taken it from his corpse. If that were the case, she would need the arcane weapon to ensure her friends' safety as they retreated from Calimport and sought the Harpers in Berdusk for assistance. Her words were strident as she commanded, "Follow me."

Although many of the eatery's patrons had left the area, a large number had remained and had formed a circle of spectators, settling less than two hundred yards away. From their vantage, they could see all that transpired without exposing themselves to danger. Myrmeen looked at the members of the crowd, the quick-tempered fighters who had started a handful of brawls and continued to battle even now, oblivious to all else, and even the eatery's staff, who had come from the kitchen to watch the proceedings with interest. She knew that every person in the area could be a Night Parade abomination in human form.

A figure appeared before her. She raised her sword instinctively, then lowered it again as she saw the look of concern in the eyes of the boy whose hair was the color of sawdust.

"Alden," Myrmeen said in relief. The young man seemed unhurt, despite the flecks of blood on his shirt. Lucius had been with Alden, and memories of the mage rescuing them from the ambush behind the counting house flooded her mind. "Where's Lucius?"

Alden shook his head and glanced at the earth. "Dead."

Fourteen

The news struck her hard. Myrmeen thought of her private talk with Lucius and the revelation that he had a family that even the Harpers apparently knew nothing about. Who would tell them? she thought, and who would be there to comfort his children when they woke in the night? Myrmeen forced such thoughts away. She could not deal with them now.

"Where's his body?" she asked.

"I don't know," Alden replied innocently.

"Alden, we have to take Shandower's weapon and leave. Have you seen Erin or Reisz?"

"I haven't," Alden said, lying expertly.

Krystin touched Myrmeen's arm. "The glove was fused to his arm. If that's the glove, then his hand is still—"

"I know," Myrmeen said in disgust, "but it has to be done."

Breaking from the others, Myrmeen closed the distance separating her from the gauntlet, which had become encased in a sphere of blue-white energy that crackled with strands of green fire. The power within the glove was blossoming out of

173

control, and Myrmeen realized that Shandower had not been summoning the power, but had been holding it in check. She knelt before the weapon. The glove was empty. If they had taken his arm to separate him from the gauntlet, no trace of meat or bone remained. Myrmeen was afraid that her own flesh would melt away if she touched the arcane weapon, then decided that she had no choice if she was going to safeguard her daughter's life.

She reached out and touched the glowing metal. It was warm, but it did not burn her. Snatching the weapon from the ground, she turned and motioned for the others to follow.

"Alden, do you know a place where the Night Parade will not follow? They know about you now. It must be a place you would not normally go."

"Yes," he said absently. "I can think of a place." She took a step in his direction and he moved back suddenly, absently cutting a glance at the weapon in her hands. Krystin and Ord had not moved at all. Alden shuddered as he looked around. "I suppose we should get out of here before more of those things arrive."

"Hold this for me," Myrmeen said to Alden, her instincts alerting her that something was very wrong with the young man. She held out the gauntlet, and Alden shrank away, raising his hand before his face.

"Go on," Krystin urged. "Take it. What's wrong?"

"Nothing," Alden said softly, sweat breaking out on his pale skin. A blanket of ochre hung above the city, beneath the clouds, and a soft breeze had gathered at the companions' backs. Alden ground his hands together. "I don't want to touch it. I'm afraid."

"Why should you be afraid?" Ord asked, suspicious.

Unexpectedly, Alden ran, waving his right hand over his head. He was signaling someone, Myrmeen realized. She heard shouts and turned her attention to the crowd that had gathered nearby. A dozen men dressed in the armor of the local guard broke through the crowd, ordering them to disperse or face a penalty. The crowd broke up swiftly and the soldiers shouted a command that Myrmeen did not recognize as they broke into a dead run, charging at Myrmeen with weapons drawn. She turned to run and saw a half dozen men who had been fighting at another table standing close, bows drawn, arrows nocked.

They were trapped. Alden had stopped less than twenty yards from the group. He watched his former allies with his lips pressed together, his hands wringing anxiously, his expression dark and cold.

"This could have been simple," he said. "Why didn't you just go along? They promised it would be quick, no pain. But they needed a human to carry the glove."

His fingers were twitching so quickly that they had become a blur. Alden shifted back and forth on his heels, moving with such incredible speed that he seemed to wink out of existence in one position and reappear in another. His teeth chattered, and his body shook with his inner conflict. He struggled not to say the words that had been left in his mind by Lord Sixx, but failed.

"My masters have instructed me to give you a message before you die," he said. "Death is only the beginning. We will take your souls and they will live on in torments worse than any found in Cyric's kingdom."

"Bastard!" Krystin shouted as she flung herself at Alden. Ord grabbed her by the shoulders and held her back, noticing the bloody gash in her arm for the first time. The soldiers were coming closer.

Ord glared at the young man. "What about your fancy words—sticking with your own kind?"

Alden smiled. "That's exactly what I'm doing."

Myrmeen thought of the ceremony they had performed, with all the Harpers touching the gauntlet. Alden had revealed himself afterward and had never touched the weapon.

The blond youth's expression suddenly changed. His cruel sneer dropped away and was replaced by a desperate, frightened look. "I only learned of my true blood today," he said in a strangled cry before he turned and ran off, leaving them to face their enemies alone.

"We're going to die here," Ord said without emotion.

Beside him, Krystin fingered her locket, anger and frustration overriding her fear of death. The mysteries of her past would go unresolved. Standing in front of Krystin, Myrmeen stared at the gauntlet in her hand. Her body quivered as she slipped her left hand inside the glove and felt a sudden surge of energy rush into her body.

The soldiers of the guard stopped four yards away. Several had raised their faceplates, revealing their inhumanity. They were Night Parade beasts, using the armor to disguise their true appearance. The sight of the glove on Myrmeen's hand made the soldier in the lead raise his hand and issue another command in their strange language.

The archers, she thought, and knew that within seconds she would be dead, her heart pierced by an arrow.

Instead, she heard the roar of thunder and saw a brilliant flash of light. Before her, the soldiers covered their eyes. She turned as the light, as bright and strong as an exploding sun, suddenly faded, and she saw that the archers had been incinerated. A hundred feet behind them stood three figures. One of them, a man, had red hair and spheres of flame for hands. Behind him were two others. Myrmeen recognized only one of them. "Lucius!" she screamed.

The mage's hand was upon the throat of a tall, dark-haired woman. His features were contorted in pain and he struggled to maintain his concentration. Although he had no weapon, he had his spells, and Myrmeen guessed that he had spoken all but the last syllable of a spell that would, if completed, take off the woman's head at the neck. Lucius's clothing was soaked with his own blood and he barely had the strength to stand. By threatening the woman, Lucius had turned the fire lord into a weapon for the humans.

The red-haired man turned and raised his hands in the direction of the second battery of warriors, those dressed in the armor of the local guard, obviously intent on burning them. Then the flames that had consumed his hands suddenly died away. His eyes rolled up into the back of his head, and he collapsed. Lucius stared at the doomed man in surprise. He had no idea what had caused him to fall like a marionette with cut strings. The woman Lucius held screamed and twisted out of his arms, no longer mindful of the mage's threat. She knelt beside her lover, taking his head in her hands. Her flesh suddenly became dark, covered with thick black hairs. When she looked up, her eyes were no longer human, but large, multifaceted blood-red ovals, and her teeth were longer, sharper. She forced down the change and became human once more as she registered that her husband was alive but unconscious. She pointed at the soldiers who hesitated before the group.

"They are the ones who have deprived us of our homes!" she screamed. "They are the ones who have driven us into the light. Take them, damn you, and feed upon their souls!"

Near where the archers had been burned Myrmeen saw that the soldiers needed no further urging. She glanced back to where Lucius had stood and realized that the mage had vanished. Then there was no more time for conscious thought. The energy trapped within the gauntlet spread through her, infusing her with a rage that bordered on madness. She did not bother drawing her sword; she knew that the glove was all she needed.

Eight members of the Night Parade advanced on her, faceplates down to hide their deformities and protect their vulnerable flesh from the magic radiated by the gauntlet. Myrmeen was vaguely aware that there were others with her. From the edge of her vision she noticed Krystin and Ord, who battled the creatures that surged around her. Myrmeen thrust out her leg and tripped one of the creatures. She drove her hand through its chest, the armor collapsing inward to worsen the damage to its body. The monster shuddered once, then was still. Before Myrmeen could free her hand from the corpse, she looked up to see a sword descending at her neck. Another sword intercepted the first mere inches from her flesh, the impact strong enough to push the defending blade against her neck, leaving a small cut.

She looked up and saw Ord grimace as he kicked at the armored stomach of the monster that had almost taken Myrmeen's head. Another creature flung itself at Ord, impaling itself on his blade as they both fell to the ground, the monster on top of Ord and still very much alive.

"Mother, save him!" Krystin shouted.

Myrmeen ignored the girl, even though she had heard the creature's inhuman squeals and had seen it beat and claw at Ord, whom it had pinned down with its weight. Rage colored her thoughts, fueled by the gauntlet's magic. Ord had nearly cost Krystin her life. Let him fend for himself.

Screaming, Myrmeen turned her back on Ord's dilemma. She described a wide arc with her brilliantly glowing hand, forcing several of the creatures back, then she plunged the weapon into the back of another soldier's head, this one approaching Krystin with a drawn sword. The creature convulsed as she withdrew her hand. Spinning, she realized that the monster Ord had impaled now was poised to crush his larynx with its heavy, misshapen hand. Her murderous thoughts cleared. She knew she had to help Ord, but too much distance separated them.

Krystin, closer by two yards, screamed a curse at Myrmeen and leapt at the creature's hand. She grasped the monster's wrist as she flipped in midair and yanked the hand in the other direction. There was a sharp crack as the bones in the monster's arm snapped and the sword impaling it was dragged several inches through its gut. Myrmeen ran for them and punched her fist through the wailing creature's faceplate. The beast shuddered and died quickly. Myrmeen dragged the body from Ord as another pair of creatures glanced at each other, hesitated as if evaluating their odds of survival, then ordered their comrades to retreat.

Myrmeen watched the creatures run. With considerable effort, Myrmeen forced the gauntlet's flames to recede. The fighter helped Ord to his feet and Krystin sprang at her.

"Get away from him!" Krystin screamed. "You were going to let him die!"

Krystin shoved her mother out of the way and took her place beside Ord. Myrmeen knew there was no time to argue or explain; that would have to come later. She led the others from the field of battle. They passed through several winding side streets, then came to the place the group had designated as a rendezvous in the event that they were ever attacked. Shandower and Lucius had insisted on these contingencies whenever they left the safe house. They entered the boarded-up temple, and Myrmeen nearly wept when she saw Reisz and Shandower waiting.

"Give it to me," Shandower hissed, pointing at the weapon with his remaining hand. The smell of burned flesh came to her suddenly and she realized that Reisz had made a small fire that they had used to cauterize Shandower's wound.

Myrmeen looked down and saw her flesh beginning to melt, her skin fusing with the weapon. She yanked the gauntlet from her arm, restraining a scream as small sections of her flesh were torn away. Shandower grasped the weapon and threw it to the floor.

"It's meant for the other hand," Krystin pointed out as she saw Shandower slide his hand into the glove, "It won't—"

There was an explosion of blue-white light and, when it faded, the gauntlet was snugly fit upon Shandower's remaining hand. Somehow, the weapon had reconfigured itself.

"Lucius?" Reisz asked.

"I don't know," Myrmeen said. "I pray he survived, but his injuries were great. He vanished at the battle. We couldn't search for him."

"We also can't stay here," Shandower said. "You may have been followed."

"We weren't," Ord said confidently. "I was checking the entire time."

Shandower laughed bitterly. A few backward glances and the boy felt secure. Shandower had been deprived of the magic from the apparatus for less than an hour, and in that time he had been overcome with the old, numbing fears. For a brief time he was able to see the threat of the Night Parade for what it had been all along, an unstoppable nemesis, an enemy that he could hold at bay for a time but never destroy. Now that he had the gauntlet back, he realized he had been foolish to entertain such dark, hopeless thoughts. His nose itched, and he raised his hand to scratch it.

The hand was no longer there. Grinning, Shandower set his head back and closed his eyes.

Myrmeen stared at his face and thought of the sensations that had coursed through her for the brief time that she had been empowered by the gauntlet: The magic had flowed through her, making her feel invulnerable, forcing away her fear and her doubts, helping her to focus on her single, driving goal, to destroy the Night Parade. Shandower was overcome by its power, she realized. If he had not been, he would have gone insane years ago.

Then she thought of Lucius, of the warm, caring man he had revealed himself to be. He would survive, she thought. He had to survive. Myrmeen shifted her gaze to Krystin, who held her arm where she had been wounded. Myrmeen went to the girl, pried her arm away from the gash, and realized that they were already risking infection.

"We have to clean and dress the wound," Myrmeen said.

"I'm fine," Krystin argued, looking to Ord for support. He shook his head and looked away. "Don't treat me like a child. Erin lost his arm, and he's not crying for help. I'll live, all right?"

"You'll live, both of you will, because I'm going to see that you get help," Myrmeen said.

"There's a healer I trust," Shandower said softly, "not far from here. We should see him before we leave the city. It seems we have stirred up too great a storm for even the Harpers to weather."

Suddenly, Myrmeen heard a scurrying in the shadows. She drew one of her blades and flung it in the direction of the sounds. A tiny squeal came from the temple's ruins. She walked past the overturned pews to find a dying rat in the corner. Shoving her boot against its quivering body, Myrmeen withdrew her knife.

Had she looked up, she would have seen a familiar pair of red eyes that she had glimpsed many times in nightmares.

"Rats," Myrmeen said. "They're everywhere."

The figure clinging to the ceiling moved carefully, making no sound as it crawled out through the broken skylight and vanished into the cold, clean air of twilight.

* * * * *

Lord Sixx had been watching the battle from a distance. All had not gone according to plan, but he had made the best of a steadily deteriorating situation. The humans knew they had been found out, and so their attacks against his people's lairs would end. This might have been enough to solidify his standing with his subjects, but the perpetrators had survived, and only their blood would answer the need he shared with his people for retribution.

There were easier ways to deal with them, of course, than the ones he had chosen so far. With the mage dead, they would be much more susceptible to his spies. All he had to do was find them in one place and have Imperator Zeal unleash his power upon them, as he had the archers during the battle.

Sixx grinned. Zeal had killed a half dozen of his own kind to protect his lover's life. He had made his personal allegiance very clear. If Lord Sixx had not used his own power to put Zeal down, he would have taken out the false members of the local militia, too. According to the stories Sixx had overheard concerning the battle this day, if Zeal had been a rival for his power, unwittingly or not, he had just lost his standing.

There were more pressing concerns for him to think about. He knew the Slayer's identity. His name was Erin Shandower, and many had seen his face. The man had been grievously injured. It was more than likely that he would retreat to the where he had secreted the apparatus. Sixx had driven the man to ground and would follow him as he went. Sixx found this course of action preferable to a direct confrontation with the man who had felt the energies of the apparatus circulating within his own body as if it were his life's blood.

Following would be difficult. The Night Parade would be expected. He felt like a fool for having allowed Alden to reveal himself. An ally within their ranks would prove invaluable just now.

Sixx thought of the girl. He remembered the distant manner in which she had treated the Lhal woman and the curse the girl had hurled at Myrmeen when the woman had not tried to save her Harper friend. She obviously was falling in love with the boy, though she had not yet admitted that to herself. The girl had proved herself in battle, and, more importantly, she had proved herself to be human. Alden had been an outsider. They would not expect betrayal from one of their own.

Ideas were forming in his mind when Tamara returned to him and told him what she had overheard at the temple. Alden had remained behind to continue the surveillance. Suddenly, Lord Sixx knew exactly how to manipulate events so that everybody would get what he or she wanted—everyone except the Harpers, who would die, but not before revealing their secrets to him. When this was over, his agents would track them across the Realms if need be and end their threat before it could even begin.

Fifteen

Myrmeen had hoped that Shandower would lead them to a cleric who could heal the torn flesh of her daughter's arm with a few simple spells. Instead, he had taken them to a run-down little house where they had suffered through a battery of questions from an obese, white-haired woman who wore a dowdy dress fifteen years out of style. Only when they had answered all her queries were they allowed access, despite Shandower's and Krystin's obviously severe wounds. Krystin had withdrawn into the shadowy world of her emerald locket.

Downstairs, the physician, a battlefield healer that Shandower once had given the money to retrieve his failing practice, cleaned and dressed Shandower's stump. The healer was in his late fifties. He had a hawklike nose, fine gray eyebrows, a heavily lined face, bushy white hair, and hands that were unusually long and thin. He had been ordered by the local officials to stop practicing medicine after he had refused to pay a tariff on his services. To all appearances he had retired, but he maintained a small practice in his cellar, behind a false wall. It was in that musty chamber that he was busy treating Shandower while the others waited upstairs.

Myrmeen sat beside Krystin, trying to think of something to say to her. That's your whole problem, she thought. Stop trying and just do it. Say whatever comes into your mind. You're certainly not going to offend her.

Myrmeen cleared her throat and said, "Even if you're left with a scar, that's not always such a terrible thing."

Krystin did not look up from the emerald locket.

"They can be marks of courage. I have several myself, each with its own story to tell." Myrmeen wondered if she was talking to herself. Krystin had honored her earlier promises regarding her theft at the Blood-Stained Sword: She had excavated and returned the remaining portion of gold to Myrmeen and confessed to the depository's owner, thus ensuring that criminal charges would not be filed against the former employee who had retrieved the gold for her.

The one thing she had not done, however, was return the locket. Strangely, it was her tenacity that had made Myrmeen begin to look beyond her own anger at the child's actions and start to wonder what it had been about the object that had driven the girl to such lengths.

Earlier that day, before they had left for Heaven's Lathe, Lucius had casually examined the locket and pronounced that it contained no magic. The object was nothing more than a chunk of metal whose seals were fused, its secrets hidden within its dented and cracked surface. Myrmeen had not excused Krystin's actions, but nearly losing the girl in battle, and her efforts to save herself, had awakened a sense of compassion that she had been forcing away for a long time.

"You did well, Krystin. I am proud of you and I will no longer doubt your abilities in a fight. Can you hear me?"

The girl nodded.

"Have you nothing to say?" Reisz added.

"Thank you," Krystin said absently. Her attention clearly was focused on the locket, her brow furrowed and covered in sweat. In frustration, Krystin allowed the locket to fall to her chest as she looked down at the gash in her arm. She felt nothing at all. Her body and mind were completely numb.

The rickety steps leading up from the cellar creaked several times, and the door opened. Shandower emerged and said it was Krystin's turn. Myrmeen had planned to go with her, but Krystin politely asked her to remain behind. She went through the doorway alone and descended to the cluttered cellar. The basement had become a dumping ground for old furniture, journals that had become damp and yellowed with age, toys that children born to loving and affluent parents would possess, and crates stuffed to bursting with old clothing, pots and pans, and more. A tarnished suit of armor rested in the corner, propped against the wall. A doorway that at first had not looked like an entrance was open, and orange light stretched out like a welcoming hand.

Krystin entered the small room. She saw a table with a white sheet thrown over it and several cabinets that were filled with herbs, vials of colored liquids, trays, and knives of every size and shape. The old physician—his name had not been given—stood with his back turned to Krystin. He was hunched over something on the small counter that had captured his attention. Krystin began to feel frightened as she recognized the distinctive smell of blood in the room.

The doctor turned, and Krystin felt her heart shrivel. His face was not human. Her thoughts slipped back to the night Alden first revealed himself to the Harpers and gained their trust. Alden had seen this man in Pieraccinni's chamber and had described him vividly. Krystin found him even more disturbing in real life. His face contained three sets of eyes, one set above and below the normal set. Lord Sixx reached up and tore off the long white smock he had been wearing. It was splattered with blood that she had thought belonged to Shandower and now realized had belonged to another. Before she could scream, a figure leapt from the shadows behind her and placed his cold hand over her mouth.

"I'm sorry," Alden whispered.

Lord Sixx advanced and clamped his powerful hands on her

shoulders. Alden withdrew as Sixx forced her back to the table, where he lifted her up and slammed her down with enough force to knock the air from her lungs. As Krystin tried to regain her breath, Alden secured her to the table with straps that had dangled over the sides. When she had been safely bound, Lord Sixx placed his hand over her mouth and ripped the locket from around her neck. The chain snapped, leaving a light welt on her throat. Krystin struggled to bite the flesh of his palm. As she tried to move her head from side to side, Krystin saw the healer's body in the corner of the small chamber, which was lighted by a pair of oil-burning lanterns. The man had been butchered. She tried to cry out, but her screams were muffled against his hand.

"You know who I am," Sixx said with a gentleness that surprised Krystin. Realizing that she could not break free, she ceased her struggles, hoping that she could lull Sixx into removing his hand long enough for her to attract help.

Dangling the emerald locket before her face, Lord Sixx whispered, "This bauble had special significance to you. It would be a shame to see it destroyed."

With a flick of his wrist, Lord Sixx slapped the locket into his palm and began to squeeze. Krystin's eyes grew wide with terror as she saw the locket begin to flatten. A look of absolute sadness crept into Lord Sixx's face. "I don't want to torment you. I don't want to give you pain. But I must be certain that you will at least hear me out."

Krystin's gaze was fixed on the locket. Lord Sixx allowed it to fall from his iron grip. It dangled once again by the chain. For a moment she became aware of the green of his primary set of eyes, the exact color of the emerald locket.

"I can make your nightmares vanish. I can give you the sweetest dreams of your life and make the visions that haunt you go away forever. But all this comes at a price." He frowned. "It is not a terrible price. I am willing to forgive the crimes you have committed against our people. Further, I will reward you by giving you that which you desire most. For you to trust me, however, you must be made to see that you have misjudged our people."

She could smell the corpse in the corner of the room.

"Humans hunt us because we are different. We are beyond their understanding. Without the apparatus, they cannot harm us. All we want is to be left alone. You can help us. In return, there is much I can give you. I know the secrets of your past. I have been inside your dreams. I will share all with you, even the significance of the locket, if you cooperate."

Krystin stared at the Night Parade's leader, a part of her so entrenched in her own needs and desires that it forced her to actually consider his offer. If she did not learn the truth and dispel the nightmarish visions that disturbed her waking hours, she would go insane. She was certain of this.

"I'm going to take my hand away from your mouth. If you scream, I will be forced to kill you and your sacrifice will be for nothing. There are more than a hundred of our kind gathered near this place. Twice that number will arrive before your friends can fight their way to safety. If you do not cooperate, they all will die. Nod if you understand."

Krystin shook her head and Lord Sixx removed his hand. She looked across at Alden, and said, "We trusted you."

The straw-haired young man turned away.

"Poor Alden," Lord Sixx said softly. "He never knew that the blood in his veins was not human. The boy is a hunter. He has senses that a wolf would envy. It was the gift of his mother, who is long dead. And he moves with the speed of the wind, the gift of his father, Dymas, who has been summoned from exile to rear him at last. Pieraccinni fancied himself the boy's father, but he could never bring himself to tell Alden the truth." Lord Sixx shrugged. "I think Pieraccinni enjoyed the company of humans far too—"

"What do you want of me?" Krystin said sharply.

"To the point. I like that. We'll work well together."

"I'll help you, but only if it will save the others."

"Oh," Lord Sixx said happily. "Very well. Then you don't want the rewards I have to bestow upon you." He dropped the locket on her chest. "You don't need to know where you came from, if Myrmeen Lhal is your mother or not."

Krystin hesitated. Slowly, like a stone wall with a hairline crack becoming wider until it shatters from immense pressure, her brave facade fell away and she began to cry.

In a tiny voice she asked, "What do you want from me?"

Lord Sixx turned her wounded arm until the gash faced outward. He motioned for Alden to come quickly. With a shamed expression, Alden crouched before the table and opened his mouth as Lord Sixx squeezed Krystin's arm until a few drops of her blood fell to Alden's flickering tongue.

Alden fell to his knees, covering his face. "I have her scent," he said. "I will not lose it."

"Very good," Lord Sixx said. "Return to the shadows. I taught you how. Do it."

Krystin watched as Alden retreated to the room's shadow-laden corner. His body appeared to become a silhouette, then he merged with the darkness and was gone.

Lord Sixx bent over her and gently caressed her hair. His breath stank. Removing his glove, he exposed to the pale yellow light three sets of eyes lining his forearm. They blinked repeatedly, then slowly opened their lids all the way as they adjusted to the luminescence. The different sets of eyes looked out in varying directions. Then he spoke:

"I will mend your wound, just as if the healer had done it himself. Tell Shandower that the old man ordered the lot of you to be gone. He will believe the words came from the ill-tempered man and will depart gladly. From time to time, wherever he takes you, reopen your wound and allow a drop or two of blood to fall. That is all you must do."

"You'll follow us."

"Safely, at a distance. There will be no further need for confrontation. When we get to where the apparatus is kept, we will take it and go."

"Shandower," she said, slurring the word as she began to feel drowsy. Sixx's many eyes were mesmerizing her, she realized, and she was allowing it to happen.

"Do not concern yourself with him. He knew the cost."

"But Myrmeen and the Harpers—"

"They will live. We have no wish to do them harm, Krystin. I will not lie to you."

His angular features twisted up in a smile that was meant to be comforting. Instead, it made Krystin's heart beat wildly as he brought his arm to her face and instructed her to stare at the eyes. She felt the haziness of dreams quickly overtake her, then heard him laugh as he said, "Now we shall see what we shall see. . . ."

Suddenly her world was draped in shadows. When she woke, she was alone in the room. Sixx was gone, along with the old healer's body. While she had slept, her dreams had revealed the truth. She sat up, the restraints once again dangling over the edge of the table, and heard the emerald locket clatter to the floor as it slid from her chest. Leaping off the table, she snatched it from the floor, examined its surface, and held it close to her breast.

She remained like that for a time, then rose and went upstairs to greet the others. Her wound had been dressed, and she was surprised to learn that she had only been absent for a matter of minutes.

Out of the corner of her eye she saw something move in the shadows—a reminder that not all of what she had experienced had been a dream. Dully, she recited the words Lord Sixx had given her, and Shandower laughed, not at all surprised that the old healer had evicted them. As they prepared to leave, Krystin held her locket before her. With trembling lips, she said, "My locket, the chain broke."

"I can fix that for you," Ord said. "Don't worry."

She nodded. As they left the house and became one with the night, Krystin found that worrying was the only task she still had strength to accomplish. As they carefully made their way through the streets, to the stables where their mounts and supplies waited, Krystin hurried and walked beside Myrmeen. Without a word, she put her arm around the woman's waist and rested her head on Myrmeen's shoulder.

Myrmeen had been shocked and had raised her hands. She

lowered them slowly and wrapped them around Krystin, practically dragging the girl with her as they walked along, wordless, into the deepening night.

*   *   *   *   *

Myrmeen squinted in the harsh light of the afternoon sun. They had left Calimport the previous evening and had been on what Shandower described as the Dead Run ever since. The route he had chosen once had been favored by traders trying to make time and avoid the blistering stretches of desert north of the city. They had come east, on a trail of land that ran parallel to the shoreline. The route was hazardous and the name it had been given was well deserved. On several occasions, the mounts had refused to move any farther. Shandower understood that they were approaching pockets of land that had been subtly altered by the magical and physical upheavals during the time of Arrival, when the gods had walked the Realms. An apparently safe patch of land could suddenly shift, like a sink hole, and swallow an entire party of travelers without a hint of warning.

Myrmeen looked past the winding, craggy cliff to the gulf below. The waters were choppy and the afternoon sun sparkling on the surface dispelled the initial impression that the sea was as hard as glass. A hazy band of white gathered at the horizon, separating the vast expanse of the Shining Sea from the distant sky. As her mount carried her through the difficult path Shandower had chosen, Myrmeen closed her eyes and imagined that she was home in Arabel, lying in her scented bath with delicate tongues of water caressing her flesh. A high squeal of laughter from behind her sent the fantasy scurrying from her mind, and she opened her eyes to the blinding sunlight. Her skin was covered in sweat from the sweltering heat. She smelled foul, and she hated it.

Shandower rode point, Reisz had been beside her, and Krystin had been riding with Ord for the past two hours. The young Harper had honored his promise and fixed the chain on her emerald locket the previous evening, when they had stopped for the night. He had used the cooking fires to fuse the metal together, a crude but serviceable solution that had delighted the fourteen-year-old.

"Keep aware, you two!" Reisz shouted. His words were met with even more laughter. The Harper shook his head sourly as he turned to Myrmeen. "They never listen."

"Perhaps that's just as well," Myrmeen said with a weariness that made her sound and feel older than her thirty-four years. "I don't think Krystin's ever had the chance just to be a child, not to have to worry about survival."

"Ord has never had that chance either," Reisz said.

"I should ask her about it. In all the time we've been together, I've never allowed her to be herself. I think I've been putting expectations on her. You understand, it's as if I've been saying to her, 'This is what I want my daughter to be. If you don't measure up, well, then, I suppose you can take the next caravan out.' "

"Were you allowed to be a child?" he asked.

She laughed. "Most of my adult life, it seems." With a sigh, she added, "Reisz, I don't know what to do."

The swarthy-skinned Harper looked over his shoulder and said, "For one thing, you could tend to that situation before it gets even more out of control."

Myrmeen had no idea what he was talking about. Glancing back in the direction he had indicated, Myrmeen was stunned to see Krystin and Ord riding side by side, their mounts close enough that they were able to hold hands as they rode. Krystin brought Ord's hand to her lips and kissed it gently.

A hammer blow to the forehead would have been less jarring to Myrmeen. She looked away and gripped the reins of her mount so tightly that her knuckles became white.

"How long has this been going on?" she asked.

Raising an eyebrow, Reisz said, "How long have they known each other? You, of all people, couldn't see what was going on?"

Swallowing hard, Myrmeen said, "I thought they were just

friends. I wanted her to have someone she could confide in. She certainly wasn't embracing me in that regard."

"You weren't doing much to encourage her, Myrmeen. And I don't believe you had much to do with this situation either—other than pushing Krystin away whenever she needed you, that is."

Myrmeen tensed. "Have you forgotten she stole from us?"

"She stole from you. Perhaps it was the only way to get your attention."

"Strange words, coming from a Harper."

"The situation is not exactly normal, Myrmeen. Perhaps when we stop next to make sure we are not being followed, I'll take Ord to the side and give him a few gentle urgings about how he should conduct himself with impressionable young ladies, and you can have a discussion with Krystin."

Myrmeen frowned as she considered how Krystin would take it. "One of the things I've always hated most is having someone else tell me what to do."

"Then you won't accept my suggestion?"

"No, you're right," she said. Myrmeen set her gaze toward his face, noting the obvious compassion that softened his scarred features. "Reisz, there was a time when I needed to be taken care of and you were—"

"I think I should see how Shandower is faring. He could still get delirious from his wound."

Abruptly, Reisz prodded his mount forward and left Myrmeen to ride alone for a time.

Night had fallen before Myrmeen had a chance for a quiet moment alone with Krystin. Despite Shandower's warnings that they all should remain together, Myrmeen took Krystin to the shore, where they waded into the gulf's cool, refreshing waters after removing their leathers and boots. Both women were expert swimmers, and before long they were tussling in the waters, holding each other's heads below the surface and racing each other back to shore. Afterward, they lay on the beach, the cool white sand clinging to their bare bodies in the strong moonlight. They stared up at the pinpricks of light visible beyond the layer of drifting clouds that sometimes stepped in front of the waiting moon.

"Your arm," Myrmeen said. "It's bleeding again."

Krystin tensed visibly. "The healer said it might from time to time—nothing to worry about."

Myrmeen picked up a sheer dressing gown she had taken from her bags and returned to the waters. She wetted the gown and wrung it out as if it were a worthless rag rather than an expensive import. When she returned, Myrmeen took Krystin's arm and dabbed at the gash, cleaning out any sand that may have lodged in the wound.

Krystin was surprised by the softness of her mother's hands. From what she had gathered about the woman's past, she had expected Myrmeen's skin to be hard and worn by her trials, as toughened and leathery as her demeanor had been after their first day together. What she had seen tonight had made her question the validity of that appearance.

Both women could sense that the walls separating them were finally beginning to fall. They shared an excitement that was laced with trepidation as they stood together on the brink of a new and terrifying journey.

Myrmeen talked about her childhood in Calimport, her father's death, her involvement with the Harpers, her service as a ranger, and her marriage to Dak. Krystin rolled over and stared into the older woman's eyes. For a moment she thought she could become lost in the deep blue recesses of Myrmeen's eyes, or sail away forever on the sails of the bright golden ships that made anchor there.

The older woman held nothing back. She answered Krystin's every question, no matter how personal or intimate. At last Krystin relaxed and admitted that much of her imposing demeanor was nothing more than a facade, particularly in the area of romance.

"Then you've never—" Myrmeen began.

"No," Krystin replied sharply. "But you've done it a lot, haven't you?"

"If you want the truth, then I don't know how many men

I've thrown myself into bed with over the last ten years, since my second husband was killed. But I can tell you this: I know exactly how many of them I've made love with."

"It's the same thing."

"It isn't. That's my point."

"How many?"

She thought of Reisz. "Only one."

Krystin closed her eyes and began to shiver. "Do you think Ord is too old for me? Too experienced, maybe? I think he wants more than I'm ready to give. Do you think?"

"What do you think?" Myrmeen asked softly.

"Yes," Krystin replied. "I don't think I'm ready."

Myrmeen stroked the child's hair, which was much like her own. If you were a little older, we could be sisters, Myrmeen thought. She had barely mentioned the sister she had lost and her mother's tale of the Night Parade when she was a child, and she purposely avoided mentioning the night her daughter had been taken during the great storm.

"Let's go back," Myrmeen said. "You're shaking."

They dressed and returned to camp, where Shandower handed Krystin her emerald locket. The girl fastened the clasp behind her head as Myrmeen lifted her hair out of the way. Reisz came back with Ord ten minutes later, and the young man did not seem pleased. He smiled weakly to Krystin, announced that he was tired, and curled up on the other side of the small fire they had built.

"Have you seen anything?" Myrmeen asked. "Any hint that we are being shadowed?"

"Nothing," Shandower said.

"I wish Lucius were with us," Krystin said.

"We all wish that," Myrmeen said quickly, realizing she missed him deeply. He had been more than their protector; he had become a trusted friend. "Burke and Varina, too."

"I'll take first watch," Reisz said. "The rest of you, try to get some sleep."

"We should change first," Myrmeen urged as she took Krystin's hand and glanced at one of her travel bags. "My leathers became damp, yours too. Neither of us will be worth anything if we get sick sleeping in wet clothes."

Krystin agreed. They found a pair of dressing gowns and retreated behind a boulder, where they changed clothes, then returned to the fire and placed their leathers as close to the flames as they could. Myrmeen lay down first, her back turned to Krystin, who decided to sleep beside her. Neither had bothered to lace the backs of their gowns, and, in the fire's flickering yellow light Krystin was able to see a network of scars upon her mother's bare back. She said nothing about it and tried to fall asleep, but was still awake half an hour later, thinking of the wounds her mother had endured.

Krystin shifted and felt the hard, cold weight of the emerald locket slap against the top of her breasts. The chain around her throat felt like a garrote.

Why did you do it, she chided herself. You should have let the bastard kill you. You should have warned Myrmeen.

Knowing that she would not be able to sleep as long as she wore the locket, Krystin removed the cold metal amulet and placed it in her pouch. She curled up behind Myrmeen, looked at the scars on the woman's back, and remembered her words: *They can be marks of courage. I have several myself, each with its own story to tell.*

While Myrmeen slept, Krystin gently traced each of the dozen scars she counted on Myrmeen's back and tried to imagine where the woman had received each one. There were battles with the Black Robes, the Zhentarim, she was certain. Others had come from the raking talons of orcs and hobgoblins. A fall from a great height, bucked from an evil dragon, accounted for another scar, and the fiery bolts of a clan of wizards, yet another. At least one, she was certain, had come from the hand of an over-enthusiastic lover.

When she could no longer bear to stay awake, Krystin put an arm over Myrmeen, pressed her face into the woman's neck, and allowed sleep to come for her.

That night, the nightmares left them in peace.

Sixteen

By Myrmeen's estimate, they had traveled six miles along the shores of the Calim River before Shandower signaled for the group to halt. They had been driven into the mountainous regions high above the river, making casual detours to the beach an impossibility. For the last two hours they carefully had made their way along one of the many tiers of rock chiseled from a cliff above the Shining Sea. The trail had been known only to Shandower. Before long, the path dipped treacherously and they were forced to lead their mounts. Their boots and the frightened animals' hooves slid too often for the comfort of anyone but Shandower, who had grinned as they had made their way down to a midlevel rise. The cliff's edge sagged, then rose again.

They were stopped before a bare section of sienna rock. The rich blue sky played host to soft white mushroom clouds that might have been kingdoms for fairy folk, or so Krystin had imagined them, to help relieve the boredom of the journey. Far below, white foam licked at the rocks that composed the

196

sea's pleasant shoreline.

There's nothing here, Myrmeen thought, then realized, that's exactly the point. Shandower would not hide an object that could cripple an entire race of beings where people were likely to stumble upon it every day.

"Prepare yourselves," Shandower said as he leaned forward and kissed the closest stone. Before any of the travelers could wonder if he had lost his mind, the rocks faded, revealing a huge black mouth on the cliff's surface. One of the mounts reared, and Reisz quickly brought the creature under control, though the unexpected proximity of sorcery had set his own nerves jangling.

Krystin's eyes adjusted first to the sudden darkness before them. "Caverns," she said.

At the sound of her voice, the darkness was replaced by a soft yellow light that intensified as thousands of candles suddenly were lighted, one by one, in a pattern not unlike falling dominoes. The light revealed a breathtaking expanse of towering columns and branching pathways that were the soft brownish white of a dust storm, or memories faded by time. Myriad dripping stalactites, resembling icicles made of soft, burnished stone, hung from above. Craggy depressions interrupted the fine line work wrought by nature within the main gallery.

Shandower led them inside, where they found an area laid out for the mounts to graze upon. "We'll have to carry everything from here."

The friends gathered their supplies and followed Shandower as he led them through the labyrinthine depths of the caves that had served as his home when he was not waging his war.

"Can anyone follow us?" Myrmeen asked.

"No," Shandower said calmly. "The winds will wipe away our tracks, and the magic that allowed us to come inside is very particular. I don't think any of the Night Parade will be able to get past its test for admittance."

"Why's that?" Myrmeen asked.

"Because only love can open this doorway," he whispered.

He guided the party to a small cavern where a boat sat upon a small pool of water. Ord and Reisz handled the rows for the one-armed man and soon they were floating across the waters in Shandower's boat. They passed beneath a canopy of rapierlike stalactites and drifted into a darkened passage.

Krystin gasped as they entered a grotto that was lighted, not by arcane fires, but by something that appeared more majestic from a distance, and somewhat distasteful up close.

"Glowworms," Ord said with a laugh.

Krystin ignored his words. The view was spectacular. The chamber's jet-black, craggy roof was covered with tiny greenish white lights that sometimes flickered like stars and were grouped in patterns as beautiful as the constellations.

"The fibers are sticky. They attract flies. That's why the lights flicker, when a fly is caught," Ord said.

Krystin sighed. She had not heard a word.

"The wall sealed itself behind us when we came in," Myrmeen said. "If this place is secure and there is no other way in or out, why is the air so fresh?"

"There is a pit at the center of the caverns," Shandower said. "It drops to an incredible depth and the walls are unclimbable, the shaft very slick and nearly bottomless. Air comes in from a small crevice at the base and through tiny cracks all about this place."

"What about the apparatus?" Ord said sharply. "You said it's here, didn't you?"

"There's a niche on the wall of the pit," Shandower said as they passed into a well-lighted chamber. There they anchored the boat and walked to a heavy, wooden door that opened when Shandower raised his hand before it. "The apparatus rests in a box jammed into the niche."

"That's all the protection it has?" Reisz asked.

"No, it's guarded by spells purchased from the finest sorcerers in the Realms. Even I cannot touch it."

They spent several hours exploring the wing that Shandower had secured for himself, surprised by the furnishings in many rooms. There were silk sheets, plush bedspreads, and ornate chairs, tables, and bureaus. These items stood out in sharp contrast to the frequently arched ceilings. Some of the chambers had flat ceilings, others were adorned with stalactites, and many were blasted smooth by hand or magic.

Reisz urged Krystin to follow him through a small keyhole-shaped opening. They promised the others that they would return shortly, then departed. Reisz was concerned with the sudden change he had noted in Krystin's behavior toward Myrmeen. He had been encouraging Myrmeen to make peace with the girl, but now his instincts were warning him that perhaps Krystin was not to be trusted. Her acidic tongue had relaxed to allow gentle and kind words to leave the girl's mouth, and that unnerved him terribly.

They entered a glowing crystal cave. The walls and unusual formations lining the cave appeared to have been carefully sculpted from glass and lighted by a secret inner fire. Even the ground beneath them radiated a pure silver light that glowed bright in places then dimmed and resurfaced several feet from its last manifestation.

Reisz swallowed hard. He was not certain how to get what he wanted from this situation, or exactly what he hoped to prove. You're overreacting, he scolded himself. The child's been through every hell imaginable, fought at your side. She deserves better than an old warrior's suspicion.

Krystin surprised him by asking a series of questions about Myrmeen. She wanted to know when he first had met her and what Myrmeen had been like as a child. With a little coaxing, she even managed to get Reisz to relate the tale of Myrmeen's embarrassing first mission as a ranger. She wanted to know everything, and the lights in her eyes danced with fascination at Reisz's every word. When they were finished, he knew his suspicions were misplaced.

Krystin had stared into his face as he had spoken. He had beamed with pride, and the tiny scars marring his face had seemed much less noticeable. His face was relaxed, his eyes dancing with fire.

"You're still in love with her, aren't you?" Krystin said.

Watching his expression, she immediately understood her mistake. His eyes once again became dark, and he seized her wrist and dragged her from the crystal cave without saying another word.

They rejoined the others and spent what remained of the day becoming acclimated to their surroundings and enjoying a feast that Shandower prepared with their assistance from his well-stocked food stores. After eveningfeast, the Harpers and Shandower discussed the future of his private war, which he agreed could no longer remain as such. It was decided that Ord and Reisz would be sent to Berdusk in the morning to enlist the aid of the Harpers at Twilight Hall.

* * * * *

That evening, Shandower sat on a polished crystal bench in his chamber. He flexed the muscles in his remaining hand, darkly contemplating the magically charged gauntlet, which gleamed in the semidarkness. He whispered, "I wonder how many this one will kill?"

The assassin sat alone in the gloom for several minutes, until a sudden panic consumed him. He raced through the room, lighting every torch and candle, then he checked the oil in his lanterns and fired each one. Soon the room was bathed in light, the shadows fully dispelled. He paused, realizing that he was acting like a child who was afraid of the dark, or a madman.

Suddenly, he heard a sound from the corner of the room. His heart racing, he turned and held the gauntlet before him, the weapon suddenly wreathed in blue-white fire. A woman dressed in a beautiful white gown stood before him. She pulled back the shroud covering her face as she slowly approached him.

"Mahrissah," he whispered, his senses rebelling at the sight of his dead wife. A trick! he thought. The monsters know everything. They are using the past to trick me.

The woman did not slow, even when green strands of lightning flared from the glove. Her face was stunning, if slightly pale, her dark eyes reflecting the light shining from his weapon. Her eyebrows moved together as she gave him a mock frown. Then she laughed, her almost red lips pulled back in a wicked smile that he had seen many times.

"Erin," she said as she took his hand in hers, the arcane fires from his weapon snaking across her skin to no ill effect, "You don't have to worry. I've come for you. It's time for us. Finally, my love, our time may begin."

"You're not real," he said.

She touched the side of his face with her free hand. Gently she raised his hand until the gauntlet was at eye level. "Take this thing off, that I may kiss your fingers, one by one. Then you may tell me if I am real."

Shandower felt his legs weaken, and Mahrissah guided him to the bed they once had shared. "It can't come off. Don't you see, it's fused to my skin. The magic—"

"The power does as you command," she said. "You are afraid to be parted from your weapon and so it makes that a near impossibility. Will it and it may be so. Anything you will, anything you desire, may be made so. You have only to want it, only to want me."

His lips trembled as he said, "Mahrissah, you died!"

"Yes," she said as she caressed his fingers, touching only metal that was now cooling, the magic fading like the surrender of twilight to the darkness. "You buried me here, and you vowed that when it was your time, you would return here and we would be together. Erin, that time has come."

"The battle—"

"Will be fought and won," she said as she touched the stump of his severed arm. "You have already given too much. Come with me and be whole."

"I don't know," he whispered in anguish. "I can still feel it, do you understand? My hand, the one that is gone, I can still feel it."

She leaned forward and kissed the gauntlet. "Surrender your avenging sword, Erin. You have done enough. Your reward has come. Do not torture yourself anymore."

"Am I dying?" he asked dully.

"Yes. A clot of blood is racing to your brain. Your wounds were more severe than you knew. In moments your life will pass. Please, Erin," she said as she bit her lip, "You cannot face what comes next if you are determined to bring the tools of slaughter with you."

Shandower stared at the skin surrounding the base of the gauntlet. The weave of flesh connecting the two was coming apart, and suddenly his hand was no longer fused to the weapon. "Take it off for me," he said in desperation, "Hurry!"

Mahrissah did as he asked, her eyes alight with rapture as she discarded the weapon and allowed the bare flesh of his hand to close around hers. Suddenly her grip became too tight and she said, "Watch my eyes, Erin, and see the truth."

Within her eyes he saw a particular patch of darkness, which the light had not been able to ward off, a tiny splash of shadow that threatened to grow and fill the canvas of his thoughts with nightmares engineered to drive him to the point of madness and beyond.

"Kill yourself," a voice whispered from the darkness.

Shandower rose and walked to a display of edged weapons he had collected from the corpses of the monsters he had killed. His fingers were inches from the hilt of a dagger, which he planned to ram into his own throat, when he identified the owner of that voice.

By then it was too late.

Seventeen

Myrmeen found Krystin sitting at the edge of the pit where Shandower had secreted the apparatus. Her long legs hung over the edge and she kicked absently as if she were trying to swim through the darkness that seemed to rise from below. Myrmeen sat beside her, tucking her legs beneath her, afraid of the abyss waiting beyond the shaft's cleanly polished lip.

The locket was in Krystin's hand, and she stared at its emerald surface in frustration. "So close," she whispered.

"I'm sorry?" Myrmeen asked. "I didn't hear you."

"Nothing," Krystin said as she slipped the locket into her breast pocket and looked at Myrmeen with eyes that mirrored the older woman's sadness and exhaustion.

They sat quietly, appreciating each other's company, when a sudden flicker of memory came to Myrmeen, chilling her. "By the gods," she whispered.

"What's wrong?" Krystin asked.

Myrmeen hesitated, then decided she would never keep secrets from Krystin again. Haltingly, she began her story.

"Fourteen years ago I did something terrible. It was the night of the great storm. I guess I was delirious with pain. I couldn't think clearly. I know that's no excuse, but—"

"Go on," Krystin urged.

"It was a few seconds after the delivery. My mind was swimming. Dak said the baby was gone. In that moment, a nightmare came to me. I saw a madwoman in red carrying her dead child in her arms. The woman wailed her agony for all to hear as she shambled through the streets. She begged anyone who came close to her for the smallest gesture of reassurance, a hint of kindness, a compliment for the noisome, bloated body she cradled in her arms.

" 'My child,' the woman whispered, 'my child is beautiful.'

"But it wasn't a nightmare. I had seen that scarlet woman wandering the marketplace when I was a little girl. A handful of drunken guards, evil men, all of them, had threatened to arrest her for making a public spectacle of herself—and, more importantly, for frightening off the tourists and their much needed gold.

"The woman had ignored them, and finally a guard snatched the corpse from her hands and threw it to one of his comrades. The scarlet woman chased after her child, but it was kept out of her reach. When she attacked one of the men, clawing at him with her bony hands, her fingernails scraped away, the guard ran her through and left her to die slowly in an alley. He stood there and waited until she was dead before he gave her back the child."

Myrmeen shuddered at the horror of that distant morning. She looked at Krystin. "Dak told me you were gone, and all I could think about was the scarlet woman. I suppose I thought that if I had seen the baby, I would have become her. My sanity would have been lost, so I didn't ask to see the baby. I just let it go.

"I made a mistake, a horrible mistake. I allowed my fear to overtake me. If I hadn't, I might have saved you."

"Or you might have died in the attempt," Krystin said. "Besides, you don't know for sure that I'm your daughter."

Myrmeen thought about her next words carefully, afraid to say the first thing that came to her mind. That doesn't matter, she wanted to say, but she knew those words would ring false, because it mattered to a great degree. There was something, however, that had equal importance.

"Krystin, all I can say is that if something were to happen to you, I would feel as if I had lost my daughter a second time."

The young woman stared at Myrmeen in shock. She was unprepared for such an admission and had no idea how to react. With a cry of longing, Krystin threw her arms around Myrmeen and began to weep.

Myrmeen's arms closed over Krystin, gently caressing her hair and the flowing line of her back. She told Krystin how their lives would be in Arabel, of the palace they would live in, the luxury and splendor, the people who would be her friends, the subjects who would adore her. "An education," Myrmeen said excitely, "a proper one. The finest tutors, only the best. You will have everything you want. Everything."

Krystin pulled back slowly and Myrmeen wiped away the child's tears. "It sounds wonderful."

"It will be," Myrmeen promised. "Believe me, it will."

Krystin touched Myrmeen's hand. "You're shaking."

The older woman rose and kissed Krystin on the forehead. "I need to talk with Reisz and Ord. Then I'm going to get some sleep. Will you be all right here?"

"Yes, Myrmeen," she said, fighting back the urge to call the magnificent woman before her by the name they both desperately needed to hear: "Mother." Instead, she said something that rocked them both even more. "I love you."

Myrmeen dropped to her knees and hugged Krystin so tightly that she feared she would hurt the girl. "Sweet dreams," she said as she pulled away and covered her face with her hands to mask the tears that were welling up in her eyes as she walked away. She found the tunnel that led to the chamber shared by the Harpers, and disappeared from view, leaving only the slight echo of her boots on the stone floor in her wake.

Krystin sat alone, waiting for the sudden wave of sickness that had overcome her to pass. When she no longer felt the pain behind her eyes, and when the cold, metallic taste in her mouth finally vanished, Krystin removed the heavy, dead weight of the locket from her blouse and stared at its seductive, gleaming emerald surface.

There was a good reason why she could not call Myrmeen her mother: It would have been a lie.

Lord Sixx had helped her remember the truth, unlocking her buried memories with his power. It was a simple enough task, considering he was the one who planted her false memories in the first place. Exposure to the magic of the apparatus, when she took Shandower's hand in the safe house to prove that she was not a member of the Night Parade, had created fissures in the walls that Sixx had erected in her mind. Through those cracks had come glimpses of her true life, memories of friends and family.

A part of her had feared that these new memories could also be a lie, and so during the ride to Shandower's retreat, Krystin had spoken to the assassin several times, making excuses to be near him. She had found reasons to take his hand in hers, allowing the gauntlet's energy to course through her. This time, the magic had not affected her. Although Sixx had not restored all he had taken when his emissaries had kidnapped her and arranged for the desert slavers to find her, these memories were true, and he had promised that once the apparatus was in his hands, he would restore all her memories.

The images that had been haunting her were so easily explained that they almost appeared to be mundane facts glimpsed on a tired afternoon rather than sleek, sharp-as-steel revelations cutting across her darkened field of memory like swords meeting, their metal crashing during a death duel, the rain of sparks adding much needed illumination.

Her life, all the gods help her, had been dull.

Her name was Krystin Devlaine. She had never been a hunter for the Night Parade. In fact, she had never known that such creatures existed outside of tales she had heard in harsh whispers at the boarding school where she had been sent by her parents. Those stories were generally used to frighten the younger children who believed in all manner of haunts and demons who knew their names and would come for them if they misbehaved.

The kindly old man she had glimpsed had been her grandfather, who had died several years ago. He had lived in Calimport and had visited her much more frequently than her own mother and father, who were restless travelers and explorers. They had relegated the task of raising Krystin to others for most of her life. The vulgar, dark-haired man with rotted teeth, who had tried to club her with a shattered table leg, had been a nameless drunk in a tavern. She had crept away from the school and had been trapped in the bar when a brawl erupted. Physical fitness had been stressed at the school, and she had been an especially apt pupil during the lessons on self-defense. Those hours of instruction had benefited her that night. She had crushed the man's instep, left him howling in pain, and ran from the tavern with a strange girl she had met, a homeless child.

Melaine.

That night had been her only true evening of adventure until she was snatched by the Night Parade. The false memories Sixx had implanted had given her a sense of bravado that had accounted for her unbearable ego, her prickly nature, and her caustic tongue. They also had made her so much like Myrmeen that it was not surprising that there had been tension between them from the outset.

Sixx also had briefly tasted Myrmeen's memories on one of the woman's first nights in the city. It had been after Myrmeen's narrow escape from death at Kracauer's "orphanage." Sixx had been disgusted with Zeal's decision to leave the humans alive, and so he had gone to Myrmeen's quarters to finish the Harpers himself. He had found Myrmeen sitting before her open window, sound asleep. He had entered her mind to kill her, but soon reversed that decision when he learned who she was and the power she had at her command.

Shandower's first instinct had been correct: Sixx had placed Krystin with the Harpers in the hope of eventually gaining control of Arabel through the girl, when she succeeded her "mother," who would die from an accident they would arrange in a few years. Sixx had not revealed all of this to Krystin, but he had shown her enough so that she could fit all the pieces into place.

But Lord Sixx had refused to give her all of her memories back, and she knew there must have been a reason beyond the one he had given; there was something he did not want her to know, a part of her past that he did not want her to see.

"Your parents are alive," he had said within her mind. "Once they know you have disappeared, they will search for you. I can lead you to them. I can give your life back to you, child."

"What about your plans for Arabel?" she had asked.

"It would probably have been more trouble than it was worth. And the apparatus is far more important to me. Work with me and the humans will live. Defy me and they will die, even Mistress Lhal."

Suddenly, Krystin felt a sharp pain in her leg, as if she had been bitten by an insect. The sensation had shaken her from her memory and she brushed at her leg absently.

Staring into the locket's emerald depths, Krystin realized that the bauble somehow had acquired the power to reflect her memories, thoughts, and dreams. There had been one last set of images that had not been explained by the revelations caused by Lord Sixx's magic, memories of figures chasing her. She cleared her mind and began to concentrate on them.

Time slowly drifted past and soon she found herself staring at movement within the locket's surface. Krystin stared at the images and allowed the world around her to fall away. She saw a half dozen men chasing her down an alley, vengeful, evil men who were quickly gaining on her. As Krystin concentrated more deeply, she was able to see that they wore uniforms: their leathers were black and on their breasts they wore the insignia of a company, a silver dagger dripping with blood.

Suddenly her view of the world altered with dizzying speed.

She saw the wall to her left flash by and suddenly she was staring at the other end of the alley, where three more men waited. All movement stopped. Krystin became aware of a woman's sharp breath coming in gasps. The men closed more slowly now, enjoying the terror they inspired.

Her world view shifted again, this time jerking upward sharply and spinning in a wide arc. The opposing wall came into view and she was turned once again and lowered gently to the ground. A woman, her face too close to be seen properly, kissed her once, then withdrew and faced her assailants.

Krystin's vantage point was close to the ground and she felt as if she were watching the dance of giants. The dark-haired woman who had set her down drew a blade and lunged at the closest of the men. To her credit, she wounded three men before they ran her through.

Suddenly a sword was buried in the soft earth before her. In the reflection of the metal she saw that she was perhaps a year old, no more. A baby. One of the men reached down, picked her up, and laughed. He spoke, but his words were gibberish. Beyond him, she could see another man holding up his empty gold purse, making a joke she could not understand. Suddenly her attention was riveted on a prize that hung around the neck of the man holding her, an object that he had taken from the woman he had killed: A beautiful emerald pendant.

The images suddenly dissolved.

Krystin once again sat on the edge of the shaft in Erin Shandower's cavernous retreat. She looked down at the locket in disgust, then hurled it into the darkness below. She thought she heard it strike the side of the tunnel, but there was no sound to signify that it had reached the bottom. No matter. The locket was gone, but its terrible gift had remained behind and would never leave her.

Myrmeen Lhal was not her mother. The Devlaines were not her true parents. She was, in truth, an orphan, with more in common with the Krystin Lord Sixx unwittingly had manufactured than she ever would have guessed.

She had to tell Myrmeen, had to warn her that she had betrayed them to the Night Parade, that time was short. But she could not make herself move. Her limbs were too sluggish to respond to her mental commands, and when she tried to rise, she nearly toppled into the pit. She fell back, darkness stealing over her. She was unaware that the deep, thin wound in her leg from the "insect" that had bitten her was now black and swollen. As her consciousness faded, she glimpsed a single nightmarish flash of the creature that had inflicted the wound as it climbed out over the lip of the pit, the emerald locket caught in its vicelike pincers.

Within seconds, Krystin was unconscious. If she had remained awake for another few moments, she would have been witness to a sight that was at once horrifying and beautiful. Where a monstrosity had been only moments before now stood a tall, lithe woman with long, dark hair and an ethereal beauty.

Widow Tamara, the Weaver, stopped before the sleeping girl. Her poison snaked through the child's system, incapacitating her without stopping her heart. She had no quarrel with Krystin. Tamara went down the corridor where she had heard Myrmeen walk some time earlier. The child's locket was clutched in her hand. She smiled and hurried to the long overdue reunion that she had left Calimport to experience.

*   *   *   *   *

Less than five minutes earlier, Erin Shandower had heard a voice that had nearly driven him to suicide before he identified its owner. He turned and was startled to see the familiar, gaunt face of a man he had presumed dead.

"Lucius!" Shandower said as he rushed to the mage, whose white smock was covered in blood from his wounds. Lucius Cardoc stood with open arms and buckling legs. Shandower caught the mage as he fell to his bed. The sorcerer's eyes lolled back in his head; his lips trembled.

Shandower suddenly realized his mistake. "You're—you're not breathing."

Lucius looked up at him with a sad, tortured expression, a deep, powerful sympathy in his eyes. The lanterns Shandower had lighted started to dim, the candles dying one by one. Suddenly the room was wreathed in shadows. From the darkness Shandower heard skittering and laughter.

Turning, he found a man he had never seen standing between him and the gauntlet, which he had allowed his dead lover to remove from him earlier. In a startling moment of complete lucidity, Shandower understood that it had been Lucius who had appeared to him, Lucius using his magic because the sorceries of the Night Parade would be worthless against him as long as he wore the gauntlet. Lucius had betrayed them, but why he had done so was a mystery to the assassin, and would remain as such.

"Greetings," Lord Sixx said with a smile. Shandower tried to dart past the Night Parade leader, but Lord Sixx grabbed him and slammed him against the wall. He repeated the maneuver several times until Shandower was delirious with pain, the stump of his arm bleeding from the impact.

"We found your ally trying to follow you. He died during questioning, but I was determined not to let that stop our little game," Lord Sixx said as several figures strode forward from the shadows. They were misshapen figures that would never be taken for human, even in silhouette. Lord Sixx looked over his shoulder and said, "This is the man who has killed so many of your brethren!"

The creatures advanced in a murderous frenzy, halting only when Lord Sixx held out his free hand to order them back. Shandower glimpsed the deformities of the first few monsters and thought he might gag in disgust.

"Now," Lord Sixx said, "you can tell me what you've done with the apparatus, or you can tell them."

Shandower anxiously looked over Sixx's shoulder, then whispered, "Go back to whatever hell you came from."

"I would, but I'm not welcome there anymore," Lord Sixx said as he flung Shandower with inhuman strength toward the monstrosities. They reached out for him with claws and tentacles, the razor-sharp teeth in their eye sockets grinding in anticipation. Shandower tried to scream as he was dragged into the shadows, but something cold and wet was jammed deep into his throat, preventing him from warning the others. Lord Sixx sighed as he watched his minions consume the man.

"I glimpsed your secrets when you slept," Lord Sixx said. "I was merely hoping to make you feel the anguish of betraying all you believed in before you died. Ah, well. I would say you left this world with dignity, but that would be a lie."

The creatures Lord Sixx had taken with him giggled obscenely as they feasted on the assassin's hot flesh.

From the bed, Lucius moaned. "Release me. I have done what you asked. I am dead. Release me!"

Lord Sixx grinned. He took a staff standing in a corner and stabbed at the gauntlet until he was able to slip one end into the glove and raise the deadly item into the air.

"Please," Lucius begged. "You promised that you would spare my wife and children and that you would release me!"

"Not just yet," Lord Sixx said as his gaze slithered across the undead mage's face. "I still have plans for you."

Eighteen

The nightmare was always the same:

Myrmeen was a child, living at home with her parents in the boarding house she one day would burn to the ground. Her father was trying to perfect a new composition, plucking notes on his lute with passion and skill, while her mother allowed her to help stuff a pillow that she would place inside a beautifully woven slipcover and sell in the market. They lay together on the sky-blue rug that Myrmeen loved so much. All she had to do was roll onto her back and look up to see the painting she treasured, the portrait of her parents, with her sandwiched between them.

I didn't want a sister anyway, she thought. Then we would have to get a new painting.

The notes her father played suddenly changed. The music became discordant and a heavy thumping replaced the light strum of his fingers upon the strings.

"I'm dripping," he said in a murky voice.

Myrmeen looked up and saw she was an adult dressed in silver armor with a phoenix headdress. The sword that had been forged for her by her second husband was in her hand.

"I'm dripping," he repeated. "I hate that."

This time she saw what he meant. His flesh was leaking from his bones, his eyeballs drooping to his jaw.

"Honey," he said insistently, though his tongue was now curling up in the back of his skull, "can't we do something about this?"

Her father had always wanted her mother to *do something* when a situation distressed him. Myrmeen was never quite sure what that meant. At the moment, she did not want to find out.

"All right," her mother said, in a voice that made it clear that she no longer was her mother, or, at least, no longer human. Myrmeen heard a thump beside her and refused to look up. Another thump. Then another. Something leathery brushed against her and she felt its texture despite the armor she wore. Myrmeen twisted out of the monster's path, refusing to believe that this was her mother.

The thing reared up to its full height, tall enough to scrape the ceiling with the top of its head. Its body was thin and skeletal, a burnt sienna mass of twisted bones and looping muscle filled with gobs of pure white feathers. Wings with the patterns of spider webs branched out from the small of the creature's back, and its head still contained the gentle features of her mother, marred by insect eyes and pincers that had been driven outward through the cheeks.

"Sweetheart," her mother said as she turned in Myrmeen's direction—the word came out slurred and sounded more like *Swuuud-harddd*—"Sweetheart, give Daddy your arm to chew on. He's hungry."

"Stay away," Myrmeen said.

"Honey!" her father bellowed. "It's getting worse!"

Myrmeen made the mistake of looking back in her father's direction. He was telling the truth; his dissolution was increasing. Even his bones were becoming soft and oozing. She realized in perverse fascination that his body was not so much melting as it was changing, becoming huge strands that reached out to the ceiling and floor, sticking to the walls, and forming an intricate web whose sinewy strands emitted the odor of rotting fish.

"Get in there, sweetheart," her mother urged. "Get in there and set that terrible knife down first—"

"It's a sword," Myrmeen interrupted.

"It has an edge!" the woman shrieked. "It cuts. It's a knife. You don't want to cut your father to pieces do you? Not like the way you cut our hearts to pieces, not the way you did before. You remember, before, when we told you the other one was dead and you would be our one and only. You smiled. You thought we didn't see you, but we did and it cut our hearts out. So don't do it again. Be a good girl. Get in the stinking web and let us eat your heart!"

The creature advanced on Myrmeen and she woke suddenly, bolting forward in bed. She tried to scream and could only force a high, quiet squeal of terror from her lungs because she had been breathing so hard that she no longer had the air inside her to muster a scream.

Myrmeen squeezed her eyes shut. She was alone, dripping with sweat. The nightmare was just that, a bad dream, nothing to worry about. She knew that she should be used to it by now, but it continued to affect her deeply, cutting furrows into her heart each time it returned to her. The dream was a lie. She had not been happy when she learned that her baby sister had been stillborn, or when she knew that her own daughter was dead.

Of course you were.

She had not smiled, not even a little bit.

Admit it. You were relieved.

No! she screamed in her mind, her hands clamped over her face. She tried to say the word, but no sound came.

Something in the darkness made a scratching noise.

Myrmeen looked up suddenly, her warrior's instincts taking control. The darkness in her chamber would have been absolute if she had not left the door slightly ajar, to make it easier for Krystin in case she decided she did not want to sleep alone.

Myrmeen's eyes adjusted to the semidarkness rapidly and she saw an object the size of a man clinging to the far wall. She could make out very little detail other than that it was alive and moving.

My sword, she thought, and remembered that the weapon had been hung on the bedpost to her right and she was lying near the edge of the bed's left-hand side. She considered bolting for the door, but knew that whatever the creature was that had been waiting for her, it would certainly be upon her before she could reach the knob.

"Want you to . . . see me." The voice sounded familiar.

Myrmeen heard the striking of flint and saw a tiny flame light near the wall. Suddenly a torch flared to life and in her mind Myrmeen heard the voice of Burke, her first tutor in the art of fighting, who said, *Now, while both of its hands are occupied. Go now! What are you waiting for?*

Who's to say it has only two hands, Myrmeen thought as she scrambled deeper into the room's shadows and drew the sword from its scabbard, thankful that she had learned to sleep in her leathers. She was smelly and uncomfortable and would remain that way until she bathed, but at least she was prepared to fight. She tried to cry out for Reisz and Ord, but her throat constricted and words would not form, just as the scream had refused to leave her mouth instants before.

"Look . . . can't scream . . . touched you while slept . . . Look!"

Myrmeen felt as if she were back in the world of her nightmares. She looked at the creature on the wall. The torch that had been lighted sat in its holder on the wall, forcing an orange-red blossom of light to caress the gruesome monster's body. Myrmeen had been trying not to look at it directly, afraid that if she gave it what it wanted, it would have no reason to wait before it leapt at her.

"Pretty," the woman-thing sitting on the wall said, indicating its rapidly transforming body with a flourish of a pale hand. The human part of it—its face—was beautiful, with dark, exotic features, long and slightly curly hair, and soft, creamy skin. Its eyes were elongating, becoming large ovals pocketed with myriad chambers, which glowed blood red. The woman-thing's lips pulled back in a sneer to reveal long, curving white fangs, and its jaw began to expand outward from side to side. Traces of a fine silk wrap clung to its body. A pair of sandals and a small pouch lay on the floor. The thing's torso was changing, growing into large, bulbous brownish black sections covered with fine hair. Each of its four human limbs were splitting in two, the flesh falling away to reveal long, thin spider's legs that spread from one another as their sockets moved into place on the body. Small red blotches appeared on the monster's torso, and its face suddenly split as pincers emerged.

Myrmeen leapt forward, thrusting her sword at the creature's heart, praying that she could catch it unaware as it continued its bizarre transformation. With a scream, the woman-spider pushed away from the wall and jumped over Myrmeen, onto the bed, which collapsed with its weight. Myrmeen had not anticipated the monster's speed. Her sword struck the wall, sending sparks of pain through her arm. She felt a rush of air at her back and heard a ripping sound. A moment later she felt the hot, wet trickle of blood down her back and realized she had been slashed. Crouching to avoid another swing of the monster's scythelike limbs, Myrmeen launched herself at the door.

She did not make it. A long, thin cord erupted from the creature's mouth, catching one of Myrmeen's legs in midstride. Myrmeen fell to the floor in a heap, then turned and hacked at the sticky web that had fastened to her leg and was now dragging her backward. By the time she cut through the webbing, she had been pulled to the foot of the bed, where the woman-spider was trying to extricate herself from the soft mattress, which had proven an equally difficult trap for the creature. Myrmeen scrambled back, refusing to take her gaze from that of the creature, her hand sliding on the slime trail that had been left by the webbing attached to her leg. Her view of the monster receded and, just before she turned to see how close she was to the door, she felt her shoulder strike the wood and slam the door all the way shut.

Issuing a curse that came out as little more than a hiss, Myrmeen grabbed at the door handle, trying to bring herself to her feet despite the slippery floor. The monster was ripping the mattress to bits, screaming in its high-pitched wail of frustration, and a cloud of feathers rose into the air. A slight laugh that sounded like a catch in her throat escaped Myrmeen, and she wondered if she had gone mad, being able to laugh at a sight such as this.

Her smile faded as she realized the woman-spider was transforming again, replacing some of its monstrous aspects with human attributes that would allow it to free itself and take full advantage of the close space.

If it wanted to kill me, it could have done so in my sleep, Myrmeen thought. It wants me afraid. It wants me to suffer.

"You destroyed my home!" it shouted.

Myrmeen wondered which of the many lairs she had helped burn had belonged to this being.

"You took everything! Every memory I had!"

Dragging herself to her feet, Myrmeen saw that the woman-spider had sprouted long, sinewy human legs that were covered with fine brownish black hairs, and its torso had reduced in size. The monster's face had become more human, but it had retained the pincers and four of its eight spider-limbs. Myrmeen knew that in the time it would take for her hand to pull the door open, the monster would be upon her, driving its swordlike arms through her body.

I'm going to die, she thought, I'm going to die for nothing. My death will have no meaning.

The thought gave her the determination to fight. Anchoring herself, Myrmeen raised her sword and waited for the woman-spider to leap from the bed.

The creature moved with blinding speed. To Myrmeen, it was standing still, then it was before her eyes, and suddenly it vanished in the time she had to take a single swipe with her sword. There was a large gash in her upper arm, and she looked up to see the woman-spider sticking to the wall beside her, wiggling her tongue obscenely. Myrmeen turned and struck with her weapon, the sword slamming into bare wall where the monster had been only instants before. She heard it skittering across the ceiling and wondered how she could win in a battle against this creature.

The torch, she thought, and suddenly thought and action were one for the statuesque fighter as she snatched the flaming torch from the wall and threw it upon the bed, setting fire to the remnants of the mattress and frame. Then she grasped an oil lantern from a nearby table and threw it upon the bed. A cloud of flames rose up and scorched the ceiling. She felt her lungs strain to deal with the sudden lack of air in the room and heard the woman-spider wail again. Keeping her sword before her, Myrmeen opened the door and felt the rush of air from the hall as it briefly sucked the flames in her direction. Before she could escape, though, she felt a slight impact on the back of her neck and she was yanked upward.

The woman-spider was staying close to the ceiling, having transformed almost entirely into a seven-foot-long spider with pincers that opened and closed in rapid, hungry movements. Threads had caught Myrmeen by the space between her shoulders and by the fleshy part of her right calf, keeping her off balance as she was lifted into the air. Myrmeen's hand closed tightly over the hilt of her blade and she swung at the threads that were yanking her steadily upward, slicing apart the strands that secured her back when she was four feet in the air. Suddenly she was supported only by her leg and she fell back, her head scraping against the floor as she found herself hanging upside down and completely at the woman-spider's mercy. Driving her sword into the partially opened wooden door, Myrmeen pushed the door closed, trapping herself in the room once again. Then she pulled with all her weight until she felt a section of her flesh tear from her calf. Suddenly she was free, dropping to the ground with enough impact to drive the wind from her.

Before Myrmeen could regain her footing, the woman-spider ran down the wall and attacked. The warrior was able to bring up her sword, jamming it between the incredibly strong set of pincers that jutted from the woman's face. The pincers threatened to close over her features, shredding the skin of her face if they connected. The creature screamed. Myrmeen used her leverage to push against the creature, driving toward the rapidly spreading flames.

The woman-spider hollered as the flames licked at its back. Myrmeen grabbed at the door handle, ripped the door open, and stumbled into the hall, hoping to pull the door shut and trap the creature in the burning room. Just before it shut she heard a scream and felt the hard wood slam against her as it exploded outward, jumping off its hinges, sending her from her feet. When she looked up, the woman-spider was standing in the doorway, the burning room at her back. As it advanced on her, Myrmeen scrambled to her feet and raised her sword in time to ward off the first strike of its spider limbs. Myrmeen felt as if her blade had connected with an iron club. The creature was moving more slowly, its lightning-fast reactions dulled to the point that Myrmeen and the hybrid could battle as equals.

Myrmeen's sword flashed as she forced away her fear and concentrated on hacking at the woman-spider, which advanced on her with clicking pincers and burning eyes. The monster had retained its human legs, leaping nimbly back and forth as it pressed the attack and retreated. It used its four spider arms to fight with the skill of a quartet of trained swordsmen and refused to allow Myrmeen an opening to drive her blade at the creature's face or the sensitive, soft places between its hard, sectioned torso.

The woman-spider advanced on Myrmeen with a feral expression, its eyes glazed with the pure, sensual delight of the battle, the joy of the anticipated kill.

Myrmeen understood why the creature was grinning: It was regaining its strength as it launched itself against the fighter, while Myrmeen was becoming worn and tired. Suddenly the creature used all four of its arms to gather Myrmeen's sword arm above her head. The woman-spider took a step forward and slightly beyond Myrmeen, then brought one of its legs between the fighter's, trapping Myrmeen with her dark, powerful limbs. A hoarse whisper—a would-be scream of fear and defiance—left Myrmeen's throat as the woman-spider brought its face close to the fighter's, its pincers moving close to Myrmeen's soft, vulnerable eyes.

With her free hand, Myrmeen reached back and grabbed the woman-spider's hair, pulling as hard as she could to keep the monster's awful pincers from blinding her. Myrmeen instantly regretted that she had not tried to put out one of the creature's eyes instead. The woman-spider's face inched closer as Myrmeen leaned back in the deadly embrace and felt the muscles in the small of her back begin to ache. The woman-spider parted its lips and spat a stream of white ichor at Myrmeen's throat.

Why not my face, Myrmeen thought, then understood that the creature had wanted Myrmeen to see the pincers coming, desiring the numbing fear Myrmeen would experience instants before the crablike claws parted one last time then closed, their sharp tips piercing her soft, moist eyeballs.

The webs constricted around Myrmeen's throat and slowly drew her face forward as the woman-spider allowed one of its arms to fall away from the other three, which continued to keep Myrmeen's sword at bay. The free limb poised near Myrmeen's stomach, the tip pricking her flesh as it bit through her leathers and slowly drew blood.

"Do you know why?" the creature named Tamara asked. "Tell me. Try to scream. I bit you while you slept. Your neck bears my mark. My venom is within you, but soon you will be able to talk. Tell me, do you know why?"

Myrmeen could not answer. All of her attention was riveted to the limb that was about to skewer her and the pincers that were about to blind her. Even if she could have responded, she had no idea what the woman-spider meant.

"She is not your daughter," Tamara said with a hiss. "Krystin is not your little girl."

Despite herself, Myrmeen relaxed slightly, the fight slowly trickling out of her. Then she noticed the way Tamara's head was cocked to one side, the inquisitive stare of a wolf that had all the time in the world to devour its prey. Myrmeen realized the woman-spider was trying to magnify her anguish to the highest degree possible before putting her to death.

"It's all a lie," Tamara said.

It doesn't matter, she thought, that won't change the way I feel about Krystin. But what if it's true?

Myrmeen was able to rip a single battle cry from her lips despite the toxin Tamara had injected into her throat when she slept. If she was going to die, she would die as a warrior, a prayer for vengeance for herself and her daughter on her lips as her life was claimed.

The pincers did not blind her. The spider-arm did not run her through. Tamara released her hold on Myrmeen and backed away, rapidly becoming human once again.

A child shouted, "Myrmeen!"

The fighter knew Krystin was behind her. She motioned for the girl to stay back as she fixed Tamara with her gaze. A strange look passed between them and, with horror, Myrmeen identified the nature of the expression both women shared: recognition.

Tamara fled into the shadows and was gone. Myrmeen turned and took Krystin in an embrace. The girl's repeated contact with Shandower's gauntlet during the long trek from Calimport had infused her with some of its power. That power had been enough to burn much of the poison from Krystin's system.

"Love," Myrmeen whispered. "Love you, too."

Krystin stared at her, sadness welling in her eyes, overcoming her shock. She opened her mouth to speak and found herself silenced by Myrmeen's raised hand.

"The others," Myrmeen croaked. "Must warn them."

"But—"

Myrmeen took Krystin's hand and dragged the girl with her. "Now!"

Nineteen

As they followed the winding corridor that led to Reisz and Ord's chamber, Krystin vainly tried to force Myrmeen to stop and listen to her, but the fighter silenced her each time.

"You have to know. You have to understand—" Krystin began. A hiss came to them from around the next bend, where they could see flickering yellow-orange torchlight and nothing else. Myrmeen froze and Krystin swallowed her next words. The hiss sounded again, revealing itself to be more of a whisper that was paradoxically very loud, as if the speaker had been next to each of the women.

Myrmeen looked down and saw the shadow stretching off from her boots shorten and deepen. The torches behind her were being snuffed out, one by one. Shadows suffused the corridor, stealing across the walls, moving into the cracks of doorways to seal them. A terrible voice came to them:

"Did you know that when I was a little boy I used to burn the other children? They told me to stop, told me that they'd feed me into the flames, and you know what? They did. I liked it."

Myrmeen had heard the leathery voice before, in her nightmares. She was not surprised when the light before her grew more intense and a long, thin shadow suddenly stretched out, piercing the splash of yellow-white light that insinuated itself upon the stone floor.

A red-haired man covered in sweat turned the corner, his eyebrows and hair burning as smoke leaked from his nostrils and mouth. He wore a red shirt that was opened to the waist and belted with black leather, then ran to midthigh. The rest of his body was bare, revealing his intensely muscled physique. The patches of tight, curly red hair on his chest, arms and legs, glowed bright orange and seemed to smolder. Flames licked at his clenched fists. He smiled knowingly at Myrmeen as he said, "Your presence is requested."

Although exhausted from her battle with Tamara, Myrmeen raised her sword. The fiery-haired man frowned and lifted his open palm, revealing a seemingly endless tunnel that appeared to be a gateway to a dimension of flames. A tongue of fire leapt across the distance separating them and flicked the sword from her hand. The metal was molten slag before it struck the ground and Myrmeen yelped as her brain registered that her hand was burned and soon would blister. She could feel the rush of displaced air and the taunting presence of unnatural heat even though the flames had retreated into the monster's hand.

"That was rude," he admonished, his features twisting cruelly as he fought to contain the murderous energy within him. The call of the flame rose to infuse his entire body with a white, pulsating glow. "But, then, I have not been entirely given to proper etiquette myself, have I? My name is Imperator Zeal. I have been instructed by Lord Sixx to escort you to a private audience. Please follow me."

Myrmeen did not move. As the man before her spoke, she heard the skittering and laughter of creatures emerging from the shadows at her back and became determined not to look over her shoulder. Krystin held on to the fleshy part of her upper arm, the girl's nails biting deeply enough to draw blood.

She also was trying not to look back.

"Do not make me repeat myself!" Zeal snarled as he pointed in their direction, his index finger losing its consistency and becoming a wavering line of fire. "Come with me or you both die!"

The corridor was becoming stuffy. The air was changing, taking on an unnatural consistency as the darkness drew closer. Myrmeen realized that in moments she would be enveloped by the living shadows of the night people.

"Are my friends with you?" she asked quietly.

"They're all here!" he bellowed. "It's a party! A celebration of our new beginning! Come one, come all—come now or I will boil the moisture from your bodies and have you dragged!"

Myrmeen shuddered involuntarily. The shadows surrounding her grew cold and she felt something that might have been a hand brush against her leg.

Imperator Zeal aimed his hand at Krystin's face. "Come now or I will disfigure the child."

"All right," Myrmeen said quickly.

"Good decision," Zeal said, his features relaxing slightly. "Besides, we don't have far to go."

They walked through the twisting corridor to the pit where Myrmeen had found Krystin several hours earlier. The chattering creatures at their backs occasionally nudged them on. Sometimes the monsters whispered taunts meant to provoke Myrmeen into turning and facing the gathering of darkness that followed close behind, but she ignored them. When she stepped into the open theater surrounding the pit, Myrmeen was not surprised to find a host of creatures every bit as grotesque as the ones she had imagined at her back. Most were human enough to stand on two legs and look out through lumps of flesh that could, from a distance, be mistaken for heads.

More than a hundred of the inhuman tormenters of dreams were gathered around the pit. Myrmeen saw beings with mouths covering their entire bodies, creatures that shook uncontrollably, and men and women with skin of every color—

including one woman whose flesh changed color whenever she moved or laughed. Colors rippled through the voluptuous frame of the naked rainbow woman as she kissed a tall man's arm. His flesh was covered with eyes that his black leather and armor were designed to protect with crystal coverings woven into his suit.

Lord Sixx was extremely relaxed and seemed only mildly interested when Myrmeen and Krystin were led into the room. Imperator Zeal's entourage remained in the corridor's shadows, then spread out to block every avenue of escape other than the shaft at the center of the large chamber.

Finally Sixx looked over and smiled, his arching brows and widow's peak pointing at the three sets of eyes peering out from his skull. Zeal approached Lord Sixx with the prisoners, the fiery-haired man bowing as he reached the dark man who held dominion over them all. "Lord Sixx, may I present—"

"You may not," Sixx said as he dismissed the rainbow woman with a gentle pat to her bottom and approached Myrmeen. "I know who this is, you idiot."

Myrmeen noticed that not all of his eyes moved at the same time, and she was unnerved by the sight.

Imperator Zeal lowered his gaze and backed away. "Of course, milord," he said.

"Myrmeen Lhal," Lord Sixx declared in his rich voice, "ruler of Arabel, a fine city. Who sits upon your throne, Myrmeen? One of yours? Or one of ours, perhaps?"

The implication caused her heart to leap into her throat as she thought of Elyn, the Harper who had masqueraded as Myrmeen, ruling the city in her stead.

"Ah," Sixx said softly as he tasted her fear, "sweet."

Myrmeen understood her mistake.

"Don't worry," Sixx muttered assuredly, "your friend is safe. But you might be surprised to learn how many of our kind have replaced humans in positions of power throughout this world. I'll give you a hint: Zhentil Keep is more for us than an excellent hunting ground."

The Zhentarim, Myrmeen thought, the Harpers' blood enemies. If the shadow people could infiltrate ranks such as those, then no agency in the world was safe from their spies. She considered that even the Harpers could be compromised.

"He's lying," Krystin said. "He always lies."

Lord Sixx turned his gaze to Krystin in amusement. "Have we met?"

"That's what Alden said," she muttered.

Sixx shrugged happily. "Alden is a confused child. You can't take his rambling to heart. It may prove fatal not only to you."

Krystin looked away, something in Lord Sixx's words seeming to strike home.

"Where are the others?" Myrmeen asked.

"Bring them," Lord Sixx said as he raised his hand, slapping his fingers against his palm as if he were summoning a waiter in an expensive dining establishment. The crowd of monstrosities parted and the two remaining Harpers were brought forth. Myrmeen could tell from the fresh cuts and contusions lining their bodies that they had struggled bravely before they were subdued, but they were only flesh, and the members of the Night Parade were much more. Ord refused to walk of his own accord and had to be dragged. Reisz held himself with a quiet dignity, despite the roughness of the talons and claws that shoved him forward. Both men had been gagged with sashes of black silk.

"Let them speak," Myrmeen commanded.

"No," Sixx said lazily, "I'm tired of their ranting."

Myrmeen looked at him, stunned to have been refused.

"Let me explain," Lord Sixx said as he lowered his head like a snake inspecting its latest kill. "You are not in control here. You breathe because I wish it and for no other reason."

"Do not anger him," a voice said from behind Myrmeen, "It will only make it worse."

The fighter turned, recognizing the voice of the mage she had presumed dead. When she saw his pallid skin, drawn lips, and blood-drenched smock, she knew something was terribly wrong with him. "Lucius?"

"Shandower is dead," the mage said, his voice appearing to

have emerged from the base of a tunnel, as if he were speaking from a nearly unreachable distance. "I helped them kill him, Myrmeen. They threw his gauntlet into the pit, with his bones." He turned to Lord Sixx. "Please release me. My time is done."

"In a just world, perhaps," Lord Sixx said. "When you reach such a place, you will have stories to share with the other complainers, those who suffered unnatural ends. Now be quiet or I'll kill them all."

Lucius felt a trace of his old strength flow into him as he said, "You promised to spare them if I cooperated."

"True," Sixx said and laughed, "but your involvement is not yet finished and their lives are still in the balance."

Myrmeen could not believe what she was hearing. "Lucius, you must not help them. If you give them what they want, they'll have no reason to keep any of us alive. What happened to you, that you could betray us like this?"

The mage hesitated. "I am dead."

The fighter drew a sharp breath and suddenly identified the smell of rotting flesh among the putrid odors of the monstrosities gathered near the pit.

"They have trapped me here between this world and the next," Lucius said. "Cyric's emissaries call to me, screaming curses because I will not come, but I cannot, though I am dead."

Myrmeen spun on Lord Sixx. "What do you want of him?"

The Night Parade's leader glanced at her as if her intelligence had suffered an instant, rapid decline. "He must retrieve the apparatus, of course. Shandower was not a powerful mage. He merely employed them. His skills would have been useless in sorting through the puzzle box of wards surrounding the apparatus."

Lucius shook his head. "You have denied me use of my spells. There is nothing I can do."

"What I made you forget, I can make you remember," Sixx promised.

Krystin hugged herself so tightly at these words that she

forced blood to leak from the wound in her arm. A figure burst through the crowd of abominations, a flaxen-haired youth who leapt to her feet and licked her blood from the floor.

"Alden," she whispered. When he looked up in response, she saw that he was no longer human. His eyes gleamed bright red and his teeth had become wolflike canines. The lower half of his face had lengthened, jutting straight outward to accommodate his snapping jaws. Alden's features had shortened, his brow becoming considerably more brutish. His hair stood out in wild patterns, matted in tangled clots near his sopping mouth. He latched onto her leg with a single hairy claw, and Krystin screamed.

"Child!" Lord Sixx shouted.

Alden's head snapped around, his eyes wide with fear. He panted like a frightened dog.

"Do not embarrass me before our guests," Lord Sixx said as he struck Alden on the back of the head, causing him to release Krystin and scamper into the recesses of the crowd. "You must forgive him. He was just happy to see you."

"What have you done to him?" she whispered.

"He is becoming," Sixx said with a touch of pride.

Krystin waited for him to finish the statement. When it was clear that Sixx felt he had answered sufficiently, she asked exactly what Alden was becoming.

Lord Sixx opened his hands. "Who knows? Perhaps his father, Dymas, will have an idea when he arrives. For now, we have other matters to consider." He looked at the mage. "What is your decision, Cardoc?"

Lucius whispered, "I am weak. I cannot help you."

"Then everyone dies and we are delayed slightly longer until we find someone who can." Sixx shrugged. "I've only chosen this tack because I am impatient."

"You said you did not want me to use my magic against you," Lucius said.

"I would still prefer that to be the case," Sixx said honestly. "I am the only one who can release you from your torments, and the lives of all you care about are in my grasp. The decision, however, is yours."

Myrmeen touched the dead mage's arm and immediately drew her hand back in disgust at the cold flesh her fingers encountered. Lucius looked at her sadly.

"I must do as he asks," he said.

"I know," she said, trying to clear her mind of the idea that was forming. "But you said it yourself, you're weak. You're going to need help. Let me help you."

He nodded and trained his gaze on Lord Sixx.

"I don't care how you do it, just get on with it," Sixx said, annoyed. He gestured, and Krystin was thrown to the creatures guarding Ord and Reisz. "Try to betray me, and their deaths will be works of art that we will talk about far into the future."

Myrmeen looked to Krystin, who was trying to control her fear, then turned her gaze to Sixx. "I understand."

Lucius stared into the pit and said, "Let us begin."

The mage gave a short list of objects he would need, stressing that the most important items were a silver mirror, a box that Sixx felt was large enough to contain the apparatus, and two lengths of extremely strong rope, so that he and Myrmeen could be lowered into the pit, where the apparatus waited. In the time it took to fulfill the mage's requirements, Lord Sixx had released the dampers he had installed in the sorcerer's mind, allowing Lucius full memory of the battery of spells he had memorized over the years and constantly replenished. The mage considered the spells he could use to gain vengeance on Lord Sixx and the creatures near the pit: he could rain acid upon them, draw their breath from them, or use a spell of wilting—but all these evocations would harm those he was trying to protect as well.

Soon a pair of makeshift harnesses was fashioned with the ropes. Several of the Night Parade's strongest members held the ropes as Myrmeen and Lucius crept backward, yanking as hard as they could to test their protectors' mettle. The ropes might as well have been secured to boulders. Lucius backed to the edge, then leapt into the darkness, his boots catching the upper rim as he tugged on the rope and was gradually fed enough line to make his descent. Myrmeen quickly followed him, disturbed by the leer of the first monster that held her rope. She restrained herself from making an impolite gesture and quickly vanished into the pit.

"Zeal, you simpleton, don't just stand there. Give them some light," Lord Sixx roared. The fiery-haired man flinched at the insult, then proceeded to follow his master's command, crouching at the lip of the pit and allowing his hands to be consumed by twin suns of flame that lighted the shaft for a depth of nearly thirty yards.

"They're fifty feet down, but I don't see any niche," Zeal said.

"We don't need a commentary. Let the humans accomplish their task," Lord Sixx chided.

Within the pit, Lucius and Myrmeen descended another twenty feet before the mage motioned for the fighter to stop.

"It is here," he called as he clapped three times, indicating that no further rope should be given.

Myrmeen saw a section of smooth rock that looked no different from the rest of the shaft. Suddenly she realized what was different about this patch of stone: On its surface were the mummified remains of several dozen insects, a few roaches, and even a butterfly that might have been pinned in the album of a collector.

"Do not touch the stone," Lucius warned.

"Have no worries," she responded.

Lucius appeared to be no longer listening; he was casting a spell. Suddenly a glowing, silver ball of light materialized over their heads. A cloud of blue flame burst from the surface of the stone and was absorbed by the spell trap, which also provided all the illumination they required.

Above, Imperator Zeal allowed the fires consuming his hands to fade and he returned to the crowd, standing well apart from Lord Sixx.

In the pit, Lucius touched the newly polished rock surface and spread his fingers upon the stone. Uttering a few simple words, he dispelled the magic holding the small section of wall in place. The burned umber stretch of rock disappeared and was replaced by the niche Shandower had mentioned. The box containing the apparatus was in plain view, three feet inside the hole into which a man could comfortably fit, provided he remained in a crouch. Myrmeen resisted the urge to reach inside and snatch the box, which was large enough to house a crossbow. The box they had brought with them was black and plain, the steel container used to protect maps and scrolls in the event of a fire. Myrmeen found it strangely comforting that these unnatural creatures could get lost as easily as any human.

The box housing the apparatus was bright gold, with arcane runes etched upon its surface. The grooves were filled in with tiny, crushed rubies. Representations of men and women suffering the torments of the damned rose from its slightly dull surface, and, when viewed from a distance, the figures meshed together to create a face that was screaming in terror. One of the eyes looked as if it had been put out. A sky-blue marble flecked with crimson had been placed in the remaining socket. The box's sides had strange figures that gave the overall impression of hands that had been fused to the metal by touching a red-hot surface.

Her instincts told her that this was far too easy. Lucius looked over at her and nodded, as if confirming her thoughts.

"The easier it looks, . . ." he said, his voice trailing off sorrowfully. He cleared his throat and said, "Perhaps you should go back."

"My place is with you," she said.

Lucius turned away and said, "What will you tell my children of how I met my end?"

"That you died to save others."

He nodded, then completed another spell. Myrmeen shuddered in surprise as her field of vision took on a crimson hue. She looked down to see a glowing field of energy surrounding her body, an aura of protection.

"Spirit armor," she said angrily. "This spell steals some of my life's essence!"

"It may be worthwhile if it saves your life later."

"Or you may have just taken a few precious days, a month, or more, for no reason. Next time, ask me first."

"You would have refused," he said dryly.

"I notice you didn't cast this spell on yourself."

Lucius shook his head. "I have no life essence to utilize. I am a dead man walking."

Myrmeen had no reply. The damage was done. All they could do was get on with the task at hand.

The gaunt mage took a handful of loose stone from the edge of the niche and threw them at the box. The stones crackled, and a blinding flash of light consumed them as the rocks were vaporized against an invisible wall of force.

"Get back!" Lucius shouted as he shoved at Myrmeen, forcing her to swing out of the niche as the spell trap's small, glowing orb rushed in and collided with the unseen wall. The explosion sent each of them hurtling toward the opposite wall of the shaft, where they groaned with the impact, then found the area once again wreathed in darkness. Myrmeen could no longer see her red aura, and wondered if the spell had saved her already. Her body drifted in a pendulous motion, swinging back to the alcove where the box had been stored. A hand gripped her arm and she allowed herself to be dragged into the small niche.

"Hold out your hand. This won't hurt you," Lucius said.

Myrmeen did as the sorcerer asked. She heard him whisper in the darkness, then jumped as a flaming sphere appeared in her hand. Her head struck the hard ceiling. Lucius had kept a tight grip on her arm, and she quickly calmed herself, realizing that the flames were not harming her. "Whatever you do, keep away from the box."

Myrmeen nodded. The mystical blast from the destruction of the spell trap had left the mage shaken, his flesh burned, lacerations visible beneath his shredded white smock. Myrmeen could see the wounds that had killed him, and turned away in disgust from the sight. She once had desired this man, but she did not want him now.

A part of her hated herself for these thoughts, but she knew that Lucius was already gone. She had to adjust to his death, even if that meant distancing herself from him while his soul was still trapped within his rotting shell.

"The signs are there," Lucius said, admiring the craftsmanship of the mages who had preceded him.

"What signs?" Myrmeen asked. "What do they indicate?"

"The sleep of ages. If we are not especially careful, we could be enveloped in a stasis field, frozen forever, eternally aware, damned for all time—similar to what Lord Sixx has done to me, only much worse. The art of what has been done here is that Phezult's spell is only the first page in a long tome. Dispelling this bit of magic will act to trigger several worse spells. Brilliant."

"What other spells?"

"There is no way to tell. I would guess a mindkiller spell, tentacle walls, fear contagion—anything is possible."

"So what do we do?"

A weak smile crossed his features as he told Myrmeen what to shout upward, to the night people. Soon they heard the sound of heels slamming against the stone above and grunts of exertion as one of the creatures was lowered to where Myrmeen dangled, just outside of the niche. The creature appeared to be human, which bothered Myrmeen, until it started scratching the side of its head and peeled back a section of human flesh to reveal scales. She ushered it into the pit, where Lucius politely asked the monster to help them, as they were not strong enough to lift the box containing the apparatus. The monster laughed at their human frailty and clutched the hand rests at either side of the box. The creature then stumbled back, where it collapsed into an eternal sleep.

"We made a mistake," Myrmeen shouted. "Lift him back." She looked into the niche and grinned at Lucius. "We have more work to do."

As the night people hauled up their fallen comrade, Myrmeen crawled back inside the niche, holding her flaming hand before her. "Could you have restored him?"

"Of course. That is what the silver mirror is for. With it I can summon any elements I might need, such as a vial containing seven drops of holy water, which it would have procured from a temple. But why should I waste the effort on such as these?"

Myrmeen smiled, reminded of what first had attracted her to the man: his attitude. "What's next?"

"The box," he said calmly, though his hands trembled. Myrmeen understood the reasons for his fear. If one of the spells managed to destroy them, she would be killed instantly. Lucius, however, would suffer eternally, his body destroyed and his soul set adrift, beyond the reach of the evil god Cyric or the monster who had killed him, Lord Sixx. To die this way would mean that he would never know peace.

"Can I help you?" she whispered, surprised by the calm, reassuring sound of her own voice. Although she was on the brink of instant death were the mage to make a mistake, she was not afraid. She had confidence that he would proceed calmly and logically, and that he would protect her.

Lucius seemed to relax as he said, "Avoid the marble in the eye. Touching it will send you into another dimension. I would not be able to retrieve you."

"I'll be sure not to touch it," she said quickly. "What are you doing?"

"I am going to try to transfer the remaining spells from the box containing the apparatus to the one we brought with us," Lucius said as he picked up the silver mirror and summoned a blue marble. He secured the marble to the second metal box with a spell that made the steel grow hot and soft long enough for the marble to be implanted. After Lucius explained that the casting of this last spell would take close to an hour, Myrmeen settled back, staring at her flaming fist, of which she had hardly been aware.

The fighter maintained her silence, giving Lucius the chance to concentrate, but her own thoughts were not so mercifully silent. They assaulted Myrmeen with the intensity of the storm that had been the herald of all the worst tragedies she had suffered through her life.

She had been betrayed.

During her career as a politician, betrayal was an accepted factor in her day-to-day existence. She had come to expect it and knew precisely how to deal with a certain lack of integrity on the part of her associates. That had been tolerable only because she had been trained to rely on no one but herself; as long as she decided well in advance that no one could be trusted in a given situation, she was never hurt by their unscrupulous actions. Give someone an opening and invariably they will hurt you.

From the moment she had summoned the Harpers, Myrmeen had been forced to surrender her trust, and had paid dearly for the mistake. Lucius, with whom she had been emotionally and sexually intrigued, had revealed a loyalty to his family and a fear of eternal torment that had caused him to hand their lives over to the creatures from whom he had sworn to protect them. Even Varina's sacrifice was difficult for Myrmeen to accept. To spare her husband a worse death, she had taken Burke's life, then given her own to help her friends escape. Myrmeen knew that on the surface her sacrifice was noble and heroic—but a part of her could not help regarding Varina's actions as cowardly and selfish. Varina did not want to face life without her husband at her side and so she chose to have no life at all. Myrmeen was ashamed of her feelings. However, she could not deny that she was angry.

Everyone goes away, a taunting voice whispered in her mind. *You can trust no one.*

Not everyone, she thought desperately. Reisz would take me back. He still loves me. He always will.

But you don't love him, and you know it.

She thought of the woman-spider and its unexpected generosity, sparing Myrmeen's life when the beast easily could have taken it.

Perhaps that was the point, Myrmeen thought. This way I know it can have me at any time. I live or die by its wishes.

No, that was not it. The look on the woman-spider's face

before it retreated had revealed that it had been as confused by its own decision as Myrmeen had been.

Thinking about the mysterious woman-thing caused Myrmeen to recall her strange dream, then she moved beyond such unpleasantness, to gentler memories of her parents and their life before that fateful morning that her father was convinced would change all their lives forever. He had been correct, but not in the manner he had anticipated.

Suddenly she remembered the lonely nights after his death, when bizarre nightmares plagued her and she woke up screaming. Don't abandon me! Don't go away! Don't leave me for the shadow people to come crawling up from the floor when the lanterns are blown out! Father, please don't—!

"I am finished," Lucius announced.

Myrmeen looked up in shock, glancing away from the pulsing, hypnotic fires that were dimming in her hand. She looked at the pair of boxes on the ground, darted forward with the speed and ferocity of an animal, and clutched the sides of the arcane box holding the apparatus. Before Lucius, who was trembling with fatigue, could stop her, Myrmeen hurled the box over the edge, into the pit.

The lazy sound of swords scraping against one another rose from the darkness outside the niche. Myrmeen had heard the sound only a few hours earlier, in her room, when the woman-spider had tried to kill her. The creature appeared on the opposite wall, the box clutched in two human hands. Myrmeen looked over the edge of the niche and saw that, fifty feet below, the monster had spun an intricate web. When she turned her gaze back to the box in Tamara's hands, she saw that white, sticky strands clung to its sides.

"Sudden movement," Lucius said, horrified.

Myrmeen spun in his direction to see the second box flaring with a rainbow of colors. The mage covered his mouth, his brow furrowed as he rifled through his vast mental library of spells, hoping to find one that would purchase their lives.

"The spell," he whispered, "was not yet fixed. No sudden movement, or it would all be undone."

"By the gods," she whispered, suddenly aware of the cost of her actions. The flames in her hand flickered out and several strands of lightning reached from the second box like newly awakened hands eager to explore. "Lucius!"

Myrmeen was aware of nothing but the feel of powerful hands on her back as she was dragged back from the niche, into the darkened shaft. She was quickly carried upward as an explosion sounded from where Lucius had remained.

The walls of the pit shook and Myrmeen looked up to see that she was in the woman-spider's arms. Tamara desperately tried to hold on as clouds of light and smoke billowed up from beneath them. Suddenly they were at the rim, over the top, stumbling forward. A beautiful shaft of greenish white light shot up from the pit and licked at the cavernous theater's ceiling, charring the stone black before the stream of light faded abruptly and was gone.

There had been no sound. Lucius's body had been destroyed, and he had not even issued a scream. Myrmeen scrambled to her feet and clutched at Lord Sixx. He held her at bay with ease.

"Help him!" she shouted. "Release your hold on his soul, before it is too late."

"It is too late," Lord Sixx said with genuine regret. "I prefer to keep my word, but there is nothing to be done."

My fault, Myrmeen thought. It's my fault he's gone, his soul wandering forever in torment. Lucius, I'm sorry.

Behind Myrmeen, Tamara had regained her human form. She approached Lord Sixx, the box containing the apparatus in her hands. Before she handed the box to her leader, she glanced in her husband's direction, hoping for a sign that he would be willing to take the box instead. Imperator Zeal stared at her in displeasure and angled his head in Sixx's direction. Tamara felt her arms grow heavy as she presented the box to Lord Sixx and withdrew quickly. Myrmeen stood beside the dark man.

"Now," Sixx whispered as he held the ornately designed gold box high over his head, intoxicated by the end of the quest and the security this object brought him: No challenger would dare usurp him. "Now we may begin again."

A roar sliced through the theater surrounding the pit as the Night Parade creatures cheered Lord Sixx. Myrmeen ran to Krystin and embraced her. Tamara watched them, her arms folded over her breasts. She was the only member of the Night Parade whose gaze was not riveted to the object Lord Sixx held out to his subjects. Her husband, Imperator Zeal, glanced at her and hoped that Sixx would not become aware of the woman's distraction.

When he was certain that the moment had passed, Lord Sixx allowed his people to break off into smaller groups, friends and allies congregating to discuss in hushed, excited tones the importance of this event to each of them. Although the conversations were diverse, many conducted in languages spawned by cultures that had not originated on this world, the content of each was invariably the same: With the apparatus back in their leader's possession, the long delayed Festival of Renewal finally would be held.

Lord Sixx went to Myrmeen, who held Krystin tightly against her. "You may live."

"And my friends?" Myrmeen asked.

"Yes, whatever. I'm feeling benevolent, and you've certainly done me a service." He gestured grandly. "Zeal, Tamara, take them outside. Make sure they get what they need for their journey, wherever they wish to go. Any who harm the humans will answer to me."

The fiery-haired man and his wife brought Reisz and Ord forward. Zeal gestured, and the creatures that had followed him in the hallway retreated from the corridor.

"Wait," Krystin said, surprising Lord Sixx and Myrmeen equally. "You owe her more than that. You should tell her the truth about her daughter."

Lord Sixx's many eyes narrowed uniformly. "Why don't you do that, child? You know as much as I do."

"What's he talking about?" Myrmeen asked, despite her instincts, which told her to leave this place before Lord Sixx changed his mind and slaughtered them.

Krystin turned to face Myrmeen. "I'm not your daughter. I never was."

Myrmeen swallowed hard. "When did you learn this?"

"Days ago, in Calimport. It's my fault they're here," Krystin said, watching Myrmeen's features grow hard and cold. Despite this, she could not bring herself to stop. "I led them here."

"You didn't," Myrmeen said flatly, becoming numb.

"Alden followed the traces of blood I left behind."

Myrmeen felt as if she were about to pass out.

"In the beginning, all they wanted was for you to think I was your daughter and take me away," Krystin said. She wrung her hands and explained in full the deception that Lord Sixx had perpetrated and the part she unwittingly had played in his schemes. Then she told Myrmeen of how the locket had related to her stolen and bastardized memories. Finally she spoke of the deal she had made with Lord Sixx to save all their lives in Calimport.

"You're a fool," Lord Sixx said, aghast at the child's stupidity. He wondered how he could use it to his own advantage.

Tears soaked Krystin's face as she said, "Myrmeen, forgive me, I'm sorry—"

"What she's told you is true," Lord Sixx said, "but it's not the whole truth. For example: What happened to your true daughter? I can tell you that."

Myrmeen shook her head and said with a quavering voice, "I don't want to hear any more lies."

"You don't understand," Lord Sixx said as he motioned for Zeal and Tamara to come closer. "I also don't have any reason to tell you a damned thing. Give me some incentive."

Myrmeen almost laughed. "I'm not playing any more games."

"You're not?" Lord Sixx asked quietly. "Do you mean to say that you have traveled so far, been through so much, lost friends to horrible deaths, seen living nightmares that will scar your dreams until you die, and now that the truth is before you, you would turn away?"

"Yes," Myrmeen said. A part of her wished to hear Lord Sixx's words, even if they turned out to hold only a glimmer of truth, because now she was left with much less than she had before entering the city.

"All I ask is a favor now and then, nothing of great import," Lord Sixx said, his delivery powerful and seductive.

That was his mistake. Myrmeen had dealt with men who had tried to use her all of her life. She knew how to resist them. "I'm not interested."

Lord Sixx frowned. "Fine. If you ever wish to find me, you will not have difficulty. And if you ever wish to know the truth of what happened to your child, the price will be the blood of this one."

His hand moved quickly, a dagger shaped like black lightning slapping into his palm. He pressed the knife against Krystin's throat as Zeal grasped her arms from behind. Tamara's arm's already had transformed, and the point of a steely spider-arm suddenly was pressed against the hollow of Myrmeen's throat.

Krystin's hand brushed hers, and Myrmeen realized that despite what the girl had revealed, she still meant what she had said to Krystin earlier that night. Losing her would be like losing her daughter a second time.

"Go to hell," Myrmeen said.

"Only if you'll join me," Lord Sixx said as he held her with his dark-eyed gaze. He then withdrew his blade and instructed Zeal and Tamara to lead the humans to safety.

Twenty

Imperator Zeal and his wife led the humans to the makeshift stables where Shandower had secured their mounts. The gags maintaining Ord and Reisz's silence had been removed, but the Harpers had said very little during the journey. Myrmeen had surprised Krystin by taking her hand while they were being ferried across the tiny lake where glowworms laid glittering traps for their prey. When the troupe had reached the shore, each of the humans was given an armful of provisions for the long ride to Calimport.

Tamara's dark eyes followed Myrmeen, her gaze clinging to the woman with the strength of the webs she had expelled while in her other form.

"I don't understand," Myrmeen said. "Why are you letting us go?"

"Because you no longer are of any consequence," Zeal said coldly. "And this is what my lord desires."

The wall leading out to the cliff vanished as Tamara kissed its cold surface, revealing a shoal of stars above the gently surging waters of the sea below. The humans led their mounts to the difficult trail outside, Myrmeen intentionally going last so that she could face Tamara, who remained close to her at all times.

"Why didn't you kill me when you had the chance?" Myrmeen asked. Tamara raised her hand, and the wall appeared, separating them.

Myrmeen, the Harpers, and Krystin led their mounts along the rise, where they retraced their steps and eventually made their way to the top of the cliff. They mounted their horses and rode toward the city as if the red-haired man were chasing them, spitting fire at their heels.

Near the cavern's entrance, Imperator Zeal confronted his wife. The candles and torches lining the walls flared as if they were about to explode. "What was the Lhal woman talking about?"

"I went to her room," Tamara admitted.

"You were going to kill her?"

"I had planned to, yes," Tamara said. "She burned our home to the ground, destroyed all I had, all that was important to me."

"Those were just objects. They can be replaced."

"You never had a family," she whispered. "You wouldn't understand."

The fiery-haired man touched her arm with a gentle caress, his anger fading. Upon the walls, the brilliant light waned until the fires resumed their normal intensity.

"What stopped you?" he asked.

"You did," she said, burying her face in his hard, muscular chest, "I thought of the displeasure you would face from Lord Sixx if she were found dead. I couldn't do it."

He knew she was lying but held her close. "I love you, wife."

"And I love you," she whispered.

These words he believed. As he brushed her hair with his nearly smoldering hands, Zeal formed another explanation for his wife's actions. He decided that his wife had grown tired of having him ignore her urging to take Lord Sixx's power. She had planned to assassinate the Lhal woman to force the two men into confrontation. Sixx would have wanted Tamara's life for her actions, and Zeal would have murdered the man to protect her. At the last moment, she had changed her mind, granting Zeal the opportunity to decide for himself if he would try to usurp Lord Sixx, something that would be nearly impossible now that the man had the apparatus.

Imperator Zeal pulled back and kissed his wife's hungry lips. As he felt the flames of passion stir within him, several torches exploded, startling them both. Once they realized what had happened, Zeal and his wife began to laugh uncontrollably. They sank to the ground, their arms still around one another as they rolled on the hard stone, giggling like children.

Between gasps of laughter Zeal said, "Yes, I will do it."

The smile faded instantly from his wife's face. "What are you—what do you mean?"

Cupping her face in his hands, Zeal whispered, "I would die for you, Tamara. If you ask me, I will kill for you as well. I know why you wanted the Lhal woman dead."

"You do?" she said in a small voice.

He explained his theory, and she did not deny his words, though he was completely incorrect in his assumptions. "It will be difficult, and we will have to wait until the night of the festival, but that will give us time to plan and make our plans a reality." He kissed her hard on the lips. "This is what you want, isn't it?"

"Yes," she said softly, imagining the sheer joy of watching Lord Sixx die, for reasons that even her husband knew nothing about. She threw her arms around him and held him tight. "Yes, my love, this is what I wanted."

Around them, the light grew brighter. Had they been more aware of their surroundings and less lost within each other, they might have noticed a patch of darkness in the shape of a slightly hunched, long-haired figure that suddenly detached from the wall. The creature stole away quickly to the comforting shadows where it allowed itself to become enveloped. It huddled in the forgotten cavern where it had gone to hide and wondered what it should do with the knowledge it had acquired.

The being that had been Alden McGregor pulled up its knees and began to cry.

* * * * *

Miles away, as the hours quickly stretched toward dawn, Krystin rode beside Myrmeen. She said nothing to the older woman and Myrmeen acknowledged her presence with only a weak smile, but the gesture was enough to keep them together for the entire following day, their conversation picking up where they had left off before Shandower's death.

Evening was approaching, and Myrmeen had found shelter for the party behind a group of towering gray obelisks. Reisz sat atop the tallest of the stones, watching for any signs of the night people. Myrmeen, Krystin, and Ord tended the mounts and prepared the evening meal.

Krystin knew that eventually they would have to talk about what had happened and the revelation that she was not, in fact, Myrmeen's daughter. The girl fully expected Myrmeen to raise the subject, and when she did not, Krystin decided she would mention it. Before she had the chance, Ord surprised her by breaking the silence he had shared with Reisz as he strode before her and stopped. He stared at her with a flat, disinterested expression that suddenly gave way to a mask of rage. He struck her in the face with the back of his hand, knocking her from her feet. She landed with a grunt of surprise, her head striking the ground inches from a sharp stone jutting from the soft earth.

"Whore!" he shouted. "That I ever could have been attracted to such as you . . ."

Myrmeen was upon him instantly, shoving him back and away from the fallen girl. "That's enough!"

"She betrayed us to the monsters who killed my parents!"

"She did it to save our lives," Myrmeen said. "It's not the

same thing, and you know it." Ord looked away. Myrmeen could not tell if her words had gotten through to him or not.

"I don't care about her reasons," Ord said, refusing to look at Krystin, who had picked herself up from the ground. "None of it makes up for what she did."

"It does to me," Myrmeen said. "You're young, Ord. Wait until you've made a few mistakes of your own."

"She's right," Reisz called from his perch. "Hating Krystin isn't going to bring Burke and Varina back. She didn't cause their deaths, and if it wasn't for what she had done, we all would be dead."

"Ord, I'm going back to Calimport with Krystin," Myrmeen announced. "If you don't want to come with us—"

"I'm a Harper, like my parents before me," Ord said. "We are the lord protectors of the Realms." He looked at Krystin. "I'm not going to let my personal feelings get in the way of that."

Myrmeen nodded. "Your parents would be very proud."

Ord left her and scrambled to the perch where Reisz was waiting. The olive-skinned man put his arm around the boy.

Krystin approached Myrmeen and said, "Did you mean what you said just now? Will you give me another chance?"

"No more lies," Myrmeen said firmly.

The girl shook her head, and the two women stared at one another. Forgiveness would be difficult, and it would take time, but from the feelings that passed between them in that single moment, they knew it would not be impossible.

* * * * *

The next day, the group rode into the city. This time, Myrmeen gave her true name and demanded that she be given an audience with the ruler of Calimport, Pasha Rashid Djenispool. By late afternoon, her request had been granted, and she stood with Ord and Krystin before Djenispool and several members of his ruling council, many of whom had met with Myrmeen in Arabel. The older man's son, Vizier Punjor

Djenispool, stood to the side, an emotionless observer to the proceedings.

Myrmeen spoke for the group. The pasha and his men listened to her impassioned plea, nodded politely, and informed her that they were in the midst of a much needed upsurge in tourism. The panic that would be caused if they tried to act on her warning—words that she could not substantiate with anything more than the integrity for which she was known—would create more damage than even the shadow beings that Myrmeen insisted were real.

"Bring one of them to us," she was told by the aging pasha. "Let us see it meld with the shadows."

"Yes, we have a dinner party scheduled at the manse next week," said one of his men. "Bring it to us by then. The entertainment in this town has been a bore lately."

The veneer of respect for Myrmeen fell away as the half dozen men before her became consumed with creating jokes about her claims, ignoring her as she tried to get their attention once again. It was a tactic she had used many times on troublesome visitors who did not realize that their audience was at an end. Myrmeen removed the sword she had been given by the night people and buried it in the wooden table behind which the council members sat, the blade striking directly between the pasha's hands.

Silence flooded the room as the old man's son started forward and was stopped by Reisz, who drew his knife and assumed a defensive stance before the vizier.

"The great storm of fourteen years ago is about to come again," Myrmeen said. "People will die, and you are doing nothing about it."

The aged pasha cracked the knuckles of his right hand. "Do you need an armed escort from the city, or can you find your own way?"

Pulling the sword back, Myrmeen turned from the assemblage and gestured for Krystin and the Harpers to follow her. The guards at the heavy door parted for them. Vizier Djenispool, a handsome man in his thirties, watched them with flat, unreadable eyes.

Behind her, Myrmeen heard the old man attempting to recover the dignity she had taken from him. "You see, this is what I mean. By allowing our rulers to be deigned by the act of succession, we end up with barbarians on the throne, fools that wouldn't understand civilization, pouting women with more muscles than brains who run around with weapons held high, acting like children before their betters. They come here expecting—"

Myrmeen turned and the old man leaned back in his seat. His eyes widened at the sight of the golden slivers in her eyes, which widened with murderous intent.

"I expect nothing from any of you except that you will bleat like the dying sheep that you are when the Night Parade comes out of hiding with a taste for blood," she said, then left the room with her companions.

"Very adult handling of that situation," Reisz chided as they walked the streets, trying to come up with a plan of action. The afternoon sun waned as storm clouds gathered.

"We have escorts," Myrmeen said, ignoring his comment and indicating the guardsmen who followed in a less than subtle manner.

"That means that if we try to rouse the people's attention, we will be slapped in chains before we have accomplished anything," Reisz added.

They walked a few blocks, and Myrmeen fumed over the old ruler's comparison of her to a child. Krystin stopped suddenly, clutching at the glass window of a nearby shop as realization struck her like a fist.

"The children," Krystin said. "It's the children they're going to want, just like they did last time."

Myrmeen blanched at the girl's words. "Why?" she whispered softly as she touched Krystin's shoulder.

"I don't know why," Krystin said, shrugging off the soothing touch as she hugged herself.

Myrmeen saw a sidewalk eatery with tables just ahead. She led her companions to a table and sat down hard, gesturing for the guardsmen to join them. The hard-looking men stood at a respectful distance, about a hundred feet away, and did not acknowledge the invitation. Myrmeen ordered a round of the strongest ale on the menu as she thought about the danger to Calimport's children.

"I don't know what to do," Myrmeen said. "If we knock on doors and walk around with signs, we'll be laughed at or thrown out of town. The council doesn't believe us."

"Perhaps this is why Lord Sixx let us live," Reisz said, "to let us face the humiliation of failure, to watch the suffering and not be able to stop it." The swarthy-skinned man shook his head. "We're going to need help. If we can't do anything to stop the festival, then we're going to have to be prepared to fight—"

"Six thousand," Myrmeen reminded him. "How can we fight that many?"

"Shandower did it," Krystin said quietly. Everyone stared at her. "Erin took the apparatus. It's something they need. You saw the way they reacted."

"Are you saying we should steal it back?" Ord asked.

"Or destroy it," the girl replied.

"Shandower must have tried," Myrmeen said. "With his wealth, he would have tried everything, every form of magic available."

"There are mages who aren't for hire," Reisz said. "Elminster, for one."

"I thought you said he was an old nag," Ord remarked.

"That aside," Reisz said with a grin.

"We don't have time to reach the Dales," Myrmeen said. "The festival is long overdue. They're not going to delay any longer. I wouldn't be surprised if preparations were already underway by the ones who were left behind."

"No," Reisz said, "Lord Sixx wouldn't have wanted the humiliation if he returned empty-handed. We have some time."

"What do you suggest?" Myrmeen asked.

"I have a friend who owes me a favor in Teshburl," Reisz said. "It's not far from here."

Ord rolled his eyes. "Vitendi? You would call upon that lout, after the way he treated you, after he threatened you in front of us all?"

"That's just his way," Reisz said, dismissing him.

"Really?" Ord said. "That's like saying that a mass murderer who consumes his victims' flesh is not a bad person—that's just his way!"

"Why are you so against this?" Krystin asked.

Ord ran his hand over his face. "It's going to be a waste of time. Vitendi will never—"

Reisz leaned over and cupped his hand over Ord's ear as he whispered to the nineteen-year-old. Ord's expression changed, and he nearly laughed.

"Admiral Mond Vitendi has his own fleet, a marvelous navy that rarely gets a chance to fight anyone," Ord said in a complete turnabout. "Excellent choice."

Myrmeen wondered what Reisz had on the man, then shook her head. "So how do you intend to get to him?"

With a smile Reisz said, "Do you have any more gold?"

* * * * *

Several hours later, at twilight, Myrmeen, Krystin, and Ord stood beside Reisz near the docks. He had chartered a small vessel and was preparing to depart. Two new guardsmen made their presence known without engaging the group. "They're charging us a fortune," he said. "They tell me there's a storm on the approach, a bad one."

A mass of clouds had gathered over the city. Myrmeen forced away memories of the night she had lost her child.

Reisz shrugged. "Of course, the interesting thing will be the Djenispools' reaction when Vitendi's ships arrive in their port."

"They'll probably welcome them as tourists," Myrmeen said. "Keep the men on the ships, or their discipline will be corrupted by this city within an hour of landfall."

"Provided they'll come," Reisz said with a wink to Ord.

"There are no guarantees."

Ord looked away, grinning.

"I'll see you soon," Reisz said as he turned.

Myrmeen glanced at the child who might have been her daughter. "Reisz, I want you to take Krystin."

"Absolutely not," Krystin said.

A single eyebrow rose on Reisz's worn face. "I'm not going to drag a prisoner behind me. Krystin, do you want to come with me or stay behind to face the night people?"

"I'm not stupid," she said. "I don't want to die, but the couple who adopted me is in the city, looking for me. I have to get them to safety first."

Myrmeen felt a heavy weight rise from her heart, lodging deeply in her throat.

"Then I'm going to tell them I want to return to Arabel with Myrmeen," Krystin said, "if she will have me."

Staring at the girl in total surprise, Myrmeen whispered, "Of course I will. But I still need to know what happened to my daughter."

"I understand," Krystin said, taking the conversation no further. Reisz nodded and walked down the pier.

"Wait," Myrmeen called, running after him. She stopped before Reisz, her chest heaving. "I just—I don't know. You've been so good to me over the years, Reisz."

"I know," he said. "I'm a wonderful man."

Her shoulders sagged.

"Let's not beat it into the ground," he said. "You know how I feel about you. Nothing's changed."

Reisz leaned in, kissed her, then turned and walked away. Myrmeen was speechless as she watched his receding form become swallowed by the shadows. Krystin and Ord came to her side.

"Do you think he'll make it?" Krystin asked.

"I hope so," Myrmeen said, but she knew why the girl was concerned. The storm promised to be terrible.

Night was almost upon them. Watch fires burned along the dock. Myrmeen was about to leave when she sensed a familiar presence. Someone was watching her. As if answering an un-spoken summons, a woman eased from the shadows. It was Tamara. Myrmeen spun, blade in hand, as Ord and Krystin readied themselves for battle. The guardsmen who had been watching them had vanished.

"He seems like a good man," Tamara said.

Myrmeen's heart raced, but she could tell from the dark woman's relaxed manner that no attack was pending. Tamara held out her hands to show that she carried no weapons.

"I thought we should talk," Tamara said. "You see, the time you thought was yours is gone. The festival will commence tonight."

"No," Myrmeen said. She was certain she had a span of days ahead of her, time enough to fulfill Krystin's mission and send the girl away to safety; time enough to do something for the children who were in danger.

"We returned much earlier than you," she said. "Listen. The opening movements of our grand composition have be-gun."

From above Myrmeen heard the roll of thunder. Tamara spread her arms wide as she spun like a child, her head thrown back with a rapturous smile as the heavy wind blowing from the coast lifted her hair and ran through it with invisible fin-gers.

"By night we can ride the shadows, we can navigate the winds of darkness. A hundred strong, a thousand strong, we could breeze past you and steal the flesh from your bones with ease. Without a mage you would never sense us."

Myrmeen wondered where the other members of the Night Parade were hidden. She had not forgotten that Tamara had tried to kill her; she also had not forgotten that the woman-spider had stepped back, allowing Myrmeen to live. An odd sensation had passed between them, something that Myr-meen desperately had tried to forget.

If Krystin is not my daughter, who is?

Recognition.

Impossible, Myrmeen thought as she stared at the lithe,

dark-haired woman with red specks in her eyes. She looks too old to be my daughter. But, then, these creatures' appearances often are deceiving.

A flash of pure white light shocked Myrmeen from her thoughts and she registered the sizzle of lightning as a bolt reached down from the darkened skies and struck a building a few blocks away. Krystin eased into her arms in a natural embrace. Myrmeen wondered if Tamara had killed the pair of guardsmen assigned to watch them or if the soldiers had run to get help. The latter was unlikely, as Tamara appeared completely human in this form.

"I know you're thinking about running," Tamara said as she made her final turn and stopped abruptly, her hair whipping around to obscure one side of her face. "If I meant you harm, you would know by now."

Myrmeen tensed as thunder rolled again, louder, closer.

"I want to help," Tamara said. "I was wrong about you. I was wrong about so much I believed about you."

The fighter could not stop the flood of thoughts that filled her mind and might drown her if she were not careful: The Night Parade took my daughter. Krystin is not that child. Tamara could be. She has more of Dak in her, but she could well be my child.

"How do you expect us to believe you?" Ord said.

Tamara gazed coldly at the man. "What you do is of little consequence to me. My concern is for Myrmeen."

"Why?" Myrmeen asked, shocked that the words had leapt from her mind to her tongue with so little restraint.

"I have my reasons," Tamara said. "Do you hear it?"

The first drops of rain began to fall, heavy, violent splatters of liquid.

I'm dripping. Honey, I hate that.

Myrmeen shook the image from her nightmare away. Above, a blanket of storm clouds had covered the city. She thought of Reisz and knew that they had acted too late.

"The children," she said, hoping there was time enough to find one orphanage and try to save the infants from the Night

Parade.

"Yes," Tamara said darkly, "the children will suffer this night if you do not listen to me."

From somewhere far off Myrmeen heard the dulcet sounds of a harp intertwined with a sweet, joyous voice that was accompanied by a flute and the delicate reverberations of a triangle. The sounds were carried on the wind, and Myrmeen suddenly felt weak. As her knees turned to liquid and she fell, Myrmeen was vaguely aware of Krystin and Ord also succumbing to the lure of the strangely beautiful music, a lullaby more irresistible than any they had ever heard before.

Tamara snatched up the blade that Myrmeen had dropped. The music was not harming her. She slashed Myrmeen's palm, then her own. Pressing her wounded hand against Myrmeen's, Tamara threw her head back and repeated a phrase in an ancient language that humans could never speak. As their blood mixed, Myrmeen's eyes fluttered and suddenly she pulled away from Tamara, scrambling back in fear and distrust.

"Bellophat's music cannot harm you now," Tamara said. "You will not be another human cow to be slaughtered. My blood has touched yours, as yours touched mine, long ago."

Myrmeen did not have time to ask Tamara to explain her cryptic statement. "Protect the others, too."

"As you wish," Tamara said, taking Krystin's and Ord's palms and sharing blood with them. As Krystin and the last Harper shook off the sudden, numbing effects of sleep, they dragged themselves to their feet and stood beside Myrmeen, whose hand was outstretched to catch the rain.

Krystin touched Myrmeen's arm. "The Devlaines."

"Don't bother," Tamara said. "The Devlaines are dead. Doppelgangers have taken their place."

Somehow, Krystin was not surprised to learn that Lord Sixx had lied and that he had murdered her adopted parents. What shocked her, however, was her own lack of emotion at the news that they were dead. She felt very little for these people, her memories of them hazy and indistinct. It would strike her later, she was certain of that. For now, her mind seemed willing to protect her from the shock.

"Bellophat," Myrmeen said absently.

Vizier Bellophat promised us sustenance.

She had heard those words on the black ship that had been smuggling inhuman cargo into the city's port. She remembered the monstrosity that could twist its body into instruments and produce sounds she had never heard before.

"We killed Bellophat," Myrmeen said, "drowned him."

"Not all of our kind need air to breathe," Tamara said. "You inconvenienced us, that's all."

"The children," Krystin said insistently.

"Yes," Tamara agreed, "they are the most vulnerable. The only chance you have to save them is by killing Bellophat. If you silence his music, the people will wake and take arms against my kind. It is the only chance humans have this night. The festival is overdue, and Calimport will be gutted much worse than during the last storm."

"Which had not been a storm," Myrmeen said, wondering if the rain she felt also was an illusion. Thunder clapped and lightning crackled over the water.

"I still don't understand," Myrmeen said as she heard the music grow even louder. "Why are you helping us?"

"For selfish reasons," Tamara said. With those words she turned and leapt toward a nearby wall, which she scaled and vanished over before Myrmeen could ask her question a second time.

Myrmeen looked at the child who might have been her daughter had circumstances been different, and the young man who had been thrust into a life he had not chosen for himself, and said, "We have to end this if we can."

Krystin and Ord nodded in agreement, and together they ran toward the music, the sounds of the storm and the encompassing fingers of rain closing over them as they disappeared into the night.

Twenty-One

"That you are my son disgusts me."

Alden McGregor tried to keep his own revulsion at bay as he stared at the red-skinned man who had spoken. The man's flesh appeared to have been flayed, leaving only bare muscle and tissue. Alden could tell that the man before him in the darkened chamber once had been a beautiful physical specimen that had literally been turned inside out and stitched back together. He wore a black leather tunic, stitched up the front, his arms and legs exposed. Rubies adorned his waist sash and the bands around his arms and thighs. His eyes were sky blue.

He was Magistrate Dymas, he explained, Lord of the Dance. When he performed, his motions could cause even the casual observer to experience vertigo and lose all motor functions. The nightmares he could provoke began with the fulfillment of fantasies and ended with the most humiliating of disappointments. The feeling of loss after even one such dream could drive a person to suicide.

The elegance of his movements were balanced by the

crudeness of his appearance, speech, and manner. Although
he was intelligent and educated, his speech often lapsed into
the gutter slang of his youth. He was like an animal who
fiercely labored to maintain a civilized appearance. Alden
loathed him.

"These is my powers," Dymas said. "What's yours? You're
a dog. You hunt and sniff and follow the scent of blood. You
ain't one of us. You're fodder. I weren't happy when your
mother died, but at least she didn't see the wretch you are!"

Holding back his tears, Alden looked away from the man
who claimed to be his father. Dymas moved with unbelievable
speed and agility, leaping to his son's side and kneeling beside
the boy as Alden recovered from the slight dizziness he felt
after watching Dymas in motion.

"I want to see Pieraccinni," Alden said firmly.

"That old woman has hawked you enough. Don't you mention his name."

Furiously whirling on the flayed man, Alden shouted,
"Pieraccinni was there for me. Where were you?"

Dymas laughed. "You call yourself his, but you ratted on the
pig when you knew he was one of us. I bet you weren't
pleased none to learn you wasn't exactly much better." He
frowned. "Come on now, boy. Admit it. Ain't you happier
knowing your blood ain't tainted with humanity?"

To the night people, humans were monsters, Alden knew.

Dymas's features softened. "Ah. You never seen the lands
of your people. Our kingdoms make this world look like nothing. If I could take you there, you wouldn't act like this at the
thought of your true sire. You'd be happy with what you are.
You would, you know."

Raising his misshapen hands before him, Alden found he no
longer could hold back his tears. His gentle hands, which had
caressed the soft flanks of a dozen women, now would tear
bloody gashes in their skin. He was becoming more of an animal with every hour.

"If it was such a paradise, why leave?" Alden asked.

"We didn't have no choice," Dymas said ruefully. "The prey

we had ate for as long as we could remember was dying off. All we could do was eat off each other or find new worlds with new prey. There was somethin' of a war. All this energy was released. The sages said our reality was torn. Doors opened, gateways to other realms, like this one. Most of us fought the new order. I mean, it would've bred the hunter from us, would've made us less than we are. We left our homes for these new worlds. We've been quiet, secret like, you know, but we've grown. Don't fool yourself, we've—"

"What is the apparatus?" Alden said, interrupting.

Dymas smiled. "That you'll know tonight."

Alden thought of the scene he had witnessed at the cavernous retreat, the plans Tamara and Zeal had made to betray Lord Sixx. He had kept his silence. Staring into the flayed man's deceptively soft eyes, Alden said, "I look forward to that, father. I do."

"Maybe there's hope for you," Dymas said as he took the young man in an embrace that startled Alden.

"Yes," Alden said as he looked out over his father's shoulder, his red eyes blazing, his sharp teeth grinding. "Perhaps there is, after all."

From outside he heard the sound of thunder and the siren's call of Bellophat's music, which raised a longing in his heart that sickened him. A familiar scent came to him suddenly, one that he had not expected to breathe ever again.

Krystin was nearby.

The proximity of her blood made him tremble. Overwhelmed by new and terrible desires, he clutched at his father, praying that he would be able to keep his inhuman needs under control long enough for Krystin to escape.

* * * * *

Myrmeen, Krystin, and Ord could tell they were getting close. They had taken shelter beneath an overhang of a warehouse overlooking the docks. The music overpowered the thunder and the driving, insistent strumming of the rain. They had passed dozens of men and women who wandered about entranced, and Myrmeen wondered if Calimport would become a city of sleepwalkers; even the dour men of the city guard had succumbed to Bellophat's sweet music, their eyes squeezed shut, smiles of transcendence on their faces. In the harbor, ships had floated toward the docks and crashed, the men on board falling over like dolls on an unsteady surface. The survivors calmly drifted into the water, many approaching shore, where they were drawn by the music.

Myrmeen could feel the intoxicating lure of Bellophat's call. She took Krystin's hand and said, "I'm betting there will be no guards with Bellophat. No one is expecting a fight. I want you to stay here."

"That's suicide," Krystin said.

"No," Myrmeen said, Tamara's blood causing a swelling of confidence within her breast. "I can do this alone."

"If there's no risk, why not let us come with you?" Ord said as he felt his own need for action rise.

Krystin touched Myrmeen's arm. "You said you would never doubt my abilities in a fight again. You said—"

"Just shut up and wait, all right?" Myrmeen screamed, her rage bringing her to the verge of embracing an all-too-familiar sensation: The last time she had experienced such a killing frenzy, such a taste of ecstasy, of blind animal release with no human guilt and no human feelings to bar her from her pleasure, had been the time she had slipped on Shandower's gauntlet and felt the apparatus's magic surge through her.

Myrmeen bit her lip hard enough to draw blood. She shuddered as she fought the impulse to run screaming through the streets, killing anything that moved in her way.

"It's not just Tamara's blood," she said softly. "Bellophat's music affects the night people, too. It helps release what's in their hearts."

And what's in ours, Krystin thought, frightened by what she saw in Myrmeen's eyes.

"Please," Myrmeen begged, "I don't want you to see me like this. Let me go alone."

Krystin backed away.

"Protect her, Ord!" Myrmeen cried. He nodded. Unable to contain her murderous desire any longer, Myrmeen bolted from them, her boots splashing through rapidly forming puddles as she hurtled through the streets and vanished.

Ord touched Krystin's shoulder. She looked up and saw that not all the moisture on his face had come from the steady flow of the rain.

"They're gone," he said, "all of them."

Krystin knew that Ord finally was allowing himself to feel the grief he had been denying over his parents' deaths. She wondered if perhaps Tamara's blood and the call of Bellophat's music had pried loose his buried emotions. For whatever reason, he had begun to cry.

Krystin felt a strength and compassion in her heart that was bold and true. She reached up and smoothed away the tear that was drifting past his cheek, then took Ord in her arms. They held each other, Ord whispering that he was sorry, so very sorry, for the things he had said and done, and Krystin's words echoed his. The rain lessened slightly and they became aware that they were no longer alone.

"A Harper and his slut," a voice called.

Krystin whirled to see a horribly wounded man standing before her on the street. The glow of lanterns created pools of light on the cobbled street where rainwater had gathered. The maze of buildings surrounding them suddenly felt tight and claustrophobic. Staring at the man who was lighted from behind by an overhead lantern, Krystin saw that he was not wounded, but had been burned or flayed.

"Time to come out and play, my son," Dymas called.

Ord spun and stared straight up as he heard the scrape of claws on the fragile roof beneath which they had taken shelter. Krystin clutched at his arm as the roof was torn in half. Above, the creature that had been Alden McGregor looked down at them and licked its lips.

Krystin had time only to scream as Alden leapt.

* * * * *

Several blocks away, Myrmeen crouched in an alley, where she had forced her berserker's rage under control. These are not the thoughts of a rational woman, she had repeated in her mind until she was able to think clearly. The irony of the statement that brought her under control was not lost on her; these were hardly normal, rational circumstances. At the end of the alley she saw people gathering and realized that she had come close to one of the many outdoor shopping pavilions. Naturally, this is where the greatest concentration of people would be found in the city at night.

From her vantage she saw the crowd grow thick, obscuring her view of the street. A couple walked past her in the alley, another pair of somnambulists, and Myrmeen cursed her dulled senses; she had not even heard their approach. Falling in behind them, walking slowly and sluggishly so as not to attract attention, Myrmeen reached the mouth of the alley. The sight before her registered with a dull, aching shock. People lined both sides of the street. Lines of human spectators stretched as far as she could see in either direction. Others went about the business of destroying the many stands and shops in the street. They swung hammers and axes with a fervor that was a marked contrast to the glazed stares of the other humans. Details of men and woman cleared away the wreckage.

"The Parade is coming," a small boy whispered, "the parade of spectacle and wonder."

"The beautiful ones are coming," a man said in a wistful voice, as if he were reliving his happiest memory.

Beside the man, a woman said, "The men will be so handsome. They are brave and strong."

"The women lovely, lovelier than words can say."

"I cannot wait," the woman said, and she sighed wickedly. "Bring them on. Bring them on now."

"Yes, let us admire them. Let us love them. Let us bathe in their splendor. Bring them on."

"Bring them on," another man added, and soon the chant was taken up by the entire crowd. The human voices blocked out the steady drizzle that soaked them. Many had left their homes wearing the thinnest of night dresses or nothing at all. By morning, they would be left with pneumonia or worse. Myrmeen stripped off her cloak and covered a naked, shivering girl with the soft fur.

When the woman rose, she was surprised to see movement from the end of the street. Even from a distance she could tell she was looking at a vast cavalcade of monstrosities. The Night Parade was about to fulfill the promise of its name. Myrmeen was entirely certain that if she stood rooted to where she stood, she would see Lord Sixx leading the procession, the box containing the apparatus held in his hands. Already she could make out various members of the group breaking off and surging into the appreciative audience that greeted them with whoops and cheers, laughter and applause, love and acceptance.

Myrmeen turned and ran down the alley. She had to find Bellophat. She had to stop the music and force the people to wake up before the parade reached its conclusion and the monsters began their night of destruction and murder, a night they had waited years to enjoy. Letting the music guide her, she traveled through a maze of streets until she finally came across a deserted plaza lined with trees at the far end and marked by a closed wrought iron gate. She stood before the Plaza of Divine Truth, an open-air temple erected to the glory of Bhaelros, the god of storms and destruction known in Arabel and elsewhere in the realms as Talos. The temple's fortified walls were four feet thick and, traditionally, guards were posted at every corner and gate. Tonight, however, the temple was deserted.

Myrmeen had been here as a youth and knew that the plaza was divided into three interlocking courtyards. If she could have seen the plaza from the air, she would have seen three hollow squares with doorways in the north walls of the middle and bottom courtyards and a gate at the plaza's base.

The storm grew worse as Myrmeen scaled the first gate

and leapt into the spacious, open area of the Inner Plaza, as the first court was known. She landed in a roll. A handful of human corpses had been propped in the far corner of the open space—the missing guardsmen, Myrmeen concluded. Before her, the middle gate and the far gate beyond it had been left wide open. Myrmeen drew the sword that the night people had given her and entered the second court, the Initiates' Plaza. Carefully checking her blind areas to either side and behind her, Myrmeen slipped around the wall and saw the beautifully sculpted shrines, eight in all, to her far left and right flanks. She glanced upward to check the walls, concerned that Bellophat might have guards or followers such as those she had glimpsed in the black ship. She feared that his worshipers might leap down at her, tearing her to pieces that would comfortably fit in the massive jaws lining Bellophat's stomach. Lightning struck a nearby tree, adding much needed illumination.

The second court was deserted, the walls secure.

Slowly she approached the final gate, which led into the Chosen Plaza, the third and last court, where those willing to make the proper donation could kneel at the altar built before Bhaelros's idol. A wall set twenty-five feet inside the Chosen Plaza blocked her view of the statue, as it would for all nonpaying callers. She peeked around the edge of the gateway, saw nothing unusual, and chose to go right. She stayed close to the stone wall and followed it another twenty feet before she reached the end and peered around its side. Sitting upon the space that once had contained the idol to Bhaelros—a god that would have been pleased with the strength and intensity of the storm wrapped around Calimport this night—was Vizier Bellophat's sprawling mass.

The monster did not look up. Bellophat's eyes were shut as it concentrated solely on its craft. It was as enraptured by its own music as the entire populace of the city had been. Myrmeen surrendered to the call of blood, allowing the berserker's rage she had been repressing to take control of her. She raced toward the seemingly helpless monstrosity. Sud-

denly, a dozen smaller creatures left their waiting shadows and
converged on her. She was ten feet from Bellophat when they
brought her down without any apparent exertion. Myrmeen
screamed as she was overcome by the pack of abominations.
Before her, Vizier Bellophat opened one lazy red eye, smiled,
then closed it again.

* * * * *

Moments after Myrmeen had left Krystin and the young
Harper, Magistrate Dymas and his son, Alden McGregor, had
revealed themselves. They knew that by attacking the humans they would forfeit their chance to be a part of the grand
procession, but Dymas was convinced that bringing his master
the beating heart of a Harper would help cement his recent
return to favor with Lord Sixx. He had thought of his years of
exile, and the memories had spurred him on.

Alden crouched above Krystin's and Ord's heads. He was
more monstrous than either of them had ever seen him. He
leapt down and landed a few feet ahead of the humans, raising
his claws in his father's direction. Despite his inhuman appearance, Alden was recognizable as having been the young,
charming, flaxen-haired youth who had helped the humans in-
flict destruction on the night people.

"Father, please, no," he said in a guttural voice. "These are
my friends. Don't make me."

"Don't make you what?" Dymas asked, indignant. "Harm
them? Taste their blood. You know you want to."

"Please," Alden begged.

"Make your decision," the flayed man said as he started to
dance, his movements deliciously slow at first, then gaining in
speed and complexity. "It's them or us."

The dance Magistrate Dymas performed held surprising
beauty for the humans who suddenly found themselves unable
to stay on their feet. Ord's head lolled back as he fell to the
ground, trying to ward off the intense vertigo that gripped
him. Krystin had looked away, catching Dymas's movements

with only her peripheral vision. The sight had dropped her to her knees, but she regained her balance.

Alden was barely affected by his father's display, though his anger was causing his body to vibrate so quickly that he appeared to be in several places at once. Ghost images, blurs, remained in the spots he had vacated.

"You're no faster than I am," Alden said.

"I'm not, am I?" Dymas said as he raced forward.

Krystin was barely able to glance to her left, where Ord lay, before it was over. From the corner of her eye, however, she saw everything. The flayed man moved in a blur, crossing the distance between Ord and himself, dancing past his son in the process. He took Ord's grasping hand and yanked the nineteen-year-old into the air, hoisting him above his head as if he were a rag doll. With blinding speed, Dymas snatched the Harper's short sword from his scabbard and impaled the young man. Ord choked and flailed, a cloud of blood exiting his mouth as Dymas held him high. Suddenly, the Harper stiffened and went limp.

The sound of steel piercing flesh came to Dymas from somewhere close and suddenly he did not have the strength to hold the Harper's body aloft. He registered the slight shove he had felt and looked down to see the hilt of a weapon jutting from his own chest. As he crumpled to his knees, Ord's dead weight collapsed upon him. The Harper's body snagged on the weapon in the flayed man's chest, inadvertently yanking the blade downward to slice again at his delicate organs. Dymas felt a cold, cruel delirium wash over him, and he caught sight of his killer: Krystin.

Dymas sank to the ground, his body tangled with the Harper's. The girl screamed and Alden helped to extricate Ord from his father's twitching form. Krystin shoved Alden out of the way and pressed her head against Ord's chest. There was no heartbeat. He was dead. Tears fell from her eyes as she wailed in grief and clutched at him.

Behind her, Alden's animal senses had been inflamed by the nearness of the blood, but his cherished humanity forced his growing feral nature to remain under control.

Finally, Krystin sat up. The part of her that had been a frustrated schoolgirl felt light-headed with shock. Ord's face was relaxed in death. Struggling to force away the emotions that crowded in on her, Krystin realized that the last of the Harpers to journey to Calimport was either dead or gone. By the time Reisz came back, provided he was not killed or grounded ashore by the storm, the morning would have come, and the Night Parade's Festival of Renewal would be at an end. The word renewal thundered in her mind.

"Have to find her," Krystin murmured. "The children, I understand about the children!"

Alden reached out, his claws coming inches from her flesh before he said, "Before you go, there is something you must know, something about Tamara and Zeal."

Krystin listened intently as Alden relayed what he had learned when he had spied on them in Shandower's lair. She looked away from him and glanced down at Ord's body. Krystin touched Ord's dead lips, then leaned down and kissed him. Then she whispered, "Alden—"

"I won't leave him in the open," Alden promised. "I'll take care of it, then join you. Go!"

Krystin took one last look at Ord, then ran off, her boots splashing through deep puddles as the storm grew more intense, a wall of rain quickly obscuring her retreating form. Alden looked back to Ord's body, then froze as he saw that Dymas's no longer lay beside it.

"Good-bye," a voice whispered from behind.

Alden tried to run, but he was too slow. A pair of hands gripped his wrists from behind and thrust Alden's claws deep into his own chest.

"Thank you, my son," Dymas whispered. "For what you've revealed, I'll make your death quick."

Crying out with pain, Alden shuddered as his claws were ripped to either side of his body, tearing the cavity of his chest to pieces as blood sprayed upward, mixing with the rain. He fell facedown in a puddle that soon turned crimson. Ord's body was beside him. For a moment he thought he saw Ord move. The boy couldn't have survived a wound such as that, Alden thought. Or could he?

Alden was about to train his animal senses on the Harper when death came for him. He did not hear the slap of his father's bare feet on the pavement as the wounded man left to seek his master.

* * * * *

In the courtyard of the Chosen Plaza, Myrmeen shook off two of the creatures that had overwhelmed her. One had stalks rising from its flesh, with either tiny, piranhalike jaws protruding from the stalks or rapidly blinking eyes. The other had been a snake-woman she first had seen at Shandower's retreat. Myrmeen's grip on her sword had been tested, but she had not released the weapon. With a grunt, Myrmeen sliced off the top of the snake-woman's head. Then she turned and ran her blade through the monster with more eyes and teeth than it ever would need again. She screamed as she hacked away at another monster, a bony, balding man with a closed knot of flesh for a face, who was gripping her thigh. Whirling, she gutted an old man with pulsating gaps of flesh throughout his head.

The creatures that had brought her down had acted as a cohesive whole at first, exercising their great strength of numbers. After Myrmeen had dispatched several of them, the creatures stumbled over one another in their attempts to escape Myrmeen's wrath. They were not protectors, she realized, merely adoring worshipers of the globular monstrosity behind her. She killed two more, then let the others flee. Myrmeen turned after she watched the last of the creatures escape and saw that both of Vizier Bellophat's egg-shaped crimson eyes were open and following her.

"You ugly bastard," she said as she raised her blood-drenched sword and tripped over one of her victims' bodies. Her own body trembled as she giggled and rose once again, stepping onto the first tier of the massive altar where Bellophat had been deposited. "How did they haul your fat, disgusting bloat of a body in here, anyway?"

Bellophat's music became more chaotic, the rhythm suddenly frantic, the notes off-key. Myrmeen thought of the god whose temple had been violated, and she prayed fervently that Bhaelros would help her destroy this monstrosity. They blamed it all on you, she thought. The great storm, the deaths and devastation, everything!

But even as the thunder rolled and the lightning crackled, striking close enough to light up the plaza, Myrmeen knew she was on her own. Bhaelros was ignoring the affront.

Myrmeen raised her sword as Bellophat swatted at her with the harp it had formed from its pink, sweaty mass. The fighter was swept from her feet, her head striking the marble altar when she fell. As she tried to ward off the lancing pain she felt behind her eyes, Myrmeen heard Bellophat's music resume its original patterns, the lovely composition a stark contrast to the disgusting mass that was performing the piece. Then she heard flesh tearing, bones cracking, and looked down to see Bellophat altering his body once again, this time creating hands that clamped down on her legs and arms and hauled her into the air as the creature's jaws snapped in accompaniment to the music it was creating.

Swinging blindly with her sword arm, Myrmeen was stunned to hear a scream that appeared to have been torn from a howling whirlwind. Her body was unceremoniously dumped at the foot of the altar. The music had stopped.

Myrmeen saw that she had severed the fleshy strands that made up the harp's strings.

Even as Bellophat roared in pain, its pink, rolling skin turning red with anger, she registered that the strands were reaching back and soon would meld together once more. Trying to stand, Myrmeen felt a coldness on her ankle and tried to pull away. She was too late. One of Bellophat's hands still gripped her. It yanked her forward, tipping her from her feet once again. A jolt of pain raced up through her back as she struck the edge of the altar's first step. She pulled herself to a sitting position and hacked the limb from the creature.

For the first time she truly paid attention to the number of instruments Bellophat had created from its elastic body. There were more than a dozen in all. The music suddenly resumed and Myrmeen darted out of the way as a thin, rapierlike bow shot out toward her face. She felt the breeze as it passed her. With a hollow scream, Myrmeen leapt at Bellophat, her boot catching in the triangle it held. She used it as she would the first step in a ladder. She kicked herself higher, her blade whipping around to thrust directly toward Bellophat's right eye.

Myrmeen drove the sword through the creature's head. Her body slammed against the monster with a soft, sickening noise, then she lost her grip on the borrowed weapon and fell back into Bellophat's huge lap, stopping inches from his wildly snapping jaws, which slowed, then stopped. The music died with its creator.

Then there was no more time to think. Bellophat's body began to dissolve, changing into a dripping mass. Myrmeen felt as if she were being sucked into a mountain of gelatinous flesh, about to be drowned in an ocean of muck and gore. Her flesh sizzled as the heat of the monster's body rose substantially and turned acidic.

"Take my hand!" a familiar voice called.

The fighter looked up and saw Krystin standing on the remains of Bhaelros's idol, which had been hidden behind and beneath Bellophat's immense form. Myrmeen snatched Krystin's hand and allowed the child to yank her out of the boiling mass that had been the creature's body. In seconds they crouched on the storm god's chest and clutched at each other as the rain washed the blood and gore from them.

Around them, the storm raged on, indifferent to their suffering.

Twenty-Two

 Some time earlier, Tamara had dutifully taken her place beside her husband in the procession. Her scheme to take vengeance on Lord Sixx called for both conspirators to remain in full view of the monstrous throng who would be their followers once Sixx was dead, thus erasing any possible accusations of guilt.

As they walked through the streets, Tamara stared at the emerald locket she had retrieved from the pit of Shandower's cavernous lair, finally understanding the fascination the object held for the girl: The locket was not a magical item. The mage, Cardoc, had proved this. It was, however, magic sensitive. With no real power of its own, it could assimilate the power of its owner and fulfill whatever need the mage holding it required. The locket responded to desire, an alien emotion to the mage while he was in the course of performing his duties, thus, despite his great power, for him it had remained a useless lump of metal with a shining emerald surface.

Krystin had needed to know her past, and the locket had

revealed it to her. Tamara wanted to know only her future, and the images that she saw within its emerald depths confused and disturbed her. With time and effort she knew she could force the locket to show her the future in such detail that the meaning of the glimpses would come clear, but it did not appear that she would have such time, not tonight, in any case.

"Stop looking at that thing," Zeal whispered.

Tamara tore her gaze from the locket and smiled as she waved to the entranced humans on either side of the street. She felt slightly embarrassed that she, the originator of the plan to depose Lord Sixx, had to be reminded to follow their script. Sixx walked directly before them, holding the box containing the apparatus high over his head. Bellophat's music eased through the streets, carried to all parts of the city by his will.

As the procession wore on, the music changed, becoming heated and out of control. Then it ceased altogether. Tamara forced back a smile of triumph. Myrmeen had succeeded in her task. Bellophat was dead.

Lord Sixx slowed, looking around in anger and surprise. He drew the box to his breast and stopped in the middle of the street. The procession, moving in perfect time with him, also stopped.

"Tamara," Lord Sixx said with a nervous edge in his voice, "Find Bellophat. Make him begin again."

She hesitated. This had not been according to plan. Tamara had been certain that Sixx would send her husband away to check on Bellophat. As they both were aware of what had happened to the monstrosity, Zeal instead would have secretly followed Lord Sixx and remained hidden until Sixx opened the box containing the apparatus. Then he would have performed the task they had discussed; Tamara had wanted to be near Lord Sixx, to see the look of surprise on his face, to laugh as he died. Instead, she would have to watch from a distance and Zeal would have to look his victim in the eye—an ironic turn of phrase considering their leader's many-eyed condition—when he dispatched the man.

Lord Sixx shouted orders, reminding all of his followers that the matter of paramount importance was the children. They were to search the city and bring him the living bodies of any babies that had been born tonight. He took Zeal and a handful of others as private guards and prepared to go on to the predetermined end of the parade, the shrine to Sharess on the docks overlooking the Shining Sea.

Sixx looked at Tamara and growled, "What are you waiting for? Go now!"

Tamara broke from the procession, wading into the stream of slowly waking humans. She smiled broadly as she heard the first shrieks of terror from the men and women who had been the Night Parade's adoring audience.

The people of Calimport were waking up.

* * * * *

Across the city, in the basement of a school that had been ravaged by two members of the Night Parade, the survivors of the attack were huddled in the semidarkness as one of the tutors, a dark-skinned woman from the south, wailed in agony as she gave birth. The music drifted even here, keeping the handful of men and women and the dozens of children, all in their midteens, happily at bay. The people waited for their new masters to debase them sexually, or simply kill them outright, feasting on their flesh while their still living bodies twitched. They would die as hapless idiots, entranced by the sounds.

"This is good," the first creature said. He stood slightly over seven feet and all of his appendages were greatly exaggerated in length. His flesh was orange and as hard and dry as an elephant's hide. His long, thin fingers, each a foot long, were caked in human blood. "I know it isn't safe to wake so many of them, but I prefer to taste their fear and hear their screams, don't you?"

"Of course," his companion said as he held up his own hand. The man was a sickly, pale color, almost ivory. His flesh consisted of maggots that wriggled obscenely on his bones. "I think I broke a couple of nails, though. I'd hate to break any more."

They laughed together as the child's head suddenly showed and the midwife grasped it.

"Be very careful," the first creature said, "We need—"

Suddenly the music died.

"That's not supposed to happen," the maggot-infested man said warily. The humans who were now waking up were bunched at the foot of the stairs, blocking the only route of escape.

The baby's scream broke their temporary paralysis. The monsters looked at each other, understanding that the only way to make it from the basement alive was to use the child as a hostage. The carrot-skinned man darted toward the baby, his claws poised to sever the cord attaching the infant to its mother's body.

Neither creature reached the baby. A swarm of children engulfed them and dragged them down, paying them back in blood for the pain and the nightmares they had caused.

* * * * *

A mile away, a young actress named Kohrin-dahr reached up and caressed the sides of her lover's face. The man moved over her, leaning down to cover her mouth greedily with his own. Their hearts thundered in synch and their bodies strained in passion. She was dimly aware of the hard wood of the stage beneath her bare form and the laughs and applause of an audience, but she did not care. She was with the most beautiful man she had ever seen, a stagehand she had barely noticed until this night. The storm's violent sounds spurred on her passion as she raked at his sides.

The music that had been their accompaniment suddenly ended. For the first time, the young actress saw the true nature of the monstrosity above her. Shocked and repulsed, she bucked wildly, trying desperately to free her body, but the creature held on tightly, its own pleasure increased by her squirming. She struck out blindly, her fingers curled into claws, and dug her hands into the golden, honey-combed chambers of his soft, glowing eyes. A rain of ichor splattered her naked body as the creature rose, screaming in pain. It was stunned by the sudden onslaught of darkness. She scrambled back, detaching herself from the monster. The actress grabbed at the first object that came into range, a heavy lamp that had not been mounted.

Kohrin-dahr smashed at the creature's buglike head, driving it to its knees. She struck it again and again until she was covered in its blood and the monstrosity finally stopped moving. Then she looked out into the theater and saw close to a dozen monsters watching her in surprise. Before any of them could vault toward her, the actress turned and ran.

*   *   *   *   *

In the glass counting house of the financial district, the rainbow woman had come to make a withdrawal of pain and suffering, torment and blood. She had not bothered to disguise her appearance; the rapidly changing colors of her flesh always proved to be an ample enticement to men of any species—along with her stunning beauty and magnificently proportioned body.

"Gentlemen," she said to the entourage that had followed her through the streets and broken open the doors to this building, simply because it had intrigued her. "I would like each of you to find something to cut with, preferably a dull knife. When each of you has found such an object, I wish for you to line up against that far wall."

Within minutes, her demands were met and each of the men stood ready with a blade.

With a lascivious grin she said, "Tonight you will be my paladins, my protectors, and more. I will share with you sensual delights the likes of which you have never imagined. In return, you will murder the women you love and bring back their heads. To show that I have your complete loyalty, I wish for a small display. Each of you will cut off one of your fingers. I'll tell you which one. You will scream with pain, give your suffering to me. Is that understood?"

The men did as she requested. Soon each of them was drenched in agony and blood. The rainbow woman had absorbed every moment of their pain and felt overwhelmed by the sensations. She smiled. "Now go and bring me the heads of your loved ones. Then I will show you pleasure and pain as you have never imagined it, never dreamt—"

Outside, as the rain beat even harder, Bellophat's music suddenly fell away. The rainbow woman looked back at her perfect soldiers, who now advanced on her, blades ready. She screamed as they fell upon her, hacking away at her until the rainbow swirl of colors surging throughout her body coalesced into a nightmare black.

* * * * *

Lord Sixx and his entourage traced the route they had planned through the docks to the waterfront temple of Sharess, the goddess of lust, free love, and sensual fulfillment. The building was elegantly designed, with dark marble columns, jutting spires, and crystalline statues, many of which had been shattered. Lord Sixx passed the sentries he had posted around the temple's perimeter and paused on the spacious veranda outside the main doors.

"Is anyone inside?" Sixx asked. "Any humans?"

"Not anymore," his inhuman guard replied. "We cleaned it out when Bellophat's music began. There is one we spared, though. I thought you might want to have a look at him."

Vizier Punjor Djenispool was brought out, his hands tied, a gag stuffed in his mouth. His cold, unreadable eyes made Lord Sixx uneasy.

"He is the son of the pasha," Sixx said, "next in line to rule this city. I've had my eye on him for some time. Keep him safe this night. After the festival I may wish for some time alone with him."

The guardsman understood. Lord Sixx would take the man's memories and replace him with one of the Night Parade's own, securing Calimport as a safe haven for another thirty or forty years. As he was led away, the flesh around Djenispool's eyes crinkled as the man smiled broadly. The sight would have bothered Lord Sixx more if it had not been for his excitement over the event that was about to take place.

"Perhaps he thinks his goddess will rescue him," Imperator Zeal said with a smirk. A few of the creatures smiled with him.

Lord Sixx turned slightly. "Did anyone ask for your pathetic display of humor, Zeal?"

"No, milord," the fiery-haired man said stiffly. Those who had joined in his amusement became expressionless.

"Personally, I do not wish to suffer it," Sixx said. "It's bad enough that I must endure the company of imbeciles like you simply because the Draw favored you in infancy." He turned to the guards. "Call out the acolytes," Sixx said. "I want to see the children."

One of the guardsmen nodded. Sixx waited with impatience as footfalls sounded from within the temple, along with the screams of human infants. Finally a string of hooded women carrying babies emerged from the building. They gathered in a circle around the many-eyed man.

"Only a dozen?" Sixx asked.

"The evening is still young," one of the women said, her black robe adorned with a long slash of crimson, marking her as their leader. Within the shadows of her hood Lord Sixx saw her withered face, her flesh drawn tightly to her skull. "Your followers will bring more to us before dawn arrives. Or do you have so little faith in their abilities?"

Faith is not an issue, he thought, still disturbed by the premature end of Bellophat's music. The rain engulfing the city was driving and steady, soothing in its own way, but lacking the sweet complexities of Bellophat's creations. A figure approached in the rain, carrying the thirteenth child for the night. Suddenly a wad of darkness appeared and expanded before the monster carrying the human baby. It pulled itself into the form of one of the acolytes and reached with ancient hands for the child. The creature carrying the baby had slaughtered nine people for this child and was reluctant to give it away. It looked in Lord Sixx's direction and saw the dark man nod. The creature surrendered the baby and retreated into the night in search of others. The new acolyte took her place in the widening circle.

"Now you have enough to begin," the old woman said.

Lord Sixx absently noted that beneath their hoods each of the acolytes was a perfect duplicate of the elderly woman. He lowered the box to the floor and commanded Zeal and the guardsmen to leave the spacious veranda. In moments he was alone at the center of the gathering.

Sixx knelt on the floor, the box before him. His hands shook as he reached for the clasp on its side. He was unaware that as he did this, Imperator Zeal stepped behind two other creatures in the crowd that had gathered on the dock to witness the apparatus's unveiling and the Ceremony of Renewal's beginning. The sweat that had suddenly burst out upon his flesh was washed away by the chilling rain. Steam slowly rose from his skin as the droplets of water hissed upon contact with him. His task was difficult, requiring total concentration so that the call of flames would not overcome him and force him to reveal his guilt once Lord Sixx was dead.

The dark man with many eyes fingered the clasp and nearly leapt back in surprise as he heard his name shouted from the creatures gathered in the rain, before the temple.

"Lord Sixx!" the voice called again.

From his place in the crowd, Imperator Zeal looked over to see a shambling creature, its body arched like a bow, approach with a child in its arms.

"I have another one!" it called.

Zeal shuddered as he tried to force down the rising heat within his breast. He had to maintain control.

On the veranda, Lord Sixx exhaled in disgust. He had been frightened enough at the prospect of opening the box and revealing the apparatus. The interruption had not been appreciated. "Mistress," he said, his voice wavering more than he would have liked, "deal with this."

A new acolyte sprung into existence, took the child, then hurried to join the circle.

"Soon," Zeal whispered, stunned that he had spoken the word aloud.

"I doubt it," a voice sounded before him.

Before Zeal could turn, he felt a slight breeze and saw a blur of movement. A figure raced past him and appeared on the veranda, before the leader of the Night Parade.

"Dymas," Lord Sixx said dryly. "Magistrate, if you do not wish a return to that frozen hell I exiled you to—"

"Lord Sixx, please," Dymas said, clutching at the wound Krystin had carved into his chest. Although his body's healing mechanisms were ultimately much faster and more efficient than those of a human, he was not immortal. The strain he had placed on himself to arrive at this place and remain conscious long enough to issue his warning was now beginning to show. Sixx could see the genuine desire to serve and protect in the flayed man's eyes. He straightened and ordered the man to speak.

Zeal watched from the crowd, impatient with the delays. He did not know what knowledge Dymas had gained; if he had, he would have boiled the man's blood before he could have spoken, or drained the moisture from his body. Dymas would have fallen over, apparently succumbing to his wounds. The fiery-haired man did not expect the words that followed:

"There's a conspiracy to kill you," Dymas said. "Zeal and his bitch want you dead. He planned to—"

"That's a lie!" Zeal shouted.

Sixx suddenly noticed the way the rain hissed and dissolved into steam as it struck him. Zeal had answered the call of flames. He was preparing to strike.

"The second you opened the box, he was gonna burn you," Dymas said, "then say it was the magic of the apparatus that done it, like you'd been unworthy. He'd have fried you, then taken your place. No one would've known it was murder."

The creatures to either side of Zeal moved away. The red-haired man stepped forward, his hands outstretched. Steam flooded from his body, wreathing him in fog.

"Lord Sixx, I have served you faithfully," Zeal said, the flesh of his palms dissolving as the burning gateways suddenly appeared in his hands. "Would you believe the word of a man who killed one of his own?"

"And said that it was because the man was a threat to you, that he planned to usurp you," the old woman said.

"A claim I did not believe at the time," Lord Sixx admitted. "Perhaps I should have."

"I'm tellin' you the truth," Dymas pleaded. "Look there. His woman waits on that rooftop, watching us!"

Lord Sixx saw the form of the woman-spider on the roof of a nearby warehouse and knew suddenly that it was true. Zeal and Tamara had betrayed him. Tearing off his breastplate, Lord Sixx revealed the Eyes of Domination. With these eyes Sixx could enslave the will of others and force them onto a landscape of the mind, where their battle to the death would be slanted in the dark man's favor. Zeal was too powerful to engage in any other manner. The Eyes of Domination flared in the darkness and captured Zeal's gaze.

The fire lord's will was incredibly strong. Sixx knew he would not be able to pull Zeal into the psychic battlefield he favored unless he could weaken the man. In seconds he would lose his hold on the fire lord, but those seconds would prove to be all that were necessary.

Surrender to the flames, Sixx urged. Let them overwhelm you.

The fiery-haired man shuddered. His arms were engulfed in flames so intense that the rain was burned away before it came within six feet of him.

Turn and release them! Sixx commanded silently.

Zeal felt his body pivot as the flames struck from his hands, reaching across the distance that separated him from his wife. He screamed in horror as he saw the tongues of flame strike Tamara, sending her shrieking form backward, into the darkness.

"No, I couldn't have. I couldn't have—" Zeal began, stopping suddenly as he spun around and caught sight of Sixx's eyes for a second time. This time, Zeal had little defense against the Eyes of Domination. He stiffened, and his own eyes became blank, though his flames continued to burn.

For long moments, Lord Sixx and Imperator Zeal remained motionless as the crowd watched. Their duel was being enacted in a private place that only Zeal and Sixx could experience, a dimension solely of mind.

Lord Sixx broke from his trance and smiled. He raised his hands as if he were conducting a symphony. Zeal jerked and trembled in time with Sixx's motions, then fell to his knees as his power became novalike. The fire lord had been the first of his so called Inextinguishables. Only one being among the Night Parade possessed the power to destroy him: Zeal himself.

Suddenly, the fire lord turned his flames upon himself. He threw his head back in a silent scream as the fires that had always been his allies choked his breath and incinerated him. In moments, all that remained was a smoldering corpse.

Lord Sixx turned to Dymas. "It seems I owe you my life."

"My duty's to protect you," Dymas said.

Sixx nodded, searching the other man's eyes for ambition. He saw nothing, but Zeal had fooled him also. When this night was done, he would enter Dymas's mind. If he found a trace of duplicity, he would kill the sleeping man. For tonight, he felt better with Dymas alive.

* * * * *

Across the docks, Myrmeen and Krystin had been trying to locate Lord Sixx and the apparatus. They knew that somehow they had to find a way to stop the ceremonies. A torrent of flame had struck a rooftop a block away. Moments later, a second burst of light reached up and touched the sky. They ran to the warehouse, unaware that it had been the one upon which

Tamara had crouched, and came upon the woman-spider's smoldering remains. They watched in fascination as Tamara quickly became human once again, though she had been horribly burned, most of her hair singed away.

"Myrmeen," Tamara said weakly. "I'm glad you came."

"We saw the light on the roof, decided to see what had caused it," Krystin said distractedly, her gaze fixed on the item around Tamara's neck, which had been burned but was still recognizable. "You saved my locket."

"Not worth much now," Tamara said, each word bringing pain that she could not mask. "Sorry."

She reached out to Myrmeen, who drew away. Tamara shut her eyes and said, "I know what happened to your child."

The words nearly drove Myrmeen from her feet. She reached out and grasped Krystin's shoulder for balance. The child wrapped her arm around Myrmeen and helped the woman kneel beside Tamara.

"Have to tell you now," Tamara said. "Lord Sixx will send someone to make sure I am dead."

"Speak," Myrmeen said, unable to force more than the single word from her mouth. She listened to Tamara's faltering narrative, the flow broken as the woman paused to cough, blood spitting out with her words, her eyes becoming glassy, her body shaking.

"I said you had destroyed my home," Tamara said. "*Our* home, where you lived as a child and I called home as an adult."

Myrmeen thought of her return to her childhood home, the Tower Arms. The building had been in ruins except for her old quarters. They had been perfectly, impossibly restored to the way she remembered them. Then she recalled the nightmare, the screeching monstrosities her parents had become, and their horrible words: . . . *we told you the other one was dead and you would be our one and only. You smiled. You thought we didn't see you, but we did and it cut our hearts out.*

Not true, she thought. Please, it's not true.

Then she remembered when she first had heard of the Night

Parade. Her mother had been explaining what had happened to her baby sister. She had been taken to a place where she would be loved and happy, where she would be with her own kind.

Where she would be a monster.

"You're my sister," Myrmeen said breathlessly, her emotions going numb at the realization.

Tamara nodded. "Twenty-eight years ago, two members of the Night Parade wanted a child but could not conceive one. In this plane they cannot reproduce by natural means. They purchased a child and brought it to the Festival of Renewal. It was placed with the others, so many others.

"Myrmeen, the apparatus transforms human children into Night Parade creatures. I was raised to believe I was one of them, given the traits during the Draw of my adopted parents, themselves part human, part spider. Many years later, they died. Zeal, who was ten years older than me and had loved me from the first time he saw me, told me the truth. It was difficult to learn the names of my human parents, but I found them, and I found you. I came to you many times, but I could not bring myself to confront you."

"The nightmares," Myrmeen whispered. "The people with limbs of spiders—"

"My parents," Tamara said softly, "and me."

"Wait," Krystin said as she looked at Myrmeen. "You said your sister was stillborn, that your mother told you—"

"She lied," Tamara said bitterly. "I had been born sickly, and the physicians gave me only a few hours to live. The slavers came and offered our parents a fortune for a child that would die soon anyway. They looked to their other child, to you, Myrmeen, who was starving because they could not provide for her, and accepted the slavers' gold."

"You should have come to me," Myrmeen said. "You should have told me."

Tamara shook her head. "I tracked you. I watched you with envy, my human sister who could go where she wished, do as she liked, and experience this world as a native creature, not a predator. As much as I wanted to be human, I had needs and appetites that were not."

Myrmeen's lips curled slightly in disgust.

The muscles in Tamara's face tightened. "I did not think I would be able to bear seeing your revulsion. It's strange, sister. Somehow it doesn't bother me."

Covering her face with her hands, Myrmeen said, "I'm sorry."

"You can't help it," Tamara said. "I understand. Besides, would you have believed me if I had told you the truth then?"

"I don't know," Myrmeen said honestly. "Why did you try to kill me at Shandower's retreat?"

Tamara shook her head. "I thought you had been party to the sale of your child. All my life I had convinced myself that you were noble and decent. When Dak sold the baby I thought you were party to the deal, that you had done to this innocent what our parents had done to me. I thought you had chosen to abandon her."

"I never would have done that," Myrmeen said.

Tamara glanced at Krystin, then back at her sister. "I know that now."

Hardness returned to Myrmeen's eyes, the golden slivers within the deep, troubled sea of her pupils shining like avenging swords. "What happened to my child?"

"Zeal and I wanted a baby," Tamara said. "We purchased yours."

"No, please," Myrmeen said. "My baby can't be like you, it can't be, please—"

"It's not," Tamara said. "I wanted to raise your daughter myself. Her place was arranged for at the Draw, but then it all came to me, the horrors I had witnessed and the evil inside me. Sanity overwhelmed me. Somehow I was able to be merciful. I told Zeal to give the baby to a human. He chose one from the Council of Mages in Suldolphor who could not have children. He and his wife have provided the child with the life of a princess. Your daughter is royalty."

Krystin took Myrmeen's hand and squeezed it as Tamara

gave Myrmeen the name of the man who had raised her child.

Tamara whispered, "I was angry with you for giving up your baby, Myrmeen. If I had known you had been deceived, that you wanted the child, I would have taken you to her long ago. I thought you came back to Calimport only to cover up your dirty secret. But when I saw you with this one," she said, pointing weakly at Krystin, "I began to wonder if I was wrong. And later I came to know I was. I'm sorry, Myrmeen."

"Why did you want to kill Lord Sixx?" Myrmeen asked.

"For the children," she croaked. "With Sixx dead, it would be decades before another rose to power and made the journey to our homeland to learn the secrets of the apparatus and the Draw—decades of life for children that would have suffered my fate."

Tamara shuddered. Death was close. Suddenly the images she had glimpsed in the emerald made sense; they had been of her life after death, had revealed her soul's destination. She was pleasantly surprised to learn that she did not face the dark gods of the Night Parade's world, but instead the peaceful kingdoms, the afterlife to which humans aspired. In that moment, she knew where she belonged. She knew she had always been human, despite the evil that had been pumped into her veins, the darkness imposed over her soul.

"Take care of your daughters," Tamara said urgently, then surrendered to death, leaving Myrmeen to question the nature of her final statement.

Light flared from the docks, an explosion of blue-white flame racing high into the air.

"Come on," Myrmeen said, taking Krystin's hand.

"We can't just leave her," the girl said, gesturing at Tamara's body. "She's your sister."

"We'll be back for her," Myrmeen said as she saw bright green strands of lightning lick the sky. She followed the length of the warehouse and peered around the corner to witness a sight that her mind could not at first assimilate. When the shock subsided and she understood what she was looking at, Myrmeen finally began to cry.

Twenty-Three

 Throughout the city, the human resistance grew stronger. The members of the Night Parade had not been prepared to fight a war. They had been lazy, confident in their abilities. Bellophat's music had made them drunk with thoughts of their own power. They had never dreamt that the humans' sheer numbers would prove to be their doom.

Human parents fought like wild animals to save their children's lives. The rich battled alongside the poor to destroy the nightmare people. The militia rallied the citizens into troops of fighting men and woman. Petty squabbles were put aside as they faced their common enemy. Buildings where the monsters had been trapped were set to the torch without a second thought. The streets filled with people whose fear had caused them to turn away from the day-to-day horrors of life in Calimport, people who refused to allow fear to control their lives any longer.

There were losses, of course. Some members of the Night Parade proved to be vulnerable to steel, and they died as easily as their human prey. Other creatures took a dozen or more human lives before they surrendered to death, while still others could be hacked into a dozen pieces, then rise to escape or slaughter their tormentors.

Despite the high cost of victory, the humans fought and won against the nightmare people. Each time one of the monsters was killed, the humans cheered and howled in triumph. They had no idea that near the docks, a drama was being played out that would decide all their fates.

*   *   *   *   *

Myrmeen and Krystin stared in horror from the mouth of the alley as they saw that the temple of Sharess had vanished. In place of the temple stood an edifice that appeared to be in a constant state of transition. Although each of the building's complex configurations lasted no more than a few seconds, every incarnation bore common aspects:

The support structures were made of searing blue-white energy. Emerald lightning snaked parallel to the ground to create various tiers within the rapidly shifting structure. The building itself had no walls to speak of and was always at least three stories high. Stairways led between the tiers, odd blood-red stretches of linkage that were either too far apart or too close together to easily accommodate humans. Standing before the structure were Lord Sixx and a ring of hooded women in black. In the dark man's hands was a glowing blue-white object that also reconfigured itself in motions identical to the larger structure. Lord Sixx was sweating, chanting loudly enough to be heard over the rain. The black-robed women chimed in at appropriate moments, adding a chorus to his strangely beautiful song of yearning and loneliness.

Myrmeen realized she was not looking at a building at all. This was the apparatus. The object created a whirlwind of shapes, each configuration more unusual than the last. Suddenly she became aware of the children in the acolytes' arms. She felt her body shake as revulsion coursed through her. She was witnessing the opening procedures in the ceremony that once had been enacted to metamorphose her sister into the progeny of darkness. She finally understood the true purpose of the apparatus: it was a machine for conjuration, a creation that evoked spells too complex for humans to manage.

Myrmeen did not want to know what the spells would bring into existence. She only knew that somehow she had to stop the ceremony before it reached its conclusion and the infants' humanity was sacrificed. The beautiful fighter studied the situation as calmly and rationally as she could under the circumstances. Getting to Lord Sixx was her first problem; directly before him lay the structures created by the apparatus, and close behind him was a gathering of monsters, including the flayed man whom Krystin had described, Ord's murderer. To make her task more difficult, the dark man was wreathed by the circle of robed women. At their backs lay the churning waters of the Shining Sea. From above, the endless daggers of rain created a shimmering curtain that lent a dreamlike quality to the proceedings.

This was not a dream, she reminded herself. People were dying, and if she did not develop a plan quickly, the children born in Calimport this night would become monsters.

"Don't jump," a voice called.

Myrmeen felt her heart stop as she spun and stumbled back. Krystin's movements echoed her own. They both were stunned to see the rain-drenched, swarthy-skinned face of the man they had sent away to find help.

"Reisz," Myrmeen said as she launched herself at him and threw her arms around his neck. He tensed, placing one hand on her shoulder to hold her back. "What's wrong?"

Reisz stepped back and proffered a small bundle to them, a child wrapped in blankets. "I didn't want you to crush the little one."

Staring in wonder, Myrmeen saw that the baby was asleep. "What happened?"

"My boat capsized while I wasn't far from shore. I swam back, then fell victim to that strange music. When it ended and

I regained my senses, I started to scour the docks looking for you. I'd have missed you completely if not for that flash of light on the roof. I thought of the fire lord and feared you might have engaged him. I hunted until I found you."

"What about the baby?" Krystin asked.

Reisz hunched over slightly to protect the infant from the rain. "I found a monster carrying the child and had to persuade the thing to part with the little darling—and its life, of course."

Krystin stood beside Myrmeen, watching the tiny baby's movements as it slept. Sadness overcame her as she said, "Myrmeen, there is a way for you to get close to Lord Sixx, but I don't think you're going to like it."

*   *   *   *   *

A quarter of an hour later, Myrmeen was walking in the direction of the conclave of monsters. She tried desperately to force back her fear of the creatures, her fear of dying, and her revulsion at her own decision to go along with Krystin's plan. Although the child she carried in her arms was very light, she strode as if she were weighed down by the burden of a lifetime spent with guilt.

Don't do it, she thought, don't give them the child. If you fail, it is a life that might have been spared, and your soul will be plagued for all eternity.

But she knew there was no other way. She steeled herself for her confrontation with the monsters. The heavy winds accompanying the rain licked at the hood she had procured from the creature Reisz had slain and threatened to pull it back and expose her humanity. She had disguised her features by covering her face in the gore of the city's gutters. The weapons she had looted from a shop two blocks away slapped against her waist and thigh.

Reisz had positioned himself on the rooftop where Tamara had been struck by Zeal's flames. Krystin had promised to remain in the alley and wait for Myrmeen. If she was killed, Krystin had been made to swear that she would turn and run, never looking back. Reisz was fairly certain that once he performed his task, the night people would not allow him to escape alive. He told Krystin that he would draw them away from her so that she could escape.

"It is my duty as a Harper to die if necessary in the task of protecting others," Reisz had said. "If you try to take vengeance on the Night Parade, you'll end up dead, too, and no one will be left to tell the tale. You must get back to Arabel and warn Elyn—she will tell the other Harpers, and they can rally an army to ferret out these killers."

Krystin solemnly had agreed, then held her mother and kissed Reisz lightly on his cheek, which had been softer and more inviting than she ever would have guessed. She even had made a comment to this effect when she had been left alone with Myrmeen.

Myrmeen had touched the girl's hair lightly as she said, "My father told me he wanted to make the monsters go away. He didn't know about the Night Parade. That isn't what he meant. There are things in our hearts that only we can dispel. If I don't come back to you, it's not because I don't love you. It's not because I don't want to come back. This is something I have to do, something I have to try to stop, or the nightmares that I've had will seem like pleasant dreams compared to what dreams may come after this night. I pray they don't come for you, Krystin. You don't deserve them."

"Neither did you," the girl had replied.

Myrmeen had smiled sadly and kissed Krystin's forehead, then gathered the baby to her and raced from the alley. Now she was yards from the gathering, trying to divorce her thoughts from the horror of what was about to occur.

"Another one," a bilious creature more smoke and mist than flesh and blood shouted.

The crowd parted to let Myrmeen through. She trained her gaze downward and registered that the baby was awake, squirming madly in her arms, but it was not crying. A strange sucking noise came from the child, competing with the heavy winds, the shouts of Lord Sixx and his acolytes, and the

steady drizzle engulfing them. She parted the folds of the
soggy blanket obscuring the child and saw two small marks on
the infant's neck.

Her vocal chords, Myrmeen registered in dull, throbbing
waves of shock. The child's vocal chords had been severed or
pinched to prevent the little girl from screaming.

I can't do this, Myrmeen suddenly decided, but then she
understood that it was too late, and that she had committed
herself. If she tried to turn back now, she would be captured
and killed with no chance to redeem the children like the one
who now depended on her.

She walked past the gathering of monsters, passing directly
before the flayed man. She was about to lay a single boot upon
the slight rise where Lord Sixx and the acolytes had gathered
when a glob of darkness burned the fabric of reality before her
and stretched itself into a perfect replica of the first acolyte.

"She's hurt," Myrmeen said. "She may not be worthy—"

"The Draw will heal her," the acolyte said, reaching out with
her pale, withered hands.

You know what to do! Burke's voice raged in her head. You
have no choice. You have to save the children. Go ahead!

Myrmeen lifted the baby slightly and hesitated. Suddenly
she felt as if she had been returned to the quarters she had
shared with Dak fourteen years ago. She once again was turning away, taking the easy way out: Our child is dead. You don't
want to see. Close your eyes. Close them.

Lifting her head so that the hood fell back slightly, Myrmeen
felt her mind suddenly disconnect from her actions. Her face
was set with determination as she slipped into the role she had
agreed to play and handed the baby over with open eyes and
an unfeeling heart. Now it was a matter of timing, skill, preci-
sion, and luck.

Lightning struck at the edge of the docks, causing shouts of
surprise from the gathering. The new acolyte had turned for
just an instant to glance in the direction of the lightning strike.
Sixx had squeezed his eyes shut as he chanted. The flash of
light made him look out to the dock. Myrmeen knew he would

see her face, which was illuminated from the apparatus's brilliance, when he looked back. Her opening would last for only a second or two.

Thought and action merged as she pulled back the folds of her cape, lifted the twin loaded crossbows that had been tied to her waist sash, and fired both weapons. The first shaft plunged into the cluster of eyes in Lord Sixx's chest; the second struck the apparatus, knocking it from his hands. The smaller blue-white construct hit the marble at their feet. Its counterpart wavered slightly, the palace of lightning shuddering, then regaining its form and brilliance.

For a moment, Lord Sixx teetered in shock, his words of evocation halted in midsentence. Myrmeen heard a slight whistle of air and prayed that the shaft Reisz had fired from his perch would strike true. She felt a sudden rush of wind at her side and saw a blur of motion as Lord Sixx was thrust out of the way of the shaft and Dymas suddenly appeared with a grunt of agony and surprise, Reisz's arrow buried in his skull. The flayed man went down, his lifeless body falling upon his master's wounded form.

"This one dies for your crime," said the acolyte.

Myrmeen turned to see the old woman to whom she had handed the infant. The woman's charred black nails suddenly extended into claws that were positioned to descend and tear the infant into bloody ribbons. Before Myrmeen could act, a sword arced through the air and severed the head of the old woman. Myrmeen rushed forward and snatched the baby as the headless body fell.

Krystin stood before her, chest heaving, the sword she had used to kill the acolyte scraping the docks' wooden surface. She was trembling, covered in blood. Although they knew they were dead, that no one would rescue them from the angry mob of creatures that was just now assimilating the shocking events of the last few moments, Myrmeen and Krystin smiled. A strange, insane look passed between them.

"You really should have been my daughter," Myrmeen said with a laugh as barren as the giggle of a man being led to the executioner's blade. "You're as arrogant and stupid as I ever was."

"I love you, too, Mom," Krystin whispered.

Before them, Lord Sixx was being helped to his knees by the remaining acolytes. The woman with the splash of red upon her black cloak had retrieved the apparatus. Another acolyte was dragging away Magistrate Dymas's body. Myrmeen had no time to react as Lord Sixx produced the edged weapon he had displayed in Pieraccinni's lair, the one Alden had described to her. He pressed the center gem of three rubies on the jagged blade's hilt, and the two knives that had been squeezed together sprang apart, revealing a strand of razor-sharp wire that stretched between them.

Myrmeen knew she could not leap out of the way with the baby in her hands. The fighter clutched the child and turned her back on Lord Sixx as he threw the knife. Krystin screamed her mother's name.

Pain suddenly exploded in Myrmeen's shoulder. Her left arm went limp, forcing her to hold the baby with one arm. She fell to her knees as she pressed the child to her breasts, determined to shield it with her own body. A single thought raced through her:

Reisz, shoot them! Damn you, Reisz, where are you?

Lightning struck, and from the sudden illumination she saw that the rooftop where he had been perched was empty. From his vantage it must have appeared that Sixx had been struck, and Reisz was scrambling down to help her, not realizing that he had left her to die.

Her entire back was soaked with blood and she quickly became light-headed and dizzy. A moment later it occurred to her that she had not been engulfed by the creatures gathered on the dock. She looked up to see that the monsters had come as close as they could with any degree of safety.

The magic of the apparatus is fatal to them upon contact, Myrmeen thought. Only Sixx and the old woman were safe because they had recited spells of protection against the energies. Dymas had gone to Sixx's side even when he knew it would mean his death; Reisz's arrow had been unnecessary.

"Take her," Myrmeen said, assuming that Krystin was close. The girl appeared before the fighter and took the child from her arms. Myrmeen dragged herself to her feet and turned to confront Lord Sixx.

Behind them, the structures formed by the apparatus suddenly revealed an open center. In that void, a large, rolling cloud of nebulous energy appeared. At the center of the sphere that was forming Myrmeen could see a second round patch of darkness and understood that she was not merely looking at the absence of light, but at entropy, the unraveling of all physical principles known to humanity. The black dot at the ball's core grew until it resembled a pupil.

An eye, Myrmeen thought in shock. She realized that she was staring at the detached eye of something large enough to dwarf the docks, a creature that looked out with eyes of darkness and absorbed reality in its wake, changing the laws of reason to suit its own desires.

"Lord Sixx, it is time!" the first acolyte screamed.

"No," he hissed. "This one dies first."

Myrmeen drew her stolen sword, which she had taken from the shop they had looted, and advanced on the man, her legs nearly giving out with the exertion.

"Not that way," Lord Sixx said as he yanked her crossbow shaft from the cluster of eyes in his exposed chest. The Eyes of Domination flared. "Watch closely."

The five remaining eyes on his chest suddenly locked their gazes with Myrmeen's and changed color. All five suddenly took on the cast of her own eyes—deep blue with golden slivers—and suddenly she was no longer on the docks. The rain had stopped, and her wound had vanished. Darkness surrounded her.

She wondered briefly if she were dead. She knew that it could happen very quickly: an explosion so instant and devastating that she would have no time to become aware of her moment of death. In her mind she ran through a catalogue of other ways in which she could have been dispatched that would explain her presence in this noiseless, formless void.

"What's happening?" she cried. "Where am I?"

She recalled the eyes of Lord Sixx, the eyes she had seen in a nightmare. Suddenly she understood. He had used those eyes to transport her to another place, a land of the mind. None of this was real.

But how could that be? she wondered. It felt real. It tasted real. The sounds were very real. Music slowly drifted in her direction. Bellophat? No, that was impossible. He had been destroyed, his music stopped forever. She recognized the lullaby, played on a lute, one of her father's compositions.

"Help me," a distraught voice called from behind her. She turned, fairly certain that what she would see would be a horror that would inflame her nightmares for years, should she survive this encounter and escape this place.

Her father was there. His body had been pulled apart, stretched to impossible elasticity as it had been in her dream. But this time his face and chest were still intact, while the rest of his body had been ripped to steaming bands of muscle, bone, and bleeding tissue.

"I went there because you were hungry," he sobbed. "I didn't want to die. I wouldn't have if not for you."

She was not moving. Her legs were not in motion, but she was getting closer to the web. In a sudden, instinctive burst of understanding, she knew that this gibbering creature before her was not her father. It was nothing more than a nightmare Sixx had dredged up from her past. This isn't real, she thought. Sixx is trying to get at me though my weaknesses, my fears. But I'm tired of being afraid. I'm sick of feeling guilty.

Sixx could shape this place to suit his needs. She understood that if he broke her will here, he would control her forever. And if he murdered her in this place, she would die in the real world. A smile came to her face, because she knew that it also worked both ways.

"I've had enough," she said, pressing her hands together as if she were clutching a sword. Suddenly a long, burning silver shaft sliced itself from the darkness and she felt the weight of her phoenix armor.

I want to make the monsters go away, a voice from her locked up memories called. Myrmeen identified the voice and realized that what she had told Krystin was wrong; her father had not spoken those words, even though he had loved her very much and would have echoed the sentiment, given the chance. It had been her second husband, the man she had loved until the day he died, though she had not realized that until this very moment. He had been the one to forge this armor. He had given her the strength to wall herself up emotionally until she was ready to deal with the horrors of her past, ready to face her private pain.

Staring at the bastardized image of her father, she knew she had faced it already. She had dredged up all the terrors she had been hiding from, confronted them, and survived. What was before her now was nothing but a lie, an illusion of the mind and the heart.

She had been a victim. All of her life she had blamed herself for tragedies that were beyond her ability to control. She had not sent her father off to be murdered. She had not asked to have her daughter stolen from her.

Myrmeen raised her sword and cleared her mind. She no longer heard either her father's music or his pitiful wails. The man he had been would never have cried in this way. He would have met his end with dignity. Staring into his eyes, she planted her legs firmly, held the sword parallel to the unseen floor beneath her, and held out her left hand, assuming the first position of defense that the man who had given her the name Lhal had taught her.

The screaming monstrosity racing toward her no longer resembled her father. It had dark hair, a widow's peak, and eyes covering its entire body. The creature was not a mere construct that Sixx had created to fool her, it was Sixx himself in disguise, terror painted upon his face. He had exerted too much power and could not arrest his flight as he raced toward Myrmeen. As Sixx thundered close, Myrmeen shifted her

weight and thrust the sword forward, impaling the screaming
figure.

An explosion of blood engulfed her senses, and she suddenly
found herself back on the docks, moving in midstride, Lord
Sixx's scream echoing in her ears. The dark man was before
her, his many eyes glazing over in shock. Myrmeen stood as if
she still held the sword, and Sixx's chest had been mangled,
blood streaming from a terrible wound that had been opened
on the psychic landscape. She had no idea if such an injury
would have harmed him in this reality—he might have laughed
at being impaled—but this wound was different. This one he
had suffered within his mind, and even he could not argue with
its results. Each of the man's eyes turned blank as he fell and
struck the ground.

Lord Sixx was dead.

"You're too late!" the first acolyte howled as she held up the
apparatus. "You're—"

She stopped, a stream of blood spewing from her mouth as a
sword sliced her heart in two from behind. A gloved hand
reached forward and snatched the apparatus from the woman
as she sank to her knees, the remaining acolytes mimicking
her motions. Myrmeen stumbled forward another step as she
saw the laughing, burned face of Reisz Roudabush, his blood-
drenched sword in one hand, the apparatus in the other.

A sigh that reminded Myrmeen of the gentle call of a hawk
came from the acolytes as each of the children was gently laid
on the marble slab. The acolytes then folded themselves into
black shapes that shrank to the size of a fist and winked out of
existence.

"I took a gamble," Reisz explained. "These forces didn't
hurt us when we touched Shandower's gauntlet, so I thought
they might be harmless to us now."

From the charred flesh, the burned clothing that hung on
him, and the halting manner in which he moved, Myrmeen
knew that the energies gathering behind them were far from
harmless to any human. Myrmeen's attention suddenly was
drawn to the sphere gathering in power and intensity behind

them, a rolling fireball of arcane energies. The smaller, equally volatile ball of magic that lay within the cage of the apparatus was growing larger in Reisz's hand.

The old woman had said they were too late. The sacred words had already been spoken. The energies would be released, but without the steady stream of spells the old woman and Lord Sixx were supplying, they would have no focus. Their purpose would be only to consume, or so Myrmeen was willing to wager.

"It never occurred to me that some of these damned things could fly. One of them swooped in and knocked me off the roof after I fired my first arrow," Reisz said nervously, cutting glances at the shimmering object he held. Desperation tinged his next words. "I never would have abandoned you, Myrmeen."

"I know that," she said, certain that the energies from the apparatus in this undistilled form would prove to be poisonous even to humans. Reisz was dead. The last of the Harpers was about to fall.

Suddenly a battle cry came from the crowd of monstrosities that had been forced to wait before the palace of lightning. They were being engaged by human guardsmen. A handsome, dark-haired man appeared before Myrmeen, and she recognized him instantly: Vizier Punjor Djenispool.

She gathered that he had slipped his bonds and run to get help. Hundreds of humans had responded to his plea. His small army fought the creatures of darkness, keeping them well away from the infants near the apparatus.

"We have to take this thing out to sea," Reisz said. "It's going to explode—I can feel it—and when it does—"

He decided not to finish. Reisz had no idea what actually would happen if the fireball escaped its cage and sent its energies throughout Calimport. Perhaps a purge would commence, the energies destroying all the creatures of the Night Parade that infested the city. There was an equally reasonable chance that all the humans caught in its wake would perish or be transformed. If the latter occurred, two million new members of the Night Parade would look out to the coming dawn, after the storm had passed.

"It's not going to be far enough," Krystin said, holding the voiceless child to her breast. "There isn't time, can't you sense it?"

Vibrations rose from the dock. Unchecked, the dark magic of the apparatus was reaching a critical stage. The energies were boiling over, burning away the rain engulfing the city, charging everything within their reach with heat.

Myrmeen glanced at the crying children lying in a circle and felt the greatest sadness for them. Her life had been full, if tortuous at times, and she had made peace with her past. The children would not be given that luxury. A single gallows laugh escaped Myrmeen.

"What's wrong?" Reisz asked. "What is it?"

"A strange thought," Myrmeen replied. "I've always prided myself on paying all my debts. I swore I would go to my end without owing anyone, but it seems I still owe Pieraccinni a small fortune."

Reisz's stricken expression vanished, replaced with an odd glimmer of excitement. Without explanation, he suddenly ran from the marble slab and raced past a collection of monstrosities that darted out of his way, the glowing energies of the apparatus causing them to recoil in fear.

"Reisz, where are you going?" Myrmeen called.

Instants before he vanished down a narrow side street, Myrmeen turned to Krystin and said, "I don't know what might happen. Protect the children."

"I will," Krystin said. Myrmeen turned and only barely heard Krystin's next words: "I will, Mother."

* * * * *

The storm engulfed Myrmeen's senses, and she forced herself on, through the rain, ignoring the lancing pain that came to her with every movement. After several minutes had passed without any sight of Reisz, Myrmeen feared she had lost him.

She ambled forward, Lord Sixx's blade still trapped in her shoulder. Blood leaked down her back, the sting of rain in her wound causing a throbbing to begin in her head. Myrmeen recognized the area into which she was running, amazed that she had found the strength to move so quickly despite her injury. She wondered if her sister's blood coursing through her veins was responsible for her sudden strength and dismissed the thought. She knew her true motivation was her resolve to pay Reisz back for the kindness, love, and devotion he had given her so many years earlier. She only wished there was something more she could do for him above being at his side when he passed on.

A flood of creatures emptied into the street before her. They raced past Myrmeen without giving her any notice. She pushed herself to move beyond them and venture into the building that had spewed them into the night: the Gentleman's Hall. Dragging herself through the main chambers of the establishment, Myrmeen found the door to Pieraccinni's lair thrown open, the merchant on his knees before Reisz. Pieraccinni was no longer human. He was as Alden had described him: His skin was dark blue, like that of a shark, the smoothness interrupted by bulging red and green veins. He had an oblong head, hooded eyes, and flaps at either side of his neck for air. His body shook as if he had palsy, and she recalled the phrase Alden had used, comparing him to a sea creature under unremitting pressure.

Myrmeen's offhand comment about Pieraccinni apparently had caused Reisz to think of the night Alden had joined their war. The boy had described the disturbing sight of his employer, Pieraccinni, transforming into a monster. Lucius had suggested that Pieraccinni was a living siphon of magical energy with immense power. Power enough, Reisz obviously had gathered, to absorb the destructive forces emanating from the apparatus.

"Myrmeen, get out of here!" Reisz barked.

"Leave the apparatus and join me," Myrmeen said. "He can't get out of this room."

"I don't want to take that risk," Reisz said.

"Reisz," she pleaded, her voice cracking, "please! Don't leave me."

He squeezed his eyes shut for a moment and bit his lower lip until it bled. Then he turned back to her and said, "Myrmeen, get out before it's too late."

At his feet, Pieraccinni babbled incoherently. Myrmeen recalled Alden's description of what he had seen, and she suddenly understood Reisz's plan. Pieraccinni's curse was that he drew magical energy into himself. Lord Sixx had created this room to dampen any arcane power. With those wards removed, magic would come flooding in, overwhelming the man. Reisz hoped that Pieraccinni could take inside himself the apparatus's magic and spare the city its imminent destruction.

"Reisz, I—"

She stopped. I love you, she wanted to say. She finally wanted to give him the words he had needed to hear, the words he deserved to hear, especially now.

"Don't lie to me," he said.

"It's not a lie."

He nodded. "And you."

Suddenly the walls buckled and a long fissure snaked across the roof. Through the crack that had been created Myrmeen saw the rolling fireball that had been contained within the three-story-high cage at the waterfront. It had broken free of its cage and followed the apparatus.

"Myrmeen, run!" Reisz hollered.

She scrambled from the room. Passing through the doorway, Myrmeen hesitated and looked back to see the bloated, quivering body of the arms merchant ripple and become insubstantial. The creature wailed in unimaginable agony as a hole appeared in its chest and grew larger. The gap was filled by a vortex of rapidly changing images: a lake of fire; a dominion of jagged, roughly hewn clouds; a city built entirely on the remains of its dead, bones for supports, skin for covering; and a long desert trail being crossed by hooded creatures taxied in chariots that were alive and screaming under an aqua sky. The abominations were no more repugnant than the ones the Harpers had encountered in Calimport, but they existed in such numbers that as Myrmeen anchored herself in the doorway and stared at the dying creature's lair, she felt she might be sick with fear.

All paths lead here, a voice called. *I am the doorway.*

Pieraccinni was not a man—he was not even alive by her standards; he was one of the portals that the Night Parade had used to make the journey to the Realms. To disguise the portal, he had been cloaked in flesh, given a personality and memories, but they were nothing but lies.

Within the portal lay a swirling, chaotic mass of hellish images. Myrmeen saw demons yanking their eyes from their heads and consuming them, colonies of monstrosities waging war against one another, and landscapes where a human being would have burned the moment he touched the ground. Near each of the shifting images were creatures staring at the portal in fascination. Myrmeen wondered how long it would be before one of them decided to reach through the doorway and enter the small room.

Through the fissure in the roof Pieraccinni was able to leech the magic of her world to feed the rift, giving it strength to grow wider. She realized that without Lord Sixx's dampers in place, the portal would continue to expand until all the magic in the world had been depleted. That meant it could grow large enough to engulf continents, perhaps even the world itself.

"Reisz, we have to close the gateway!" Myrmeen shouted.

The Harper nodded, steeling himself as he hurled the apparatus into the yawning pit before him. Suddenly the lightning cage dissolved, releasing the ball of energy as it shot forward, bursting into one of the shifting tableaus. The portal was engulfed in blinding blue-white energies.

Reisz turned to run from the room when Pieraccinni's arm shot out, the force of the creature's will making it corporeal. He grabbed the Harper by the heavy belt at Reisz's waist and dragged him toward the swelling portal with inhuman force. Before Myrmeen could race to his side, the roof was torn from over their heads as the three-story-high counterpart of the sphere of entropy lowered itself into the room. The fiery, over-sized eye was no more than a dozen feet above their heads and closing. Myrmeen watched in horror as Reisz was yanked toward Pieraccinni.

"Give up the quest, Myrmeen," he called to her. "You're not going to find what you're looking for until you do!"

Before she could take a step in his direction, Myrmeen saw Reisz throw his head back and stifle a scream as he was consumed by the portal that had been Pieraccinni. The arcane energies snapped his body apart and ate him alive. All traces of the merchant's humanity vanished, leaving only the portal and the massive sphere of light that continued to descend, trying to follow its smaller counterpart. Whatever it touched disintegrated instantly.

Tears streaming down her face, Myrmeen pulled herself away and raced from Pieraccinni's lair. An implosion of sound and light knocked her from her feet and sent her body rocketing across the dining hall. Turning, she picked herself up and saw that the portal and the sphere had connected. The vortex seemed to be consuming the ball of energy, the fiery, magical lace that made up its outer edges straining to weave itself around the sphere.

This was no time for gawking, she reminded herself. Heavy gusts of supernatural winds racked what was left of the Gentleman's Hall. She ran for the door and in moments she was on the street, stumbling to the ground half a block away. She chanced a look back at the Gentleman's Hall and saw that the establishment no longer existed. The vortex had grown to encompass the entire building, and the blue-white sphere was now half swallowed up, its lower part emerging in some other world, some nightmare dimension safely away from her own.

The gigantic eye then began to shudder and lose its form. The pressures being exerted by the portal were too much for the sphere. Its pupil spun wildly as if it were searching for a glimpse of the being that had been its undoing. The dark iris stopped for a moment as it fixed its gaze on Myrmeen.

Fear gripped her. She wondered if the sphere really was the eye of the night creatures' god, as she had imagined earlier. If so, had it seen her? Had it sent an image of her face to its own counterpart in a dimension of undreamt of horror? Would it remember her and seek vengeance?

The street began to shudder, and she scrambled to her feet, prepared to run, but there was no time and nowhere for her to go. The vengeance of the dark god was at hand, it seemed. Suddenly the sphere exploded, spreading a cloud of blue-white energy that resembled shimmering sand released from a shattered hourglass. The energies licked at the sky above Calimport, tinging the heavy rains. Before the unnatural rains could fall, the vortex spread even wider, cutting across an area two blocks in diameter. Buildings were cut in half, their upper portions disintegrating.

The vortex sat there, only five feet over Myrmeen's head, and she felt as if she were experiencing the worst possible gale winds. She found a post buried deeply in the ground and hung on, even though its upper half had been eaten away by the vortex. Staring up at the wildly changing kaleidoscope of color, Myrmeen felt an intense heat wash over her. The vortex was translucent, and through it she could see the glimmering blue-white raindrops fall to the yawning, hungry void, vanishing as they struck its surface. The portal shuddered as if it had gorged to the point of explosion, but it swallowed the darksome energies released by the sphere anyway. When they were gone, the vortex trembled, as if it was now addicted to the energies of the apparatus.

Myrmeen shook as she watched the vortex. She wondered if it still retained some of Pieraccinni's mind, or if it operated solely on instinct, need, and lust. The city was rich in magic, and if the vortex still hungered, it might yet attack the city.

Without warning, the vortex shrank with incredible speed and collapsed in on itself. It dwindled until it once again hovered over the remains of the Gentleman's Hall, then it became too small to see through the heavy rains and vanished. The portal apparently had followed the rest of the apparatus and its power to the dimension where it had sent the mystical object.

Myrmeen began to laugh, and soon her laughter gave way to tears of thanks that were washed away by the storm raging on around her. After a time, she became vaguely aware that people were coming. She hoped they were human. There was no fight left in her. Only the steady, insistent drumming of the rain upon her back kept her from losing consciousness. Soon she felt hands on her back, and she angled her head to see that the men who had found and were helping her to her feet were indeed human.

She stared up at the sky and smiled as she realized that the night had not left them. In the fairy tales her mother had read to her when she was a child, and in the stories that Reisz had recited on the long nights when he had held her in his arms and she had quaked in terror at the storm, the dawn always arrived with the expulsion of evil.

There was no dawn. There would be no perfect day for a very long time.

Myrmeen turned to the faces of the men surrounding her, stunned to recognize the dark-haired nineteen-year-old she first had glimpsed at a table in Arabel. "Ord?" she asked.

He nodded weakly, explaining that he had been wounded but not killed. He was found by the men who had come to help her, a band of adventurers who had several vials of healing potions and felt obliged to pour them all down Ord's throat when they saw the pin that marked him as a Harper. A cleric was with them, and his magic had completed the task of restoring the young man.

Ord reached to his breast and removed the pin, gesturing for Myrmeen to come closer. "You should be the one to wear this for a time. It's what my parents would have wanted."

Myrmeen did not object when he secured the pin to her leathers. She took the young man's hand as they went out into the rain-swept night to find Krystin.

Epilogue

 Myrmeen stared into the face of Pholuros Argreeves, a tall, handsome, brown-haired man in his early forties. Argreeves ran a private temple for the worship and study of magic, and he had been a member of Suldolphor's highly touted Council of Mages for two decades. He had a forceful personality coupled with a fairness and a gentle nature that had surprised Myrmeen.

She had arrived at the city with a military force large enough to show the council that her request for an audience with Argreeves and his daughter would not be denied. Her show of force had turned out to be completely unnecessary. The mage acted as if he had been expecting her and explained that he had always known this day would come. He made no excuses for his actions and did not beg Myrmeen's forgiveness. They met in the beautifully adorned audience chamber of his temple, statues of the great fallen sorcerers of the last two decades lining the walls—including one of the archmage Elminster, who had "died" and been resurrected so many times that the council found it easier to leave his statue on display, just in case. Weapons and arcane items that once had been rumored to contain spirits or curses were hung on the wall or preserved under glass. Murals had been painted on the arched ceiling, depicting great moments of triumph and tragedy for their kind, the births, lives, and deaths of the most revered mages in recorded history. Elminster once again took up more than his share of space.

Through a handful of windows on the right-hand wall Myrmeen saw Krystin walking through the garden with Ord, who was too busy enjoying the pleasures of life and allowing his wounds, both physical and emotional, to heal before he launched himself on a new quest.

Calimport had survived the second coming of the great storm, and this time the citizens were well aware of the Night Parade and its activities. Without the apparatus, the creatures could not reproduce, but many thousands of the monstrosities had survived and escaped, and there were doorways still to be discovered leading between their world and the Realms. All of the creatures who had been near the temple of Sharess had been consumed by the gigantic eye of entropy that had been released from the apparatus's cage.

Vizier Djenispool had formed a special arm of the military to deal with the city's infestation, and warnings about the night people had been spread throughout the Realms. The war was far from over, but Myrmeen's part in the battle was finished, at least for now.

"Are you certain you want to do this?" Pholuros Argreeves asked.

Myrmeen stared at the mage before her. "No," she said, "but I have to do this."

Argreeves lowered his gaze. "Then what you tell her is up to you," he said, his words gossamer as he turned and walked to the end of the long corridor, leaving Myrmeen to absently admire the many artifacts on display until she heard a soft, feminine voice call to her.

"Milady?"

Myrmeen looked up. The child approaching her from the double doors at the end of the hall was dressed in a white, flowing gown with a frilly bodice and elegantly styled sandals. Her soft brown hair was pushed back in a bun, held in place by a jeweled headband with white and red roses tucked into her hair. Her skin was pale, her eyes jade green, and her lips were touched with only a trace of scarlet.

Myrmeen's first thought was that the child did not even look like her, and she wondered if she had been deceived. Then she looked closely and saw that the deep emerald eyes were those of Dak, the hair jet black at the roots and dyed to appear the same as that of her adopted parents. The child's hands had been at her side, but Myrmeen could see that they were soft and delicate hands that clearly had never been sullied by the hard lessons of manual labor or the artistry of sword wielding and combat. The girl wrung them nervously as she approached.

"Father said you wished to see me," she said as she bowed with an unexpected grace, bending to one knee as she spread the folds of her gown like an imported fan, displaying the beautiful designs that had been etched into the fabric, invisible at first because they were off-white against ivory. "My name is Lynelle Argreeves, daughter of Pholuros and Mia Argreeves, granddaughter of—"

"Yes, I know," Myrmeen snapped impatiently.

Stunned, the child looked at her with wide, hurt eyes. Apparently, a harsh word was rarely spoken to this girl.

Myrmeen could hear Reisz's amused and somewhat admonishing voice in her head: *Well, here you are, Myrmeen, at the end of your quest. You have your daughter—so what are you going to do with her? Have Krystin teach her the discipline of the sword?*

"Are you happy here in Suldolphor?" Myrmeen asked.

"Oh, yes, milady," Lynelle said with a bubbling enthusiasm that erased any hint of her earlier reserve. "Here I have my studies, my parents, and my suitors—each and every one a true gentleman."

"Your studies," Myrmeen said, grasping for some common ground with this alien child. *She is to become a mage, perhaps, and such pursuits certainly would help to grow some callouses on her far too trusting and vulnerable soul.*

"Yes," Lynelle said brightly, "our library contains the works of the poets from all the ages—not that I believe that my humble scribbling will ever gain such recognition, but there is an art to be admired, a beauty forgotten by many, that must be explored—particularly the poems of love, for without them our world would be a barren and lifeless place. Don't you agree?"

Myrmeen stared at the child, finding it incomprehensible that this could be her daughter. The longer she watched Lynelle's pretty face, the more subtle clues she discovered that made her believe this was her child.

This girl wouldn't last five minutes alone on the streets of Calimport, Myrmeen thought. She felt as if she were about to crush a beautiful flower underfoot in her blind race to pursue her own fulfillment.

"What do you know of me?" Myrmeen asked.

Lynelle smiled. "That you are the ruler of a shining city called Arabel. Why you wish to waste your time with my lowly presence, I do not know."

"Why do you think I'm here? Hazard a guess."

"My father often has strangers come and speak with me, sharing their views, imparting their wisdom, so that my life is not so cloistered—or so he says. Frankly, many of them are bores. I do not sense that you would be such."

"You are most kind," Myrmeen said in a halting, arduous fashion. The enthusiasm that had gripped her on the journey from Berdusk was now fading. Even her memories of the ceremony at the Twilight Hall, where she officially had been brought into the ranks of the Harpers, did not bring comfort.

What did you think you would accomplish here, Myrmeen? Reisz's hearty voice asked in her mind.

I wanted to know that she was safe and happy.

You already knew that.

Myrmeen realized that this moment had played a thousand times in the theater of her mind. In her fantasy, she told Lynelle the truth and the girl embraced her, turning her back on the life she had led for the past fourteen years. Tearfully, they rode off together, beginning a cherished journey of exploration, embarking on a quest that would have no conclusion, as the raising of a child was an adventure that lasted until a parent's final days, no matter what age mother and daughter attained.

"Mistress Lhal?"

Myrmeen was abruptly snapped from her revery by the child's voice.

You are my daughter. Say it.

"Mistress Lhal, you haven't said why you wished to see me. I am—very curious."

The child was becoming worried. There was no other reason for her slip of etiquette, at least by the standards of Suldolphor. It was not proper to ask a caller his or her business; a decent host waited until visitors felt that the time had come to announce their purpose. The child would know this and understand the breech in conduct.

Tell her.

Myrmeen hesitated, looking into the deep jade-green eyes of her daughter, and was reminded of Dak. Each time she had found Krystin staring into the emerald locket, she had wanted to say, Your father had eyes like this. They were the first thing that attracted me to the man.

Myrmeen felt it odd that she was thinking of Krystin at a moment like this. Suddenly she understood why, knew what Reisz had been trying to tell her all along:

All quests had an ending. If they did not, they would not be quests, simply life, the seemingly endless stretch of days leading to twilight and eternal darkness. By filling her mind and her heart with an endless string of quests, she had been ignoring her life, and it was going on without her. That was why she had felt so hollow and empty that night in Arabel, when she looked out at the storm with longing and desire for something she could not identify. That explained why she had felt that, despite her many achievements, she had accomplished nothing with her life.

Staring into Lynelle's eyes, she knew she had to make a choice, embark on a quest that would shatter this child's peaceful existence, or walk away from it finally, content with the knowledge that her little girl had been raised with love and had been given from infancy more than Myrmeen ever had been equipped to provide for her.

There was no choice.

"My father was a poet," she said softly, "a lyricist. I had hoped that perhaps you had heard of him, and that your vast libraries might hold some of his work, something that would help me remember him, now that the past is slipping away."

Lynelle nodded slowly and asked Myrmeen her father's name. The fighter told her, then added that there was no reason to hurry in this pursuit. Myrmeen would be in Arabel for a very long time. If the girl came across anything, her kindness in forwarding copies of the poems would be appreciated.

"It would be my honor, Mistress Lhal."

"You may go. My time is short, and I have a pressing engagement."

"Of course," the child said as she bowed again, the top of her head showing the roots beneath her resplendent headdress.

"I have one last question," Myrmeen said. "Why do you dye your hair?"

Lynelle blushed. "To look more like my mother. It seems I inherited the hair of my grandmother on my father's side, who died giving birth to my father. It's vanity, I know."

"Not at all," Myrmeen said. "You're very lovely."

With a wide, embarrassed smile, Lynelle half bowed and left the room with a lightness of step that she had not displayed when she had entered. Two figures, Krystin and Ord, stood in the doorway as Lynelle departed.

As Krystin entered the hall, Ord drew back and shut the door, leaving them alone together.

"Was she everything you had dreamt she would be?" Krystin asked.

Myrmeen swallowed hard. "No," she said, trying to hold back the tears welling up inside her, "but you are."

Krystin was shaken. She had no idea how to respond. She surprised them both by throwing her arms around Myrmeen and holding the woman as tightly as she could. The tears came, and Myrmeen clutched Krystin's back tightly. Krystin responded with strength matching that of the older woman.

There was a dawn somewhere in this bleak, terrible world, and Myrmeen knew she would no longer have to search for it alone.

FORGOTTEN REALMS
FANTASY ADVENTURE

▪ THE HARPERS ▪

A Force for Good in the Realms!

Red Magic
Jean Rabe
A powerful and evil Red Wizard wants to control more than his share of Thay. While the mage builds a net of treachery, the Harpers put their own agents into action to foil his plans for conquest. Available now.

The Parched Sea   Troy Denning
The Zhentarim have sent an army to enslave the fierce nomads of the Great Desert. Only one woman, the outcast witch Ruha, sees the danger—and only one Harper can counter the evil plot. Available now.

Elfshadow   Elaine Cunningham
Harpers are being murdered, and the trail leads to Arilyn Moonblade. Arilyn must uncover the ancient secret of her sword's power in order to find and face the assassin before he finds her. Available now.

The Ring of Winter   James Lowder
Harper Artus Cimber travels to the jungles of Chult to find the fabled Ring of Winter, but the Cult of Frost also seeks the ring, which contains the power to bring a second Ice Age to the Realms. Available October 1992.

FORGOTTEN REALMS®
Fantasy Adventure

THE LONG-AWAITED SEQUEL TO THE MOONSHAE TRILOGY

Druidhome Trilogy
Douglas Niles

Prophet of Moonshae — Book One

Evil threatens the islands of Moonshae, where the people have forsaken their goddess, the Earthmother. Only the faith and courage of the daughter of the High King brings hope to the endangered land. Available March 1992.

The Coral Kingdom — Book Two

King Kendrick is held prisoner in the undersea city of the sahuagin. His daughter must secure help from the elves of Evermeet to save him during a confrontation in the dark depths of the Sea of Moonshae. Available October 1992.

The Druid Queen — Book Three

In this exciting conclusion, the forces of the Earthmother are finally united but face the greatest challenge for survival ever. Available Spring 1993.

FORGOTTEN REALMS
Fantasy Adventure

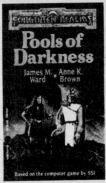

Pools of Darkness
James M. Ward & Anne K. Brown

The entire city of Phlan has vanished, ripped from the surface of Toril by dire creatures and magical forces. While the minions of the evil god Bane bicker over the spoils, the denizens of Phlan mount a stubborn defense.

A ranger thief named Ren seeks his missing friends, Shal and Tar, spellcasters nonpareil. Ren bands together with a mysterious sorceress, Evaine, her intrepid shapeshifter cat, a couple of droll druids, and a fearful knight who is absolutely, positively dead.

The novel *Pools of Darkness*, also a best-selling computer game by SSI, revisits the heroes of Phlan ten years after the city was saved in *Pools of Radiance*. Available now.